Ride the Blue Riband

Books by Rosalind Laker

RIDE THE BLUE RIBAND

THE SMUGGLER'S BRIDE

ROSALIND LAKER

Ride the Blue Riband

DOUBLEDAY & COMPANY, INC., GARDEN CITY, NEW YORK, 1977

ISBN: 0-385-12416-3
Library of Congress Catalog Card Number 76–29791

Ride the Blue Riband

1.

On the brow of the hill Oliver Marlow reined in his horse and looked down at the Hampshire village of Hartsworth with a feeling of intense well-being. Thatched roofs and some of slate lay clustered together around the gray stone Norman church and the green with its duckpond. He was home again. After a full season at the races, which had taken him away from his cottage in March and had allowed him to return on this crisp, amber-hued fall afternoon, he was about to be reunited with his wife and family. No dark sense of premonition touched him, no chill concern that all might not be as he had left it. Ruth was a good wife and used to managing in his lengthy absences. All would be well.

"Come on, boy," he said aloud to his horse in his deep, throaty voice as he dug his heels into its scrawny flanks. "We're almost there."

With a clop of hooves on the hard, rutted surface the nag jogged on down the winding lane. Oliver did not press his tired mount to greater speed, being content to take his time and look about him as he rode along, his light-blue eyes under the forward-tilted brim of his tall beaver hat keen and alert, missing nothing. He had a good seat on a horse, natural and easy in spite of his bulk, and altogether he was a fine-looking man and knew it. Thick, wheat-colored hair and heavy brows gave dramatic impact to a well-molded, leonine face much weathered by hard living. Deep lines ran from the straight nose to the corners of a fleshy, mobile mouth, which looked as if it enjoyed many things, not least of all laughter, and its corners were relaxed in amiability as he took note of the changes that had been made since he had last ridden the dusty lane. Over there the flint wall had been repaired, and in the copse a quarter of the trees had been felled. An extra rick in one of the fields told him that the summer had been dry and no excess rain had spoiled the hay crop.

He always savored the last half hour of home-coming. It was a breathing space spiced with anticipation that settled on him comfortably, without excitement, but with contentment, knowing that the gifts he had in his saddlebags would delight his children, who would show their joy, no matter that all four had grown into young adults. He had a double-barreled fowling piece for his son, lengths of silk, lawn, and light wool for his daughters—he always thought of the eldest as his own child—and there was velvet for Ruth, who was also to receive a fine Cashmere shawl, its muted shades well suited to her fair coloring. Not that she would wear it, except to try it about her shoulders after taking it from its wrappings, simply to show Judith and Tansy and Nina, who would want it displayed. Then it would be folded away in a drawer with most of the other peace offerings he'd given her, always reluctant to adorn herself in any way that might inflame his ever-swift desires.

Ruth had changed much since he had first taken her in the silent, green woods half a mile from her home amid the scent of fern and leaf and waving willow herb. She had loved him and he had been wild for her, that frail sprig of a girl with the pansy-dark eyes, whom he had waylaid and haunted at every turn, having been barred from calling on her at her home through his own scalawag reputation, for all that he came from a great house and was better born than she. He was the younger son of a strait-laced Yorkshire family, rebelling at an early age and taking to gaming, wine, and women with a gusto that had appalled all except his paternal grandmother, who doted on him and alone refused to condemn him as a black sheep. After her death, he had cause for gratitude to her. Ruth was the only child of a first wife, resented by the second spouse, who had time only for her own brood, and ignored by her dour, Bible-thumping father, a banker by profession, who held her responsible for her mother's death in childbirth. No wonder Ruth had been starved for love and affection, her natural desires warring with her strict upbringing, but eventually he had coaxed her into secret meetings and had known it would not be long before he had his way with her. Never before and never since had he waited thus to possess and be possessed, for in the end she caught him on the hook of love and there had been no other thought in his head but he must marry her. They had eloped together, and from that moment forth they had been rejected and disowned by their respective families, he for this final evidence of his profligate ways, she for daring to defy her overbearing parent. She had never cared for the traveling existence that had followed, for he had been forced to earn a living out of the only two assets to his credit: a knowledge of horseflesh and skill at cards. He had always had a wanderlust and reveled in the freedom of it, but she had become more thin and wan with every move, suffering several miscarriages. Eventually he had bought her the Hartsworth cottage, where she had struck tenacious roots, never again venturing out of the village, content to let him come and go at will with never a word of reproach for a lack of letters, knowing it was purgatory for him to put pen to paper, for he had no scholastic or literary turn of mind whatever. Yes, she understood him. Too well for her own peace of mind, but he was as he'd been made and there was no changing him now.

Sometimes he wondered if in her heart she had never believed what he had told her about their foster child and remained convinced that the girl, now twenty-eight, was his by-blow, but she was wrong there. Judith Collins had been ten when he'd brought her to Hartsworth, seated before him on a horse far superior to his present mount, for he had been in the money on that occasion. Her mother had been a wanton creature, who had come to a bad end, and her father had been a notable jockey in his time, but had succumbed to the bottle and gone downhill after his wife deserted him; then, on a soft, misty day at Aintree, he had taken a fatal tumble during a steeplechase. Judith, seeing him fall, had screamed and darted under the rails to reach him before anyone could stop her, and was knocked flying by the hooves of one of the other runners taking the fence after him. Miraculously she had not been killed, but had suffered broken bones that were to leave her permanently crippled and ever to walk with a stick. Discovering that the child had nobody to take charge of her, he had paid for her to be treated for her injuries and looked after until the day when the last race of the season had been run and he returned to take her home with him to join his family. Ruth had stared from him to the child and back again with stark, unhappy eyes, no doubt thinking to see some similarity in their features, in spite of listening to what he had to say, but when he lifted Judith down from the saddle that good wife of his had put all else from her in consideration for the child, who stood shy and frightened and bewildered, leaning on a stick, her outgrown dress revealing beneath its hem the terribly twisted foot. Holding out her arms, Ruth had said softly, "Come to me, Judith dear. I've been wanting an older daughter just like you to help me care for my baby. Her name is Tansy. Let's go indoors and see her, shall we?" Judith had trusted and loved Ruth from that moment forth, and there was not one of his three children who did not look to the girl as an older sister. It was a pity she had not married, for she had a sweet nature and would have made some man a loving partner, but her disability had been against her chances and now it was doubtful that marriage would ever come her way. Not that it seemed to trouble her, and with her quiet good humor she had shared the ups and downs of his fortunes with the rest of the family and had helped Ruth shoulder many a burden when the others had been growing up.

He could not help wishing he'd had a better season during this year of 1847. Then, as he had done so many times before, he would have come home on a thoroughbred with sovereigns weighing down his pockets, and looped across his waistcoat there would have been a new gold watch and chain to replace the one he'd had to hock for a final flutter on the last race. He should have known by long experience that he couldn't turn his luck at such a late hour and must wait for it to smile on him again when the next season started. That was the way of it. Ah, but he'd had some strokes of good luck in his time! Take last year's Derby, for instance. He'd lost disastrously this year, but not on that previous sweet day in May, which had made him a rich man for a while. In his mind's eye he could see again his winner romping home while he cheered and shouted and threw his hat into the air. The roar of the crowd seemed to echo once more in his ears, that multicolored sea of people from all walks of life, who flocked annually to the lush, green slopes of the Epsom Downs within easy reach of London for the grandest race in the world. Nowhere else was such a supreme test of speed, strength, and endurance put to the best three-year-olds in the land, and so greatly had the occasion fired the imagination of all that the race had become an unofficial national fete, even Parliament retiring for the day to allow Members to attend. Gentlemen mostly arranged their wagers privately, ladies were beginning to place their bets discreetly in pairs of gloves, and the bookmakers in the Betting Post handled the money of common folk, but no matter if the bets were in hundreds of thousands of guineas or as little as a tanner warm from some costermonger's pocket, every punter shared on an equal footing the glorious thrill of watching a field of thirty runners or more thundering along the horseshoe-shaped, undulating course to the winning post. In the Grand Stand, the private stands, and the elegant carriages drawn up at vantage points at the rails, the elite in their tall silk hats and befrilled bonnets roared their enthusiasm with the humbler spectators who clustered about the course and covered the famous Hill with no room to spare. It was a day when class was forgotten, when a Duke could rub shoulders with a gypsy, and all mingled freely in that superb setting. How the flags and the bunting waved! What a trumpeting of bands and a jingling of bells and a merry screeching of individual fiddles! Never empty of customers were the striped booths offering refreshment, the gaudy canvas enclosures of the sideshows, and the brightly hued beer tents. And what a hubbub of delighted noise came from the swings and other fairground pleasures! Derby Day at Epsom was unique, an experience not to be missed. Long may it continue! Oliver smiled to himself, his thoughts reaching out to a certain long-legged colt, gamboling in a faraway paddock, a future winner if ever he saw one. May it bring home to him in the not too distant future the great fortune that any punter worth his salt determined to make one day! May it win the wonderful Derby!

Lost in his reverie, he had reached the bottom of the hill, and when the horse brought him over the hump of the stone bridge that spanned the river he saw to his surprise the slender figure of his elder daughter stumbling to a breathless halt in the middle of the lane ahead of him. Tansy! She must have spotted him on the hill and come at a run from wherever she was to meet him. A grin of pleasure spread across his face and he did not find it amiss at first that she did not dart the last few yards to reach him, but stayed hesitantly where she was, watching him approach, and twisting round and round with nervous hands the wide brim of the hat that she held, which was dusty as if it had flown more than once from her head and been retrieved from the ground. Exuberantly he urged the horse into a canter to shorten ˙ the distance between them as quickly as possible. At the same time he was struck anew by the beauty of his dear child, his special pet, and pride soared up in him. Her luxuriant hair, windblown and tumbled, was a richer, brighter shade than his own. Not for the first time he congratulated himself on having chosen the perfect Christian name for her, for even as a tiny baby her wispy curls had been the color of the little meadow tansy, which spread its gold amid the tall grass and along the wayside under summer skies, and he had swept aside all Ruth's wishes on the matter and been ever glad of it. He marked how tall she was, how graceful, and how her black dress accentuated the exquisite pallor of a skin immune to freckles. From him she had the high forehead and straight nose, although with her the nostrils had an almond curve and were delicately molded above a generous, soft-lipped mouth, but in the shape of her chin there lurked a stubbornness that reminded him of Ruth, and there was a marked resemblance across the eyes, which were more violet than blue, dark and glistening, full of secret thoughts.

"Tansy, my child!" he explained boisterously when he came within earshot. "Trust you to be the first to welcome me!"

Only then did she come forward with reluctant steps, and she stood looking up at him as he drew level with her. With compassion she saw the easy grin fade from his ruddy face, comprehension dawning on him that all was not as it should be, and it was some terribly serious mission that had brought her there. Slowly and deliberately he swung himself from the saddle and took hold of her by the shoulders. She could smell the dust of travel on him, sweat and leather, and the pungent aroma of tobacco on his breath.

"Tell me!" he ordered harshly.

A great wave of filial love swept through her and with it came the tears she had not dared to shed before, filling her eyes, half-blinding her. With a gulp she dropped her hat and threw herself against him, her haven, her refuge, her adored father who was the tower of strength she needed in this hour of trouble. The others had looked to her to succor and comfort them, and yet at heart she had been the weakest and the most sorely grieved. She clutched the lapels of his coat, twisting them, her face pressed into the hollow of his shoulder. The words wrenched from her.

"I wanted you to hear the news from no one else. Mama—is dead."

She felt rather than heard the gasp that shuddered through him. "How? When?" he demanded in a hoarse whisper.

"Seven weeks ago. At night. There was a fire. The wall behind the kitchen range ignited—the one in need of repair"—her voice faltered and became choked by sobbing, but he gave her a kind of angry shake, forcing her to go on—"and the flames took hold before Roger woke and raised the alarm. It was too late. Mama was trapped in her room. The thatch burned like a torch. People came and formed a chain with buckets from the well, and someone put a ladder against a window to get us out. There was nothing we could do. Nothing anyone could do. The staircase was ablaze. Roger nearly went insane. They say it must have been over quickly for Mama. The smoke. Perhaps she knew nothing."

An awful animal-like groan of despair broke from him. With a swiftness that caught her off balance he thrust her from him, making her stagger and fall, but although the result of his violent action must have been unintentional he made no move to help her up again and threw himself back into the saddle, bringing his whip down with such force across the horse's rump that it leaped forward with a startled whinny into a full gallop, thundering off in the direction of the village, leaving her in a cloud of dust that stung her eyes and was gritty in her mouth.

Fear gripped her. What was he going to do? Where was he bound? She scrambled to her feet, vaguely aware that she had grazed her elbow in the fall and that her palms had been cut and pitted by stones on the lane's surface, but she did no more than brush them clean against her skirt, breaking into a run to follow after her father, who had already vanished from sight.

Ever after, the rest of that day seemed a nightmare to her, and indeed it was to return to her many times in dreams that made her cry out while she searched in vain for a distraught man who blundered about somewhere ahead of her, his frantic hands taking up one piece of charred wood and then another as if by putting the burnt timbers together again he might restore the home he had lost and bring back to life the woman who had lived in it.

It was a full two miles from where Tansy had been left on her own to the far side of the village where the blackened ruins of the cottage still stood, an ugly jumble of scorched inner walls, fallen beams, and powdery cinders. She came to it at a stumbling run and knew he had been there. The only door still left on its hinges had been kicked in and the ash and pieces of debris lay disturbed where he must have trampled them under a ceiling of open sky, which was already fading to dusk. Where was he? Where had he gone? To the churchyard. That was where she would find him.

She turned with a swirl of petticoats and followed the footpath that led to it, slowing her pace when she came to the gate, which opened with a faint screech, for she did not want to intrude on his private moments of grief, but now that he was home she could not bear to be far from him. Yet at first glance she saw he was not in the churchyard and when she looked into the church itself he was nowhere to be seen.

Retracing her steps she hurried down the cobbled street of the village where most of the shops were still open, although there were few people about. When she came to an arched passageway near the green she went through it, making for the wide green gates at the end of it, on which was painted in white lettering the name of the owner and his business: *Edgar Webster and Son, Builder and Contractor*. It had occurred to her that her father could have sought out her brother Roger, who at the age of fifteen was apprenticed in the carpenters' workshop there, not through his own choice, but through pressure from their mother, who had distrusted his love of horses. She hated his hanging around stables and riding as though born on horseback whenever the opportunity presented itself, and it was her fear that he would follow his father into the racing world that had made her deal somewhat unjustly with him, committing him to a trade that he worked at obediently, but with little heart. After the cottage had burned down Mr. Webster had allowed him to sleep under the workbench at night and he was fed in the household's kitchen. Whether it had been Mr. Webster's own idea that Roger should do two extra hours of work a day in return for his keep Tansy did not know, but she suspected it was at Mrs. Webster's instigation, for the woman was as tightfisted as she was snobbish. It was well known that she held the purse strings, it being her money that had enabled Mr. Webster to establish himself and build her a grand house, keep a carriage and pair, and accumulate a stable of good hunters which he and his only son, Adam, rode to hounds. Tansy felt sorry for Roger having to work such a long day, but it had been necessary and he had done it without complaint.

But in a way things had gone harder for Nina, who was two years older than Roger and a year younger than herself. Tansy had secured a post for Nina as dairy maid on one of the farms where the farmer's wife had offered, in lieu of paying her wages, to feed and accommodate Judith at the same time. It was not a very satisfactory arrangement, but Tansy had been thankful to have both girls housed for the interim period until her father came back. Unfortunately Nina had found the work hard and distasteful, hating to have the odor of the byre upon her skin and clothes, being fastidious in every way, and she grumbled incessantly to Tansy whenever they met that her hands were ruined and so much bathing in icy pump-water would give her the lung fever before she was finished. She declared she would gladly change places with Tansy and take up the daily vigil to ensure that their father was sighted as soon as he came over the hill, but Tansy knew her sister well enough to have no doubts that at the first drop of rain Nina would have taken shelter somewhere under trees where she could no longer see the road, or else, becoming bored, taken time off for an hour or two, ignoring the risk that their father might have gone riding by in her absence. Admittedly Tansy's own small job was far less arduous than Nina's, for she had taken on the duties of night nurse to an elderly woman, giving the son in the house and his wife a chance to sleep at night, there being little the matter with the old crone apart from stiff joints. After an initial battle of wills, the old woman, whose main enjoyment was tormenting her daughter-in-law, had acknowledged Tansy's authority and ever afterward slept like a log in her presence all the dark hours through. This had enabled Tansy to get the sleep she needed and be fresh for her daily watch directed toward her father's return, for all along she had wanted to guard against his coming upon the burnt-out ruins of the cottage without being forewarned by his own kin. But she had bungled the breaking of the news to him. She must have. Why else would he have reacted in such an extraordinary way?

Wrapped up in her own confused and troubled thoughts she had pushed open one of the wooden gates and was through it into the yard before she realized that she had come upon a tempestuous scene not uncommon on the Webster premises. Several workmen stood grouped about, eyeing warily and uncomfortably their master and his son, who stood facing each other with all the fury of two enraged lions a few feet apart in the middle of the straw-strewn, cobbled enclosure. Edgar Webster, a portly, bald-headed man dressed in loud checks, was crimson with temper, his clenched fists shaking at his sides as if it was taking all his will power not to smash one of them into the lean, bold face of his offspring, whose deep-set dark eyes were narrowed with suppressed violence into flashing slits, the blatantly sensual mouth so tightened that the skin about it showed white. Two of a kind were the Webster men. None crossed their paths lightly and their quarrels with each other were notorious.

"Damn you, Adam," Edgar roared, "I've bin in buildin' all my life, and you can't tell me nothin' about bricks and mortar!"

"I'm not disputing that." Adam's speech was far removed from his father's coarse dialect, but he looked equally ready to resort to a primitive exchange of blows should the first move be taken. "It's your antiquated methods I abhor. When are you going to get it into that thick head of yours that we're wasting time and money with that out-of-date brick kiln and if we only invest in the new process I've outlined to you—"

"Shut your jaw! Or I'll shut it for you! You think money grows on trees just because your mother had her way and sent you to them fancy schools. Made a namby-pamby of you. I left a dame school afore I was twelve and could read, write, and cipher. That were good enough for me and it should have bin good enough for you."

"Don't sprout such nonsense at me. I'm sick of your ignorance. Are you going to take my advice about the brick kiln, or aren't you?"

"Never. I'll see you in hell first."

"You're a blundering old fool."

It could have been the flash point for blows. The foreman, who had worked many years for his master, winked meaningfully at some of the other men and they moved unobtrusively but purposefully a few steps nearer father and son, ready to leap forward and part them should the calamity of fisticuffs, so far avoided by a hair's breadth on many previous occasions, come about at last. But even as Tansy, who had been at a loss whether to stay or go, decided she must withdraw and return later to see Roger, it was her brother himself who created a timely diversion.

Unnoticed, he had come to the door of the carpenters' workshop, woodshavings clinging to his apron and lying like golden snowflakes on his fair, curly hair, to stare with the rest of them at the angry scene, and now, absently leaning a hand against some planks stacked upright against the wall, he caused them to slip and come clattering down with a great din. Edgar swiveled around with an oath to see what had happened, and let out a bellow.

"Idiot boy! That's best timber!" He stomped toward Roger, his wrath temporarily diverted to this new target, and he drew up his hand in readiness to deal out a swiping backhander across the face of his youthful employee. With mingled admiration and anxiety Tansy saw that her brother did not quail, in spite of the fact that he was exceptionally short for his age and small-boned like their mother, but stood his ground and faced Edgar squarely and without insolence.

"I know it is, sir," he said bravely and openly. "The fault was mine."

Unexpectedly Edgar's hand faltered. It could be that he remembered in the nick of time that this was the lad who had behaved with the courage of a man on the night of the cottage fire and had had enough grief to bear as a result of it without being punished physically for what was, after all, a harmless accident. He lowered his arm, but spoke no less fiercely, bushy brows lowered. "Why the devil was it stacked there in the first place?"

It was the foreman, well used to dealing tactfully with his irascible master, who came over in time to answer first. "Beggin' yer pardon, sir. It were you who said to leave it there."

"Hmm. Did I?" Edgar's eyes shifted and he shrugged his big shoulders irritably. "Well, I only meant during unloadin'. See that it's set where it belongs." He went striding out of the yard and the atmosphere immediately relaxed, although Adam stayed where he was, glaring after him, showing himself to be dissatisfied with the way the clash between them had ended. The workmen dispersed homeward and the foreman only remained long enough to give Roger a final word about the restacking of the wood before departing too.

Roger had not noticed Tansy and was stooping to get a grip

on the end of a plank when she came to a standstill at his side. "Hello!" he exclaimed, taken aback. "What are you doing here?"

"I came to find out if Papa had been to see you."

He straightened up, dusting his hands on the seat of his trousers, and he frowned with deepest concern, catching a distressed undertone in her voice. "No, he hasn't. He's home then. Now—how did he take the news?"

"Badly, I'm afraid."

"It was to be expected. Why did you part from him?"

"He rode off on his own."

"He would want to be alone for a while," he commented sagely on a sigh. "I'll be glad to talk to him when he does come into the yard. Tell him if you see him again before I do, will you?"

"I will. Well, I'd better not keep you from your work."

"No, you'd better not." He spoke with private bitterness, leaning down to start lifting again, and she drew away with a backward glance over her shoulder at him. He had become singularly restless and resentful of his work since the fire, with wild talk of going to sea or emigrating or taking to the road. All the time she had told herself that her father would know how to cope with this strange, mutinous attitude when he came home. But now he was home and she had no idea where he might be.

"I couldn't help overhearing what you said." It was Adam falling into step at her side, and her heart gave an unbidden little leap. "I gather your vigil was rewarded?"

Tansy had long been attracted to Adam, despite his reputation for being the village heart-breaker, but early in the autumn he had become Nina's beau, and she'd had to crush down her own feelings. Yet she knew herself to be still vulnerable to his easy charm and especially susceptible to his ever flirtatious eyes, which had the power to make any girl think it was she alone whom he found beautiful and desirable. Even though he was being sober and respectful at the present time in his questioning, she gave him no more than a quick glance as she answered him.

"Yes, I was. As you know, it was my fear that someone else would blurt everything out to him on the road, but"—she shook her head sadly, slowing to halt as he leaned forward to open one of the gates for her—"I don't know that I did any better."

"Nevertheless, he must have been thankful not to have heard it from other than his own kin," he said kindly in an attempt to console her.

She nodded, biting deep into her tremulous lip, and met his eyes. He smiled seriously at her and again she gave a nod, hurrying through the gate and down the arched passageway back into the street.

She tramped the rutted track under the first stars to the farmhouse where she found Nina sluicing out the dairy at the end of her day's work. Her sister turned at her approach, bucket in her hand, her dark red hair hidden under a frilled cap, and stood with one hand on her hip, her whole stance one of physical tiredness and dejection.

"Whatever brings you visiting at this hour?" Nina greeted her coldly, and then added on a note of sarcasm: "Nothing to do but take an evening stroll, I suppose."

It was enough to tell Tansy she had made a wasted journey and Oliver Marlow had not discovered his other daughters' whereabouts and gone to them in his grief. Wearily she covered the last stretch of distance between them and thought as she did so that Nina's complaints about her dairy work had been justified, for the girl looked wan and exhausted, the bloom gone from her face, her dark blue eyes shadowed, her cheeks hollow. Thank heaven, it would all come to an end in the morning. She reached the dairy and leaned against the doorjamb.

"I've good tidings," she said, hoping that no bleakness sounded in her voice. "Papa has returned."

Nina dropped the bucket with a clatter and wiped her fingers on her coarse apron. No joy showed in her unusual, elfin-eyed face. Only resentment was registered there. "And none too soon! Why isn't he with you?"

Tansy made an indecisive little movement with her hands. "Let's find Judith first and I'll explain."

Nina nodded, pulling the cap from her head and releasing her hair, which tumbled down her back like polished silk. She led the way along the path into the farmhouse kitchen where they found Judith alone in the lamplight, her neat head bent over some linen she was busily stitching for the farmer's wife, her thimble flashing, and she looked up at the sound of their footsteps on the flagstones.

"Tansy!" she exclaimed with smiling astonishment, lowering her sewing and putting it aside. "It's late for you to come calling." Then her gentle face tightened anxiously. "Is anything wrong?"

After their bereavement she, always the calm and docile one, had become taut and overwrought in a way quite unnatural to her, nervous of anything that was slightly out of pattern, but gradually she was recovering from that stress and developing into a stronger personality, almost as if, much as she had loved Ruth, she had been dominated too much by her, just as a bud is prevented from opening into full flower by a shadow between it and the sun. Tansy, anxious that there should be no relapse, had made up her mind not to burden either of the girls with unnecessary worry. "I've seen Papa," she said simply.

Judith released a shuddering sigh, closing her eyes briefly. "He's going to need us now."

Tansy gave her a curious look. How strange that her foster sister should have expressed in such an odd manner her relief that he was home, when it was they who had been in such desperate need of him as head of the family to take all matters into his charge. He was the pivot around which their lives had always turned.

"How slowly the weeks of waiting have gone by." Judith's throat was full and she blinked at the glint of tears on her lashes. "He's home, and I can hardly believe it's true."

"It's true enough." Tansy went to her and they hugged each other spontaneously in the emotion of the moment, Tansy secretly in want of comfort, Judith expressing her affection for them all.

Releasing Tansy, she looked expectantly toward the door as she reached for her stick and hauled herself to her feet, a tallish figure, thin and small-breasted with a swan-like neck and pretty hands. "Is he waiting outside? Oh, tell him to come in, do!"

Tansy shook her head and the strands of hair dangling about her face reminded her that she had left her hat in the lane, but it had probably been crushed under cart wheels by now. "He's not here. I met him beyond the village as we had planned, but the news was hard for him. He wants to be alone for a little while."

Judith's expression became tragic as she shared mentally the widower's anguish. It made the skin go tight over the pointed bone structure of her face, dulled the fawn-colored lights in her hazel eyes, and made her lips look pinched and full of pain. Compassionately she whispered her own special name for him: "Poor Papa Oliver."

"You'll be able to see him tomorrow, I'm sure," Tansy assured her.

Judith gave a nod, absently brushing back a light brown tendril that had slipped from the coil at the nape of her neck. None of them suspected how great a void had opened up for her with Ruth's going, causing all the insecurity of her early childhood to come surging back to undermine all her stamina. For days she had been unable to check her copious tears, and she was ashamed that she had leaned too much on Tansy for succor instead of giving her the help she needed at such a time. But she had recovered herself and was determined that never again would she fail her or any of the other Marlows. With her resolve had come a peculiar sense of freedom, which was inexplicable to her, for she was as bound by her disability and her surroundings as she had ever been.

"Would you like some tea?" she invited. "The kettle is on the hob. They let me make a cup for Nina when she comes in at this time from the dairy. There'll be enough for three."

"Yes, I would." Tansy would have dealt with the steaming kettle, but Nina motioned her to take a seat.

"I'll do it. *Tea!*" Her rosy lower lip curled scornfully. "It's only the tea leaves left in the pot from earlier today. They eat and drink like the peasants they are in this house. And their table manners. Dear God, the pigs in the sty make less noise."

"They're kind people," Judith pointed out firmly, "and farming folk have no time to waste at table."

Nina, having poured the boiling water into the teapot, put on the lid and stood waiting for the leaves to infuse. "You always make excuses for everybody," she mocked her foster sister. "Be thankful that Mama saw to it that each of us learned to conduct ourselves mannerly, and it's due to her that none of us has those crude local vowels to sully our speech. Not only can we be grateful that she spent hours teaching us herself to supplement the education we received at the village school, but she also ensured that we'll be able to choose husbands a cut above the average when the time comes. Even Roger can do well for himself if he goes into business on his own when his apprenticeship is finished, making elegant furniture perhaps, and employing others."

Judith was silent. She considered both the Marlow girls to be exceptionally beautiful, Tansy with her dramatic golden loveliness, and Nina with her fascinating changeling looks, and knew they would get their choice of suitors when they wished it, but for herself she must relinquish all hope of marriage and the children she had longed to bear, knowing no man found her desirable with her thin body and wasted leg. Tansy, seeming to divine her thoughts, which was not surprising, for they had always been close, gave her a cheering smile.

"Whoever gets you one day, Judith," she said with complete sincerity, "will have the best wife of all. Neither Nina nor I have your sweet patience and forgiving nature. We have much to learn from you."

"The tea is ready," Nina announced, rolling up her eyes at virtues she had no desire to possess.

They sat at one end of the long wooden table where the grease stains gave evidence of the table manners that disgusted Nina, and talked as they drank the tea. Tansy was careful to parry all questions about Oliver apart from how he looked and if she thought he had had a good season. The tea was abysmally weak, but warming and not without flavor. She felt quite refreshed by it when she left the farmhouse to return to the village once more. Surely she would find her father looking for her. He would have forced himself to overcome that first terrible shock and his thoughts would have come round to his children again. He would remember how he had thrown her from him and be anxious about her, for he had never dealt harshly with any one of them, leaving matters of discipline to their mother, and the fear that he might have hurt her accidentally would press him sorely. She must find him quickly and reassure him. Perhaps he would want to discuss plans with her, deciding everything as he must have done so often in the past with her mother sitting quietly, listening to all he had to say.

She came to a halt. The village street was deserted. Not a soul to be seen and all the shops shut with only a few lights showing in upper windows, except for the tavern on the other side of the green where the windows shone brightly and the noise of drunken singing could be clearly heard. There was a good bass voice, somewhat slurred by alcohol, leading the other singers and in full command of the notes of the bawdy song. She had never heard that voice sing such a song before, but she knew to whom it belonged.

Numbness took hold of her. Not anger or outrage, but a state of disbelief without feeling. Almost mechanically she stepped from the street onto the grass and it clung damply to her skirt hems as she moved in a direct line across it until she stood in the rectangular pattern of light thrown down onto the forecourt by the window of the taproom directly in front of her. It was too high to see in, even if the lower panes had not been made up of coarse, green bottle glass, but any last doubts she might have been harboring about the identity of the singer were completely dispelled.

Without hesitation, although it was a place for men and none but the coarsest of womenfolk would ever enter it, she went up the steps and through into the crowded taproom, which was lit by lamps in brackets on the walls, the atmosphere so thick with tobacco smoke that for a few moments it was difficult for her to get her bearings. At first nobody noticed her, all attention focused on Oliver Marlow, who was lolling against the bar conducting the singing with one hand and holding a tankard of ale in the other. The raucous chorus came at her like thunder from all sides, assailing her ears.

She had time to study the scene. Her father's face was crimson with heat and alcohol, sweat trickling down his face, his hat stuck on the back of his tawny head, spilt ale staining his waistcoat. He appeared to have struck up a singing acquaintanceship with a well-dressed, black-haired stranger in a tall stovepipe hat, whose broad back was toward her, an arm resting on the bar with long fingers curled about the handle of a pewter mug, his voice deep and strong. Had her father not been in his cups and the scene a quiet parlor instead of a common taproom, their singing together would have made pleasant listening. As it was, she could only stare across at them with the numbness within her being taken over and consumed by a white-hot temper at a pitch she had never known she possessed, a violent trembling seizing her limbs and churning her stomach.

Gradually the company was becoming aware of an alien presence and voices fell silent around her, one man and then another sensing that something was wrong and turning his head with a start of recognition toward her. Only those pressed close about the bar took longer to notice the change in atmosphere. Among the first of them was the stranger, whose gaze suddenly riveted onto her reflection in the mirror on the wall behind the bar. He saw a white-faced girl with eyes tearing and ablaze, standing like a black-gowned Fury from some Greek tragedy, with a mass of shining, spun-gold hair in glorious disarray.

Between the opaque letters on the mirror, which made up the name of some brewer's ale, their eyes met and it was as though she had found a target at which to direct all blame for the agonizing situation that had been created. No local man would have drawn her father into the tavern, for all knew of the tragedy that had taken place, or—when he was drunk enough—tossed him the song that he must have taken up with gusto, forgetting he was in mourning, oblivious to everything but the flowing ale and the noisy carousal centered around him. The stranger had been responsible! She hated the tanned, hawk-like face held reflected there in a glow of lamplight, his hard stare unwavering. She thought his handsome features ruthless and saturnine. The narrow, brush-lashed black eyes were flint-bright under thick brows, the nose forceful, the jaw square and obdurate, and the firm lips were slightly parted as though briefly he held his breath in a kind of wondering surprise, showing teeth that were strong and white.

All this she had noticed in a matter of seconds. Then abruptly his reflected face swung away from the mirror and he had turned to rest both elbows on the bar behind him, looking directly at her. At the same time the last of the singing fell silent, except for the voice of Oliver Marlow, which faltered and faded as he came to the realization that all was not as it should be.

"Whassar m'tter?" he demanded pugnaciously with the unpredictable swing of an alcoholic mood. "Why aren' you blood' well singin'? Whas'us happened to your blood' throats? Too blood' dry, eh?" He reeled about to crash a clenched fist on the bar, bawling out his order to the landlord. "Drinks all round! D'you hear me? Fill 'em up, I say!"

The landlord, whose wary gaze was also fixed on Tansy, made no move, except to continue wiping the same little patch of the bar surface in front of him where some ale had been spilt, waiting to see what she would say or do. With the exception of those who were shuffling back to leave a clear path between father and daughter, all present were still, watching with the landlord to see what would happen. Oliver fumbled in his pocket and brought out a handful of change which he slammed down on the bar, and some of the coins rolled and fell with a chink into the sawdust on the floor. Only then did he see her there on the far side of the taproom. His mouth fell open as though he could not gather his befuddled thoughts into an understanding of why she had appeared, and he wiped a trickle of saliva from his chin with the back of his hand. But gradually comprehension dawned enough to bring horror blended with rage that she should have come into such a place and be present amid such foulmouthed company. His face congested, his color deepening almost to purple.

"Get out!" he thundered at her, giving himself with one hand a thrust away from the bar, and he stood with feet set apart, reeling slightly, with his head lowered as he glared at her from under his bushy brows.

She remained motionless and silent. Wanting to hit him for the insult inflicted on her mother's memory. Wanting to scream. Wanting to beat with her fists at his drink-sodden face. Seeing that she showed no signs of obeying him, Oliver reached out before anyone realized what he was doing, snatched up the nearest object that came to hand, which was an emptied glass on the bar, and hurled it toward her with all his strength, so that it smashed into a thousand sparkling shards at her feet.

"Get out, I tell you!" he roared louder than before. "Go home!"

She bit deep into her lower lip, bringing the salty taste of blood into her mouth, and her eyes narrowed on the pain of what he had said in his drunken stupor. Then she spoke at last and her words came like a whiplash at him.

"We have no home! And you have no respect for the dead, Oliver Marlow! You shame my mother's memory!"

Whirling about, she turned her straight and furious back on him and the whole company to rush from the taproom, letting the door slam shut behind her. Down the steps she darted, grasping the iron balustrade, and her hand slid down, following the curve at the end of it to bring her round into the shadow of the steps. There she leaned her forehead against the cold bricks of the building and rested both palms against the rough surface on either side of her face.

She was shaking so much that her teeth were chattering. And she was remembering. Scraps of the past, momentary impressions that had registered more deeply than she had known, snatches of conversation overheard without interest, but now having a new significance, all jumbled together like a new dissected picture puzzle that her father had brought home once for Judith and the game had been to put all the pieces together again.

She was putting everything together! No wonder his homecomings had been received so phlegmatically by her mother. There had been no joy in those occasions for her. She had known that he cared nothing for her, nothing for any of them. He had tossed his gifts about, showing off like some returning hero, basking in the adulation of his offspring, and staying only for as long as it suited him before going on his selfish way again. Tansy mocked herself for ever having thought her parents' runaway marriage romantic. He had won her mother with his glib tongue and false affability, but the times when he had been at his wife's side in days of trouble could be counted on the fingers of one hand, and then her concern had always been for him, for his feelings, for his well-being.

Overhead the door of the tavern opened as someone came out, releasing a rumble of talk, subdued now with no more singing, before it closed again. Footsteps began to lurch along down the flight to the forecourt. She clenched her hands and turned in the dark shadows as her father took the final step, paused as though to steady himself, and then staggered away out of her range of vision. Above her a man spoke.

"Go after him, Tansy."

She looked up sharply. The stranger stood there under the lintel, lighting a cigar with a lucifer, which flared and spluttered, marking pearly planes of his face before he blew it out. He must have accompanied Oliver out into the open air and remained to make sure he did not fall and crack his addled skull. She considered it small atonement for having got him in drink in the first place. He spoke to her again on a note of authority, which riled her anew.

"I've been told you're his daughter. Follow him. He needs your care."

"My care?" she echoed explosively. She stamped to the foot of the flight and faced him furiously. "Who are you to give orders to me?"

She had not meant her words to convey a literal meaning, intending them only as an exclamation of contempt, but he answered her, coming leisurely down toward her.

"Forgive me. I should have presented myself before addressing you." There was the faintest edge to his voice as though he were unaccustomed to anyone adopting an imperious attitude toward him and it was not to his liking. "My name is Dominic

Reade. I had a matter to discuss with Mr. Marlow and we were to meet by appointment tomorrow. Hence my decision to arrive today and stay overnight. I need hardly say that in view of what has occurred in his absence—and I offer you my most sincere condolences—I'm departing now and another meeting can be arranged at some future date. He knows my address and where to get in touch with me."

"Surely it is a little late for such finer feelings, Mr. Reade!"

His cigar stopped short on its way to his mouth. "I'm not sure that I understand you, ma'am."

She jerked her chin. "You had been informed of the circumstances and yet you encouraged my father in his outrageous disregard of everything but his own selfish desire to drown his sorrows in ale. In public and with the greatest vulgarity."

His eyes had steel in them behind the drifting curl of cigar smoke. "I have never seen a man more broken by grief," he stated without expression, his face immobile. "The Oliver Marlow who was your father—and with whom I've been acquainted over the past five years—has gone. You will find you have someone on your hands whom you have never known before."

For a moment fear stabbed at her, but in the same instant she dismissed it. However many faults her father had he was too resilient a man to be cut down by a misfortune that she coldly believed to be no worse to him than others he had suffered in his time. When he had recovered from the effects of his debauch he would be the same as before. Only she would be different. The blinding trappings of childish adoration had been ripped from her eyes. She felt suffocated with humiliation.

"You're wrong," she retorted. "Utterly mistaken in every way. I know. That's why I'll not go following after him. I should say things to him better left unsaid. Let him vomit where he will and not look to me to hold his head as doubtless my mother would have done."

Unexpectedly the man reached out and grabbed her by the arm, his grip almost bruising her. "Have you no pity in that bigoted little heart of yours? No compassion? For all your womanly appearance are you still so immature that you only see life in the starkness of black and white without its endless shadings of grays? Do as I bid you and go after that unfortunate man. Then, when we meet, I'll be sure of finding that you are truly possessed of the warm and loving nature that your looks proclaim you to have."

She gasped at his audacity and tore her arm from his grasp, stumbling back a pace. "There'll be no next meeting, sir. Nor for my father either if it lies in my power to prevent it. You've done enough harm already, corrupting him into a drunken debauch that will be ever to his disgrace. I hope never, never to set eyes on you again!"

Abruptly and defiantly she spun away from him with a snarl of petticoats into the direction directly opposite to that which Oliver had followed, and taking to her heels she ran as fast as she could from those tavern steps. In confusion and anger and misery she half-expected the obnoxious Dominic Reade to give chase and haul her back to follow his instructions. But the night remained silent except for the clatter of her own heels on the cobbles. She did not stop until she reached the gates of the house where her night duties at the old woman's bedside awaited her. The gates clanged behind her when she flew up the path and thumped hard on the knocker to be admitted without delay.

She did not sleep at all that night, although the querulous old woman in the bed gave her no trouble, apart from upbraiding her for being late, and slumbered peacefully with her usual snorts and snores. Tansy rose time and time again from the couch where normally she slept quite well, and she paced the room, pausing only when she came to the window. There she looked out at the starlit night and wondered where Oliver Marlow was spending it, chiding herself for not having fetched Roger to attend to him. Was he sprawled in a gutter or lying face downward on the green? Had Dominic Reade gone after him and—like the Good Samaritan—seen him into lodgings at the tavern?

She wished she knew. In vain she tried to convince herself that she did not care where he was, but the longing to know his whereabouts became intense as the night wore on, and fear for his safety grew in her as it occurred to her that he might have fallen and hit his head or suffered some other harm. Suppose he had blundered into the duckpond and gone under the dark water with a splash that nobody had heard!

Never before had she welcomed the first signs of dawn with such thankfulness. Hoping that her charge would not hear the church clock strike and know the right time, she fetched water and soap and clout to bathe the wrinkled face and aged limbs, her own toilette long since completed. It was with relief that she finally snatched up her shawl and swung it about her shoulders as she left the sleeping household, which would soon hear the rapping of the old woman's stick upon the wall when breakfast failed to arrive at the hour she would imagine it to be.

The village was bathed in the pinkish light of sunrise, the shadows long, the air crisp and autumnal. When she crossed the green her skirt hems created a swath of deeper color when the dew was swept aside. Oliver was nowhere to be seen. Somebody was astir in the tavern and she tapped the glass panel of the entrance door. When the bolts were flicked back and the chains unfastened, a shake of the head from the yawning landlord was all the answer she was given after asking if her father was staying there.

Her search went on while the sky grew brighter overhead. She looked down every alley, turned into all the lanes and footpaths, peered into ditches, under hedges, and went right round the duckpond. Finally she found his hat lying just inside the churchyard gate. Slowly she bent and picked it up, knowing now where she would find him. The hat was damp with dew and she smoothed the ruffled nap with gentle strokes of her fingertips as she turned in the direction of her mother's grave.

Coming round the side of the church she looked toward it and thought for a moment with a lurch of despair that he had already left again. Then a terrible cry broke from her and she threw herself into a run. He was lying face downward across the grave, quite motionless. When she reached him and fell to her knees to turn him over she saw that she was too late. A seizure of the heart had taken him from her, the tears he had been shedding still wet on his lashes. By the headstone lay a bunch of ferns, berries, and other autumn foliage, all of the varieties that Ruth had loved best, and it must have taken him all night to gather them.

2.

Tansy saw Dominic Reade at the funeral. When she moved away
from the graveside with Nina on one side of her, a weeping but
head-high Judith on the other, an arm through Roger's, she noticed him with a heavily veiled woman on the outskirts of the silent crowd of mourners and sympathizers who had gathered
there. Bareheaded, he bowed to her, but although she acknowledged his courtesy with a slight dip of her head she could not
bear to look at him, for she blamed him for everything. Had her
father not been drawn into drink by him, he would not have
gone blundering about throughout the night, falling and grazing
himself on sharp stones and against rough tree trunks, the evidence of which had been borne out by the ripped state of his
clothing and his poor, gashed hands, but would have taken sensible shelter under a neighbor's roof, getting the rest and sleep he
needed after such a great shock, and the seizure of the heart
could have been averted. He would have been alive today, sharing this quiet noontide with his children, and knowing that she
loved him more than ever with no last angry words lying between them. She knew now she had shrieked at him in the pub
out of her own fear, her own panic-stricken realization that he
was never going to face up to the responsibilities that his wife
had borne for him and they were to fall on her youthful, unprepared shoulders. Some part of her had known that for the first
time she was seeing the man he had always been within that
bright shell of flamboyancy and bumptiousness and the cock-o'-
the-walk air that he had always presented so blatantly to the
world. Intuitively, Judith had been aware of his true nature and

turned instinctively to the stronger of her two foster parents, loving him but finding the security she sought in Ruth, which had made her utter those enigmatic words at his home-coming, their meaning now all too clear. Ruth Marlow had known and understood the true Oliver with all his weaknesses and had loved him in spite of them in her own quiet, undemonstrative way, she alone his support and his anchorage. With her going he had become a lost soul.

Tansy, remembering what Dominic had said about him from the tavern steps, knew he had only put into words the truth that she had been refusing to acknowledge, and she had hated him for bringing her face to face with it, and for seeing her in her fright and anguish.

The funeral tea was held at the Rectory. When the Rector and his wife had offered their parlor for it, Tansy had accepted thankfully. It was a small party of mourners who gathered in the house, there being no relatives to attend other than the Marlow offspring themselves, and only those who had known the late departed best were invited to drink tea and eat the cherry cake, sponge fingers, and the gingerbread, which Tansy and the Rector's wife had made ready between them. When the modest repast was over the guests made their farewells and left, glancing over their shoulders with curiosity at the lawyer, Mr. Cooper-Evans, who had timed his arrival to coincide with their going, but he ignored them, busying himself getting out his papers while a maidservant cleared the remains of the tea swiftly out of sight into the kitchen.

On the parlor's leather-upholstered sofa Tansy took her place between Judith, whose hand she held between both her own, and Nina, who had not shed a single tear. Roger lifted forward a small table to place beside the lawyer's chair before seating himself on a carved stool and setting a youthful, tool-scarred hand on each knee. The black brim of Tansy's bonnet, the veil thrown back over it, accentuated the pallor of her face, shadows like bruises under her eyes, and she sat stiff-backed and motionless, expecting nothing. The lawyer cleared his throat in preparation and hooked on his spectacles.

There in the stillness of the Rectory parlor with its slightly musty aroma and the background sounds of the ticking of a clock and the faint clatter of crockery from the direction of the kitchen, Tansy and the other three heard the last will and testament of the man who had loved them all dearly, no matter how great his faults.

It was a short will drawn up some years previously in which everything was left to his wife and after her death the residue to be equally divided among their surviving children, with whom he included Judith. But there was little to be shared, most of the items having been disposed of long since in bad times and never replaced, probably forgotten about, and the rest had been destroyed with the cottage itself in the fire.

"There is a codicil," the lawyer added, clearing his throat in readiness to continue. "It is as follows: 'To my beloved elder daughter, Tansy, I leave the house known as Rushmere, in the village of Cudlingham, in Surrey, together with all the contents, household effects, and land appertaining to it. It is my dearest wish that she will use her heart and her head and deal kindly with all she finds in it.'"

Mr. Cooper-Evans looked over his spectacles at the dumbfounded girl. "This is the property that he inherited some years ago from his widowed grandmother. She was a Hammond before her marriage, and the house had come to her from her side of the family, built—so your father told me—by one of her forebears for use as a small country seat within easy distance of London. Some of the furniture in the house is from the time that ancestor of yours lived there."

A sharp nudge from Nina's elbow jolted Tansy out of her stupefaction at hearing that she owned a house. A whole house. With furniture in it. A home to replace that sad, blackened shell. A place where the four of them could be together again.

"My father never mentioned Rushmere to any of us, Mr. Cooper-Evans," she exclaimed, leaning forward in her amazement. "And I know I speak for all of us when I say that I'm sure our mother never knew of its existence."

"Indeed?" The lawyer raised his thin, gray eyebrows. "I find that hard to believe. Judging from the number of receipts in the iron box saved from the fire it appears to have drained his resources in upkeep from time to time. Roof repairs, interior decorations, and so forth. Yet to the best of my knowledge it has been untenanted, there being no record of any rents paid or a lease of any kind being transacted. Unless your mother was kept in complete ignorance of the late Mr. Marlow's financial affairs it's difficult to see how she could not have known of it. It is my belief he was keeping it in good repair against the day when he would retire from his life of journeying and settle down. It is possible that he would have removed there with your mother if she had been agreeable when the house became his in"—here he referred to a document—"1835 and you were all twelve years younger than you are now. But ladies are often reluctant to leave friends and neighbors and familiar surroundings for the unknown. If the matter was a bone of contention between your parents it would explain why you never heard the house mentioned."

Tansy's bewilderment did not lessen. Her mother had never been one to make friends or hobnob with neighbors, always keeping herself aloof and all outsiders at a distance. It was more likely that she had refused to consider living under a roof gained through the generosity of a member of the Marlow family, never having forgiven them for shutting their doors on her husband as her own family had done to her. But could she not have understood that his grandmother must have felt differently about him from all the rest to leave him a house that had once been hers? But Tansy knew the answer to that: Ruth Marlow had a stubborn streak in her. Pride was a tree with many branches.

"I still can't understand why my father should have left it untenanted," she replied, puzzled that Oliver, whose finances had been so often at low ebb, should have allowed a sound property to remain uninhabited when he could have relied upon it to keep his head above water at many a time. "An empty house deteriorates. No wonder he had to keep spending money on it."

"I agree. Unfortunately I can offer no other explanation. Your father never confided in me, and apart from consulting me on minor matters and getting me to draw up his will I never saw him from one year's end to the next." He stroked his chin thoughtfully. "There is always the possibility that the property is not attractive in appearance, lacks certain amenities, or is situated in a somewhat inaccessible spot. It may be that you will decide to sell the property after you've seen it."

"I hope not," Tansy replied earnestly. "To me that codicil read like an appeal that I should cherish Rushmere, and that means he didn't want it sold." Privately she wondered if originally Oliver had intended it as a dowry for her. True, he had set nothing aside for Judith and Nina, but he must have hoped with his unbounding, ebullient optimism that he would have scraped together something else for them to add in further codicils in case of his demise before their respective wedding days dawned.

The lawyer nodded, and then looked at Judith. "As the eldest, Miss Collins, you will be an excellent chaperone to Miss Marlow and Miss Nina in these new surroundings."

"A duty I welcome, sir," she replied, feeling a sense of pride in being appointed officially such an important role. Without her it would have been difficult socially for two young girls to live alone, and she felt she had come into her own at last, no longer a rootless addition to the family, but a strut to keep them secure.

"But shall we be able to afford to make a home of this particular house, sir?" Roger intervened bluntly, an aggressive note in his voice. He was feeling a need to assert his male presence. His lack of height was a sore point with him, and it often resulted in his being treated as if younger than his fifteen years. The codicil seemed to deal out that same treatment again in his eyes, it having been a bitter blow to him that the house in question had been left to Tansy. As the only surviving son it should have become *his*. Jealousy and resentment were high in him, for in addition he saw himself chained to a trade that had not been of his choice in the first place, while the three girls went off to a new county and a new world of interests that would not include him. It was grossly unjust. He tried not to hold Tansy responsible in his own mind for their father's death, but it was all her fault really. If she hadn't left him as she did when he was in his cups a doctor might have been fetched when the attack occurred and had time to bleed him and save his life. "Some of these old country places encompass areas of land that in upkeep would be far beyond our meager resources."

"In the past Rushmere did dominate a good many acres, but your father sold them off, leaving the house with a modest garden and orchard. As to your financial state, that brings me to the next point I have to discuss. As I mentioned to you, he has left you all but penniless. He was a man to whom money came and went with equal ease, and we must remember that he had expected many years yet in which to lay aside provision for the future. But the house is a good asset, and you will have enough on which to live modestly for a little while. I admit that it is obvious that your father did not wish Rushmere to be sold, but he would not have wanted you to starve in comparative grandeur to keep it in the family."

Tansy spoke thoughtfully. "I'm not so sure about that. My father must have tightened his own belt many a time to find funds for Rushmere."

"And at our expense, too," Nina muttered bitterly, speaking for the first time.

"Be thankful that Father did keep the place in repair." Roger retorted with a sharp glance at his sister. "At least it will be sound and dry, and you won't be going to a ruin."

"You can be sure of the property's good condition," the lawyer endorsed, "and your decision to move into the house, at least for the time being, is exactly what I intended to advise. It will reunite you under one roof and give you a respite in which to recover from your sad bereavements, one following so close upon the other, and at leisure you can make plans for the future." He glanced again at some papers on the table and took up a letter. "This brings me to the final matter. From the papers in the strongbox I discovered that your father owned a half share in a colt—a yearling to be exact—and at the present time it is being trained and stabled by the other half owner, a Mr. Dominic Reade, at his stud at Ainderly Hall in Cudlingham." The lawyer paused, looking over his spectacles at Tansy's involuntary gasp of dismay, but when she said nothing, only lowering her head and biting her lip, he assumed she had merely been taken aback of yet another surprising piece of information, and he continued with what he had been saying. "I wrote to the gentleman and received this reply, which I will read to you."

Tansy clenched her fists in her lap. That she should find herself inextricably linked with Dominic Reade through this business over a young race horse was a cruel trick of fate. She wanted to forget him, to put him from her mind. With dismay she listened to the letter, which was brief enough, stating that the late Mr. Marlow had wished to negotiate terms to purchase Dominic Reade's own share. Incredulously she learned that the sum of three hundred guineas had been bandied about by her father, who must have been bluffing his way through on the basis of a hoped-for loan that he had been counting on from an unknown source, but this had been a first offer and refused. However, in conclusion, Dominic Reade announced his willingness to discuss the colt's future with Miss Marlow at any time when a period of her mourning had elapsed and she felt able to consider the matter.

"Three hundred guineas!" Nina expostulated, her face contorted with a furious indignation. "How dared Papa! How dared he! A mere handful of sovereigns clinking in his money belt and he strutting about as though he were a millionaire."

"Hush, Nina," Judith implored in deep distress. "Don't say anything you'll regret."

Roger, his face rapt, had risen to his feet and he spoke half to himself and half to the lawyer. "A colt! And at such a price! Papa must have known there was something special about it. And it's stabled in Cudlingham. I'd like to see it. And soon. Do you think—"

"No, Roger!" Tansy's voice cut across his. She had sprung up from her chair and he had never seen her look more resolute. "Put away your daydreams. Papa told me once it's an old trick in the racing world to boast of a colt's high purchase price and chances when it's entered for a race—and then the owner bets on another, less favored horse which he knows has more chance of

winning and gets far greater odds. Mr. Reade can buy *our* half
share. I'm willing to agree to that—and without delay!"

Roger screwed up his eyes in mutinous exasperation. "What's
happened to you, Tansy?" he demanded heatedly. "I've never
known you show prejudice against the Turf before. Mama hated
it and all it stood for, but that was natural, I suppose. But I'm
not interested in the tricks of the racing world. It's the horses
I've wanted to be with. I thought you always understood that.
You—and Father. Is it so wrong to want to see—just to see and
clap and perhaps even ride once—a colt that he picked out,
whatever his reasons might have been?"

"I'm not against racing. I never have been. Do you think I've
ever forgotten the wonderful outing I had with Papa years ago
when he took me on my own with him to Goodwood?" She gave
a choked, emotional half laugh, half sob. "He won on a horse
called Harkaway, and riding home afterward we cried out the
name like a huntsman's tallyho at everyone we met. To me the
Turf *is* Papa. But it's vital to my peace of mind that we get rid
of the colt."

"It is right and proper that you should dispose of the half
share in this horse as soon as possible," Mr. Cooper-Evans interposed approvingly, "but I feel bound to point out that Mr.
Reade's letter gives no indication that he is prepared to buy—
only the matter of *selling* is referred to. If you could persuade
him to sell the animal on your mutual behalf, then that would
settle the whole business swiftly and amicably." He began to
pack up his papers, making ready to leave. "By all means get in
touch with me if you should need advice on the matter. I am not
a sporting man myself and find it incredible that the total value
of the yearling appears to be six hundred guineas, but even if it
fetches a smaller figure on the open market you will still receive
an acceptable little sum to invest and tide you over any unexpected difficulties or expenses incurred at Rushmere. Now I shall
take my leave of you."

They all stood to say their goodbyes, and Roger went to fetch
the lawyer's coat, which he held for Mr. Cooper-Evans to thrust
his rather long arms into it, and then handed him his top hat and

cane. The lawyer held them at his side as he had a last word with Tansy.

"I must warn you that getting rid of the colt will not sever altogether your connection with it if it should ever run at Epsom Racecourse. I omitted to tell you that the village of Cudlingham lies no more than a mile away from that famous spot, and it's possible that you may be able to see it from the windows of Rushmere."

Roger saw him out to his brougham and the three girls were left alone in the parlor. Tansy, still ashiver inwardly from the impact of all she had learned in the past hour, slipped an arm tightly through Judith's, and spoke in awed tones: "Just think! We have a home to go to. We're going to be reunited as a family."

Nina, patting her hair into place before a looking glass above the mantel, watched their reflection and felt the old tug of deeprooted jealousy. Tansy was quick enough to turn to Judith on every occasion, but it was a different matter when it came to her. Well, she was determined not to let bereavement dampen the prospect of moving to a new home in a new district, which had excited her instantly in spite of her feeling of outrage that her comfort had been sacrificed over the years for it. She intended to cast aside her dyed black mourning clothes at the first opportunity. It was not that the death of both parents had left her untouched; indeed, she had sorrowed deeply and in private, but more for the tragic manner of their passing than from a personal sense of loss. She had longed too often to be free of her mother's strict control not to accept the situation now there was no changing it, for Ruth had been the only one difficult to deceive with her inventive lies, and sometimes only by biting the inside of her cheek till it bled or nipping the skin of her wrist with her nails was she able to keep the guilty color from flooding up into her cheeks under her mother's clear and steady gaze. As for her father, she had been fonder of him than anybody realized, but she had never been his favorite and the knowledge had embittered her. Tansy had been the shining apple of his eye, and always she had felt shut out, the least important of his children in those exu-

berant home-comings when he flung gifts from his saddlebags as
though each were a cornucopia of never-ending surprises. So she
had deliberately shown less enthusiasm for the presents received,
no matter how they delighted her, unable to control the hurt and
jealousy that rose in her at being the last to be picked up and
kissed and swung around in the air. She took hard the times
when the gifts were less lavish and poverty lay like a shadow
over the cottage, feeling that he had failed her more than the
others, for he knew it distressed her to be shabbily dressed in
Tansy's made-over garments and to go without treats or pleasures, and she laid all blame for everything at his door, seeing it
as a further denial of his love.

It was small wonder she had grown up the odd one out, never
pouring out her heart to the other two girls as sisters often did at
bedtime hours when they shared the same room. She and Tansy
should have been close, there being no more than eleven months
between them, but instead Tansy drew more to Judith than to
her, albeit unconsciously, and even Roger showed that he preferred their company to hers any day.

"But how can we be reunited?" Judith was saying. She was
feeling her new position already, but did not want to push her
advice. "Roger has to serve four more years of his apprenticeship, unless"—here her eager hope started in her eyes and
she clutched at Tansy's wrists—"you'd buy him out of his indentures and let him come with us."

Nina, retying her bonnet strings, gave a delicate snort. "He'll
never stick another four years at Mr. Webster's anyway, I can
tell you. He'll turn foot-loose like Papa and make a similar mess
of his life."

Tansy knew that Nina was only voicing a possibility that she
herself had considered. Roger's restless mood boded ill, but during the long weeks of her vigil she had confidently awaited her
father's decision about what should be done to settle him, never
dreaming that the responsibility would be hers alone when the
time came. She wanted him to have nothing to do with Dominic
Reade or the colt, but it went against her whole heart to think of
leaving him behind in the village where daily he would see the

sad, blackened shell that had once been their home whenever he
went in and out of Webster's brickyard, quite apart from everything else there was to consider.

"I'll—I'll speak to him about it," she promised Judith.

The door of the parlor jerked open again and Roger came
back into the room to stand facing her, his lean body tense, his
fists balled at his sides, his snub-featured face compressed into
an expression of mingled defiance and determination.

"I want to go with you to Cudlingham," he announced with a
pugnaciousness that showed he expected argument and refusal.

Tansy nodded and lightly clasped her hands. "I think it would
be best—but on one condition."

Roger's whole face changed, incredulous delight washing over
it, his eyes almost vanishing in crinkled exultation, his grin a little shaky. "I never thought you'd agree. I can hardly believe it.
Does it mean—could it be—?"

He did not dare to voice his most secret hope, and Tansy put
it into words for him with a smile. "I've no objection to your
finding work connected with horses, if that's what you want to
know. But what would you do?"

"I'll be a jockey!" he announced triumphantly.

"Rubbish!" Nina taunted, giving Tansy no chance to answer.
"Nobody starts off as a jockey, you should know that, except for
gentlemen who own their own race horses and can do what they
like. You'd have to serve an apprenticeship as a stable lad, and if
you're lucky—and only if you're lucky—you may become good
enough at riding and handling horses to be tried out eventually
in a race, but that's only if you don't grow too tall or too heavy
or fail to achieve what is expected of you. We heard Papa talk
enough about it all, heaven only knows."

His complacent, exhilarated air did not diminish. "Well, now
I'll tell you something that was a secret in the family between
Father and me—and heaven too, of course." It was obvious that
he could scarcely contain the joyous wonder of what he had to
tell. "I have been trained already. Not to a professional peak yet,
but trained. Every time Father came home he arranged for me to

get hours of riding in over the hill at Squire Brompton's racing stables. You should have seen me on the gallops there!"

"Mercy me!" Judith exclaimed, sitting down in the nearest chair.

Tansy raised her eyebrows in bewilderment. "So you didn't go along to reload Papa's fowling pieces when he went shooting with the Squire!"

"I used to join the shooting party after riding," he explained hastily. "It was the same when Father and I went coursing or out snaring rabbits or fishing in the river. I just used to ride *first*. Neither Father nor I ever told Mama a lie about it. We didn't have to, simply because she never knew."

Nina's lip curled scornfully. "It wasn't easy to keep anything from Mama. She was probably getting suspicious, and that was why she was quick to set you to a carpenter apprenticeship last March as soon as Papa left for the season."

"She was wrong to do it," Judith said quietly. They all looked at her. Never before had she uttered a word of criticism against their mother, but a new Judith was emerging, almost as if she had found the power to speak out after years of remaining silent in the background. "Everyone should have the chance to live their own lives. I want to see Roger become a fully fledged jockey."

Tansy, getting over her surprise at Judith's outspokenness, nodded. "I agree with you." She turned toward Roger, holding out her hands wide in a warm, expansive gesture. "Without doubt the Epsom district is the place for you. Would the trainer at the Brompton stables give you a letter of recommendation, do you think?"

"I'm sure of it," he answered promptly.

"You must give me your solemn promise on one thing and one thing alone," Tansy insisted, seriously.

"Yes, yes! Anything, anything!" He was throwing himself about in his happiness, much like a gangling young colt himself, and he hugged Nina and Judith in turn, and then threw himself down on the sofa with feet outflung as though exhausted already by the excitement of it all.

"You shall see the colt," Tansy said. "It is right that you should be with me when I discuss the selling of our share to Mr. Reade, but that must be an end of it. You must give me your word that you'll not ask Mr. Reade for work in his stables. This is all I require of you."

Roger sat forward and laughed at the simplicity of her request. "I make an oath on it! If the colt is sold I'd have no interest there anyway. There'll be other racing stables where I'll find employment. Have no fear about that. I'll do well, I promise you. I might even be a trainer myself one day."

He was on his feet again and he crushed her in a jubilant bear hug, making her fear for her ribs, and then he was pacing with a springing step up and down the room, telling them all the still more grandiose plans that were coming into his mind, which ranged from owning a string of race horses to riding a winner in the Derby. She knew she had acted wisely in letting him have his way, and hoped with all her heart she would continue to make the right decisions in the time that lay ahead.

The four of them stayed another half hour in the parlor making plans for the earliest possible departure for Cudlingham, and the morning two days hence was settled upon.

"Provided all goes well with Mr. Webster," Roger said, suddenly anxious.

"I'll go to his house straightaway," Tansy answered.

"I'll come with you," Nina said quickly, never having seen inside the Websters' house and curious to know what it was like.

Roger volunteered to walk Judith home to the farmhouse where she and Nina had continued to be housed since the tragedy, and after Tansy had thanked the Rector and his wife for their hospitality the four of them went their separate ways.

At the Websters' house, from a window, Adam happened to spot Tansy and Nina approaching and he opened the door to them before they had a chance to ring the bell. His face was serious in deference to the funeral that had taken place that afternoon, but his eyes showed he was glad to see them and went from Tansy to Nina, revealing his deeper pleasure in the sight of her.

"Good evening, Adam," Tansy said in answer to his greeting. "I've come to see your father and Nina is keeping me company. Is he at home?"

"Yes, he is. Come in." He stood aside for the girls to enter and showed them into the best parlor. It was chill, there being no fire to offset the cold dampness of the evening, a pleated paper fan spread open in the grate. Nina glanced about her before sitting down on a horsehair sofa. Tansy remained standing, facing Adam.

"Thank you for coming to the funeral," she said to him in a quiet voice. "I saw you at the graveside."

"What happens now?" he inquired with a genuine concern.

Her face became radiant. "Papa left me a house! A house called Rushmere where we can make a home together again. It's at Cudlingham in Surrey. Near the town famous for its salts and its racecourse."

"Epsom, you must mean. That's splendid news. I know Cudlingham." Then he corrected himself. "Well, that's not strictly true. Better to say I rode through it a couple of times when I went with a party of friends to the Derby and we stayed in a tavern in the village of Ewell nearby."

"Is it a pretty area?" Nina questioned eagerly from the sofa.

He looked blank. "Yes, I think so. We went to the races, y'know, and not to look at the scenery, but there are woods and a fine span of rolling Downs and they say you can see the dome of St. Paul's in the distance on a clear day."

"How wonderful!" Tansy said on a satisfied sigh. "That's why I'm here to see Mr. Webster. I want Roger to come with us. Do you think your father will raise any objections? I'm prepared to pay, of course."

Adam shrugged easily. "I shouldn't think he will. Roger has tried hard, but he'll never make much of being a carpenter. It's my belief that Father won't be sorry to see him go. Er—don't take offense at my plain speaking."

She raised a hand reassuringly. "Indeed not. We've all known that Roger's heart has never been in it."

"I'll tell my father you're here." He was gone from the room for a matter of seconds and returned with Mr. Webster, who himself invited Tansy to adjourn with him to his study. Adam and Nina were left alone. He sat down on the sofa beside her. Her large, almond-shaped eyes, a lighter shade than Tansy's, regarded him with their aloof, enigmatic look that he found fascinating and intriguing.

"I'll miss you, Nina."

"Will you?"

He thought with exasperation that she never gave anything of herself away. Either physically or mentally. She had given him no indication as to whether or not she would miss him, and the kisses he had managed to gain from her over the past weeks had been hard won, the few chaste caresses she had allowed even more so. Yet there was a pulsating sexuality in every move she made, every turn of her head, every flicker of her lashes, and it emanated from her like the bouquet of a rich wine. There was gossip about her in the village. There always was about girls who looked like Nina. He remembered hearing it said once that when she was younger she bartered favors to boys of her own age for a silken hair ribbon, a fairing, or pretty buckles for her shoes. He doubted the truth of it, but could not be wholly sure. One could never be sure of anything about Nina.

With a gap of five years between them he had never paid her any attention, scarcely recognized her, in fact. Then one hot September day he had come across the two Marlow girls resting on the grassy slope by the blackberry woods, the baskets full of the fruit they had gathered set down beside them. He knew he would never forget the sight of them there, one sitting a little higher than the other, their muslin skirts billowing lightly in the breeze, and all the brilliance of the sun behind them concentrated in the rich abundance of their marvelous hair, Tansy's the color of spun gold and Nina's fired to a flaming copper-red. Briefly he had stood in indecision, not knowing which of them attracted him more, amazed to discover that while he had been enjoying himself elsewhere these two girls, who had always been overly protected by their dignified but intensely strict mother and made to keep apart from the more rowdy village children, had grown up into young womanhood. Nina had spoken first. "Since you have come all the way up here, Adam Webster, you may carry my basket down for me when I'm ready to go." That piece of impudence, coming as it had done with that cool, tantalizing look of hers, had tipped the scales. She had offered him a challenge that Tansy had not, a challenge he had taken up with no success, and now she was going away.

He directed his dissatisfaction into a halfhearted expression of envy. "Roger is fortunate to be escaping from a trade that never suited him. I hope he realizes his luck."

Nina, who had been counting the objects of silver on display in the room, raised her eyebrows at him. "Why do you speak on that note? You wouldn't change your work, would you? You told me once you had building in your blood."

"I have." His mouth tightened, his eyes smoldering. "But I'm not my own master. My hands are tied."

"Then you should break away." Her tone was matter-of-fact and she looked from him toward a pink glass epergne that she thought extremely pretty.

He narrowed his eyes at her lovely profile, the curve of her throat, and the high, sweet tightness of her full, young breasts straining against the black cloth of her bodice under her opened cloak. She looked tender and vulnerable in her funeral clothes and the black brim of her bonnet gave her face the innocence of a nun's. The young animal desire that he felt for her, although not nulled in any way, took on momentarily a gentler aspect, which made him wonder if he was in love with her. The thought had come upon him previously at other times, but he had never given it any serious consideration.

"Suppose I come with you to Cudlingham," he said, testing her dangerously. His patience was running out. He wanted to know once and for all what her feelings were for him.

Deliberately she chose to misunderstand him. "We shall have no need of an escort when Roger is with us, although it's kind of you to think of it. It was fortunate that our wagonette in the cottage's outhouse escaped the fire, and we'll be traveling in it with Papa's horse in the shafts. I think it will be an agreeable journey if the weather is kind to us, and Tansy has planned that we take it in easy stages not to let Judith get overtired." She got up from the sofa and went across to run an exploratory finger along a rosy glass frill of the epergne. "What a charming thing this is!"

She had driven him too far. With a wrathful exclamation he sprang up and went across to grab her by her shoulders, snatching her about to face him. "I didn't mean just for the journey! I have thought of cutting free from my father many times. Cudlingham would be the ideal place for me to set up on my own as a builder and contractor. I noticed when I was there that whole areas are ripe for development. The Brighton railway line was extended to Epsom itself this year, the first time there has been a railway station nearer Kingston and Croydon, and that means the district is really going to grow with easy travel to London. As it is, Epsom has become rich on the races and grown from a village into a town in a remarkably few years, and there's no greater magnet for crowds in all England than the racecourse when the Derby is run. I'd make my fortune—not on the horses, but with bricks and mortar."

She gave a faint, patronizing smile to show she thought his enthusiasm was running away with him. "Have you the financial resources for such a venture?"

"Enough to get started. What do you say, Nina? Let's start a new life together."

His words startled them both, the significance of what he had said plunging home. Too late he realized he had made the irrevocable step of offering for her, and the clang of the matrimonial trap seemed to resound in his ears, but then he saw that her reaction was not what he would have expected, something close to panic sharpening her features and making her eyes dilate in alarm.

"What are you talking about?" she gasped.

Then he knew he did love her. He loved her as he had never loved before. There was no going back and he did not care. He lowered his tall head to bring his eyes on a level with hers, smiling into her face, amused to think she should have imagined his intentions not to be honorable, and excited by it, his body stirring, his blood beginning to pound hot for her.

"You and me, Nina—and a wedding ring." His arms went about her slim, pliant body and he caught her close, crushing her when he felt her involuntary jerk of resistance, and his mouth jammed down on hers, taking from her surprised mouth the kind of kiss he had sought in vain so often before. He had hardly time to savor the warm, moist sweetness of it when she became steel-like in his embrace, thrusting up fists and arms and elbows to wrench herself free of him. They broke apart.

"I'm not in love with you." Her voice held a note of incredulous shrillness in it as if she were astonished that he should have harbored such an illusion for even the briefest of spells. "Nor do I want to be. I don't want you anywhere near Cudlingham either, if it comes to that. Do what you like with your life. Don't try to link yours with mine."

He could scarcely believe what he was hearing. She was turning him down. And savagely, too. Rage burst within him. Her very rejection inflamed still further his passion for her, he who had never known a girl's ultimate refusal of anything he had ever wished for. His pride was outraged, his ego offended to the limits of endurance. He wanted to strike her. Wanted to shake her until her teeth chattered and her bonnet fell off and her hair went awry. Wanted to throw her down on the floor and take brutal and bloody possession of her.

She drew back another step from him, not cowering, but alert to all she saw in his congested face. "I'm going on my own way at last," she cried defiantly, able to think of nothing but the one stark fact that he had wanted to intrude and stake a claim on the lovely new life she was planning for herself amid new surroundings and new people. "I've never had the chance before. Far from this village. Far from the tongues of the people in it. Far from you."

Then he did strike her, catching her a hard blow with the flat of his hand across her cheek that made a scarlet mark leap to the surface of the pale skin. "Go to Cudlingham on your own and be damned!" he exploded at her. Then he went from the room and slammed the door after him with a force that made everything in the room dance. The pink glass epergne went on tinkling after everything else had stopped, jolted afresh when a second slam in the hall followed Adam's storming from the house.

Tansy, emerging from the study with Edgar Webster, was in time to see Adam's coattails disappear into the darkness and guessed immediately that something was severely wrong. Ignoring Edgar's mutterings about there being no doubt who had closed *that* door, his son having no respect for anything or anybody, she went swiftly into the parlor and stood with hand on the knob in the open doorway. Nina had drawn the black veil of her bonnet down over her face again, but there was something about the set of her head, the vibrating tenseness of her whole figure that told Tansy that her sister was only a step away from hysteria.

"Mr. Webster has kindly agreed to let Roger go," Tansy said evenly, as if by keeping all expression from her voice she might lower that tension like a gentle breeze smoothing a rough sea. She did not add then that he had made a show of reluctance to release Roger from his indentures in order to demand greater compensation, pointing out that several months' tuition had been wasted on the lad. But in the end he had suggested a sum larger than she had hoped for and less than she had feared, so that she had paid out readily and thankfully, Roger's freedom being all that mattered. "Come along, Nina. We won't take up any more of Mr. Webster's time."

Nina straightened her shoulders, regaining full control of herself again, and moved forward obediently, the veil wafting against her face. As she passed through the full glow of the lamplight it seemed to Tansy that one of her sister's cheeks held a burning color, but then the shadows took over and she thought she must have been mistaken.

Outside in the lane before Nina branched away to go up to the farmhouse, she gripped Tansy's arm. She had been silent since they had left the Websters' house, although barely listening to all Tansy had been telling her about the interview with Mr. Webster. "I wish we were leaving tomorrow. Don't let anything delay our departure, Tansy. I don't want to see Adam ever again."

Only then did Tansy realize the extent of the trouble between them. A throb of regret assailed her for what might have come about between herself and Adam if Nina had not coquetted with him that day on the hill. But it was folly to think of that now.

"We'll get away on time, I promise you," she said. Nina gave a trusting nod and set off up the winding track that led to the farmhouse, her veil still covering her face.

The day of the Marlow family's departure dawned crisp and clear. Roger, the reins in his hands, was in the driver's seat of the wagonette, Tansy beside him. Judith lay with her feet up on one of the passenger bench seats, a cushion behind her, a crocheted rug donated by a neighbor over her knees. Opposite her sat Nina, straight-backed, her head held proudly, trying to ignore the fact that she was sharing the seat with an ungainly bundle of their belongings, another boxful by her on the floor of the vehicle.

Although it was early, a number of well-wishers gathered at doors and garden gates to wave to them as the wagonette clattered over the cobbles. Hopefully Tansy scanned the faces for a glimpse of Adam, but she was doomed to disappointment. Judith, her quick tears making everything a sparkling blur, clutched to her breast a posy of flowers that someone had darted forward to hand up to her. Few spoke to Nina, whose haughty ways, like those of her late mother, had always kept them at a distance. Nina did not notice that the shouted farewells included her only through old-established country courtesy, and she would not have cared if she had. She was rejoicing inwardly that she was leaving at last.

The wagonette rolled on and soon the village was left behind. Tansy swallowed when they passed the spot where she had met her father on that fateful day, which now seemed months instead of a mere ten days ago, but she made no comment and neither did any of the others. The wheels rattled over the bridge that spanned the river and the countryside spread out all around them. A mile farther on Roger reined in briefly, giving his sisters the chance to catch a last view of the village lying in its hollow before the hills folded together and hid it from their sight. Only Nina did not turn her head in its direction, but kept her gaze set rigidly ahead. None of them spoke. Then Roger slapped the reins and the horse moved on again.

From his vantage point on horseback higher up the slope under the trees Adam watched the wagonette trundle on along the lane. His love for Nina burned in him like an angry torch, and he half-wished he had ridden down and waylaid her with a few well-chosen words, not of apology for having struck her, but a simple statement that would have let her know she had not seen or heard the last of him. It would have given her something to think about on the journey and made her realize that no girl spurned Adam Webster except to her cost.

The wagonette vanished from his view. With hard hands he jerked the horse about, digging in his heels and adding the sting of his riding crop for good measure. The hooves thudded on the grass, carrying him away through the coppery woods and back toward the village, and the steady rhythm was like the echo of a name to his ears. Nina! Nina! Nina!

Jogging along the road Tansy shivered and glanced skyward to see if a cloud had blotted out the thin warmth of the sun, but the only ones to be seen were gathered far in the distance. The chill persisted like a sense of premonition, knotting her stomach, and a quiet dread of what the future might hold for all of them settled heavily upon her.

3.

They came to Cudlingham in early evening when the sun had gone long since from the day and heavy rain threatened a storm. The three girls had pulled the hoods of their cloaks over their bonnets, Nina and Judith sharing the additional protection of a tarpaulin, which had been taken out from under one of the seats where it was stored in readiness for times of inclement weather. Apart from the rain, which had started to fall in midafternoon, the journey had gone well. They had stayed overnight in some cheap and comfortable lodgings and, contrary to Tansy's earlier fears, Judith had taken the traveling remarkably well, the fresh sights and scenes keeping her lively and attentive and forgetful of her small physical aches and discomforts.

The village of Cudlingham had a Saxon church with a square bell-tower, and one inn, called The Winner in deference to nearby Epsom racecourse. The rest of it consisted mainly of thatched cottages with a few grander houses set back in wide grounds behind high walls. It was a richly wooded area with tall elms, poplars, and thick groves of beech and ash and oak. A woman hastening in through her cottage gate paused to direct them to Rushmere and then stood, heedless of the pelting rain, to stare after them with open curiosity.

Tansy was never to forget the first sight of her new home. Gloriously surrounded by trees like those she had already seen, it appeared behind iron gates, the graveled drive short and straight, opening into a narrow forecourt. The house, framed by the dancing branches, was Elizabethan; built of stone mellowed by time to a greenish gray, it had projecting bays enhanced by a grid of mullions and transoms, gabled dormers running their own pattern along the entire front of the house, the tall chimneys lost from sight behind the treetops.

Jumping down from the wagonette before Roger could bring the horse to a complete standstill, Tansy saved herself from stumbling into a fall and ran with her cloak billowing to the gates, but before making any attempt to open them she gripped two of the rain-wet iron bars and looked through at Rushmere with cautious, critical eyes. It was somewhat larger than she had expected, but nevertheless it was still a house of undaunting size, most probably built originally to be the unpretentious home of a country gentleman of modest means, for it was not large or grand enough to have been the residence of some local squire of the time or any other person of more distinguished standing. She tried to analyze her feelings toward it: mainly relief that it looked manageable, but underlying that relief was a nagging doubt, a curious throb of—not fear, but something more complex —a wariness born of simple intuition that Rushmere represented an additional burden to her shoulders and was far from the haven she had hoped in her heart that it would be.

She had expected the gates to be padlocked, and took her father's bunch of keys out of her cloak pocket, but when she turned her attention to opening them they swung in freely on oiled hinges. A new uneasiness assailed her and with quick running steps she hastened up the drive, framing her hands about her bonnet brim for additional protection against the slashing rain as she glanced upward at the chimney pots. A thread of smoke! It was as she might have expected, but hadn't given thought to beforehand. How typical of her father's carelessly generous nature that he should let traveling acquaintances of his, particularly his friends in the racing world, have access to the property and use it whenever they were passing through the area. All she could hope for was that she wouldn't find that every room had a guest in it.

Roger drove through the gates, following Tansy, but his eyes were on the house. The well-kept appearance of it and the garden in which it stood was startlingly offensive to him in a way he could not have imagined possible, and he regarded it with a hostility that had nothing to do with his previous disappointment that it had been bequeathed to Tansy and not to him. He knew Nina begrudged the money that had been spent on it because she felt it had deprived her over the years of sundry fripperies that were all-important to her, but he was remembering other, more serious privations that had encompassed them all. He thought of the countless times that his father had declared he had no money to spare when the leaking cottage most needed a new thatch, or there were rotten floorboards to be replaced, or fresh plaster wanted over the cracks. A shaft of almost unbearable anguish pierced him when he recalled the crumbling wall behind the cooking range where the ancient beams had caught fire through lack of repair and reduced their home to charred ashes with all the terrible consequences. Everything had been spent on Rushmere. The sooner it was disposed of the better. Had it been his he would have arranged to have it sold without even stepping inside it. Maybe that was why it had been left to Tansy and not to him. His father would have known that he'd harbor no sentimental attachment for it simply because it had been owned by his forebears. If Tansy had any sense she'd not allow herself to be tied down by their father's last wish, but he knew her well enough to guess she'd do what she could to abide by it.

"It looks gloomy, doesn't it?" Judith commented with a shiver from her seat in the wagonette. "The sort of place where a ghost might walk."

The house frightened her. She did not know why, but she wished herself far from it, back within the confines of the Hartsworth cottage with its age-polished furniture and the comfortable ticking of the grandfather clock—but the cottage was gone, and there was no going back for any of them. Her hands were shaking in her lap and she tightened them together, being stern with herself and forcing herself to banish her fears with the reminder that once long ago the cottage had been strange and alien to her, but she had soon settled down. So it must be with Rushmere. She saw that for a few heart-sickening moments it had caused her to lapse back into the abyss of insecurity that change inflicted on her, but this was going to be her home and she would not shrink when she crossed its threshold.

"I like it," Nina said with satisfaction. She alone had no misgivings. In such a house she would be established socially, no matter that they were poor as church mice. Her sharp eyes had not missed the other good properties that they had passed on their way through Cudlingham. She intended to get invited to those grand houses at the earliest opportunity. Oh, yes, she liked Rushmere. From it she would be able to fulfill her long-cherished ambition. She had learned at first womanhood that she had the beauty and breeding and sexual magnetisim to get—given the right circumstances—the kind of husband she wanted, a man of wealth and position, who would lift her out of the life of poverty that was abhorrent to her. From Rushmere she could do it. At Rushmere she would come into her own and be the lady that she was born to be.

Roger had alighted from the driver's seat, and he came round to open the little door of the wagonette. Nina stepped out quickly and ran across the forecourt to peer in one of the windows, cupping her hands against the glass to see better into the evening-darkened room. To her surprise there were no dust sheets covering the furniture and she could pick out the polished gleam of wood, but before she could see more Roger gave her a shout to call her back to the wagonette where she linked hands and wrists with him to form a bandy chair for Judith, whose limbs were stiffened by lack of exercise during the long day of traveling. Together they swung her swiftly to the entrance steps and set her down, both still supporting her.

"Hurry up," Nina said impatiently to Tansy, who was trying to find the right key for the door out of the bunch she held. "We're soaked already and I'm chilled to the bone!"

"I have it!" Tansy rattled the key triumphantly. Unaware that she was holding her breath she inserted the key in the lock and turned it. The door swung wide into the hall and the air smelt warm and welcoming after the damp coldness outside and there was the fragrance of apple-wood smoke.

"Somebody's in here!" Roger said sharply, stepping forward defensively in front of his sisters.

At the same moment a door opened, letting through a shaft of lamplight from the kitchen quarters, and a young maidservant with a crisp, frilled apron tied about her narrow waist, a cap with streamers pinned to the top of her head, stood there gaping at them, one half of her in shadow, the other bathed in the golden glow. In her hand she held a lighted taper.

Domestic staff, too. Roger thought with fury. Servants to keep this hateful house clean. Had there been no end to his father's obsession for Rushmere? "I'm Roger Marlow," he announced in a hard, fierce voice. "My sisters and I—"

"Yes, sir! Yes!" She came hurrying forward, her apron rustling. "You're expected. Your aunt said you would be coming. She would like to speak first with Miss Marlow on her own."

"Our aunt!" Roger exclaimed in astonishment, the girls behind him giving gasps that expressed their similar reaction to the amazing piece of information. "But—"

Tansy's sudden sharp grip on his arm silenced him, making him turn his head quickly to her, and her warning glance told him not to blurt out anything about the old family rift before a servant. Whatever they were shortly to discover it must be kept to themselves. "I'm Miss Marlow," she said to the girl.

"One moment, if you please, miss. I was about to light the rest of the lamps and I mustn't let visitors wait in the gloom." She opened another door into a drawing room and busied herself putting the taper to the wicks of several lamps before showing Roger and his two companions into it, and they took seats on an enormous sofa amid the other newish and ornate furniture. Tansy, looking about her through the doorway after them and in the hall itself, could see no sign of the antique furniture that the lawyer had led her to believe she would find in the house and a surfeit of small paintings in heavy gilt frames, some of them executed by artists of little talent, almost covered the walls.

The maid closed the drawing-room door and bobbed to Tansy with a smile. "Come with me, please. I was told to take you straight to Mrs. Marlow when you arrived."

Mrs. Marlow! Tansy hid her bewilderment as she followed the maid down the hall. Her father's only brother had died several years ago—she well remembered hearing her parents talk of it, Oliver having been given the news by an old acquaintance whom he had chanced to meet on his travels. Was it her late uncle's widow whom she was about to meet? But what need had her aunt to live in another's house—especially that belonging to one who had been the black sheep of the family.

The maid opened double doors into a long room, which stretched the length of the rear of the house and was of fine proportions with a wooden bossed ceiling. Here standing lamps were already alight, glowing in patterned, globe-shaped shades, and a cheerful fire blazed on the hearth, the flames reflected on the mahogany surfaces of the many large pieces of furniture, all highly polished and elaborately carved, which managed to crowd the room in spite of its size. On every flat surface there were lace mats and tasseled runners, covered in turn by vases of dried ferns and pampas grass, porcelain figurines, silver dishes, candlesticks, wax flowers under glass, and fancy knickknacks of every kind. A plush pelmet covered the mantel shelf on which stood a tall clock with a floral-painted face, flanked on either side by a host of ornaments and a pair of stuffed parakeets under glass domes. All these things Tansy noticed in a startled, sweeping glance as the maid ushered her into the room and announced her.

"Miss Marlow, ma'am." The girl withdrew, and Tansy was left alone with the sole occupant of the room, who rose slowly from a velvet-upholstered chair by the fire.

Tansy's first impression was that the woman exactly matched the tasteless clutter of the room itself, which had so effectively destroyed the simplicity needed to set off the splendid ceiling and paneled walls. Small-waisted, full-bosomed, and with pale, floating hands, the woman wore a flounced and frilled gown of black silk, with bows and buttons and tucks ornamenting it, a brooch pinned at her throat and several rows of jet beads looped about her neck. Her hair, a suspiciously bright tea color, was dressed in fussy little curls and ringlets over which flowed the narrow, black streamers of her dainty little mourning cap. She was no longer in her first youth, but her doll-like features had retained a cherubic plumpness of cheek and her exceptionally fair complexion was as smooth as her white throat, and under deep lids now quivering nervously, her blue eyes were round and girlish. She spoke first, her voice carefully modulated.

"How do you do, Miss Marlow—or may I call you Tansy? I have heard so much about you from poor dear Oliver. Pray come and sit down, do."

Then in a flash of revelation Tansy understood. How or why it should have come to her so quickly she could not begin to comprehend, but she knew for a certainty that this woman was no aunt of hers, no relative of any kind. This overdressed, voluptuous little creature had been her late father's mistress. Shock turned her cold and made her immobile. She stayed where she was as though the soles of her shoes had become glued to the crimson-patterned carpet, and she stared across the room at this sudden personification of a secret part of her father's life that she had never suspected existed.

Though her throat felt stiff and frozen she managed to speak, trembling with the shock of her discovery. "Your surname cannot be Marlow through any blood relationship to me. I suggest you have no right to call yourself by it. I want to know who you really are and by what right you occupy this house, which my father bequeathed to me."

The answer came with some dignity and a dash of bravado, although the woman's voice quavered. "I changed my surname by deed poll before I came to live in this house twelve years ago. I am Amelia Marlow. Nobody can dispute that. Everybody in Cudlingham believes me to have been Oliver's legal spouse and they now consider me his widow." Unexpectedly a sob overtook her and she put up her shaking hands to form a peak of fingertips over her nose and stroke away the spurt of tears that had overflowed to trickle down her cheeks.

Tansy scarcely noticed that obviously genuine submission to sorrow, for she was staring at those cared-for hands with the polished, manicured, almond-shaped nails and she was remembering her mother's calloused palms and swollen knuckles, which in winter became raw with chilblains, the flesh breaking red and sore. How could her father have allowed his wife and family to struggle against poverty in the bad times while putting this woman first, seeing that she was well-clothed, well-fed, her every comfort catered for! Suddenly Tansy was certain that her mother, an intelligent, farsighted woman, must have known of her husband's unfaithfulness. Yet he had truly loved Ruth in his heart and been broken by her death. Nobody could have made him a whole man again. Perhaps Amelia least of all.

Maybe the woman guessed part of Tansy's train of thought and sought to turn her ponderings to advantage. With a shaky attempt at a conciliatory smile, her lashes left wet and glittering, she made one of her graceful, nervous little gestures toward a chair opposite her at the fireside.

"Please sit down," she urged coaxingly. "We cannot talk with you at one end of the room and myself at the other, and there is much that has to be said between us."

Tansy accepted the common sense of the woman's remark and moved toward the chair indicated. As she sat down the fire cast its warmth over her set face and quiet hands, which she folded in her lap, but the feeling of having turned to solid ice within persisted, giving her a kind of rigid calmness, which she saw was having a disconcerting effect on Amelia, who showed that she felt herself at a disadvantage, having given way already to a display of emotion. When the woman had reseated herself in her own chair Tansy spoke, combining a host of questions in a single word:

"Why?"

Amelia made no pretense about not understanding and replied in a rush with equal simplicity. "Oliver loved me."

"Did you love him?"

"I did."

"Yet you knew he was married."

Under the pale lids the blue, shifting gaze steadied as though in complacent, prideful satisfaction before the sandy lashes quickly lowered. "I was more wife to him than Ruth Marlow ever was."

Tansy's eyes were bewildered. "How could that be? It was she who wore his wedding ring and bore his children."

The sandy lashes remained lowered. "I repeat, I was more wife to him than she ever cared to be."

The significance of her words made Tansy's cheeks dye crimson. Whether or not the situation between her parents had been as the woman had implied she did not know, nor did she want to, but there leaped unbidden into her mind her own remembrance of the way her mother's cool reticence had ever contrasted with her father's bombastic, demonstrative nature.

Had the rift developed through her mother's discovering that there were other women in his life, or had it come about through the opposite cause? She realized now in her own new, worldly attitude that her father, being the man he was, could never have lived like a monk on his travels and she guessed he had been no more faithful to Amelia than he had been to Ruth Marlow. Firmly Tansy changed the course that the conversation had been following. "Had my father prepared you for the loss of this house in the case of anything happening to him?"

Now the lids lifted sharply and tears swam again. "He always wanted you to have Rushmere, I knew that. There was a clause in your grandmother's will that the house should go to one of Oliver's children. He promised to make provision for me."

Tansy gave a nod. Whatever private financial arrangement Oliver had made with his mistress was no concern of hers. Her glance flicked lightly toward the innumerable knickknacks on all sides. "I can see that many of the things in this house are your own personal property and you must tell me whatever else you wish to take with you—"

"It's all mine!" Amelia sprang to her feet, snatching up a silken cushion from the chair and clutching it to her as if to demonstrate her ownership. "Every stick of furniture in this house belongs to me!"

Tansy, surprised by the unexpectedness and vehemence of the

woman's reply, rose too. "Rushmere and its contents were left entirely to me."

"The old stuff that was here in the past has all gone." Amelia tossed down the cushion and darted across to run her palms possessively and almost sensually over a black table inlaid with mother-of-pearl, which was one of many dotted about the room. "I chose all these pretty things." She moved on to touch one piece of furniture and then another. "They were all gifts to me from Oliver."

"Is there nothing left of the antique furniture that once was here?" Tansy asked, dismayed.

Amelia made a little grimace. "There are one or two broken pieces in the stable loft, I believe. They weren't worth selling. The rest of it Oliver disposed of from time to time when he'd had a run of bad luck and needed money. That's when he sold off the land around Rushmere. It was only the keeping of the house that had been stipulated in the old lady's will—nothing about the land having to be retained." She reached a display cabinet and stood with her back to it, fingers of one hand looped on a rim of one of its glass doors. "It's amazing how much gentlemen will pay for those ugly, antique chests and four-posters and uncomfortable chairs. I was glad to be rid of it all."

"Surely my father regretted the going of such heirlooms!" Tansy exclaimed.

"He never said he did," Amelia blustered. "In any case, why should he when I was able to refurnish in such an agreeable way?" Again the tears shone bright. "I made him happy. He was always happy here."

Tansy refrained from pointing out that her father's huge capacity for enjoying life made him content wherever he was when things were not going seriously against him. "In that case, you will need time to get everything packed up and removed," she said fairly, determined not to let her own personal antipathy toward the woman make her act unjustly or without due consideration. She was totally unprepared for Amelia's reaction.

"You can't turn me out!" Amelia's face was distorted with panic and her hands fluttered as though they had taken on a life of their own over which she had no control. "I've nowhere to go. No one to turn to."

Tansy looked incredulous. "That I cannot believe. You knew the house was to be mine and you must have given some thought to the future over the past few days, if not before. Did you not tell me yourself only minutes ago that my father had made provision for you?"

"Not made it, only promised!" Amelia almost shrieked in her agitation, nuances of a coarser accent showing through the genteel veneer. "It was always going to be done when he had his next lucky streak, his next big win! He never came around to putting anything down on paper."

The truth rang in the woman's words. Tansy could well imagine her father making promises to Amelia, which he would have had every intention of keeping, but always there would have been other demands on his resources, and with the confidence of the robustly healthy he had ever chosen to postpone setting aside some part of a good win for his mistress when he was convinced he would live to be a hundred and could indulge her extravagances for many years yet.

"You surely had the foresight to put aside some portion of whatever my father allowed for yourself and the upkeep of this house," Tansy replied levelly.

"Nothing, I have nothing!" Amelia struck her bosom over the heart with a flattened hand to emphasize that her statement was no lie. "My jewelry is not lavish. Merely a few pieces that I treasure for sentimental value like the brooch I'm wearing now with a lock of dear Oliver's hair set in it. He didn't win at the races all the time. There were less prosperous periods when I made do with the same gown many times over for balls and parties, trimming it up with this and that. I had to see Oliver through the rough patches as well as the good. Never think that it was only at your home that he was loved. He was everything to me." Whirling about, she collapsed sobbing in one half of a tête-à-tête chair, sprawling her elbows over the arm of it, her forehead resting on her wrist while the huge tears made dark blotches on the striped, purple silk upholstery. "Oh, Oliver! Why did you have to die? Why? Oh, oh, oh, why?"

A lace-edged handkerchief protruded from a beaded reticule left on Amelia's vacated chair by the fireside and Tansy pulled it out and handed it to her. The woman took it blindly and pressed it to her eyes, her shoulders continuing to shake with grief. Tansy stood momentarily at a loss. Even if the whole house was as stuffed with furniture as the room in which she was standing, the sale of it would never raise enough for Amelia to live on for more than three or four years at the most. Such pieces, solid and well made though they were, fell in value the second they left the shop in which they had been purchased and Tansy could see nothing that might fetch the original price paid for it. But she told herself that it was no concern of hers. There were limits as to what she could be expected to tolerate, and having her father's mistress under the same roof for even the minimum length of time it would take the woman to pack up and depart was all she could endure.

She turned, intending to leave Amelia alone to recover from her weeping while she returned to the others, who must be wondering what had happened to her, although what she was going to say to them she didn't yet know, but she had taken no more than a couple of steps toward the double doors when she was halted by Amelia leaping up and hurling herself down at her feet in a billowing of silk and a trembling of frills and ribbons.

"Don't make me leave!" Amelia clutched two handfuls of Tansy's skirt, gazing up into her face through reddened eyes and streaming tears. "I'd be destitute! Nobody would employ me! I don't know how to cook or clean or sew. I've no qualifications to be a governess. I'd end up on the streets or in the workhouse. Is that what your father would have wished for me?"

Tansy stared down at her in mingled pity and revulsion, her own face tight with a new knowledge that had come to her. Amelia wasn't aware of it, but Oliver had made provision for her future—through a codicil to his will, through his own daughter. Perhaps a twinge of conscience or a sudden dip of mood had caused him to go on that particular day to his lawyer's and have the fate of Rushmere set down. He had known that Amelia, weak, foolish, and as improvident as he was himself, would be unable to cope with life on her own should he lose out one day to death itself, and neatly and guilelessly he had put his last request on paper, knowing it would not be refused, a gentle imploring of his daughter to use her head and her heart and deal kindly with whatever she found at Rushmere. Amelia! That was the additional part of the legacy not bargained for. Tansy shuddered, and Amelia, taking it as a rejection to her plea, screeched out wildly and threw her arms about Tansy's ankles, groveling at her feet, cap askew, ringlets awry.

In weary exasperation, not far from tears herself, Tansy wrenched herself free and leaned down to haul Amelia to a sitting position and give her a resounding slap across the cheek to silence the mounting display of hysteria. It had effect. Amelia looked at her in gulping silence.

"I'll not turn you out, Amelia. For as long as we're able to live at Rushmere you shall have a home here, but more than that I cannot promise at the moment." Tansy helped the woman to her feet and led her back to the fireside chair where she sat down obediently and dabbed her eyes with her soaked handkerchief. When Tansy asked if she kept any brandy in the house she nodded toward a small buffet. Tansy went to it and took out a decanter and a glass. When she had poured out some she handed the glass to Amelia, who took it with a shaking hand and sipped it with every evidence of appreciation.

"How good you are, Tansy," she said gratefully. "I thought when I saw you at the funeral how like your dear father you were—"

Tansy interrupted the unwanted flow of flattery. "You were there?"

Amelia nodded. "A kindly neighbor, the very same who brought the news of Oliver's death to me, took me in his carriage."

Instantly Tansy recalled Dominic Reade standing with an unknown, heavily veiled woman at some little distance from the graveside. "Was it Mr. Reade who escorted you?" she asked quickly.

Amelia looked astonished. "Yes. Is he acquainted with you? Until Oliver took him into his confidence on the eve of his death Mr. Reade was as ignorant as anyone else of the true state of affairs, and believed me to be Oliver's wife."

Tansy was frowning deeply. "It was a chance meeting I had with Mr. Reade. If he said nothing of it to you we can assume he is a man to keep his own counsel on all accounts."

"Oh, he is."

"What explanation did you give other people about my father's death?"

"I told the truth—that he had died of a seizure. They understood it was to be a quiet funeral some long distance away at his birthplace."

"But my father wasn't born in the village."

"I know, but it was all I could think of to say in my distress. Everybody was so kind. I had no end of letters of sympathy . . ." Her voice trailed off as she saw the expression on Tansy's face and hastily she took another sip of the brandy, knowing she had let her tongue run on too fast.

"I must warn you," Tansy said firmly, "that I can tell no lies to cover all your deceptions and never again must you refer to yourself as my father's wife in my hearing, but neither will I answer any probing questions from outsiders. It is a private matter and must remain so. I know my father would have wished it."

"Yes, how right you are. How wise." Amelia nodded her head vigorously, overeager to agree to anything at the present moment to please her youthful benefactress. "Nobody will be surprised at your presence here. They know the house was to be left to someone in the next generation. Now if you could just persuade your brother and the girls to address me as Aunt—"

"No." Tansy felt she had come to the end of her tether. "I'll do no such thing. I don't even know yet whether they will tolerate living in the house with you. It is to that end I must use my powers of persuasion."

Amelia's small, pink mouth trembled moistly. "Don't speak

harshly to me. I know I deserve it for my thoughtlessness, but I've never been able to endure hard words. Oliver never talked crossly to me. I'll try not to aggravate you, but you must be patient with me."

Taking little notice of the promise, Tansy spoke of another matter. "I'd like some supper served. My brother and sisters must be as hungry as they are tired. There is also our horse to be stabled."

"Rooms have been prepared for you. I'll ring—"

Amelia would have risen to go to the bellpull, but Tansy motioned that she should stay in her chair. "I'll go myself to the kitchen. It's best that you meet Nina, Judith, and Roger tomorrow when they've had time to think over all I shall say to them. Later in the day we must talk again most seriously of how this house is to be managed. Good night, Amelia."

"Sleep well, Tansy."

When the door closed after the girl Amelia gave a shuddering sigh and sank back against the cushion, exhausted by the strain of the interview, which she had dreaded for days, starting every time she had heard the clip-clop of horses' hooves anywhere on the road or the drive. Stretching out her feet, exposing at the same time her slender ankles below the frills of her petticoats, she pushed off one shoe with the toe of the other and when the process was repeated she wriggled her stockinged feet in the fire's glow.

If only Oliver had been able to leave Rushmere to her the ordeal would never have had to take place, but he had told her at the start it could never be hers. Looking back over the years she realized she should have pressed harder for him to purchase a house where she would have owned the door key, but he had enjoyed his coming and going at Rushmere, being fond of the place, liking its proximity to Epsom, and enjoying the company of those in Cudlingham who had become their friends. Well, his friends more than hers. She had always felt herself to be accepted for his sake, Oliver being so obviously a gentleman of true birth and breeding, while she—although she played the lady to the manner born—always sensed that with the special recognition of their own kind inherent in the upper classes they saw through her and hid their arrogant smirks behind her back. Only in rare moments of complete honesty did she face up to this unpleasant fact and it caused her unbearable anguish, which in the past Oliver had always kissed and comforted away, making her believe she had imagined the small slight that had caused her distress. She had observed at the funeral that Tansy had the same air of aristocratic breeding that Oliver had had. Nina had it too, and Judith's delicate frailness made her look like the princess in the fairy tale who had felt a single pea through the thickness of a stack of goose feather mattresses. Any one of them could wear sackcloth to a ball and none would doubt that they were gentlefolk. With the boy it was difficult to tell. He was at that plain, spotty stage of early manhood, and although short and undersized for his age, his arms and legs appeared to be trying to grow independently of his body with its own new, problematic force and power.

Amelia sighed again and drained the last drop of fortifying brandy. Reflecting over the interview with Tansy she supposed it had gone as well as could be expected. Everything she had told the girl had been true. Well, almost everything. If Tansy had turned her out she would have been incapable of earning any kind of honest living and she had been away from the theatrical world too long to return to it now; not that she believed she had lost the power to put on a good performance. Yet she hadn't been acting this evening. A very real fear that Tansy was not to be swayed after all had turned her knees to jelly and made her heart pound. What she had she wanted to hang on to, her comfortable home, friends among the well-to-do in the village, and a position of respectability that was all important to her. She felt she had a right to salvage anything she could now that Oliver had been cruelly taken from her. She had not lied when she said she had loved him. For him she had left her own actor-husband, which in truth had been no great sacrifice, but that was beside the point. For him she had led a life of lies. For him she had suffered torments of loneliness and jealousy. For him she would have gone through everything all over again.

A great sense of loss swept over her once more and she put her hand across her eyes, but with it came a notion of bitter grievance that Oliver should have died more or less through his own folly, throwing his life away by allowing himself to get overly upset by the loss of his wife. He knew—had always known—how she needed him. But he had put Tansy first by giving her Rushmere. In the end it had been as she had always feared: he had loved Ruth Marlow and her children better than he had ever loved her.

In the hall Tansy stood with her face in her hands, dry-eyed, but taking time to regain her strength and courage, wondering how best to tell the others how and why Amelia came to be living in the house. She now had to look after not only her brother and two sisters, but Amelia as well. She gave a thought to her father. Had he always seen some inner resilience in her that she herself had never realized she possessed until recently and for that reason had chosen to give her and not one of the others full responsibility of Rushmere and its occupant? It made her feel close to him, he of the generous heart and generous mind whose worldly follies had been so numerous. Men were strange creatures. He had been infatuated with Amelia's physical charms while loving Ruth with an abounding devotion.

She let her hands fall to her sides, straightening her shoulders and giving her mind to immediate, practical matters. Better to let the others eat first before she broke the news. She had no idea how they would react, and if the girls gave way to tears and wailing, the good food that they needed after their long journey would be wasted. Crossing to the baize-lined door that led to the kitchen quarters she pushed it open and the warm smell of broth and roasting beef and spicy cheese and salted ham brought the saliva into her mouth, making her aware of how hollow her stomach had become. As she followed the flagged passageway toward the steps down into the kitchen itself she steeled herself to the face another difficult task, which was to inform however many members of staff might be gathered there that their duties at Rushmere were at an end.

Unexpectedly it was Nina who took hardest the information about Amelia, all color draining from her face, for privately she saw it as further proof that parentally her father had cared nothing for her or her well-being, allowing her to endure spates of abject poverty while his whore had wanted for nothing. Her stillness and white lips alarmed the others, but she made an effort to recover herself and by inclining her head indicated that they had nothing to worry about with her, although she did not speak again that evening except to bid them good night. Judith, used to keeping her thoughts to herself, only said after due and careful consideration that they must for Oliver's sake try to live harmoniously with Amelia. Roger was far from silent. He gave vent to his feelings with a healthy anger, and when he eventually calmed down a little he announced his intention of looking for work early next morning, not wanting to spend another night if he could help it under the roof of Rushmere, a house he had detested at first sight.

"Not tomorrow," Tansy begged. "I'll need your help about the place tomorrow, and in any case I don't want you rushing into the first vacancy offered you. You must seek out the racing stables that can offer the best prospects."

He gave a heavy nod, seeing the sense of her argument. "Very well. When are we going to see Papa's colt? Maybe we should do that in the morning?"

She understood his keenness and by encouraging it she could divert him from his smoldering anger, which had not yet abated. "We could go in the afternoon if it proves a convenient time for Mr. Reade. I'll dispatch a note to him in the morning. The sooner the sale of our half share can go through the better it will be."

"I still wish we didn't have to sell," Roger commented mutinously, his mood still hot and burning.

That night Tansy lay dreading her meeting again with Dominic Reade. Every detail of that ruthless, handsome face was vivid in her mind. Restlessly she tossed on the pillow, wishing she could put him from her mind and find sleep.

In the next room Nina was sharing a wide pinewood bed with

Judith, and Roger was accommodated at the end of the corridor. He had protested that he would prefer to sleep in the stables rather than under Rushmere's hateful roof, but Tansy, losing patience, had given his shoulder a painless punch and said he must stop making everything more difficult for all of them.

A slight sound of someone passing her door made Tansy lift her head from the pillow. Was it Judith wandering about? Sometimes when her limbs ached in the night she found it better to get up and walk about from room to room for a little while. Throwing back the bedclothes Tansy rose from the bed and hastened to open the door. Outside, the landing and the staircase were dark, but the faint glow of a candle showed through a chink in a doorway downstairs in the hall. Thinking that Judith must have gone down to seek out the warm embers of a fire, Tansy went quickly down the flight of stairs, but when she reached the half-open door she saw it was Amelia who was in the room. She was standing on a footstool and reaching up to take a book from one of the shelves of a large, glass-fronted bookcase. Even as Tansy stepped back to return to her own room a floorboard creaked under her foot, giving her presence away. Amelia gave a cry, slammed the bookcase shut, and spun about, stumbling down from the footstool.

"Who's that? Who's there?"

"It is only I," Tansy said, taking a step into the room.

"What do you want?" Amelia was flustered and upset, her face as pink as the peignoir she wore over her lace-trimmed nightgown. "Why are you spying on me?"

"I'm not!" Tansy exclaimed. "I thought perhaps Judith had come downstairs. She does that sometimes."

"I was getting a book to read!" Amelia made a vague, nervous movement with her hands.

"Yes, I see that. Good night again." Tansy went back upstairs to her bedroom, thinking that Amelia had behaved as guiltily as if she'd had no right to help herself to a book from her own bookshelf. She gave her head a shake over it as she climbed back into bed. It could hardly be expected that any of them could behave quite normally in their present state of adjusting to each other's presence in the house. She went to sleep to dream that she was climbing a mountain of books and at the top Dominic Reade stood watching her, grim and stern and silent, waiting for her to reach him.

4.

Nina volunteered to deliver Tansy's note to Dominic Reade. "I'll take the wagonette and drive through the village," she said. "I want to have a look at everything."

"Well, don't dally in delivering it," Tansy requested, "and be sure to wait for an answer. I don't want to make a fruitless visit to his house this afternoon only to find him absent." She turned to Judith. "Would you like to go with her?"

Judith declined, saying she had had enough traveling about to last her for a few days, and Nina silently breathed her relief. She didn't want company. She wanted to savor the pleasure of being a young lady of importance driving out from Rushmere to acknowledge the respectful nods of those she passed and take another look at the grand houses she had glimpsed all too briefly the evening before. How thankful she was that her father had been extravagant in buying the neat wagonette, which Roger had kept in good trim, and she felt no shame in driving it.

As she drove out through the gates she took a deep breath of satisfaction. It was a fine morning after the previous day's rain with that special mildness that can come when autumn tips into winter and like a last reprieve the sun holds sway for a few hours or a few days as if nature had forgotten how to deck the earth with frost and snow. Nina was bonnetless, and wore instead a ribbon snood to keep her hair neat, a flat bow adorning the top of her burnished head, and for the errand she had donned a braided mantelette instead of a cloak over her green, woolen dress. She had fully expected Judith with her new authority or Tansy to question why she was not wearing mourning clothes, but fortunately she had managed to dodge her foster sister and Tansy, recovering from the ordeal of introducing the three of them to Amelia, hadn't seemed to notice what she was wearing when she'd taken the note from her.

Nina thought the introductions bizarre. She had felt only contempt for Amelia, who—pathetically eager to be accepted—appeared to have put on her best manners and her best dress for the occasion, a creation of striped, gray silk with black ruffles at the throat and wrist, sober enough for mourning without being blatantly black to remind them that she considered her loss to be as great as theirs. The three of them had been excruciatingly polite to Amelia and she to them. Nina, remembering how her father's glance would always flick in the direction of any good-looking woman, could see how he must have found Amelia alluring, especially when younger, but she despised the weakness she saw in the shifting, blue gaze under those pale lids that never met quite fully another's gaze. There was greed, too, in that soft-lipped rosebud mouth, which was a full explanation for many things, not least of all the replacing over the years of the antique pieces that should have been Tansy's, with furniture of Amelia's own. It suggested a solid determination to keep a hold on the house in one way or another. But it was too good a morning to waste thoughts on Amelia. Nina shook back her ringlets and gave the horse a little flick with her whip to increase his pace.

She looked about her as she bowled along, satisfied to see that she had been right in her first impression of Cudlingham as being a pleasing place in which to live. It was situated in a saucer of farmland with thick woods, such as those that Rushmere faced and which were bordering the lane she was following, and all around the Downs rose smooth and green and gentle to the eye. All the fine houses she had glimpsed in the previous evening's dusk and rain looked even more splendid in the bright morning, and some were so deeply set in their acres of land that they could only be glimpsed between trees at the end of mile-long drives. Cottages and more commonplace residences lined the rest of the way for her into the center of the village where the shops, most of them bow-fronted, surrounded the open market square, which was busy with traffic and people on foot. She was aware of receiving a number of male glances as she drove through, but pretended not to notice, holding her chin elegantly high. Beyond the village the lane was joined by a river that ran alongside until it swung round under a bridge, and she knew from Amelia's directions that she was not far from Dominic Reade's home. Within a matter of minutes she was driving along the private road that led to Ainderly Hall.

It proved to be a grand house of exceptional size, not as ancient as Rushmere but dating from the seventeenth century, and stood four-square, built of rosy brick, with elaborate stone scroll-work ornamenting the tall, graceful windows, and a flight of steps with curved balustrades leading up to an imposing entrance.

Nina eyed it approvingly as she alighted from the wagonette and went up the steps to pull hard on the iron handle of the bell. A servant showed her through a gracious hall with a black and white checkered floor into an anteroom to await a reply to the note she had handed over. She had plenty of time to tidy her hair in front of a gilt-framed looking glass and study everything around her before the sound of footsteps sent her whisking back to a chair as if she had never stirred from it.

Into the room came Dominic Reade himself, the delivered note open in his hand, another young man of similar height and age in his wake, both of them dressed in riding frockcoats, breeches, and top boots.

"Good morning, Miss Marlow." Dominic Reade smiled at her, a smile that creased the sides of his face attractively, but she did not respond to him. She wasn't sure why. Admittedly she had been forewarned by Tansy that he had full knowledge of their present situation, which made her wary of disclosure from his lips, but she had not been influenced by her sister's obsessional conviction that he had been instrumental in bringing about their father's death. The tragic accident had been the cumulation of many things, as was every event that took place in life. There was something else, familiar and momentarily intangible, which made all her nerves resist the appeal of his intense maleness. It was not in his handsome features or his vigorous height, but more in his confident, easy carriage, his look of being thoroughly experienced and wordly wise, his nonchalant and casual air that was belied by those dark, piercing eyes that missed nothing. Then it came to her why she felt about him as she did. It was as if in her nostrils she inhaled the gambling trait in him and, associating it as she did with all that had caused her distress, saw him as the enemy Tansy had already declared him to be, no matter that his amiable attitude made it appear that he held no such animosity toward any of the Marlow family.

"I'm Nina Marlow," she said, making a point of never being confused with Judith, who was often assumed to be kin.

He took it as an invitation to use her Christian name. "Thank you for bringing your sister's message to me, Miss Nina, but first of all, allow me to present my companion here, Edward Taylor. He's a friend of mine and lives at Cudlingham Manor next to Rushmere. Edward—meet your charming new neighbor, Miss Nina Marlow."

Nina looked at Edward with interest and saw it was reciprocated, well spiced with an obvious appreciation of her looks. She treated him to one of her rare and beautiful smiles.

"How do you do, Mr. Taylor."

"I'm honored indeed, ma'am." His face was slim with fine bones, his nose high-bridged and aristocratic, the tilt of his head arrogant, and his thin, flexible lips were shaded by a neatly trimmed moustache that was, like his brows, a little darker than his blond hair, which grew in thick, shining ripples. "You've come to stay at Rushmere, have you? Deucedly good news, I must say! My sister and I are acquainted with Mrs. Marlow and naturally we knew her late husband, too. You are a cousin of the family, perhaps?"

"Niece," Nina stated firmly. She sensed rather than saw Dominic glance sideways at her out of the corner of his eye. "I shall be living permanently at Rushmere, not just on vacation. My sister Tansy has inherited Rushmere through some silly quirk of a will that wouldn't let it go to Uncle Oliver's widow."

Beside her Dominic stood silent and the last vestige of tension went from her. Amelia had told Tansy she was certain that he would in all honor keep to himself what he knew of their affairs and she had not been wrong. The last hurdle of danger was past. She wanted to crow with triumph, but turned a suitably serious and intent face to Edward, who was giving an understanding nod.

"Nobody can tell me anything about wills, don't you know. Most families have some experience of such clauses—unfortunate for your aunt, but dashed fortunate for your sister. The Manor is similarly tied up, but in favor of the eldest son, and so I had no worries on that score when it was my turn to inherit."

Dominic made an inviting motion with his hand to indicate they accompany him out of the anteroom. "Let us go into the library. You would like a cup of chocolate to refresh you, I'm sure, Miss Nina. Something stronger for you, Edward?"

The library had books on four sides from floor to ceiling. On the paneling above the huge stone fireplace hung an eighteenth-century racing scene. Nina's sharp eyes missed nothing, taking in the Persian carpet, the soft, dark leather of the studded chairs, and the shaded lamps. Over the cup of chocolate she paid attention to Edward, who sat forward on the edge of the chair facing her. Dominic stood with one foot propped against the hearth and an elbow resting on the mantel, taking no part in the talk which flowed between Edward and her but looking into the fire.

She could tell she was making a deep impression on Edward, every smile, glance, lift of eyebrow, and flicker of lash registering with him. Entertainingly she sketched a picture of her life before coming to Rushmere, but the rest of her family would have had a hard task recognizing anything that she described. With a delicate pull at his sympathies she confessed to their impoverishment through their father's ill luck at the tables and the course, a point at which he said quickly, "No disgrace at all. A gentleman has to honor his gaming debts before all else. Damned hard on his nearest and dearest, but that's the way of it."

"It is indeed," she sighed. "It means we are having to do without servants at Rushmere."

He was deeply concerned. "Such hardship! How difficult for you. You deserve better than that. Surely—"

"Please say no more!" She tilted her chin proudly and bravely.

He was instantly abashed. "Forgive me. I have offended you. It was the last thing I intended."

She was patiently forgiving and saw that she had him exactly where she wanted him. His error in attempting to discuss her circumstances in the kindly thoughtlessness of the moment should set him on a long trail of seeking to make amends. She did not care what Dominic was thinking. Let him think what he liked. At least he would not put his thoughts into words and that was all that mattered.

She left more than half of the chocolate in the cup, knowing from her mother's instruction that no lady drained anything to the dregs. She saw with satisfaction Edward's obvious disappointment when she said she must be going.

"If you will just give me a verbal reply to my sister's note," she said to Dominic, "I'll take my leave."

"Then please tell Miss Marlow I look forward to receiving her and your brother at two-thirty, the time she suggested."

"Allow me to escort you back to Rushmere," Edward said at once.

"I'm so sorry. I have other calls to make," she lied easily.

"Another time perhaps."

Her lips curled prettily at the corners, her eyes guileless. "Perhaps."

The two men went with her out of the house and down the steps to the waiting wagonette. Edward assisted her up into the driving seat and unslotted the whip to hand it to her. "Thank you." She glanced from Edward to Dominic and back again. "Good day, gentlemen."

Her eyes held a gleam in them as she drove back to Rushmere. At the gates of Cudlingham Manor she drew up for several minutes and studied what she could see of it in the distance. It was ten times the size of little Rushmere and much larger if not grander than Ainderly Hall. It would ruin everything if Edward turned out to be already betrothed, but she must keep her fingers crossed and hope that her luck would hold.

Tansy received the news that Dominic would see her that afternoon with mingled dismay and relief. Much as she loathed the thought of seeing him, at least the whole unpleasant matter would quickly be over and done with.

"By the way," Nina added, turning at the foot of the stairs, "one of our neighbors from Cudlingham Manor was with Dominic this morning. I told him I was Amelia's niece."

Tansy was aghast. "You told such a lie!"

"It simplified everything. The man has a sister who'll undoubtedly spread the word and local people will accept it without question. I have absolved you and Judith and Roger from any awkward queries and situations. None of you need say anything. You should be grateful to me. Mama once accused me of being an accomplished liar—did you not know that? So at least I have one talent, however dubious you may consider it, with which to help this family escape a swamping tidal wave of scandal."

Her feet tapped up to her room and the door closed after her.

Tansy changed into her best dress of blue wool for the visit, her black one being shabby and tanned with much washing and pressing, and she did not want to appear at a disadvantage again with Dominic Reade. She also made sure that Roger had a neatly ironed shirt and one of their father's cravats to wear with his brushed jacket and trousers.

Dominic must have been watching out for them, for he came into the hall as they were admitted, and his eyes met Tansy's with a hooded, guarded gaze. "I bid you welcome, Miss Marlow." He bowed to her and shook hands with her brother. "And you too, Roger. I suggest we go first to the stables and you can see the colt before we enter into any discussion about him."

"Yes, sir!" Roger replied keenly.

"Is that agreeable to you?" Dominic inquired of Tansy. When she gave a nod he indicated the way they should follow and fell into step beside her as they crossed the hall, went through one pair of doors and then another, he answering Roger's questions as they went. "The colt's name? It's Young Oberon, a fine name for a colt which has already shown tremendous enthusiasm for galloping and flies over the ground as fast as any fairy prince. Anyone would think he knew he could number among his ancestors one of the greatest horses of the English racecourse."

"Not Priam, sir?" Roger demanded excitedly. "He went to America to sire a line of winners there. My father said he should never have been sold."

"No, it's not Priam, but you'll get it with your second guess, I'm sure."

"It must be Eclipse." Roger's tone was breathlessly incredulous.

"Right. Your father told you about him, I suppose."

"Yes. And I've read all I could get hold of about him, too. He's said to have sired a hundred and sixty winners. Three Derby winners among them. Of course my father never saw him run, it being long before he was born that Eclipse won every race he was entered for, but a horse like that is a legend. Do you think— is it possible that—oh, could Young Oberon become another Eclipse, sir?"

Dominic laughed, well pleased with the boy's interest. "It's a dream to cherish, but nobody could make any kind of prediction like that at this stage."

Tansy spoke emotionally. "Except perhaps my father. He appeared to have high hopes centered in him, enough to meet the tune of three hundred guineas."

Dominic gave her a sober glance, leaning in front of her to open a colored-glass door into a garden room, which they had reached. "Oliver did have some kind of hunch about this yearling, which he couldn't explain to himself or anyone else. Young Oberon is a thoroughbred, but not classically bred—that is to say, neither his sire nor his dam ever won one of the five great classic races, such as the Derby or the Oaks—and the strain of Eclipse's blood is now so thinned out as to be counted merely as a compliment rather than anything to pin hopes on." They passed through the trapped warmth of the garden room with its plants and flowers and aromatic fragrances to go outside to the stables as she made her reply.

"My father was much given to having hunches about race horses in general, and his successes were far outnumbered by his failures. It would be foolish for anyone to suppose he could be right about this one."

Her words were intended primarily to check her brother's enthusiasm, for it had worried her to see his keenness reaching new heights before he had even set eyes on the colt and it could only make his disappointment in their selling of the animal all the harder to bear, but he was quite lost in his excitement. Dominic answered her as they stepped outside to follow a flagged path.

"Oliver came whenever he was in Cudlingham to watch Young Oberon and the other yearlings in the paddock over there," he said, pointing to a stretch of green where a few horses were grazing. "Who's to say he didn't see something in the colt that nobody else has been able to define yet? Young Oberon has always been lively, and after coming to the fence to show an inquisitive interest in your father's arrival he would go galloping off again, sometimes flat-out and stretching himself to his limits through sheer exuberance. Those were the times when Oliver never took his eyes from him. But unfortunately your father never saw him ridden, because it was only last month that my trainer began to break him in, but I had no chance or inclination to give Oliver a report when I met him on the eve of his death, the poor man having nothing else but his bereavement on his mind."

Tansy looked toward the fence where her father had stood to watch one gamboling yearling with dreams of riches in his eyes and her own misted over with grief and love and sorrow, making her blink quickly and be thankful for the seclusion of her bonnet brim.

They came into the square stableyard, its flags clean and swept, the buildings whitewashed with roofs of gray slate. The head stable lad, a wiry, middle-aged man in spite of his title, which was an old established piece of racing jargon as Tansy well knew, came hurrying from the tack room to touch his cap to Dominic and the visitors.

"Afternoon, sir. It were Young Oberon you wanted to show. He's ready and waiting. I'll bring him right out."

"Thank you, Harris."

The man went hurrying off to disappear through a stable door at the far end of the west block and reappeared almost at once leading the colt, a chestnut with rangy limbs, a prominent white, star-shaped blaze in his forehead, an alert, intelligent head, and lovely dark eyes. Even as she felt herself melt, drawn to the gracefully stepping creature that had won her father's heart and fired his dreams, she heard Roger give a stifled, half-choked exclamation of wonder and saw the glory in his face. Instantly she crushed down her own feelings, determined not to weaken, and she reached out a checking hand to remind her brother that they were about to sever all connection with the colt, but she was too late to restrain him. Already he had darted forward and was running across the yard to meet Young Oberon. As she watched helplessly he was patting the curved, muscular neck and smoothing a hand over the soft nose with its delicately flaring, amber-tinted nostrils, talking to the colt in a low, quiet voice as though the two of them were quite alone.

Dominic signaled with a slight nod to the head stable lad to leave the colt and the boy to become acquainted on their own, and Young Oberon, whose ears were flicking with curiosity, nickered appreciatively when Roger dived into his pockets and brought out an apple for him, and then a carrot.

"Your brother knows how to make friends with a horse," Dominic remarked to her after they had watched in silence for a while. "I suppose one could say that mentally boy and colt are about the same age. This could be the beginning of a lasting relationship."

"That's out of the question," she replied firmly, but he did not hear her, having walked forward to speak to the boy.

"What do you think of him?"

Roger turned a rapt and blissful face, creased and shining. "Magnificent, sir. He's a born winner, I'm sure of it."

Dominic smiled, clapping the colt and running a hand over its rough winter coat. "Young Oberon has some more growing up to do and a long way to go before he can prove himself. Only three-year-olds are eligible for the Derby. I will say he's certainly quick and eager to work. He has learned to canter with a man on his back already. The other yearlings are still at the trotting stage."

"Could I ride him, Mr. Reade? Just once?" Roger held his breath as he waited for an answer.

Dominic regarded him thoughtfully, standing with his hands set low on his hips and feet apart. "How much riding have you done?"

Eagerly Roger told him about the experience he had had under his father's guidance and at the Brompton racing stables, although the slight raising of Dominic's eyebrows showed that he had no high opinion of that particular place. In a rush the boy concluded, "I could handle Young Oberon easily. I know I could."

"I'm afraid I cannot be so sure about that. Young horses can be skittish and unpredictable at this age. They often take fright without warning or take it into their heads to be playful. In Young Oberon's saddle you would have to be alert every second to check a trip or stumble, because—like all youthful creatures— a yearling is inclined to be careless about where he places his feet. Come, come! Don't look so downcast, boy. I just want to find out first how you can handle an older horse, and then it will be up to you to make a good impression on my trainer, Kirby. If he is prepared to let you into Young Oberon's saddle after seeing what you can do, then you have my permission, too. Be here tomorrow morning at seven o'clock. I'll tell Harris to give you a hack to saddle up yourself, and then you can ride out under Kirby's eye with the yearlings and their stable lads to the gallops on excercise. In the meantime Young Oberon is due to be trace-clipped this afternoon. You may stay to watch if you give me your word you won't get in anyone's way."

"I won't. Thank you."

"Well, now you can walk Young Oberon round the yard and back into the loose box. Your sister and I have some business to discuss in the house. You can come and find us when you're ready." He turned and came back to Tansy, taking her by the elbow to escort her indoors, but she broke the brief physical contact immediately by drawing slightly ahead of him, ashiver at his unwanted touch. She felt compelled to bring up the subject of Nina's visit that morning.

"My sister told a tremendous lie in your hearing earlier today, Mr. Reade—"

Briskly he interrupted her. "Don't let it embarrass you. There is no need to discuss it. I'm only thankful that you and I do not have to play out any kind of charade with each other, social or otherwise. The night we met put us on a unique footing, which cannot be denied."

That was true enough. Theirs had been no ordinary meeting, but a violent clash of wills and temperament, the memory of which made her teeth ache with hostility. He dared to remind her of it! At least to him she could speak her mind frankly without any of the pretense, abhorrent to her, which had fastened chains about her and those dependent on her.

"My family and I are in the state of having no secrets from you," she conceded with a tilt of her chin, her gaze ahead as they retraced their steps through the house. "I should like to know why my father confided in you in the first place. Nobody else— with the exception of my poor mother—seems to have suspected the fact that he had two homes, Rushmere being the one that all his racing friends and acquaintances knew about, and the cottage tucked away in Hampshire being the hidden part of his life."

"Oliver told me the truth that last night of his life. I had seen him at the Newmarket races not long beforehand and mentioned in the course of conversation that I expected to be in Hampshire about the time which—I realize now—he had planned for his home-coming. No doubt he thought to save himself a special journey to Cudlingham by arranging to meet me there. As it was, he broke out with the tragedy that had befallen him as soon as he clapped eyes on me. The situation soon became clear enough. I was astonished, to say the least."

"Talk no more to me about that night," she said on a low note of anguish. "It is a time I do not wish to remember."

They had reached a drawing room where tea waited on a small, circular table set with a lace cloth. He invited her to pour the silver teapot, which she did, and when she handed him a cup he sat back in his chair with it, crossing one long leg over the other. She sat straight, all composure regained, her cup of tea untouched on the table beside her.

"Now we must talk about the colt," she began in a businesslike manner, painfully conscious of the way he was watching her, a curious look blended of impatience and compassion behind his eyes, which she did not understand. "How did you and my father become joint owners in the first place?"

"The usual reason. Your father was short of money at the time he wished to buy the foal at a stud not known to me, and I became the owner of a half share in an animal I didn't particularly want. It was the knowledge that the foal had that faint strain of Eclipse's blood in him that did at last rouse my interest, I must admit, and I agreed to stable Young Oberon and have him trained when the time came."

"What made my father decide he wanted to buy you out?"

He put aside his cup and folded his arms. "Your guess is as good as mine. He became obsessed with the idea that Young Oberon was going to change his luck and bring him in the huge fortune that he always thought he would win in the next race or the next season. I sincerely believe that when he leaned his elbows on that paddock fence he could see himself leading in Young Oberon as the Derby winner, and made up his mind to share that moment with no one else if it should really come."

She did not dispute this idea. It was so typical of her father that she found the explanation entirely acceptable. "Three hundred guineas was a remarkably good offer," she said. "Far more than anything you could have paid out for that half share in the beginning. In fact, from the few inquiries I have made it appears to be an absurd sum. Yet you turned the offer down."

"I did."

Her eyebrows lifted mockingly. "You thought your half share worth more?"

"It was—to me. And it still is."

"May I ask why?"

"I had good reasons. There are others as well now."

His answer puzzled her, but she did not consider it important. Relaxing, she leaned forward slightly to make her announcement. "I didn't come here today to increase my father's offer, as you must have guessed." She paused while he gave a nod. "But you will be pleased to know that I have no intention of asking three hundred guineas for our family's inherited half share. I am prepared to sell it to you at a just figure such as it would fetch on the open market." She picked up her teacup and saucer to take a sip.

His eyes narrowed at her. "I'm not interested in buying or selling half shares in Young Oberon. I'm content to leave matters as they stand."

She whitened, stopping short with the teacup before it reached her lips. "But that's not possible."

"Why not?"

Suddenly she was afraid. It wasn't going to be as simple as she'd imagined it would be. She put down her cup and saucer with a little clatter. "I don't want to retain that half share. Not under any circumstances."

"You have no choice."

She drew in her breath sharply. Anger, fired by her strained nerves, surged through her. "I'll sell out to someone else. I'm entitled to do that after giving you first chance."

He shook his head slowly and drew out of an inner pocket in his jacket a folded document which he opened and held out to her. "Under the terms of this agreement, which your father and I both signed, you will see that neither partner can sell to an outsider."

She took it with nerveless fingers and saw that what he had said was true. The paper crackled as she folded it up again and returned it to him. With effort she controlled her emotions, determined not to beg or to lose her dignity. "You must see that I couldn't contribute to the cost of keeping and training a race horse. It's far beyond our family means."

"I realize that. I want nothing from you for stabling Young Oberon. If he's as good as your father believed him to be he'll bring in his own rewards."

"No. He may never win a race. Then I'll be in your debt and that I could never tolerate."

His face darkened at the animosity that had shown through in her tone. "What do you propose to do?"

"I'll give the colt over to you completely. Yes. That's it. A gift you cannot refuse."

"You obviously didn't read every word of the agreement," he commented dryly. "Money must change hands."

She decided there was nothing for it but to throw herself on his mercy. "Then change your mind and buy from me. I tell you I need the money that the half share would bring in. I need it now."

"There would be no money," he answered quietly.

She stared at him in bewilderment. "No money? What do you mean?"

"Even if I agreed to pay you three hundred guineas you wouldn't feel able to keep a penny of it with your views on the matter of being in debt."

"Please explain what you mean."

"Your father owed me a sum far in excess of that figure."

"How much?" she demanded hoarsely.

"I have his signed memorandums in my desk. I'd have to go through them to reckon the exact amount."

"How much?" she repeated as if in a nightmare trance.

"It's somewhere in the region of two thousand pounds."

She almost fainted. Her arm fell against the table and knocked her cup over, the undrunk tea spilling, and it roused her to a kind of tearful panic, which was a reaction to the greater catastrophe that had fallen upon her. "Oh, look at what I've done! That lovely cloth! Did I crack the cup?"

She started to dab frantically at the spreading stain with a clean handkerchief that she had whipped from her pocket, but he was beside her chair at once. "Leave it," he urged and found he had to restrain her wildly dabbing hand forcibly. "It doesn't matter. A cloth, for God's sake. It's unimportant."

She became very still, registering, without really being aware of it, every detail of the strong hand that clasped her wrist, its touch cool, a gold signet ring on the little finger, the faint, dark hairs that ran down the broad back of it. Slowly she lifted her head to look up into his face.

"Why did you lend him so much?" she asked brokenly.

A glimmer of gentle amusement at her naïveté showed for a moment in the depths of his eyes. Still holding her wrist he reached out for the back of his chair, twirled it forward, and sat down to lean toward her. "That's a relatively small sum among gaming men, although I realize you wouldn't appreciate that. As a matter of fact, in this case it was the residue of a much larger amount, but that's not for us to talk about. The purpose of my appointment with him at your home village, which you must forgive me for mentioning once again, was for him to settle what he could of his debt to me."

"He came back with very little in his pockets."

"I'm not surprised to hear it. The whole season had gone against him. He had hoped to recoup some of his losses out of the last flat races of the season, but it's rare that a man's luck will turn at that stage."

"Why on earth did he keep on throwing money away when he was losing all the time?" she exclaimed in despairing exasperation. "It would have been better if he'd left and come home until the spring again."

He gave a little shrug. "It's an old saying that a good win will take a man from the gaming tables, but heavy losses will keep him playing. The same adage applies to any kind of gambling."

"Would you say my father was an unlucky gambler?"

"He wasn't always the wisest of punters, but at times he had some curious flash of insight—not often enough, unfortunately—when he could win enormously by pulling off the most outside gamble. I believe he had it about Young Oberon."

She became aware that his thumb was lightly stroking her

inner wrist, almost absently but caressingly, but even as she snatched her hand away she was convinced she understood the true meaning of his words.

"So it was greed that made you refuse my father's request to buy your share of the colt," she exclaimed wrathfully, springing to her feet. "You couldn't bear the thought of his reaping alone the harvest of his foresight if that gamble should come off."

He rose from his chair and answered her with a deliberate courtesy that deflated her and made her long to bite back the accusation she had uttered. "My father owned a stud before me, and I was bred to the racing world. There's little I don't know about it and the men who people it. I understood the pattern of Oliver Marlow's ways. Had I agreed to sell he would have paid me with money borrowed from another source, and removed Young Oberon from Ainderly Hall, not wanting to risk getting deeper into debt at my stables where I might make some claim on the colt again. As I told you, he was like a man possessed over Young Oberon. Then the devil only knows where he might have placed him for training and under which trainer, all too many of them mediocre in my opinion. I believe I have one of the best, but Oliver and I didn't always see eye to eye about this, partly because he was so besotted with the colt that he thought none good enough for him."

She interrupted, having an important question to ask. "Did you quarrel with my father?"

He answered without hesitation. "There was ill will between us toward the end due to my refusal to sell, but I knew that it only needed another hard loss or two on the course or at the tables for the colt to be put up as stake or for sale. That would have been the end to Oliver's dream and everything else. Most important of all Young Oberon could have lost the chance forever of becoming a great race horse."

She threw out her hands expressively. "This I can understand. My father lost possession of a good race horse once before in a similar manner. I spoke too hastily to you and I regret it. But I'm still in a quandary to grasp why you refuse to buy the half share from me for a fair amount that can offset at least a fraction of the money owing you."

He moved closer to her, looking down into her face from his superb height. "Young Oberon is an unknown quantity and so are you, Tansy. I'm set on discovery. If I release the rein of joint ownership you'll fly from me. I can see it in your face."

She was speechless for a few seconds. Then hastily she gathered up her drawstring bag, thrusting her tea-sodden handkerchief into it, wanting only to get away from this contrary man and out of his house. "As far as I'm concerned you may do whatever you wish with the colt. He's yours to train and race. In the meantime I promise that my father's debts to you will be paid. It will take time, but I'll not have them on my conscience and I'll manage to settle them all somehow. I bid you good day, sir!"

She swung away to make her departure as Roger arrived breathlessly in the doorway, his face radiant. "They let me help trace-clip Young Oberon and put a blanket on him afterward—"

"Be silent!" Tansy ordered, astonishing him with her anger, and she caught him by the shoulder to whirl him about with her out into the hall. "Don't speak the colt's name to me ever again. We retain our half share, but on paper only. There's an end to it. Say good day to Mr. Reade. We're going home."

She swept out of the door and was seated in the wagonette when Roger emerged to shake hands with Dominic on the threshold. "Thank you again, Mr. Reade. I'll not be late tomorrow morning. Mr. Harris showed me the hack I'm to ride."

"That's good. Goodbye now."

Roger, casting sidelong glances at his sister, did not speak until they had left the grounds of Ainderly Hall and were some distance along the private road. "What happened?" he asked cautiously.

She told him everything except Dominic's extraordinary declaration in those last traumatic minutes in the drawing room, anger glowing white-hot within her. She seemed still to feel that cool, firm touch on her wrist. "So," she concluded finally, "not only are we still legally bound to half-ownership of the colt, but I also have to find two thousands pounds to pay off Papa's debts."

He responded with an incredulous half laugh at the frightening absurdity of such a prospect. "It might as well be a million pounds for all the chance you'll have of raising that sort of money. Only at breakfast you said we must have a family conference this evening to include Amelia and decide how best to economize in every possible way to keep within our strictly limited means."

She dipped her head. "I know. I'll break the news to them then. But I've thought of something. I'll mortgage Rushmere."

They gathered in the dining room for the evening discussion. Tansy took the chair at the head of the table with past household account ledgers in front of her, both her sisters on the left side, and Roger at the end. Amelia, after fussing about pouring out glasses of homemade sherry wine, which she placed before each of them on individual little crocheted mats, finally took a seat opposite Judith, who gave her a shy smile which was eagerly returned. Judith did not have it in her nature to hold a grudge of any kind against anybody, and although she knew Amelia to be an adulteress—the very word conjuring up fire and brimstone—she read her Bible daily and would have been at Christ's side to defend her foster father's mistress against the stone-throwers. As to Oliver himself, who had broken the same commandment, she was sure all the good in him had been weighed against his sins and that he was in heaven and not in hell. Judith saw God in her own image. His wrath was mild annoyance and his love innocently boundless.

Tansy opened the family meeting. "The two housemaids left this morning and Cook departed half an hour ago. The gardener, who also doubled as groom, has found another place already. Amelia gave them all excellent references. In future we'll share out the household chores as we did at home to help Mama, and Judith, who makes better bread than anybody I know, will do the cooking whenever she feels able to; otherwise I'll be in charge in the kitchen. The store cupboards are well stocked with preserves, pickles, ham, dried and salted foods, and all sorts of other good things. The cellar has racks of Amelia's homemade wine, which she has told me is her specialty. We're tasting a sample in this excellent sherry wine she has poured for us, and if the rest are half as good we are indeed fortunate. Also stored in the cellar are sackloads of potatoes, carrots, and turnips, strings of onions, and trays of apples—much like our winter cellar at home and enough to last us through until the spring. I shall see that we eke out *everything* as economically as possible. After this, evening wine will be kept for special occasions. Amelia is most anxious that hospitality to visitors should not be impaired and I'm sure we all understand her sensitivity on this point."

"We're all used to playing our part," Nina said pointedly, "but what is Amelia going to do? Playing hostess doesn't get the kitchen floor scrubbed."

"I've given thought to it," Amelia said swiftly. "I'll continue to make wine and tend the flowerbeds. I have always enjoyed doing that. I have green fingers with flowers and plants—"

"What about vegetables?" Tansy inquired practically.

Amelia was taken aback. "I never touched the *kitchen* garden or any of the hard work. The gardener always did that and took out any of the tough weeds for me. In any case," she ended flatly, "I couldn't dig."

"Why ever not?" Nina asked, bristling. She was determined to have no outdoor chores herself, having had enough garden duties in the past. "You're fit and strong. There's nothing to it."

"My hands!" Amelia exclaimed weakly, displaying their soft palms. "And I wouldn't have the strength."

"I'll do the digging," Tansy said to settle the argument, "and all of us except Judith can do work in the garden, but we'll put Amelia in charge." She looked down the table at her brother. "We're not counting on you being here, Roger. During your visit to Mr. Reade's stables tomorrow morning you can ask the advice of Mr. Harris about the best place to apply—other than Ainderly Hall."

Roger opened his mouth to speak, thought better of it, and nodded glumly. Judith turned to Tansy. "What's wrong with Mr. Reade's stables if he could get taken on as a jockey there?"

"Everything!" Tansy declared promptly. "Oh, I don't mean

with conditions at the stud. It's just that the less any of us has to do with Dominic Reade the better."

"He is a very nice gentleman," Amelia protested, round-eyed, "and he gives the most entertaining parties and balls. I wouldn't want to miss those."

"You must do whatever you wish," Tansy answered her on a tired sigh. "The rest of us hold him responsible for Papa's death."

"You do, you mean," Roger exclaimed bitterly, putting two clenched fists on the table before him. "But it was you who left Father to die alone."

There was a terrible silence. Tansy went paper-white and looked toward her sisters. Both met her eyes without accusation, blaming neither her nor anybody else. She turned to Amelia and surprised a sad look of hopelessness before the soft lids lowered, but there had been no blame. Only Roger had spoken out the personal resentment he had been harboring. She looked down the table at him again.

"I had no idea how you felt," she said in a strangled voice. "It is as well that it has come out into the open. As a family we have always been honest with each other."

He was scarlet with mortification. "I'm sorry. It was a cruel thing to say, and now I've said it I don't feel it any more." The clenched fists had become restless hands clasping and unclasping each other. "It came out because of something else. I wish I'd never made that promise not to ask Mr. Reade to take me on at his stables." His voice cracked on a note of utter despair. "Young Oberon is going to win the Derby one day and I'll not be there to bring him to it."

"What is all this?" Nina demanded impatiently, looking from Tansy to Roger and back again.

"Young Oberon is the name of Papa Oliver's colt," Judith volunteered, having been told all about him by Roger, who had always found hers to be a sympathetic ear.

In a shaky voice Tansy gave them an account of her afternoon visit to Ainderly Hall, only keeping back again Dominic's private words to her. Both her sisters gasped with dismay at hearing of the size of the debts that their father had incurred. Even Amelia was startled. She had never known Oliver without money. There had been times when he had been short of it and she'd had to wait for things she'd wanted, but he had always rewarded her patience with an additional trinket or two, and she had shown her appreciation in loving, erotic ways that had delighted his passionate, lustful nature. That he had been in and out of debt at those times had never occurred to her.

"Tell everybody the solution you've thought of," Roger encouraged Tansy, wanting—now the poison was out of his system—to make amends and heal the breach as quickly as possible. There was the chance, too, that she might relent and absolve him from that dreadful promise that he must have been mad to make. He couldn't believe she would truly deny him the opportunity of a lifetime. Not now when he had poured out his heart's longing to be with Young Oberon on the greatest day in a race horse's life.

Tansy made her announcement. "It's quite simple. I'm going to raise a mortgage on Rushmere."

Amelia piped up. "But you can't! It's been done already. Oliver did that a year to two after he sold off the last piece of its spare land. He said it was necessary at the time and I didn't question him about it. It was a private arrangement with Mr. Reade and still stands as far as I know."

Tansy leaned her elbows on the table and held her head in her hands. She was thwarted at every turn, either wittingly or unwittingly, by the one man she least wanted to associate with. There seemed no escape from him.

"Then there's no help for it," she said, lifting her head again and letting her hands fall wearily. "We'll have to turn Rushmere into a lodginghouse for racegoers at Epsom when the flat-racing season starts in the spring and accommodate others on their travels between one racecourse and another."

The pandemonium that broke out with cries of hysterical protest from Nina and Amelia ended the family meeting. Tansy, unable to endure any more that day, thrust herself up from the chair and dashed from the room. She fetched her cloak, threw it about her shoulders, and went out into the dark, quiet night, leaving the noisy hubbub still going on in the dining room.

She walked. After starting off at a frantic pace she checked herself once she was outside the gates of Rushmere and changed to a brisk tread. Down through the village she went where the twinkling lights of the large houses showed through the trees and lamps glowed in the cottage windows. The grocery store was still open, and in the lighted butcher's shop a tired boy in a stained apron was sweeping out the sawdust. The church stood dark against the night sky. By a bridge that spanned a narrow river she took a rest, going a little way down the bank to sit down on a flat stone and watch the shining water slipping by.

She had much to think over. Roger had made her see how wrong she had been to let grief embitter her, and she realized all too clearly that she had made Dominic a scapegoat for a personal feeling of guilt about her father's death that she had not dared to face up to. She was grateful to her brother for forcing her to get the whole matter into perspective. Her hostility toward Dominic on other points was fiercely unabated, there being too much conflict between them, but in all fairness she was compelled to wonder if she should give Roger the chance to withdraw his promise to her. Her quarrel with Dominic was not his. On her shoulders alone rested the burden of all the unpleasant involvement with the man who had cast a shadow across her life.

She turned her thoughts to her father's debts. Had he kept up the mortgage payments? Or was there more to be added to the amount she had to settle? Somewhere in Rushmere there must be a document and papers dealing with the mortgage, because there had been nothing of that kind in the strongbox opened by the lawyer. She would ask Amelia about the matter in the morning. Most sincerely she hoped that Nina and Amelia would have settled down by then and accustomed themselves to the idea of making Rushmere a hostelry.

She herself had seen it as a flash of inspiration. That morning while Nina had been at Ainderly Hall she had made an inspection of the house with Amelia, going into all the rooms from

basement to attic, and during that time Amelia had talked incessantly, obviously enjoying herself, a clear indication to Tansy that she had suffered hours of loneliness in Oliver's absence. Among the information that Amelia had supplied, which had included gossip about the local gentry with whom she was genteelly proud to be associated, there was a description of what it was like in Epsom and the surrounding villages when the Derby and other important races were run. Not nearly enough accommodation was available for racegoers, who crammed themselves into every available room in hotel, inn, and cottage, or else were forced to sleep where they could in barns or tents or under trees in the open air. With the roads crowded with every kind of racegoing traffic, it was, she had declared, a nightmare for all but persons of quality able to stay with well-to-do friends or relatives in the big houses in the vicinity and take places during the day in the Grand Stand. The brawls and fights, the attacking and robbing of people on foot and in carriages had, according to Amelia, to be seen to be believed. She had flung up her dainty hands, and the wedding ring that she had no legal right to wear gleamed on her third finger.

Tansy, breaking off a piece of tall grass and twirling it, recalled the moment of her arrival at Rushmere when, glimpsing the trace of smoke above one of the chimneys, she had jumped to the conclusion that her father had given an open invitation to his racing acquaintances that they should use the house whenever they were passing through the district. That was what she was going to do, but they would pay for the privilege and would receive the best food she could produce, cooked well as she knew she could cook it, and rest their travel-wearied limbs in Rushmere's comfortable beds.

Hearing a carriage coming along the road she paid no attention, and when it came to a halt by the bridge she glanced toward it, saw it to be a conveyance built for speed and driven by one man, who sat half-hidden by the raised hood, and her reaction was more exasperation at the intrusion on her solitude than curiosity as to why he should have stopped at that particular spot, but she knew she could not be seen from the road in the

darkness and hoped he would soon drive on again. But he was waiting for someone and she saw him tense when a horse and rider approached from the opposite direction, the hooves clip-clopping over the bridge. She could see the new arrival's silhouette above the parapet, black and compact, at ease in the saddle, and she followed him with her eyes until he came with a word of greeting to a halt by the carriage, the hood of it blocking him from her sight, and conversation began between the two men in low, urgent tones.

"Has the switch taken place?" demanded the rider.

"Last week," replied the other. "Bill Jemmy's had his finger in this sort of pie before . . . all went smooth as butter . . ."

She lifted her head, suddenly on guard. There was something extremely secret and conspiratorial about that meeting between the rider and the unseen driver of the conveyance there in the quiet night. Not wishing to eavesdrop she would have moved away out of earshot if she had not felt a paralyzing effect on her so that she scarcely dared breathe, the blade of grass drooping motionless from her finger and thumb. The rider was speaking again.

" . . . laid heavily against him at Doncaster . . . easily done again . . . nobble for a *pony* any day . . ."

The driver answered him. "That's a chance we must take . . . worth the risk . . . four-legged imposter . . ."

" . . . hangman's rope or transportation."

The driver gave a grim chuckle. "I agree . . . by appearing not to know me you should be absolved from all suspicion, but he's a crafty devil . . ."

The rider wheeled his horse about, and the slight change of direction enabled her to catch every quiet word of his in the still air. "I'll be at Newmarket with a runner of my own in March that day. It will enable me to keep an eye on things. The switched nag will be spirited away if anything goes wrong."

" . . . won't be necessary."

"I agree. Farewell, sir. Safe journey."

The rider cantered off the way he had come, and the hooded carriage made a sweeping turn and departed in the opposite di-

rection with a hiss of whip and clatter of hooves. The silence of the night descended again, broken only by the distant barking of a farm dog disturbed from its slumbers.

She dropped the blade of grass and stood up, her heart beating uncomfortably, and she retraced her steps up the bank to the roadside. A "pony" was racing slang for twenty-five pounds. She'd heard her father use that expression often enough, and "to nobble" was to deliberately keep from winning, usually by foul means, any race horse that would interfere with bets laid on another. But those two men seemed to have a number of unsavory racing plots afoot. Many times her father had talked in her hearing of the tricks played by rogues of the racecourse, which sullied the glorious sport of kings.

Standing in the road, she looked after the direction that the rider had taken. Not far from where she was lay the private way that led to the gates of Ainderly Hall. But she needed no additional clues to the rider's identity, having recognized his voice from the start. It was Dominic Reade who was preparing to put unscrupulous plans into action with the help of his unknown confederate when the flat-racing season was launched at Newmarket in the spring again. The fact that she had been right after all, no matter the original cause, to put up whatever barriers she could between Dominic and herself gave her no satisfaction. It was too sorry a state of affairs.

Putting her hands over her ears as though at this late stage she might block out what she had heard, she hastened homeward and wished that on this particular night she had not stirred beyond the bounds of Rushmere. The only good to come out of it was that the decision about Roger's future had been made for her. There was no question now of allowing him to withdraw his promise. The stables at Ainderly Hall were no place for him. Not when the owner of the stud was involved in the kind of dangerous racecourse dealings that led at times to violence and even death.

5.

Tansy was coming downstairs when Nina happened to hurry across the hall to answer the doorbell. A young woman in a tan calling costume, her bell-shaped crinoline in the new and fashionable width, and her bonnet trimmed with curling feathers, stood on the doorstep. She was tall, graceful, and confident, having a polished, well-bred look to her porcelain beauty, and from a center parting her hair showed glossy and smooth as black paint.

"Good afternoon," she said in a clear, high-pitched voice, giving Nina a narrow little smile. "I'm Sarah Taylor of Cudlingham Manor. My brother, Edward, made your acquaintance yesterday at Ainderly Hall. I know you must be Miss Nina Marlow by his description."

Tansy, who had been told about the meeting, saw her sister preen as she invited the visitor to step inside. Both of them turned when she reached the bottom stair and introductions took place. Amelia then appeared, paused to give a little upward flick of her hands in studied pleasure at the sight of Sarah, and came sweeping forward.

"My dear Miss Taylor. How kind of you to call."

"Dear Mrs. Marlow. I trust I find you as well as you can be in present circumstances. How are you managing to bear your sad loss?"

The conventionally sympathetic inquiry had its depressing effect, destroying the emotional uplift that the diversion of a visitor had offered. Amelia, who happened to be wearing black, immediately looked every inch the bereaved widow, her mouth becoming tremulous, her eyes pink with suppressed tears.

"I'm scarcely able to eat or sleep," she answered huskily and with perfect truth, "but I'll not burden you with my troubles. Come into my drawing room. We'll all have a glass of my elderberry wine."

Judith, reading by Amelia's fire, looked up when they entered and put her book aside. Again introductions took place and when everyone was settled Tansy poured the wine for Amelia and handed round the silver biscuit barrel, which contained a selection of macaroons and ratafias. She knew Amelia's grief to be genuine and had seen her surreptitiously wipe away a tear. But she felt decidedly less charitable when Nina, during the course of conversation, talked of their father as dear Uncle Oliver. Judith looked down at the glass she held to hide the pain in her eyes. Nina went on to gloss skillfully over their move to Rushmere as if they had traveled there in a carriage, at the same time managing to convey that their previous home, which had only matched Rushmere in age, was comparable to their new one in every way.

"Of course, our furniture was older—mostly antique," Nina stated glibly, wanting to let Sarah know that furnishing an Elizabethan house with contemporary pieces as Amelia had done was not to her taste.

"Never mind," Amelia interposed vaguely on a commiserating note. "I'm sure some of it was quite pretty."

Sarah and Nina exchanged amused glances and hid patronizing smirks. Tansy, watching them, decided that without doubt they were two of a kind. Snobbish and self-centered. The cottage furniture had certainly been antique, but not in the way that Nina had spoken of it. It was a relief to her that she did not have to utter more than a monosyllable now and again, the two of them doing all the talking and getting on famously, and she gave her thoughts up to Roger, whom she had not seen since he had set off early that morning for Ainderly Hall to ride with the yearlings on their exercise as arranged. She was not surprised that he had not come home again afterward, knowing that he was hoping to prove himself a good enough rider in the eyes of Dominic's trainer to be able to ask with confidence where he might stand a chance of getting taken on as a jockey. If given several addresses he was going to try all of them before the day was out. Crowning all his hopes was the longing that he would be able to ride Young Oberon on exercise the following morning or to be given a special short turn in the paddock. She knew that either of these privileges would only serve to cement his obsessional desire to be with the colt indefinitely, but if she told him —or anyone else for that matter—what she had overheard the night before he would think she was letting her imagination run riot, her acrimony toward Dominic making her misconstrue whatever had been said. There might even be doubt as to whether she had been right in identifying Dominic in the darkness. No, it was better to keep it all to herself, at least for the time being, and feel forewarned against the future.

Like an echo to her thoughts Dominic's name came into the conversation going on around her and she was alert at once. Nina was holding forth, once again embroidering the truth for the benefit of her new acquaintance.

"So my brother went off at the crack of dawn to Dominic Reade's stables. He has his heart set on being the most famous of all the gentlemen jockeys who ride their own horses one day."

Sarah tapped a finger thoughtfully against her cheek. "Now I wonder if it could have been Roger whom I saw in our stableyard this afternoon before I left. Edward was talking to a boy about the age of your brother. Not very tall with fair hair. He was wearing a brown jacket, if I remember correctly, and leather gaiters."

"That was Roger!" Nina exclaimed.

"I would have spoken to him had I known."

"Does your brother own race horses?" Tansy inquired.

Sarah looked at her as if surprised that she should enter into the talk at this late stage, when the wineglasses had been emptied and refills genteelly refused. "Only half a dozen, but that number does include a two-year-old which has been entered for the Derby next year. It was my father who was the racing man. During his time our stables held many more, but Edward prefers to breed his own hunters, the chase being his great interest, and if we didn't live so close to Epsom I doubt whether he would keep the race horses that he has. From what Nina has said, I should think Roger was asking Edward about his chances."

"Wouldn't it be splendid if Roger could be at the Manor stables!" Nina exclaimed gushingly.

"What is the name of the Derby entry?" Judith asked. Until now she had been as quiet as Tansy, but that was natural to her.

"Wild Wind."

"That's a good name," Judith said approvingly.

Sarah inclined her head condescendingly to show agreement. "Edward hopes to have a winner in him." She had already decided that out of the three sisters Nina was the only one whose company she considered truly agreeable, Judith being decidedly dull and Tansy too proud-looking, her dark violet eyes showing no effusive gratitude for her graciousness in calling so soon. It was as well that Edward, who had prompted the call, giving her no peace until she had promised there should be no delay, was smitten with the best of the bunch. She turned her thin smile on Amelia, whom she despised, but whose late husband had been a gentleman born, a likable rascal not above giving her waist a squeeze at every opportunity that had presented itself. In spite of the years between them, she had found him a disturbingly attractive man, his laughter-crinkled eyes holding teasing, improper, unmentionable suggestions whenever he looked at her. Ah, well, it was too late to have any regrets now, because he was gone and no amount of wondering if she would ever have succumbed to temptation could bring him back again.

"Mrs. Marlow," she urged Amelia in dulcet tones, "I know you are in deepest mourning and not able yet to face the world, but would you have any objection if your three nieces came to the Manor tomorrow evening to listen to music? A most decorous gathering, I do assure you."

Amelia shot an uncomfortable glance at Tansy, rubbing the palms of her hands together nervously. "I should like my nieces to accept the invitation. It's important that they should get to know people and make friends as soon as possible. Oliver always had their good at heart and would never have wanted them to sit at home in grief and sorrow on his account. He enjoyed life too much himself for that. But you must remember, Miss Taylor, that Tansy is mistress of Rushmere now. She only defers to wishes of mine through her gentle courtesy. You must ask Tansy to speak for herself and her sisters."

Sarah arched her neck and turned her gray-green eyes on Tansy. "What do you say? My brother will never forgive me if I take home a refusal."

"I thank you and your brother for inviting us, Miss Taylor," Tansy said formally, well aware that Nina and Judith were both holding their breath apprehensively in case she should take it into her head to refuse, "and I accept for all three of us."

"Good!" Sarah rose to depart. "Until seven-thirty tomorrow evening then." She kissed Amelia, bade Tansy and Judith good-bye, and let Nina see her to the door. As soon as it had closed after her Nina gave a squeak of excitement and rushed back into Amelia's drawing room, her eyes shining.

"I knew Edward wanted to see me again. I guessed it would be soon."

Judith gave a little laugh, sharing the girl's happiness. "It does sound as though you made a hit. Sarah particularly mentioned how disappointed her brother would be if the invitation was turned down. That could only mean it's you he wants to be there."

Nina nodded, laughing too, and the pink tip of her tongue curled triumphantly at the corner of her mouth. "He's rich and unattached. Amelia told me all about him, didn't you Amelia? Don't worry any more about settling Papa's debts, Tansy. I intend to do that for you—for all of us."

Tansy, who had been collecting the dirty glasses onto a tray, straightened up slowly. "What do you mean?"

Nina flung out both hands expressively, "I'm going to be Mrs. Edward Taylor, Lady of the Manor of Cudlingham."

"Oh, Nina!" Judith exclaimed in awe of the brave boast.

Tansy was less impressed. She picked up the tray and held it with both hands, the rim against her waist. "There's a saying about not counting your chickens before they're hatched," she said dryly. "You would do well to remember that. What's more, as I happen to be the eldest the responsibility for Papa's debts is mine, and I want no help of the kind that you're prepared to give. Follow your heart and not your head, Nina. I wouldn't want any sister of mine to marry for mercenary reasons and not for love, should the possibility ever arise."

She made to pass Nina with the tray, but her sister blocked her way. "What makes you think I'm not in love already?"

Tansy gave her a long look. "I know you're not. Not yet, anyway. I believe you're more concerned with getting me to postpone my intention to turn Rushmere into a financial proposition."

Amelia gave a low moan of despair. Neither she nor Nina had mentioned Tansy's resolution since she had fled from their protests the evening before, perhaps both of them clinging to the hope that she had had time to reconsider the project and as long as they did not bring up the subject nothing more would be heard about it. Nina's face grew taut and desperate.

"You can't, Tansy! A common boardinghouse. For all the riffraff of the racecourse."

"Don't exaggerate," Tansy replied patiently. "It will be for racing gentlemen like Papa."

"That's not the point. We are on the brink of being accepted into just the right circles—the kind of society that Mama always wanted us to mix with and brought us up with gentle speech and manners like her own and Papa's to that end—and you're set on ruining everything. Who will speak to us when it gets known that you intend to become a—a lodginghouse keeper? We shall be cut dead on all sides."

"Nina is right," Amelia wailed. "Nobody will receive us ever again."

"I cannot agree with you," Tansy said calmly. "There's really no need for you both to get so upset. As I've told you already, I intend to be selective. Without Roger, and no other man in the house, I couldn't—and wouldn't—take in anyone of dubious character. Rushmere will be a home away from home for distinguished gentlemen of the Turf."

"It will make no difference," Nina declared fiercely. "We shall be ostracized. Not even at the cottage—poor though we were at times—did we ever have to sink to the lowly status that you are planning for yourself and us, too."

"There's nothing lowly about earning an honest living," Tansy retaliated crisply. "A paper that Amelia found for me today shows that Papa failed to keep up the mortgage payments on Rushmere. I don't think you realize that Dominic Reade could foreclose at any time, and then what would happen? We should be homeless with no one to turn to and nowhere to go."

"He wouldn't do that," Amelia protested frantically. "I'm sure of it. He and your father were friends."

"Not toward the end. Dominic admitted to me that there had been differences between them."

"It was only over that wretched colt. Oliver had fallen in with someone else whom he believed could train the animal better, but I thought the man a real shyster and told your father so. However, he could be stubborn at times, and where that colt was concerned he was like a man besotted, full of fanciful dreams of the great fortune he would make on Young Oberon one day." Her voice became choked and she took out her wispy lace hankerchief to dry her eyes again. "Poor Oliver! Oh, my poor Oliver!"

Judith put a sympathetic hand on Amelia's arm and received a wobbly, grateful little smile in return. Nina, impatient at the diversion in the conversation, returned to her attack on Tansy.

"If Papa was stubborn, then so are you. Like him, you think of no one but yourself."

Judith spoke up with unaccustomed heat. "That's totally unfair, Nina. Tansy is right, in wanting to secure our home and clear our debts. Whatever she decides to do I will support to the best of my ability."

"Our camp appears to be divided down the middle," Tansy remarked judiciously, putting the tray aside for the time being, "but that doesn't change anything. Roger has no say in the matter because he won't be living at home, and as this house is mine I must do with it what I think is best. However, if either you, Nina, or you, Amelia, can come forward with any other scheme to help lift us out of debt I'm willing to listen and consider it."

"We can get rid of some of the furniture in this house for a start." Nina made a contemptuous sweep with her arm to indicate the cluttered, crowded room. "There's far too much of it. We could raise enough to make some small show of payment to Dominic."

"No!" Amelia cried, outraged. "It's mine! All mine!"

Nina rounded on her. "Only because over the years you deviously replaced everything that should have been Tansy's with an eye to establishing yourself more securely at Rushmere."

"That's a lie!" Amelia shrieked, looking frightened.

"No, it's not. You thought yourself clever, but in a court of law it would all be awarded to Tansy, because she was left the contents of the house and you have nothing to prove that Papa intended any of it to be solely yours."

"I may not have proof, but he did mean it to be mine alone."

"Why was everything at Rushmere bequeathed to Tansy then?"

Amelia burst into a hysterical sobbing that was entirely different from her previous tears, and she waved her arms about. "Why are you torturing me? We're all using the furniture, aren't we? Tansy knows she would hear no protest from me on the grounds of strangers sitting in the chairs, at the tables, and sleeping in the beds if she made Rushmere a hostelry, but it is the shame of the project that will fall on our heads that upsets me. People will think us common! Common! There's no disgrace in all the world to compare with being thought common."

"What makes you think—" Nina began dangerously.

"Nina, be silent!" Unexpectedly Tansy crashed a fist for order on the side table on which she had placed the tray, making everything on it rattle. "I will not have this stupid quarreling. Amelia, sit down and dry your eyes. The furniture is yours and there's an end to it. I appreciate your cooperation in letting me have full use of it for guests should my plan be carried out, but you still haven't said if you have anything else to suggest." She paused, looking inquiringly at Amelia, who shook her head miserably, wiped her eyes, and blew her nose. "Well, that's it then. I shall go ahead with my idea."

"But you mustn't," Nina wailed in anguish. "Oh, you cannot deny me the time I need!"

Tansy raised her eyebrows. "For what?"

"To get Edward's ring on my finger."

"Are you really serious?" Tansy questioned with concern.

Nina's face was wrenched in new appeal. "Give me six months. That's all I ask. If by then I'm not betrothed to Edward and the date set for our wedding you may go ahead with your plan for Rushmere without any opposition from me."

"Six months is a long time. That brings us toward the end of April. The racing season will be in full swing and the Derby little more than three weeks distant." Although she spoke firmly, compassion and sisterly love moved her deeply, for she saw how desperate Nina was in her plea.

"I would ask for less time if I could," the girl cried, "but Edward is twenty-seven years old—that's old enough to be wary of rushing into anything. With the exception of Dominic he's probably the most eligible bachelor for miles around—"

"He is," Amelia endorsed eagerly, all personal animosity toward Nina forgotten in a greater cause at stake. "Lord of the Manor, heir to a title, Master of Foxhounds, a magistrate. And wealthy—heaven alone knows how wealthy. I cannot tell you how many young ladies have pursued him in his time—and are still trying to catch him." She threw up her hands. "All in vain."

"—and I intend to succeed in getting him to propose to me where all others have failed," Nina continued breathlessly.

"And she can do it!" Amelia exclaimed excitedly. She took hold of Nina's shoulder and gave her a shove forward as though exhibiting a piece of merchandise. "Look at her. She has beauty and character and intelligence. She'll outshine all the little ninnies who weary him with their ogling and fan-fluttering. I know men—I've seen the bored look in his eyes sometimes. They like someone who's—different." Her voice trailed away—Nina having wrenched herself free with a withering glance that reminded her they were all too painfully aware of from whom she had been different—and her lips quivered as she fell silent.

Nina returned to her emotional attack on Tansy. "As his wife I'll receive a handsome spending allowance—I intend to make sure of that. Out of it I shall donate regularly toward Papa's debts until they are paid off." She tossed her head, becoming more defiant under her sister's quiet, assessing stare that seemed to see right into her innermost thoughts. "I'm his daughter too. You have no moral right to deny me a share of the obligation and neither can you stop me paying Dominic back all that is owing him once it lies in my power to do so. Oh, I'll fall in love with Edward, if that's what is worrying you. It must be the easiest thing in the world to love a rich young man, especially when he is tall and good-looking."

Tansy's penetrating gaze remained fixed on her sister. "Does a marriage of wealth and position mean so much to you?"

"It does," Nina answered fervently. "It's what I've always wanted above all else. Never to be poor or shabby again. To have jewels and furs and a carriage of my own to ride in, servants to wait on me and nothing to soil my hands. Don't deny me those six months. If you go ahead with turning Rushmere into a lodginghouse my chance will be gone forever."

Judith, ever soft-hearted, looked toward Tansy and spoke persuasively. "Do let Nina have her chance. It's true that people like Sarah would never call on us again once Rushmere becomes a lodginghouse. That wouldn't bother you or me, but it does Nina and Amelia."

Tansy thoughtfully picked up the tray again and lodged it against her hip before giving her reply. "You shall have your six months, Nina. I would have felt happier if your first priority had been love, but I hope most sincerely that during the time I've allowed you, you'll find love to be more important than all the rest." Her expression was gentle. "I want you to forget about Papa's debts. You must have nothing to burden you, nothing to create difficulties between you and Edward should you wed. I'll manage somehow." Her mouth twitched into an amused, self-mocking smile, her eyes twinkling. "I'm not our thrifty, penny-watching mother's child for nothing, and I'll find some way to sort things out and make ends meet."

Nina was intensely relieved that her wild and somewhat foolish offer to settle their father's debts had not been taken up. How could she be sure that Edward, whom she had yet to know and discover on a deeper level, would allow her to let money he had intended for her adornment go toward another purpose to which he might be inexorably opposed? It was one thing for him to approve of a man's gaming debts being settled, but another to be expected to contribute toward them himself. But there was one point on which she was not clear.

"If I'm not to help financially after I'm married, how can you manage?"

"You'll be helping in another way, Nina—by setting your stamp of approval on my taking in guests at Rushmere when the six months is up and in time for the Derby. You, as lady of the Manor, a position above criticism or reproach, will set the lead simply by receiving us in your home as you would anywhere and in any circumstances. Everybody else will follow suit, and Amelia need never fear ostracism again through this venture of mine." She paused as all three of her listeners gave little exclamations of mingled surprise and relief that for the present moment all foreseeable problems appeared solved, and then she gave Nina a constrained, sisterly smile. "I suppose all that remains is for me to wish you luck."

Nina came up to her and with a rare show of affection looped an arm around her neck, their faces coming together with a pressure of cheeks. "Thank you, Tansy. You wished me love, too. I hope I find it."

In the kitchen washing the glasses Tansy thought about Adam with a bittersweet longing. He haunted her more often than she cared to count up, although she knew that vain hankerings after what might have been were the greatest folly. Love. Would it ever come to her with its rich fulfillment of heart, mind, and body? Unaccountably her thoughts turned to Dominic and anger stirred again in her as she recalled his words. If only some magic, wand-like touch could free her from him in an instant! In a way he owned her. The roof over her head, the ground on which she stood, and even—indirectly—the clothes she wore on her back were all bonded to him. The debts she had to settle had become a deeply personal issue between them. It was as though she and Dominic faced each other with rapiers in a duel and although he had all the advantages, her triumph would be all the greater when she could pierce him at the heart. She paused, having taken up the cloth to dry and polish the glasses, and she daydreamed of the moment when she would throw the last golden sovereign down before him and be free of him at last. But that day was a long way off. With a shake of her head she rubbed vigorously at the crystal, making it sparkle.

Roger came home soon afterward. When he had removed his mud-caked boots at the kitchen porch he entered, tired and hungry and smelling of straw and horses. While he scrubbed the day's grime from his hands at the sink Tansy took food from the pantry for him. He was in an elated mood.

"You should have seen Young Oberon at the gallops!" His eyes glowed and he half-turned from the kitchen sink, scattering soapsuds. "He went into his canter with a proud head as if he knew he had advanced in his training beyond the others. I kept alongside on my hack and watched every move he made, every twitch of his ear. He doesn't like falling leaves. Fortunately the branches are more or less bare now, but it was a gusty morning and I saw how startled he was when an odd one came drifting past his nose. I think he can be willful, too. Once, for no reason at all that I could see—probably sheer contrariness inside his head—he went spinning off and sent some of the other yearlings into confusion. If I'd been in his saddle I would have checked him quicker than the stable lad who was riding him." He dried his hands. "Mr. Kirby—that's Mr. Reade's trainer whom he mentioned yesterday—has given me permission to ride Young Oberon to the gallops tomorrow morning, a distance of about half a mile which has been strewn with soft bracken now the frosts have come, and after that I'll have to hand over, but it's a start."

"A start and a finish, I would say." Tansy put down a dish of cold, boiled ham with a little thump. "You wanted to ride the colt just once, I remember you telling me. Tomorrow that wish will be fulfilled." Her look held a blend of anxiety and pity. "Don't reach out after more, Roger. It can't be. For reasons I don't feel able to disclose to you I know that the sooner you turn your back on the Ainderly Hall stables the better it will be."

His expression became deflated and the sullen set to his mouth as he jerked out the chair from under the kitchen table to sit down showed that he did not agree with her. "Just because we owe that money—" he muttered.

"No, it's more than that. Far more. I swear it."

He gave an uncomfortable shrug to his shoulders, which showed that whatever her belief he was certain he would not go along with it. "Today was the happiest day in my whole life," he stated stubbornly, attacking his supper.

"I'm sure it was," she said understandingly.

His eyes flicked toward her. She had taken a seat on the bench on the opposite side of the table, leaning both arms on it, and he was encouraged by her tone to mention Young Oberon again, the light coming back into his face. "Mr. Kirby told me that there's little doubt that Young Oberon's name will be written down for the Derby next spring—a whole year before the one that he'll actually run if nothing unforeseen occurs—and his selection, like all the other entries, will be based on his breeding, which in his case has that special strain of the great Eclipse's blood." He swallowed a mouthful of cold potato and ham.

"What happens if a horse which has been entered for the Derby doesn't live up to its promise over the interim period?" she asked, cutting him another slice of bread.

"There are three forfeit stages when an entry can be withdrawn," he informed her authoritatively. "There were one hundred and eighty-eight entries last year, Mr. Kirby told me, but in the end only thirty-two ran. That was an exceptionally big field, too. Usually the number is quite a few less. Think of all the hundreds of pounds in accumulated entry fees that are added to the great Derby prize when so many drop out!"

"I heard today that Edward Taylor of Cudlingham Manor has an entry running next year. His sister called this afternoon and told us she saw you talking to her brother. What happened? Any luck?"

His face fell again and his appetite seemed to wane. "That's the fourth place I went to. Mr. Harris, the head stable lad at Ainderly Hall, advised me to try a stud at Ewell first, but it was a wasted journey. I tried a couple of other stables, but even if they would have taken me on neither offered the kind of place I wanted. Then I walked all the way back to Cudlingham again and went to the Manor."

"Well?"

"I'm to go back again tomorrow. Mr. Taylor said I could speak to his trainer." He frowned, puzzled. "It's funny, but I had the impression that he wouldn't have bothered to give me a minute of his time if I hadn't introduced myself the way Mama always said a gentleman should." A grin lifted his permanently freckled cheeks. "I bet she would have been proud of me. Remember how she was always quoting that manners maketh man?"

Tansy nodded, smiling, and was glad that they were reaching the stage when they could talk about the parents they had lost with love and humor and less pain. "She had quotes for everything. I'll have to watch myself or I'll carry on the same habit. I found myself telling Nina never to count chickens after our visitor had left. You see, we learned that Edward Taylor appears to be somewhat attracted to Nina." She chuckled. "I dare say it was your surname more than your manners that won you that interview with his trainer tomorrow."

He was amused by the little joke against his own conceit, sharing her chuckles, and with a return to something of their old comradeship of the past they sat talking in the kitchen for quite a time, she telling him all that had taken place that afternoon and of the arrangement settled upon to help Nina win the man she wanted. Only then did they join the others.

When the evening ended and all had said good night, Tansy went in search of a book to read in bed for a little while. The bookcase where she had surprised Amelia late at night was full of volumes on horses, flat racing, and steeplechasing, the few she picked out at random all bearing her father's name in his own handwriting on the flyleaf. She smiled to herself, returning a history of horse racing to a shelf. In spite of a complete lack of literary interest in anything else, her father had amassed a fine collection on his favorite topic, some of the volumes being quite old and several that were surely museum pieces. A wide gap showed where Amelia must have withdrawn at least three good-sized books. The outline of them still showed in a faint edge of dust. Tansy thought it strange that Amelia should have found the subject of horse breeding or horse racing relaxing midnight reading, but there was no accounting for what other people enjoyed and she herself would prefer a work of fiction, something by Mr. Dickens or one of the new lady writers.

She was about to close the glass doors of the bookcase when she realized that her father's small library was hers, and she held the doors wide for a few moments longer, her gaze lingering affectionately on the leather-bound backs, some gilt embossed, in variegated autumnal hues, that stood neatly side by side. Out of all the contents of the house originally intended for her only these were left. She would treasure them all the more for it.

A further search of some bookshelves in another room yielded at least a dozen books on etiquette and the social graces belonging to Amelia, and a stack of somewhat lurid romances that were also hers. She was about to give up when she found among them a well-thumbed, battered book of plays. With interest she took it up to bed and read far into the night. When she closed the book, and before turning out the lamp, she used as a bookmark one of the programmes that she had discovered tucked into the back of it. A particular actress's name was featured in the cast of each one, but always in a minor role. Mrs. Amelia Rose St. Clair.

Next morning Tansy told Amelia of her discovery, and saw her give an unhappy start, her color fluctuating. "I'm sorry," she said sincerely. "I didn't mean to pry. I was hunting for something to read and chose the plays. I had looked through two or three of the programmes before I noticed that the same name was listed in every one."

Amelia's expression settled to one of resignation. "I suppose you were bound to find out sooner or later that I was once on the stage." She let her graceful shoulders rise and fall on a little sigh. "I need hardly say I toured with a traveling company of world-wide repute. That is how I met Oliver. He came to the performance of a melodrama when the day's races were over. I only had a small part—for some reason which I can't quite recall now I wasn't playing the lead for once," she interjected quickly, forgetting that Tansy, having seen those programmes, must have gained a good idea of her humble rating as an actress, "and when he came round afterward to the back of the tent—er, I mean the stage door—he said he hadn't been able to take his eyes from me and had no notion of what the drama he had viewed was about." Suddenly she sucked her lower lip under her pearly teeth in abashment, her round eyes becoming rounder. "Perhaps I shouldn't talk about my meeting with your father."

Tansy thought with irritation that Amelia may not have been very accomplished on the stage, but she was full of little actressy tricks and mannerisms. "You've told me quite enough. I should like to finish reading the plays if you have no objection."

"Read them by all means!" Amelia flung out her hands extravagantly, seeming to take Tansy's interest in the plays as an indirect compliment to herself. She looked singularly well pleased as she trotted away.

6.

That evening when Tansy was dressed and ready to leave for the Manor with her sisters, Judith waiting with her cloak on, Nina still titivating before her looking glass upstairs, she set the kitchen table with a cold supper for Roger, who had not returned home since going from it soon after six o'clock that morning. She could only suppose he was staying until the last possible minute at the stables to see Young Oberon through to the head stable lad's final check before bedtime to see that all was in order, something he had mentioned feeling inclined to do the previous evening but had come home in order that she should not start worrying about him. The sooner he was away once and for all from that place the better. When the owner of the stud was involved in racecourse villainy there was the chance that everyone employed there, from the trainer to the humblest stable lad, was tainted by it, and she did not want Roger to fall in with bad company.

Her dress rustled as she moved about the kitchen. She was wearing a plaid taffeta in rose and white, the low neckline modestly filled in with a muslin chemisette, all of which she had made herself. There had been no problem about what to wear that evening for any of them, for each possessed a share of pretty dresses made from the materials that Oliver had brought home in the past. There were lengths still to be made up, which had been discovered in his horse's saddlebags, and a Cashmere shawl, which they guessed had been bought for Ruth, was by common consent given to Judith, who was more often in need of an extra layer of warmth and possessed nothing so fine to put around her shoulders. There had been no doubt either about for whom a length of deep-blue velvet had been intended, but Nina had coveted and taken it, giving neither of the others the option, and intended to make a grand gown out of it. It was fortunate that Ruth had been skillful with a needle and had passed on her accomplishment to each one of her girls, although it was only Judith who had developed the ability to give a garment a bandbox look and in later years she had taken over the checking and fitting and correcting of the clothes that the others made. Nina hated sewing, but she had always loved new clothes, and whenever Oliver had brought home the usual lengths of fancy materials she had been the first to get down on her hands and knees to cut out a new dress. Ruth had often shown disapproval of her husband's choice, saying that more practical colors and materials would be of greater use, but to the relief of his daughters Oliver never took her advice, and continued at his home-comings to swirl out of his saddlebags the pinks and blues and greens and golds of silks and muslins, taffeta, lawn, and softest grenadine.

Tansy removed the apron she had popped on to protect her dress and went out into the hall as Nina descended the staircase, her splendid hair arranged simply but with style, and her dress was her favorite, a self-striped, amber-colored silk.

"How do I look?" she asked, always avid for praise.

It was Amelia who answered, darting forward from the open door of the long drawing room where she had been waiting. "Beautiful! Did you use some of the scent out of the bottle I loaned you? Gentlemen like a delicate perfume that is full of promise. What about your hands? My lotion softened them, didn't it. Which of my fans did you select? Ah, the ivory lace! Very pretty!"

Tansy, watching Nina turn and pirouette as much for her own benefit in the hall's pier glass as for Amelia's approving eye, thought that no Derby horse could be better groomed and encouraged toward victory than Nina was being by Amelia at this moment on the brink of her marriage campaign.

"It's time we left." Tansy, who had donned her cloak, held

Nina's out to her. "You don't object to walking the short distance, I suppose. It's a fine night, although cold."

"'I wouldn't have ridden in the wagonette anyway," Nina announced grandly. "You see, I intend to be driven home by Edward."

Amelia clapped her hands girlishly. "Well said!"

Nina ignored her and addressed Tansy and Judith. "Don't worry about anything. I prepared the way completely with Edward the day I met him. I was careful not to entangle myself with any outright lies beyond claiming to be Papa's niece. I told the truth, and simply left out the parts I didn't want him to know. That's why everything went so well when Sarah was here. I could tell he had given her all the information he had gathered about me when she mentioned the Yorkshire Marlows. I let slip to him that you and I, Tansy, are related to them, but although he knows them to be a respected and wellborn family he has never met any of them nor is he acquainted with anyone who has, which is exactly what I expected, knowing how Papa always said they were too parsimonious to go anywhere or do anything."

"What did you say about me?" Judith asked uneasily, being as unhappy as Tansy at the way they had become enmeshed in Nina's web with no chance of escaping except by destroying all her plans.

"There was nothing to evade there," Nina replied airily. "I told him you were our foster sister and your parents were dead. He knows your father was killed in a racing accident and assumed from what I said that he was a *gentleman* jockey, and not a mere professional, which put everything right for you." She looked from one to the other of them. "Is everything clear?"

Judith, happening to catch Tansy's eye, saw that she was finding Nina's pompous, school-dame attitude highly ridiculous, and felt her own giggles rising within her. It was either to giggle or to cry.

"Yes, ma'am," she replied in unison and quite spontaneously with Tansy. Then they both exploded with laughter.

Nina, more exasperated than annoyed, swept toward the door. "Oh, come along, do!"

She gave them one more instruction as they set off down the drive. "Just say 'Papa' when it fits in, and 'Oliver' when it doesn't. In that way neither of you will be straying from the truth—not that you would anyway," she added in a mutter to herself.

The windows of Cudlingham Manor streamed with light. Broughams and landaus and barouches passed the girls along the drive and drew up to let their passengers alight at the great porch entrance. When they left their cloaks, Nina dallied deliberately, whispering to them that they should go ahead of her, because she wanted to give Edward a scare and make him think she hadn't come after all.

He was receiving his guests in an anteroom that led into the music room, and when they were announced he greeted Judith and Tansy most warmly. "Miss Collins—the pleasure is mine. And Miss Marlow—this is indeed a privilege. Is your sister not with you?"

He glanced quickly beyond them to some other guests who were arriving, but seeing no sign of her he half-craned his neck anxiously. Tansy thought wryly that Nina had succeeded with her artful ploy. The coquetry had worked just as she had planned.

Judith compassionately put him out of his misery. "She is on her way."

He beamed at her in his relief, and seeing that she was fumbling a little with her stick he gave her his arm and went with them to the door of the music room where he left to go back to receiving his guests. They saw before them a setting of silk-paneled walls and fine chandeliers in which at least thirty people were engaged in conversation, some standing, others sitting already in the gilded, cushion-seated chairs that had been arranged in semicircular rows facing the palm-backed dais set ready for the musicians with harp, grand piano, and music stands.

Tansy felt someone's gaze fixed on her. She knew instinctively who it was even as her head jerked involuntarily in his direction. Dominic's jet-dark eyes met hers across the room. He stood tall in his black evening clothes against one of the jade-green panels, the glow from the chandelier above his head casting blue lights into his thick hair. He bowed to her and she acknowledged the courtesy coolly, her heart beginning to pound as though alerted by a silent alarm. She felt her color come and recede again.

Sarah, playing hostess with verve and a superficial charm, gathered the two sisters into her charge and conveyed Judith to a sofa placed to make extra seats near the dais where she could converse with an elderly gentleman whom Sarah thought too boring to inflict on anyone else, and Tansy was swept into other company. Out of the corner of her eye Tansy saw Dominic move slowly and deliberately to take up his solitary stand again where his view of her was unimpeded by those who had come between them. She felt his glittering gaze absorbing her as if on this occasion, not being engaged in talk with her, he could give himself up to finishing the appraisal of her face and figure he had first started making in the smoky atmosphere of a village tavern.

She found it difficult to concentrate on what was being said to her, knowing if she turned her head his eyes would be waiting for hers. There was surely not a wispy strand of hair straying loose from a ringlet, a ripple of the ribbon band taut about her waist, or a gather over her bodice that was escaping his penetrating gaze. It had not crossed her mind before that she was likely to meet him at any social function to which she was invited, but she was determined to find an escape from his unwanted attentions somehow.

In the anteroom Edward saw Nina approaching, her hair a glorious bronze in the candlelight, her skin creamy, and almost translucent over the lovely bones of her triangular face. She made all the other young women attending the musical evening seem pale and insignificant by comparison, their prettiness doll-like, their expressions simpering. Nina had a unique poise; in all his experience of women, which was wide, for he was sensual by nature, there had never been one who had fascinated him as much as Nina. If she liked him at all he could not tell, but he knew himself to be falling in love with her and it was a pleasurable sensation.

"Good evening, Mr. Taylor." She was extending her white-gloved hand gracefully to him.

He realized he was staring at her as if struck dumb, and he recovered himself, smiling broadly, and bowed, holding her fingers a fraction longer than was necessary. "How glad I am that you could come, Miss Nina." To his relief she was the last to be received and there were no other guests after her, and he offered her his arm. "Everybody has arrived. Allow me to take you through."

She smiled at him, warm rosy lips parting to reveal pearly little teeth. "How kind," she murmured.

Although outwardly she was utterly composed, inwardly she was riotously jubilant. Heads turned as they entered the music room together, and she saw another ripple of movement follow as people whispered or exchanged knowing glances. She was amused. Let the local young ladies pout and their matchmaking mothers frown. She, Nina Marlow, had taken the first decisive step toward getting Edward Taylor's ring on her finger.

The five musicians were taking up their places, the pianist flicking out his coattails as he settled himself at the grand piano. Sarah was ushering people into chairs. Tansy saw her loop a familiar arm through Dominic's, say something that caused him to bend his tall head to catch her low-spoken, laughing words and then unexpectedly give a wide, wicked grin, his eyes half-closing in amusement before she led him away to sit with her somewhere at the back of the room. Tansy decided there were probably many facets to his nature and she herself did not want to know one of them. She sat rigidly, gazing ahead, between two of the people with whom she had been talking. Near at hand Judith made room on the sofa for Nina and Edward to sit beside her. With clear and pure notes from a violin the concert began.

The quintet was of high repute from London and the classical selection enthralled Tansy, who loved music and had never heard such quality of performance before. When the interval came she stirred as though from a blissful dream and found Dominic standing before her.

"It's my pleasant duty to take you in to supper, Tansy."

Whether that duty was self-appointed or had been set upon him by the host or hostess she did not know and could not very well ask, seeing that they were in the hearing of others. Everyone was pairing off to go through the double doors that had been opened to reveal a long, candelabra-lit buffet table.

"I don't feel very hungry," she said distantly, rising to go with him.

"I should have thought the walk from Rushmere to the Manor would have stimulated your appetite."

She looked at him in surprise. "How did you know that Judith and I walked?"

"Because you were the only two who entered the room with roses in your cheeks that had come from the night air and not from a vanity jar."

"Nina walked too."

"After you arrived I didn't look at anyone else."

Why did everything he ever said to her play such havoc with her emotions? She had not felt pleasure at his compliment, because heaven alone knew how much she disliked and even feared him, but nevertheless the way he had looked at her had made his words touch off some deep, trembling chord within the most intimate depths of her being and she was desperately afraid that he knew it.

To her relief, although he waited on her and brought every kind of delicacy he thought she would like from the buffet, they ate with others in a little group that included her two sisters and Edward, which made the conversation general. Judith, sitting on Dominic's other side, engaged his attention for a considerable time, making Tansy wonder what on earth they could be finding to talk about at length, but it did give her the chance to discuss Roger's possible prospects with Edward, who brought up the subject with her.

"Townsend, my trainer, thinks he is a dashed promising youngster. He has seen him ride twice today and watched him handle a stallion that was fighting for his head, mouth wide open, and never once did Roger lose control. He has all the makings of a good jockey—that's provided he stays more or less the same height and weight that he is now, but there's many a disappointed fellow who starts to shoot out of his socks when he reaches sixteen or seventeen, don't you know."

"What makes a good jockey? It cannot be just a question of size and an ability to ride well."

"Indeed not. He needs plenty of courage, keen intelligence, and trigger-quick reactions."

She smiled. "I like to think Roger has all those qualifications."

Edward gave her a serious nod. "Townsend thinks he might have them too. He gave me his opinion when I saw him earlier this evening. I have agreed that Roger shall be offered a traineeship when he keeps an appointment with Townsend tomorrow morning, but in the meantime say nothing to him and keep what I have told you to yourself. Townsend has a right to tell Roger himself."

She was overjoyed. "I quite understand, and thank you for giving your sanction. All I have wished for Roger is to see him accepted by good stables where he can work hard and fulfill his ambitions."

"It's a pity your brother cannot start off with his own horses because this is a hard way for a gentleman's son. However, I have arranged with Townsend that Roger shall live with him and his wife, which will save the boy mixing more than is necessary with the ordinary jockeys and others not of his class."

"Roger wouldn't wish for any special privileges," Tansy insisted.

"Nonsense. He'll be treated as strictly as anybody else, have no doubts about that."

Tansy knew she should feel relieved that her fears of Roger's involvement at Ainderly Hall had been lifted. As a trainee at another establishment he would fall in naturally with the rivalry that existed between stables in the racing world, and she hoped he would soon make friends and settle down.

Nina, engaging Edward's attention again, continued to spin her half truths, the subject of their conversation having turned to travel. "How fortunate you are to have seen so many faraway places," she declared, wide-eyed. "My late parents never took us abroad—Judith's health would not have permitted it. Traveling tires her. But that's not the reason why I've never met any of the Yorkshire Marlows. Papa and Mama had no particular interest in them and preferred to suffer no interference from outside members of the family. Therefore I don't know them and neither do they know us."

He laughed, his eyes dancing at her. "How wise! I'm plagued with dashed more relatives than I can count. Fortunately they only descend on Cudlingham Manor for important family occasions such as weddings and funerals—and christenings."

Her glance fell away from his, and her lips parted slightly before she spoke again. "Don't they come for the Derby?"

"No, thank the Lord! None of them is a racing chap, and you'll find none of my aunts betting in pairs of gloves. They hunt, don't you know. We Taylors prefer the hunting field to the racecourse—my father was the exception. My great-grandmother rode to hounds until she was over eighty."

"How splendid! But who would surrender willingly the excitement of the chase." She sparkled with a delighted enthusiasm that managed to suggest it was customary for her to indulge in the sport from November to April.

He beamed at her. "You enjoy it as much as I do, I can see that. Capital! There's a meet at Ewell next Saturday. I trust you will join me."

Her mind raced. It would be the first time she had ever ridden to hounds and she had never possessed a riding habit in her life, but there was that length of deep-blue velvet, which the others had let her have. Judith should help her make a fine habit from it, even if it meant sitting up all night and every night to get it finished. And she could ride well and knew she looked elegant in the sidesaddle, for her father had seen to it that she and Tansy rode in the manner born. Her mouth curled prettily at him.

"I accept with pleasure."

It was time to adjourn from the supper room to take their places again for the second half of the concert. When it was over Edward expressed his wish to drive her home, intending that

Tansy and Judith should be included under his escort, but Dominic took over there from him.

"It's pointless for you two to wait until every guest has departed," he said to Tansy, "and that could be some time with the way many people delay. Miss Judith looks tired. I will take you home."

His arrogant assumption that she would prefer to ride with him than wait for Edward and Nina took her breath away. He seemed to have a knack of putting propositions to her that she had no choice but to accept. She thought Sarah looked askance when thanks for the evening's hospitality had been said and Dominic escorted them out of the door. The interior of his carriage was comfortably upholstered in dove-gray velvet with silk-tasseled blinds at the windows and carpeting underfoot, a luxurious indulgence that caused Tansy surreptitiously to slip off her shoe and test its softness with her stockinged toes. Then to her embarrassment she lost her shoe and no amount of frantic searching about with her foot could discover it, the movement of the carriage having caused it to roll away somewhere.

Dominic, who was sitting opposite the girls, paused in discussing with Judith the concert they had enjoyed and let his gaze drop to Tansy's skirt hems with a twitch of his mouth in amusement. "Lost your shoe?"

"Yes, I'm afraid I have."

"I'll find it." He dropped down to one knee and reached under the seat, finally locating the shoe in the opposite corner. Tansy would have taken it from him, but he shook his head and reluctantly she raised her foot, which swayed as the carriage wheels covered the rutted lane. Without ado, he took hold of her ankle under her petticoats with one hand and slipped the shoe on with the other. "There, that's better."

He took his seat again, not taking his eyes from her, but she looked resolutely out of the windows as if there were something of interest to see in the blustery, wind-blown night. Her face burned crimson. He had caressed her ankle with his touch. And her instep. Admittedly the caress had been light and it could have been accidental, but she herself had no doubts at all. Such an intimacy was unheard of. Skirts were at a length that protected the slightest glimpse of an ankle from public gaze and that he should dare to take hers into those stroking fingertips of his was an outrage not to be borne. He was treating her like a—like a *demi-mondaine.* Did he imagine that by living under the same roof as Amelia she was tarred with the same brush? But what could she do or say? If she challenged him he would no doubt apologize profusely and say he had not been aware of causing any offense, which would make her look and feel ridiculous, as though she were making a fuss about nothing. Or—worse still—being the man he was, he might admit to it and then whatever apology he offered could only make matters a deal more awkward in every way. She would ignore it. Ignore the whole incident and pretend she hadn't noticed. Hadn't noticed? Dear God! Considering that she had only to come near him for her pulse to race and every nerve in her to throb it was small wonder that contact with his fondling hand, however brief and passing, should make her body come alive. How was it possible to be physically attracted against one's most stubborn will to a man for whom one felt only animosity and enmity?

The ride was already over, the short distance between the two houses covered at a good speed. Judith, sensitive to atmosphere, glanced unhappily from one to the other of them and gave her hand to Dominic on the doorstep, bidding him a hasty good night, and added:

"It was kind of you to bring us home. I'll not forget what we talked about this evening. Good night again."

Tansy would have followed Judith into the house without a backward glance in Dominic's direction, but he caught her by the arms and drew her into the dark shadows of the deep doorway out of sight and hearing of the coachman and groom on his carriage.

"Listen to me, Tansy. No, don't toss your head and look away. I understand that it goes against your pride to be in debt to anyone. I should feel the same if such a misfortune ever happened to me, but for you to create a feud between us over Young Oberon is neither sane nor sensible. You left Ainderly Hall in high dudgeon the other afternoon, but I hoped you would simmer down and at least come to accept the situation. I had looked forward to seeing you this evening, knowing from Sarah that you were to be there, but as soon as you saw me you made a mask of your face and I knew we were as far apart as ever."

"That is how we shall remain," she retaliated. "No matter by what impertinences you seek to make your desires known."

He gave a soft, low laugh and moved in closer, still holding her. "Forgive me, I beg you. It was grossly unfair of me to take advantage of you over your lost shoe, but although I know you to be virtuous I hardly think you prudish."

"You don't know me at all!" she retorted, feeling trapped between him and the stone wall at her back. "Yet you are highhanded enough to make judgments about my character as if we had been long acquainted. I've not forgotten all you said to me the night we met. You were insufferable."

"Ah," he said sagely, "is that at the root of it all?"

"No, it's not." All anger against him seemed to ebb from her and she gave her head a weary shake, capitulating to her sense of fairness. "I must tell you that until Roger said something to me that opened my eyes I blamed you for my father's death."

"I?" He was incredulous. "Why? What possible reason could you have had?"

"You led him into drink."

"You're wrong. He had downed more brandies than I knew of when I came downstairs to the taproom from the accommodation in the tavern that I had taken for the night. He stood alone at the end of the bar, there being no one else there at the time, the hour early. He was weeping. I have never seen a man shed such tears. The landlord and his wife hovered helplessly, at a loss how to comfort him. It was a relief to them when I appeared and took over. After lining up a few more brandies they left us alone. Oliver told me the whole story, our differences forgotten. In truth I feared for his sanity, so wild-eyed was he and mad with grief and despair. After a while the brandy dulled pain and memory, which seemed to me the best thing possible for a man in such agony of mind, and then as others came into the taproom his mood changed to a drunken need for camaraderie on a wider, boisterous scale to help ease his torment. The landlord and I had arranged to haul him up to one of the upper rooms and put him to bed for the night, but he stayed on his feet, amazing us both, neither of us having seen a man drink to such capacity without passing out. I believe his grief counteracted the full effect of the spirit he consumed, because after your appearance in the bar he became sober in his mind if not in his body."

Her head hung. "And I didn't go after him when he came out of the tavern as I should have done. I was so angry with him—and with you."

"That was very obvious. But I followed him."

"You did?" Her head came up again, her eyes wide.

"I caught him up and talked with him. He appeared clearheaded. I told him that I would not be staying the night after all and he was to return to the tavern and take my bed. He said he would do that after he had been to the churchyard and made his peace with Ruth and been alone with her. That was the last I saw of him. I only knew of his death when the lawyer notified me, having found a copy of the agreement over Young Oberon among Oliver's papers and wanting to check that the colt had not been mutually disposed of since the document was signed."

"Sorrow must have overcome my father again at the graveside and that was why he wandered the night through."

"I can see that some measure of blame could be mine through not waiting to see him back myself to the tavern, but I thought him safe to leave."

"No, you acted with humanity and none could expect more. I only realized my folly in blaming you for what happened to him at the end when I discovered that Roger had been holding me responsible all the time. I was ashamed. I suppose I had saddled you with my own sense of guilt."

"Now we have talked out this point may I hope that we find ourselves on surer ground for our relationship?" he asked quietly.

"Nothing else has changed," she answered stubbornly. "I can have no freedom of spirit until all debts are cleared between us.

I have learned that not even Rushmere is wholly mine. There are mortgage payments outstanding to add to all the rest."

"I don't care a damn about the money," he responded fiercely in exasperation. "Such paltry, unimportant sums—"

"They are not paltry or unimportant to me," she flashed back, not daring to add that owing money to a scoundrel contaminated the debtor and her hands would not be clean until every last penny was paid in full. Her voice took on a taunting note, and she prodded his chest with her finger. "I'm now going to share a secret with you and as a gentleman you will respect my confidence."

"Naturally." He sounded pleased. "You have my word on it."

"I intend to lead a double life this winter. Nina and Amelia are so anxious to preserve a genteel façade that I am thwarted in my original plan to make some money out of Rushmere and must wait for that until the spring. So in the meantime I shall take up some daily employment in one of the big mansions in Epsom or outside it as a cook or linen maid or some other domestic post where I can at least earn something in regions where the grand lady of the house won't see me and there will be no chance of my bringing disgrace to those of my own household."

He was angered and outraged. "You cannot do that! It's unthinkable."

She was well satisfied with his reaction. Now she had it in her power to cut herself free of his attentions once and for all. In the stress of sorrow her father may have forgotten momentarily that Dominic indulged in racecourse tricks that had been abhorrent to him and brought about the gulf between them, but she had uppermost in her mind that sinister meeting she had been witness to by chance. "I shall scrub floors if I have to. Think of that! You may pass me by in future without a nod and I shall understand. No person of standing in Cudlingham or anywhere else can hobnob socially with a servant girl."

His grip tightened on her arms, which he was still holding, and he lowered his head to bring his face within an inch of hers. "You underestimate me," he warned dangerously. "The sooner you drop such ploys the better. I'm not so easily discouraged."

His arrogance dumbfounded her. Did he imagine she was playing some coquettish game of chase and capture? Or—worse—did he think to fix a price on her to level out the debts between them? Then, even as she drew breath to answer him, she was too late, for he had interpreted those seconds of her silence into some meaning of his own, and his mouth swept down to possess hers. In the cold blackness of the doorway and the rough night there was an explosive golden fire in his kiss, his lips moving with a demanding violence against hers, his passion a force so powerful that even had she wished it she could not have broken from the embrace of his arms that held her clasped to the full male length of him, body to body, thigh to thigh. With complete and utter abandonment she surrendered to the delirium of her pounding senses with a sweet and frantic wildness, all her reason flown, all her will to resist momentarily melted and gone.

When at last their long kiss that had been many kisses ended he still clasped her tight with his arm about her waist and would have touched her throat with tender fingertips, but she drew back sharply, breathless and disheveled, and reached for the ring handle of the ancient door behind her.

"It is all still as it was between us," she said emotionally. "Nothing can or shall be changed. I mean what I say."

She entered the house with a rustle of her taffeta skirt and closed the door behind her, shooting the bolt home with panicky fingers as if she feared he might decide to come in after her. Then she leaned back against the door's stout timbers, giving her heart a chance to ease its crazy beating and her limbs time to lose their trembling. The hall was in darkness. Only a chink of light escaped from the direction of the kitchen to show that Judith had not gone to bed, but was waiting for her, probably with a pot of tea ready or some other hot drink.

Outside, the clatter of departing hooves carried him away. Silence descended on the night again, except for the creak of branches outside in the wind. She knew she must make a move. It was not fair to let Judith sit waiting any longer. With both hands she smoothed her hair, took a deep breath, and went toward the baize-lined door.

In the lamplit kitchen she found that Judith was not alone. Roger stood with his weight lodged on the edge of the kitchen table, both legs straight, his arms folded. Tansy saw at once that all was not well. Judith looked white and Roger's face held a defiance that was not far from immature tears.

"What is the matter?" she asked anxiously.

Judith spoke from the bench where she was sitting. "Roger has something to tell you. He has been given the chance to become a professional gentleman jockey."

Tansy relaxed, releasing a relieved sigh. "Is that any cause for such glum faces? Edward told me this evening that his trainer had been instructed to offer you a place, Roger. Did you see the man while we were at the concert?"

Roger nodded. "I was there about half-past eight. Mr. Townsend had been expecting me back in the morning, but I called in again on my way home."

Tansy supposed that the conditions laid down were more strict than her brother had expected. Perhaps at first he would be doing less riding than he had hopefully anticipated. Another possible reason sprang to mind. "Do you have to spend an initial period in the hunting stables? I know those horses mean more to Edward than the others."

Roger's freckles seemed to stand out on his taut face. "You don't understand. I'm not going to be at Cudlingham Manor. I stopped by to tell Mr. Townsend I was already fixed up."

"Where?" she demanded in a dangerous voice. "Tell me where!"

He gulped and swallowed. "Don't be mad, Tansy. I've been taken on at Ainderly Hall."

"You promised me you wouldn't ask for a place there!" she exploded, hurt as much as wrathful. "We don't break promises to each other or anybody else in our family."

"I didn't ask, really I didn't. You must believe me. After I came back from the gallops this morning and had helped unsaddle and clean off Young Oberon, replaced his rug, and seen to some fresh bedding, I was called into Mr. Kirby's office. He offered me a traineeship there and then. I accepted." His voice shook. "I couldn't refuse, Tansy. He told me that Mr. Reade said I was to ride Young Oberon at every opportunity—and if I prove myself I'll be able to race him when the time comes."

Tansy stood very still, the fingertips of both hands pressed against her closed eyes as though fighting to gain control of herself. When at last she lowered them she spoke very calmly. "Well, no harm is done. You can go right back to Ainderly Hall in the morning and tell them that you have reconsidered the offer and find you are unable to accept it."

Roger straightened up from the table's edge and squared his shoulders. "It's too late for that. I signed the papers. Whenever I ride in a race I'll be wearing silks in the Ainderly Hall colors and no other."

Tansy made a little sound between a cry and a sob. Her indebtedness to Dominic was increasing every day. Was she never to be free of him! Turning on her heel she went from the kitchen, her heels clicking as she traversed the long passageway. They heard the baize door close with a thud after her.

7.

In the winter months that followed, Tansy's life dropped into a pattern. Every day she took the wagonette, starting out at six o'clock each morning, to travel some little distance to cook and housekeep for a retired Rector in one of the surrounding hamlets. Nina had wanted her to take employment under a false name, but that she would not do, and she confided to the Rector her need to earn money without offending the genteel aspirations of those with whom she lived. He was a kindly man, and he understood and sympathized, paying her fairly, not only for her domestic services, but for the writing she did for him in the afternoons when he dictated to her a book he was hoping to have published about the life of one of the lesser known saints.

It was not the work she did for him that played the real havoc with her hands, bringing on chilblains, but the hours she spent exposed to the bitter elements while tending the open-air stall she had taken at a brisk and weekly market in the little town of Epsom. There she sold eggs from the hens she now kept, the lace and other handiwork done by Judith—who spent the greater part of every day making goods for the stall—and the pots of cosmetic preparations that Amelia concocted with such skill, a talent developed from her theatrical days when she had found it cheaper to make her own than to buy them. It was Nina's praise of Amelia's hand lotion that had first given Tansy the thought of turning that talent to their mutual financial advantage. Unfortunately Amelia was basically lazy, forever wriggling out of doing the small chores allotted to her, and she had to be chivvied constantly into getting the next batch of scented creams and lotions ready in time, each consignment selling out on the stall before the market closed. Invariably it fell to Tansy to pot and bottle it all in the late evening when her day's work was done, but she knew it was worth it, most of the money brought in going toward food and fuel and other necessities, the small residue joining the unspent wages received from the Rector to swell the still minuscule nucleus of a first payment against the debt that burdened her. The hand lotion, in spite of its undeniable ability to soothe and soften—the reason for its rapid sale—could do little for chilblains renewed constantly, and daily Tansy longed for milder weather.

At parties and other social gatherings she felt compelled to wear white gloves or else kept her discolored and often puffy hands hidden as best she could, never once accepting an invitation to play cards or spillikins when all eyes would be on her fingers. Once she met Dominic on the stairs in the home of a mutual acquaintance during a party, and knowing they were alone in the entrance hall he caught her hand and ripped it free of its glove, his face darkening when he saw its swollen state. Outside the family circle only he knew of the work she did.

"You're a stubborn young woman," he said impatiently.

"I have obligations to fulfill," she answered, not unamused by his exasperation. She believed herself to be one of the few—perhaps even the only one—of the women he knew and had known who persistently went her own way against his wishes. She made to withdraw her hand, but he held it tight by the fingers and put his other hand under it to cup his palm against hers.

"Why don't you stop this folly?" he demanded, his eyes searching hers. "There are more ways than one of settling this debt between us."

He was propositioning her! Was there no end to his conceit? Did he think to add her to his conquests. And there were many if only half of what she had heard was true.

"Sir," she said quietly and coolly, "you should know by now that I'm set on a particular path and nothing can turn me from it. Least of all any alternatives that you may suggest. Now, if you will kindly release my hand—we are observed."

He followed her glance and saw Sarah standing at the head of the stairs, looking down at them, her face pinched and her mouth thin with jealousy. It was well known that there had been —or still was—something between them, and he did escort her to many occasions. But she was by no means the only one on whom he bestowed his attentions, and he was rarely without a pretty woman on his arm.

"So we are," he remarked dryly. Then, instead of releasing her hand, he put the glove back on it with elaborate care, turning her wrist to fasten the tiny button. Only then did he free her, but with such a wicked look dancing in his eyes that Tansy was hard put to keep a smile from her lips, and she hastened on down the stairs, leaving him to await Sarah's descent.

The hard, frosty winter weather continued until mid-February, when it gave way to cold, damp days with much rain, which turned the lanes into a morass of chocolate-colored mud. Never had the drive home seemed longer to Tansy on a particular Saturday afternoon when she came home from market in a heavy rain that had not ceased since early morning. She was soaked through and chilled to the marrow of her bones, for all the time she had stood behind the market stall the wind had driven the slashing rain before it like a curtain, making mockery of the awning, which had snapped and billowed like a sail. She had kept her head tilted against the rain, seeking some protection from her deep hat, its wide brim at eyebrow level offering some disguise against recognition for Nina's and Amelia's sakes, a calamity so far avoided. Nina did nothing to help toward the stall, accepting the domestic results of the funds it brought in as a natural right. She alone at Rushmere led a life as near to that of a true lady as was possible in the circumstances, spending most of her time at Cudlingham Manor and in Edward's company. Everything was going well between them, and Nina sang about the house, was less openly derisive of Amelia, from whom she borrowed shawls, jewelry, and other gewgaws, although she still despised her, and was altogether more agreeable to live with.

Without doubt she was—as Roger had so aptly put it in racing terms—coming into the straight with the winning post of a betrothal looming ahead.

Tansy shivered, aware that she was aching in every limb, and she peered ahead through the rain as she drove past Ashby Woods, straining her eyes for the first welcome glimpse of the gates of Rushmere. It would have been easy to have shown her authority on the night that Roger confessed to joining the Ainderly Hall stables and forbidden him to come to Rushmere again since he had flouted her most anxious wishes, but she had known that for his sake she must swallow her anger and accept that what was done could not be undone, or else such a gulf would widen between them that he would feel unable to come to her should he be in trouble or difficulties at any time. Since he was essentially an honest boy, it would go completely against his nature to find himself party to any stable dealings that were at all shady, and yet, having signed himself away, he was bound body and soul to Ainderly Hall, not able to visit other stables without the trainer's permission. There could be no buying him out of it, for Dominic would not be like Mr. Webster, relieved to be rid of him, because a trainee jockey with inside information would never be let loose to allow his tongue to wag in the wrong quarters.

Tansy was thankful that after an initial spate of awkwardness on Roger's part, during which time he stayed at Ainderly Hall and had not come home for a month, he now visited Rushmere freely whenever he felt like it and his long and busy day permitted. All the real work of training had been held up over the deepest winter when the stone-hard ground could wreck a young horse's brittle legs, but now it had commenced again. Young Oberon officially became a two-year-old from a yearling on the first day of the New Year, and Judith had baked a special cake to celebrate the occasion, which had been much appreciated by Roger. So carefree was he, so full of rosy hopes, that Tansy was sure she would spot the first signs of any unease on his part about what he might see or overhear of crooked racing practices being carried out at Ainderly Hall.

The gates of Rushmere stood wide. The horse in the shafts of the wagonette, as eager to be home in the dry as she, trotted quickly to the stables at the rear of the house. She almost fell from the driver's seat in her exhaustion and realized that she staggered as she unharnessed the horse and led him into his stall. How her face burned! And there was a strange lightheadedness that came and went. She hoped desperately that she was not going to be ill, because she could not spare the time to lie abed.

Lacking the strength to unload from the wagonette the goods that had not been sold, she left them where they were under cover and entered the house by the back door. The warmth of the kitchen hit her like a buffeting cloud, but still she shivered. With arms that seemed hampered by invisible weights she managed to hook her cloak on the peg by the door, her hat with it, and then she lowered herself onto the bench by the table, where she proceeded to empty the leather pouch that carried the day's takings, and counted out the coins.

Sometimes she felt like a miser, but every penny mattered. She knew she had less to count than usual, the rain having kept customers away, but surely there should be a little more than the figure she had reckoned up. A pain behind her eyes was confusing her, making it difficult to concentrate, but she totaled up the money again, discovered she had overlooked some shillings and a silver three-penny bit, and scooped it all into a metal box and closed it. Her shivering was making her teeth chatter. She reeled to her feet and left the table to take a seat in the rocking chair by the range where the fire glowed white-hot behind the bars. Her damp clothes began to steam in the heat and she knew she should have gone to change into dry things at once, but in her curiously dazed state she was unable to summon up the will to do it.

On the wall one of the bells jingled. Tansy looked at it without interest. Rushmere had a visitor. If it were the Queen herself at the door she would not be able to find the energy to get up and let her in. The bell could be heard faintly from the long drawing room and other downstairs rooms, so she must only hope that Amelia, whom she supposed to be in, would go to answer it,

Judith having gone with Nina to lunch at the Manor with Sarah Taylor. She closed her eyes, her limbs heavy, her head like a furnace.

The bell jingled again, making her start, and she sat forward, inadvertently setting the rocking chair in motion, and with a sigh she sank back into its soothing rhythm, hearing voices in the hall and knowing Amelia had answered the door at last. She was asleep immediately.

When she woke again the hands of the big-faced kitchen clock had moved forward half an hour, but she gave it no glance, having lost all sense of time and conscious only of a raging thirst. She lurched up from the chair, leaving it rocking wildly, and stumbled across to the sink, where she had to use both hands to work the pump handle, sweat pouring in rivulets down her face and under her clothes.

When she had drunk all she could manage, her one thought was to get up to bed, and she clutched at the edge of the table for support as she made her stumbling way across the kitchen. Never in her life had she felt so ill, and iron bands were crushing her chest. She reached the flagged passageway, the baize-lined door into the hall looking as though it were a mile away.

Then she realized she was crawling on her hands and knees. Hampered by her rain-damp skirts and enervated by her raging fever, she progressed with agonizing slowness, sometimes sprawling out flat, welcoming the chill of the flagged floor against her burning forehead. When she finally reached the door it was closed and she had to struggle upright to put her weight on the handle. Reeling with it when the door swung open, she fell full length at the feet of the man who was ending his visit and coming with Amelia from her drawing room. It was Dominic. He gave an exclamation of dismay, echoed by Amelia's shriek, and knelt at once to stoop over her, slipping an arm under her shoulders.

"Tansy! What is it? You're ill!"

She tried to answer him but could not. Then she thought she was floating, but he had picked her up, and out of the jumble that his strong voice and Amelia's whispering were creating in her head a few sentences registered in her consciousness.

"Send my coachman posthaste for Dr. Westlake. Which room is Tansy's?"

"The second door on the right. Er—about your decision?"

"Let's have no more talk of that in this present crisis, madame." He had started up the stairs, Tansy's head lolling against his shoulder, and she thought vaguely how soothing was the clean, male fragrance of shaved chin, crisp linen, and good broadcloth blended with the faint aroma of cigar. Like an arrow to pierce her pain-tormented head Amelia's sibilant whisper followed them up the stairs.

"But I must *know*, Mr. Reade!" The hissing tones took on an independent note. "Because if you're not prepared to settle the matter without delay—"

He spun round at the head of the flight and his wrathful answer rumbled in his chest under Tansy's ear. "You shall have your price! I'll contact my banker in the morning. Now let that be an end to your prattle, Mrs. Marlow. Have that call sent to the doctor."

Pillows were soft under Tansy's head. She opened her eyes once and looked into his face. He thinks I'm going to die, she thought incredulously. Never had she seen such desperate anxiety in another's eyes. She wanted to reassure him, to tell him that she was never ill and this state of affairs would be over as quickly as it had begun, but although she spoke, her steadily rising fever touched her at that moment into delirium and there was no sense in what she cried out with hands uplifted to him.

She knew little of the care that was taken of her in the days that followed. The faces of Nina, Judith, and Amelia alternated at her bedside with the bearded visage of the doctor, who seemed to be waking her continually from the blissful oblivion of sleep, although later she heard he had only come twice daily after the first day, when he had called thrice. Cold-water sponges burned her body as her sisters sought to bring down her stubborn temperature, and she sobbed when one sweat-soaked nightgown was changed for the newly ironed crispness of another, it being agony for her to be propped up and the garment pulled down over her head, one arm and then the other guided into a sleeve with a gentleness that seemed to her racked form the most rough and brutal treatment.

She emerged at last from the ordeal of her illness to a new quietness. Daily Judith sat sewing in a chair by the bed and tender rays of March sunshine penetrated the mullioned windows to make a checkered pattern on the floor. Tansy learned that she had been near death for several days and was still dangerously sick for two weeks after that, but she had no clear recollection of anything to pinpoint the passing of time. Her room was full of daffodils, and there was a fresh bowl of spring violets on the table at her bedside. Judith noticed her looking at them.

"They're from Dominic. They were delivered just now while you slept. Aren't they lovely?" Judith put aside her sewing and took her stick to come across to lift the bowl and hold it toward her sister. "Just inhale their scent. It's like having spring itself in the room."

Tansy buried her nose in their dewy depths. Their delicate perfume touched her deeply, moving her almost to tears in her weakened, emotional state, her thankfulness for their beauty also gratitude for being alive.

"I always think they're my favorite flower until the roses come, and then I'm not sure," she said with a smile, letting her head drop back against the propped-up pillows, and keeping a single violet to hold between finger and thumb, brushing it against her cheek.

Judith gave a quick little nod, replacing the bowl. "I know. But spring flowers are always special. I think it's because we seem to wait so long for their coming." She touched the trumpet of one of the golden daffodils that made a splash of brilliant yellow on the top of the chest of drawers. "Sarah and Edward sent you these. Flowers and gifts of calf's-foot jelly and beef tea and egg custards have been arriving at the house ever since people we know heard you were ill, and there's enough hothouse fruit in dishes and baskets everywhere to keep us all fed."

"Do give Roger some more to take back to his quarters and

share with the others in the stable," Tansy urged, "and you and Nina and Amelia must have all you want. Everybody has been so kind. I must write letters of thanks to all when I'm able."

Judith sat on the edge of the bed. "You're the convalescent who has to get her strength back," she said, patting the bed-covers over Tansy's legs in gentle admonishment, "but I will let Roger take whatever looks overripe. I don't think you need write to Dominic. He is waiting for a first chance to see you. You gave him a great shock when you came falling through the kitchen door to collapse at his feet. Not a day has gone by without his calling at the house to ask after you, sometimes two or three times when your condition was still critical. On that terrible night when we sent for Roger, thinking we were really going to lose you, Dominic didn't go home at all, but stayed pacing about downstairs like a caged lion until dawn when I was able to go down to him with the news that your fever had broken at last."

Tansy spoke with some distress. "Please don't ask me to see him," she implored. "I appreciate his concern, but I'm not ready to face anyone from outside the family circle yet."

"I think you're making an excuse directed solely against him."

"Perhaps I am," Tansy answered a little desperately, "but if you were in possession of all the facts you would understand."

"I have no idea what those could be, but I do believe he cares for you more than you realize. You cannot yearn after Adam Webster forever."

Tansy's head swung back in a tumble of flying strands, her startled eyes meeting that calm and wise, hazel-golden gaze. "How long have you known?"

"For a long, long time. When he rode past the cottage in the days when you were no more than fourteen years old you would stop whatever you were doing in the garden and follow him with your eyes, although he never as much as glanced in your direction. I've seen you run to the window at the sound of his laugh and more than once you blushed like a rose when his name came into the conversation. Later when he began to court Nina it went really hard with you. I could tell. It could have been the last straw to break you completely, but you bore it with all the rest."

Tansy's eyes showed tears in their depths. "I loved him more than I ever realized at the time. The feeling is still with me. I think of him constantly."

"I was afraid you did. So often I've seen you with a faraway look in your eyes."

Tansy gave a weepy smile and reached out a hand. "Is there nothing that you don't see and observe from your corner, little mouse?"

Judith took the girl's hand and folded the fingers over her own with careful concentration. "Try to put him from your mind. I know that's trite advice, but he would have been no good for you, and it's only folly for you to imagine otherwise."

"When it finished between Nina and him I confess I hoped he might think again about me. During those first weeks at Rushmere I looked daily for a letter, but I suppose you spotted that too?"

"I did, as a matter of fact."

Tansy released a long sigh. "Well, no letter ever came, nor is it likely to now." She tilted her head against the pillow with an expression blended of interest and curiosity. "Tell me, since you seem to have missed nothing of importance that has ever happened, did you ever suspect Papa of having a—having another home?"

"No, I didn't," Judith answered reflectively, "but I often thought what a sad, proud face Mama Ruth had, and her mouth seemed to get tighter and sterner with each passing year. I'm thankful she was spared ever knowing that one day we should be sharing a home with her husband's paramour."

"It could be much worse," Tansy said phlegmatically. "At least Amelia is placid and amenable and her chief fault is laziness. She is not at all the kind of wicked, scarlet woman I had always supposed mistresses to be in the past."

"You don't resent her presence at all?"

"Not any longer. Not since the moment when I realized that Papa had made a last request of me."

Downstairs the entrance bell echoed faintly. Seeing how Tansy started at the sound, Judith gestured reassuringly as she rose from the bed to go and answer it. "I don't expect that to be Dominic, since he was here with the violets less than an hour ago." She paused at the bedroom door before opening it and looked back over her shoulder with a thoughtful, pensive expression. "Don't underestimate Amelia. She has some metal in her or else she wouldn't have kept a man like your father on a string for so many years. At first her grief and a sense of insecurity, alarming to her, made her meeker and more docile than she might otherwise have been, but recently I've noticed a definite hardening of attitude and an asserting of herself that was lacking before. It has been particularly noticeable since you fell ill. Amelia has come to resent *our* presence at Rushmere. I hate to say it, but I truly believe she is on the alert to find some loophole to be rid of us."

"But that's impossible. She would have to contest Papa's will to do that, and she wouldn't have a leg to stand on."

"She might be thinking up some other way. Oh, dear! There's the bell again and nobody else is at home to answer it." She went out of the room as fast as she could manage, her stick tapping away along the landing and laboriously down the stairs.

Tansy mulled over what Judith had said. She supposed it was not surprising that Amelia, who had been chatelaine in what had been virtually her own house for such a long time, should have recovered from her initial shock to develop a resentment at the position in which she found herself. She had been told that Rushmere was to be her home until the end of her days without her needing to fear she might have to leave it other than by her own will, but that still left her in limbo, being neither head of the household nor head of the family, the ignominy of it all having come home to her at last.

Tansy gave a deep sigh. Had she owned two houses she would gladly have removed to the other one and left Amelia at Rushmere. Judith had remarked at her first sight of it that it was a gloomy house, and Tansy had come to agree with her, but she was certain that the depressing atmosphere was created by the heavy furnishings of ill taste and the clutter of bric-a-brac, which included a number of stuffed birds other than the parakeets in the drawing room as well as—horrors!—a pug with staring glass eyes, which had once been a cherished pet of Amelia's. The house seemed suffocated, unable to breathe, and even in daylight the heavy drapes at the windows gave a somber touch to every room.

The murmur of conversation in the hall reached her. Judith had been right in guessing that the visitor would not be Dominic. Instead it was a woman whose voice she did not recognize, and she wondered if it was a maidservant sent from the house of an acquaintance with more flowers or fruit.

She realized she had dropped the violet she had been holding and searched for it. It came to light a trifle crushed in a fold of the coverlet, but she carefully tucked it back into the bowl with the others. She let her mind dwell on the day she was taken so desperately ill, and found she could not recall driving home from the market. Her memory also played her false over the time she must have spent in the kitchen. It could have been hours or seconds that she was there, for it was only a brief recollection of struggling with the pump handle that had come back to her. She could recall Dominic's concerned face coming down toward her as though from a distorted ceiling height and she supposed that was when he had bent over her. He had carried her upstairs, too, and laid her on this same bed, although it could have been in any other room in the house for all she could remember of it. He had been talking to her. No, not to her. He had been answering Amelia, that was it. What had he been saying? It seemed to her he had spoken harshly, but why? And what had been the reason for his visit in the first place?

The effort of trying to recall any more was momentarily too much for her. She was almost asleep when Judith re-entered the room alone, a letter in her hand. Tansy smiled lazily, her lids drooping. "Who was it?"

"Your retired Rector's sister. She came down from Lancashire to look after him when you were taken ill and he was without a housekeeper. She has decided to stay and make her home permanently with him."

Tansy made a rueful little grimace. "I've lost my post then?"

"I'm afraid so. Would you like me to read his letter?"

It was a letter of appreciation. The Rector was going to miss her, but his sister wished to take over and would do his writing for him. Again he expressed his regret for having to dispense with her services and he wished her a speedy return to health.

Judith folded up the letter, "He doesn't put it into words, but it sounded to me as if he wasn't overjoyed that his sister had moved in with him."

"He only spoke of her to me now and again, but the impression I got was that she was something of a busybody."

"I thought the same thing myself downstairs. You mustn't worry about losing your post. It won't be long now before Nina gets Edward up to scratch and then we can go ahead with your plan for Rushmere."

"Do you think she is really going to manage it?"

"I should say there's little doubt. He is obviously in love with her."

"But how much in love?" Tansy's brows came together in a little frown of concern. "Enough still to go ahead and marry her if by some fluke the truth should come out about our relationship with Amelia and the scandal of it all break forth? It would not appear to be a very savory situation, would it? Oliver Marlow's daughters living in the same house as his mistress? People would be angry and humiliated, feeling that Papa, whom they had all liked and respected, had made fools of them by causing them to receive into their homes a woman who would otherwise never have crossed their threshold. Then they would cut each one of us for living under the same roof with her."

Judith was absently rubbing the edge of the letter she still held between her finger and thumb, her expression thoughtful. "Everything you say is true. Do you remember that time at home when Squire Waltonbury at the Grange married his housekeeper? That created a most dreadful scandal even though she was a respectable woman and there was no suggestion that he had behaved dishonorably toward her before their marriage. Even Mama Ruth was shocked and she, bless her, hadn't been received in those upper-class circles since she had chosen to settle in a humble village cottage. He was asked to leave the local hunt and after that rode to hounds with farmers from his own estate. It's small wonder that he took to drink when everybody he had ever known turned their backs on him." She gave an uncertain little shake of her head. "I hope Edward loves Nina enough to weather any storm that might break, but if he's put to the test in the face of scandal I fear that it would immediately be at an end between them.

"I share your view and I'm convinced that Nina does too." Tansy turned her glance toward the bedroom door and Judith followed suit as Amelia entered in her outdoor clothes, untying her bonnet strings and unbuttoning her coat.

"How is our invalid feeling now, then?" she inquired brightly, but she did not wait for a reply. "My! I've had the most agreeable morning. Two calls made and a most pleasant chat with Sarah, whom I met by chance in the lane. She is most anxious to see you when you feel able to receive visitors, Tansy, and sent her kindest regards. She said you must be well in plenty of time for the ball she is arranging for next month when Edward will have returned from Newmarket after the opening of the flat-race season there."

"I thought Edward wasn't particularly interested in racing," Judith remarked.

"I don't think he is as a rule, and keeping race horses at the Manor is simply part of a tradition he doesn't want to drop, but when there's a possible Derby winner in the stables anyone would be interested. Sarah said that Wild Wind did splendidly last year and Edward is eager to see him run again." She slipped off her coat and looped it over her arm. "Mr. Reade is going to Newmarket too, but then he always does. He has a three-year-old filly called Merry Day, which is expected to give Wild Wind some opposition."

Tansy was thinking that Judith was right about Amelia. She *had* changed. She had become decidedly more bouncy. "Since you have brought Dominic's name up I must ask you why he was in the house the day I was taken ill."

"He called to let me know he had met an old friend of Oliver's, who had sent a word of consolation for me, not having heard of his passing before, learning of it from Mr. Reade's lips."

Tansy was puzzled. The explanation rang false. There had been no consoling tones in Dominic's voice, but presumably they had been talking together for a while before her untimely entrance, which could have caused a change of mood to the sharpness of urgency out of a natural concern for her feverish state. Yet there had been a patness about Amelia's reply as if she had been expecting the question and had prepared herself for it.

"I thought—oh, I suppose it due to my fever—that he was annoyed and impatient," Tansy admitted tentatively. "I seem to remember there was some kind of argument."

Amelia ran her tongue over her lower lip with a little flick, leaving it pink and moist, and her smile did not reach her eyes. "You're quite right. Fancy you recalling that! He picked you up in his arms and told me to go out to his carriage and tell the coachman to go at once for the doctor. I was in such a panic that I think I was running round in circles saying he must do it and I would attend to you. He had to speak sharply to pull me to my senses." There was the slightest hesitation. "What else do you remember?"

"Nothing else. At least I don't think I do. I seem to have lost the power of concentration and I fall asleep when I lie alone thinking."

"That's nature's marvelous way of healing," Amelia said, fluffing up her curls that had been flattened by the bonnet which she had removed. "Don't trouble your head with the past. Think of the future and being well and strong again. None of us must miss the Manor ball. Of course, being in mourning I cannot dance, but enough time has elapsed now for me to attend such a function and watch from the sides with the other matrons." Her face became impish in the girlish manner that she had. "Do you think Edward might pop the question to Nina that night? Sarah didn't actually say it was being held in anybody's honor, but with half the county there it would be an apt time to make an announcement of a betrothal during the evening. That's how it's often done."

"We shall have to wait and see," Judith said in her calm way. "Now I think we'll leave Tansy on her own to sleep again for a little while. She looks very tired."

Tansy did not hear the door close after them. Sleep was drawing her down into its soft, dark depths. Then suddenly an echo of Dominic's voice rang through her brain: *You shall have your price!*

Jerked out of sleep she sat upright with a fluttering lurch of the heart and put the fingertips of both hands to her temples. Her memory of what he had said had returned to her as clearly as if he had repeated his words at a shout within the bedroom walls, and almost at once there flowed back into her mind all the rest that had passed between Amelia and him. Tansy was at a loss to understand what Amelia had meant in those persistent, truculent whispers, but what she had said could be linked to Judith's fears that the woman might be hatching a plot to take their home from them. And there was no more obvious person for Amelia to turn to than the one man from whom they had no secrets.

She tossed restlessly in the bed. Anything could happen while she lay helpless. Judith was already alert to possible danger, but Nina must be warned to keep her eyes and ears open; as for Roger, he was not often enough in the house to be of any practical help. Tansy thumped her clenched fists down on the bed on either side of her. She must get her strength back soon! She must! Amelia was the traitor in their midst. She had known her to be foolish, weak, and lazy, at times even a trifle greedy, but never once had she thought her capable of cunning and betrayal.

Whatever happened, Amelia must not suspect that they were wise to the fact that she had some mischief afoot. Nor must Dominic gain the slightest inkling that his participation in Amelia's plot—whatever it might be—was known. If only there were someone to whom she could turn at this troubled moment! Someone like Adam. The thought of him soothed her. In her mind's eye she saw him as he had looked on that sunny day when he had climbed the hill to where she and Nina had sat side by side on a grassy knoll. His hair blowing. His eyes searching her face and then Nina's as though he were Paris with the apple and two graces instead of three sitting there before him. A dream state took over. It was to her he was holding out his arms, and of Nina there was no sign. In slow motion she rose up to meet him, every tassel on her shawl lifting lazily as though lighter than air, her skirt swirling slowly out in the gentlest of ripples. She felt weightless. One foot and then the other brushed the grass tops as she went like a drifting leaf toward him. His arms enfolded her and she shut her eyes blissfully. But when she opened them again it was Dominic who held her. In despair she closed her lids again and he kissed away the tears that ran from under them.

The disturbing dream was embarrassingly vivid in her mind a few days later when, relenting, she received Dominic as one of her first visitors. He found her propped against her pillows, a shawl about her shoulders, her white linen nightgown buttoned high to the throat. She was overwhelmed that he had brought her more flowers as well as several newly purchased novels, including one by Miss Austen which she had never read.

"You are too generous!" she exclaimed a little helplessly.

"Not at all," he replied, waving aside her thanks impatiently, and he seated himself in the chair drawn up in readiness at her bedside. "How are you? I'm told you're feeling better."

Judith, who had shown him into the room, withdrew to a chair by the window, not wanting to make her chaperonage intrusive. Glancing up from her embroidery from time to time, she studied their profiles and thought them a remarkably handsome couple, and she wished he could make Tansy forget Adam Webster. They certainly seemed to find each other's conversation stimulating, and she could not think why Tansy was always so wary of him, so quick to slam shutters between them. That, at least, had nothing to do with her old love.

He had noticed a pair of field glasses lying on the side table, and he picked them up, glancing at the initials embossed in gold. "Your father's?" he said to Tansy.

She nodded. "I watch the birds in the garden and in the trees with them. It passes away the time. And every morning I use them to see as far as the hill slope of the gallops above Ashby

Woods where the strings of race horses from both Cudlingham Manor and your own stables are worked daily."

He put the field glasses to his eyes and adjusted them to look in the direction she had indicated. "Training for the season has begun in earnest now. Yes, I can see that you have a good view. Are you able to pick Roger out with these?"

"Quite easily. Soon after half-past seven he's up there on Young Oberon with the first lot of horses being exercised, and later he comes back with a second batch and rides several different ones. I've noticed two or three older men riding with him in place of stable lads, and there have been the same number on Edward's horses."

"They're the jockeys, who—including Roger—are getting the feel of the horses and trying out the new ones. It's important for them to get to know the length of stride of each horse that they're going to race, as well as being able to sum up an animal's individual capabilities, temperament, and willingness to try." He returned the field glasses to the side table. "Hasn't he told you that?"

Judith answered for her from across the room. "Not even Roger has been allowed to stay long on his visits to see her. The doctor was most insistent that she shouldn't be overtired by company."

He took the hint with a rueful smile, rising to his feet. "I mustn't be guilty of that fault, or else I'll not be allowed to come again. Good day, Tansy. It gladdens me more than I can say to see you on the road to recovery."

After that day he came often to see her, but as her convalescence progressed rapidly and the number of her visitors increased accordingly, so that he rarely found her without company, he called less frequently.

Her first outing was with Judith and Nina to dine quietly with Edward and Sarah at the Manor. Tansy would have preferred not to go, for although she liked Edward and enjoyed his company, Sarah could never resist giving her vindictive little digs in the conversation, and in her present, still weakened state she was not sure that she could suffer them. It was worse than she had expected. Sarah's attitude had taken a new turn for the evening: she was effusively friendly, overconcerned for Tansy's comfort, and constantly fidgeting about an extra cushion or a more comfortable chair while all the time her eyes flicked cold and hostile, her smiles a mere parting of the lips. She had hoped I would die, Tansy thought despairingly, and is trying to placate her conscience.

Finally Judith, who had been watching Tansy grow paler and become more exhausted as the evening wore on, rescued her. "I really think I should take you home if Edward and Sarah would excuse us," she said firmly, getting up from her own chair to help Tansy to her feet.

Edward summoned the carriage, but even as they reached the open air and stood on the steps saying good night Tansy's tired mind registered a pink star above the treetops in the grounds, which vanished almost immediately. The significance of what it meant made her catch her breath.

"Fire!" she gasped. "Over there!"

Edward and the others spun about to look in the direction she was pointing. "Dear God!" he exclaimed in horror. "The horses!"

He charged down the steps, shouting for the servants to come with him, and in the same instant the fire bell began to jangle wildly as someone else raised the alarm that the stables were on fire. Flames began to flicker, tinting the sky, and silhouetting the trees, and from all directions people were running to converge on the distant buildings, some carrying buckets and others trundling a hand pump. Sarah had gone darting off in her brother's wake, and Nina was left with Judith and Tansy, who had sagged against the pillar of the portico, shock having sapped the last of her strength. The terrified neighing of the horses reached them above the general pandemonium.

Nina spoke urgently. "Take Tansy home. She looks on the point of collapse. I'll stay and see what I can do to help."

The coachman, who had jumped down from the box to soothe his own horses, who smelled the smoke from the fire and were stomping restlessly, assisted first Tansy and then Judith into the equipage. Judith, looking back out of the window, saw Nina running toward the stables like a white wraith in the darkness.

Afraid that Tansy might have some kind of relapse, she got her into bed as soon as they arrived home. Amelia, who had not been asleep, came into the room, clad in a floating peignoir over her nightgown, a frilled lace cap on her curls, but she did nothing to help, simply settling herself down in a chair at the window to have a grandstand view of the fire in the distance, exclaiming at the flames.

"I've never seen anything like it! Mercy me! Oh, listen! That sounds like the arrival of the fire brigade! I can hear galloping hooves and a bell clanging!"

In the bed Tansy moved restlessly, agitated and upset, thinking only of the horses that might have been trapped. Judith did her best to quieten her.

"I'm sure every one of the horses will have been fetched out to safety," she said reassuringly, smoothing the fold of the sheet over Tansy. "There are always stable lads sleeping on the premises. They would have acted at once. Try to keep calm. Why not take one of those sleeping powders that the doctor left you?"

"I don't want to sleep with that terrible fire blazing!" Tansy cried, clutching at her hand. "I must know all that has happened as soon as Nina returns. Oh, Judith! That poor horse who screamed! Do you think—?"

"No, I don't," Judith replied quickly. Then, as Amelia let out another shriek at a fresh burst of flame, she rounded on her sharply. "Be silent! It's not a sideshow—it's a tragedy. And you're making everything that much worse with your foolish noise."

"Well, really!" Amelia jumped up from the chair. "I won't be spoken to like that in my own—in this house! I'll watch in another room!"

Nina came home at dawn. The aroma of smoke hung about her and she was white-faced and exhausted, having spent the night helping Sarah to dispense tea and ale to the firemen and others at work on the blaze, every male servant having been recruited into the struggle while the women servants filled urns, ran with trays, and struggled to set up the heavy casks.

"There were no serious casualties among men or horses," Nina said, sinking down wearily on the edge of Tansy's bed.

"Thank God for that!" Tansy breathed. "Is the fire completely quenched?"

"The ruins are still smoking and the firemen are checking everywhere, but those awful flames are out at last. People came from all around to help. Roger was there. I served him a tankard of ale at the height of the fire and he told me that all the stable lads from Ainderly Hall, except those on guard, had come with him. Some of them risked their lives to get the horses out."

"On guard?" Judith inquired, not understanding.

Nina gave a nod. "Apparently it would never do to empty a stable of all personnel at such a time in case a fire-raiser moved on to start up another blaze. Roger has learned that these things happen sometimes before an important race."

Judith gasped. "Do you mean that arson is committed to stop horses taking part?"

"Not horses. Usually one particular horse that represents a threat to a runner from another stable, which has been heavily backed to win."

"Does Edward suspect that this fire was not accidental?"

"He told me that the captain of the fire brigade had his suspicions. It looked rather as if it had been ignited in the saddle room and it spread quickly from there."

Judith exclaimed again and asked more questions. In the bed Tansy listened, but her eyes were not on either of her sisters. She was watching with a troubled, unfocused gaze the rosy-golden light of the rising morning that was tinting the white ceiling between the oaken beams. Finally she spoke.

"Will Wild Wind be fit to race at Newmarket?"

Nina answered. "No, he won't. He was due to leave here tomorrow and be transported by train, but he went almost crazy in the fire and was singed by some blazing straw. To race him until he is fully recovered from his fright is out of the question."

Tansy watched the pattern on the ceiling. She was certain she knew who would win the race instead of Wild Wind. It would be Dominic's Merry Day.

The following week Roger brought her the racing newspaper that she had asked for. She read first an account about the fire at Cudlingham Manor, which included the information, known to her and the rest of the village several days before, that the remains of an unidentified man had been found in the burnt-out stables. The police held to the belief that an arsonist had himself been trapped and burnt to death through his own hand, the fire being similar to others deliberately started in racing stables at various times throughout the country. Then she turned to the page devoted to Newmarket.

There had been rowdy scenes when it was discovered before the first of two important races of the day that a four-year-old colt had been falsely entered for a three-year-olds' race, the switch having been made most cunningly between the two horses concerned during the previous autumn. A phrase, which she had last made contact with when she had heard it used by Dominic's racing acquaintance in the darkness of a roadside at night, leaped from the print at her: *a four-legged impostor.* Worth the risk, the stranger in the night had said. Well, risk or no, the horse's mouth had been examined and the ruse spotted in time, but inexplicably the horse had disappeared without trace and no charge could be brought without evidence. She caught her breath, a single telling sentence confirming everything for her. *The jockey, Bill Jemmy, expressed his indignation that such deceit should have been used and was thankful that the fraud had been exposed before the weighing in, because it would have gone against his good name to ride a four-legged impostor past the winning post.*

She lowered the newspaper and leaned back in her chair. No matter how much Bill Jemmy had protested his innocence he must have been in the plot as deeply as Dominic and the unknown stranger, who had brought the news that the switch had been made. The three of them had planned to make a deal of money out of their knavery, but fortunately the plan had gone wrong. There could be no charge without evidence, the report said, but she had evidence. Enough to get Dominic brought to trial for it. She would send for Edward, who was the local magistrate, and tell him all she knew. But would he believe her? She had no proof to offer, except that she had heard two voices in the night and knew one to have been Dominic's. But Dominic was Edward's friend. Edward would accept his denial and think her mistaken. It would all be in vain.

Wearily she lifted the newspaper again and looked for the news item for which she had originally wanted it. She read that in the race that followed the one involving the attempt at fraud, Merry Day had won by three lengths at such long odds that those who had backed the filly to win must have made themselves a small fortune. She folded the newspaper. What Dominic had lost on the roundabouts he had apparently won on the swings, but it must have been a disappointment to him not to have pulled off the swindle in the previous race and doubled the amount. Some day—and somehow—she would see that justice caught up with him.

8.

On the evening of the April Ball at Cudlingham Manor the Marlow sisters with Judith and Amelia, who was aglitter with jet on black satin, arrived early by arrangement. The great house had never looked more welcoming. Hundreds of candles danced in the crystal chandeliers, creating waterfalls of light from the ornate ceilings, garlands entwined the banisters of the huge sweeping staircase, and there were sweet-scented floral displays everywhere. Nina, exquisite in honey-colored tulle with silk rose-buds in her hair, took her place at Edward's side at the entrance to the ballroom, ready to receive with him the first guests when they should arrive, and after initial greetings all round Sarah chatted to Amelia while Tansy gave a supporting hand to Judith as they crossed the wide, shining floor, her iris-blue crinoline blending harmoniously with Judith's sprigged green silk. They were making for an alcove seat where Judith could sit comfortably and watch the dancing without her view being impeded. In the gallery the musicians struck up a lilting waltz.

Hardly had they seated themselves when Dominic arrived. After speaking to the others he came straight across to the two sisters and bowed. "Good evening to you both. Pray allow me to put my name on your dance programmes."

Judith gave a surprised little laugh, having already put hers away in her reticule as a souvenir, knowing it would not be used. "Tansy's dance programme, you mean. You know I cannot dance."

"Have you ever tried?"

"Oh, yes. Papa always taught us the latest steps and dances, but with him it didn't matter about my being—er—a trifle clumsy on my feet, because he always held me tight about my waist to keep me from falling."

"Would you be kind enough to allow me that privilege?"

Tansy was eyeing him watchfully, prepared—should he be teasing Judith—to intervene promptly, but she saw that he was serious. Judith flushed uncomfortably.

"That's most kind of you, but dancing with family at home is very different from making a dreadful exhibition of myself before hundreds of people."

With raised eyebrows he surveyed the huge room and returned his gaze to her. "I don't see hundreds of people here. Only four persons whom you know well." He smiled and bowed deeper than before. "May I have the pleasure of this dance?"

Judith's color deepened painfully and she looked as if she did not know whether to laugh or cry, but she edged forward on the seat in preparation to rise. He was quick to take the hand she reached out toward her stick, letting her use his support instead to stand and gain her balance. Then his arm went about her waist and he drew her into the steps of the waltz.

Tansy watched them, torn between joy that her sister was dancing and anguish whenever she clumsily missed a step, which was due sometimes to her disability and at others to her extreme nervousness. At the door other guests were announced, but although Judith said something to Dominic in frantic appeal, he shook his head smilingly, spoke some word of encouragement that made her nod, the wild rose color flooding her cheeks again, although less tormentedly than before, and their dancing continued. A few enthusiastic dancers among the new arrivals took to the floor at once, encouraged by the sight of one couple already ahead of them, and within minutes Dominic and Judith were in the midst of dozens of other rotating couples, the ladies' crinolines swaying like multicolored bells, the men's coattails flying out.

When a final chord announced the end of the waltz Dominic held firmly both of Judith's hands, which enabled her to give a closing curtsy gracefully without fear of falling. On his arm she returned to the alcove seat, excited and breathless and triumphant. Tansy, who had been joined by a group of people whom they all knew, turned to give her a swift little hug.

"You're the real belle of the ball!" she exclaimed warmly.

"But didn't you see all those blundering mistakes I made?" Judith bubbled, seeking solace in talking about the misplaced steps that had caused her much embarrassment. "I stepped on Dominic's toes a dozen times."

"You're so feather-light I didn't notice," he declared gallantly. "Now if I may have your dance programme?"

Shyly but willingly she opened the drawstrings of her reticule and took it out and handed it to him. With the tiny pink pencil attached to it he wrote his name down for another dance before supper. Even as he would have returned it to her one of the young men in the group, who had been writing his name on Tansy's dance programme, reached out his white-gloved hand for it.

"May I?" he asked Judith.

"Er—yes," she stammered in confusion, "but you do realize that you have to hold me tight about the waist, don't you?"

The young man's eyes twinkled and his mouth twitched. "I cannot imagine anything more delightful, Miss Collins."

Everybody laughed and Judith joined in the laughter, the last shreds of her awkward self-consciousness dispersed. Tansy thought happily that she had been right in declaring that the evening was Judith's, no matter that later Nina would capture the limelight. Seeing that Dominic was waiting to take her programme from an older man now writing on it, she decided, considering what he done for dear Judith, that he deserved one dance.

"The first Mazurka, the third Gavotte, or the second Polonaise," she said with a tilt of her head, secure in the knowledge that the supper-dance was already promised.

He glanced under his brows at her, the little pencil poised in his hand to write, and answered without a smile. "The second Polonaise will be most agreeable."

When he had written his name down he handed the dance

programme straight to another man who had come forward to ask for it, and with a slight bow he departed, lost to her sight among the fast-gathering throng milling about the ballroom on all sides. Her first partner of the evening claimed her, and she was swept into the dancing. Later, when she had a chance to draw breath and glance at her programme, she saw that when Dominic had written his name down for the second Polonaise, which happened to be the first dance after supper, he had scrawled it at such an angle that it covered all the remaining dances of the evening. After that she gave him a cool look when they met in a quadrille, angry at the dark throb that pulsated through her at the thought of being in his arms for the whole of the second half of the ball.

Once she came face to face with Nina in a chain dance of linking hands and her sister uttered a thrilled whisper in her ear. "After supper is over Edward wants to speak to me in the conservatory. You know what that means!"

"I do indeed," Tansy managed to whisper back before her radiant sister passed her by.

The chain dance ended. Even as Tansy's partner would have escorted her off the floor a strong male hand seized her wrist and a voice she had not heard for six months spoke to her. "I don't know to whom you have promised the supper waltz, but on the basis of old friendship I claim it from him."

She turned to the man in evening clothes who had addressed her and gasped her astonishment. Before her, tall and broad and smiling, was Adam Webster, his impudent eyes twinkling at her, his narrow lips set wide in a show of strong white teeth. Her whole heart welcomed the sight of him. "Adam! What on earth are you doing here?"

Before answering her, he drew her arm through his and hastened her away to another part of the ballroom, seeking out one of the anterooms where they could talk undisturbed.

"I'm here at Edward Taylor's invitation," he said, glancing over his shoulder to make sure that Tansy's rightful partner was not in hot pursuit of her. "I've set up in my own business just outside of Epsom and have landed myself work for months. Can you guess what it is?"

They had passed through a draped archway into a deserted anteroom, softly lit for the benefit of those wishing to sit out dances romantically. "Not rebuilding Edward's burnt-out stables!" she exclaimed incredulously, sitting down in one of the delicately armed brocade chairs.

He gave a nod, standing with his back to the fireplace. "The greatest stroke of luck that could have befallen me. He was impressed with the way I approached him with immediate, practical advice after the fire and later he approved the ideas I laid out for the new stable buildings. Finally he accepted the competitive figure I quoted and the work commenced."

"But the fire was some time ago. Why didn't you call on us at Rushmere? You knew the address. I gave it to you myself."

His face held a stiff look. "Have you forgotten? You surely knew that Nina never wanted to see me again."

She lowered her head. "I knew it was all over between you. But you had no quarrel with Judith or Roger or me."

For a moment he stared at her blankly as if it had never occurred to him to call on any member of the Marlow family except Nina. "It's good to see you now anyway," he said, seeking to make amends and moving restlessly. "I can't say I miss anyone from home, but there's nothing like seeing an old friend."

She leaned forward, showing her interest. "What made you decide to part company with your father?"

"We had one almighty row. I knocked him down and broke his nose."

"Adam!"

He threw himself down in the chair opposite her. "You know my temper—or maybe you don't. We Websters are an unforgiving tribe, old quarrels and ancient grudges are not forgotten until avenged. My father and I have always clashed. This blow I gave him was the last straw, needless to say. I packed my belongings, took the horses and wagons that were my own property, and left the same day. I had already decided that the Epsom area was a good one. Just the spot for a man of business like me. I intend to make a great deal of money. One day I'll live in a house like this." He made a circling gesture from his wrist to indicate their surroundings.

She put her head to one side, watching him closely. "There are many such mushrooming areas to chose from. Small villages along the coast are expanding into popular seaside resorts. The cotton-mill industry in the northeast has brought a boom. You had a wide choice and yet you came here. May I ask why?" With every fiber of her being she longed for him to say that it was to pick up those snapped-off threads with her, to take up from that moment on the hill when the die had been cast in Nina's favor, but there was nothing in the way he looked at her, no special eagerness in his voice, and no extra warmth in his attitude toward her to suggest that he was more than ordinarily glad to see her. The sharp sweet hope that had soared within her at that first sight of him was sinking back into the sad, dark depths from whence it had sprung.

He answered casually. "I had been in this district before and had seen its possibilities, but"—here his whole expression sharpened, matching his change of tone—"I cannot deny that knowing Nina was in Cudlingham was the real reason why I wanted to start up in this part of England."

"Oh, why didn't you make an attempt at reconciliation as soon as you came into the area?" she exclaimed compassionately, knowing that he must be suffering the same pangs of yearning for Nina as she felt for him.

His eyes narrowed to slits, flinty and hostile. "Nina is greedy and selfish and avaricious to the core. Do you think she would have done anything but turn her back if I'd come to her empty-handed? The first months were hard. I knocked on office doors and went from one site to another. The first work I got was repairing a barn wall, and I did it in my shirt sleeves with my own hands and was proud to do it. It was a start. After that I dug ditches and laid water pipes and reslated a roof. It was then that my luck began to change. I took on two men and then a third. Soon I had half a dozen working for me. Then on the night I saw the fire engines driving out of Epsom and heard where the fire was I decided to step in before anyone else did. Taylor has already recommended my name to others. Now I can face Nina on the first rung of the ladder and show her that I'm on the way to making that fortune I once predicted would be mine."

"It's too late," she said in sorrow at having to disappoint him. "Nina and Edward will become officially engaged during the first dance after the supper interval."

His grim expression did not change and he showed no surprise. "Since I arrived here this evening I've heard whispers on all sides that an announcement is expected at any time. I was honored with an invitation simply because two of Taylor's cousins were at school with me, otherwise I should not be among the elite of the county at this moment." His tone was cynical and it did not change as he continued. "I knew this betrothal was in the wind weeks ago. It's been a high topic of speculation among the local people. You see, I made it my business to find out all about Nina as soon as I had unpacked my good and chattels. It wasn't difficult. I came into Cudlingham and made the first of many calls at The Winner. The tongue of the barmaid there wags with all the gossip for miles around. I soon learned all I wanted to discover about the Marlow family, although," he jibed cuttingly, "I must say I was amazed on that first occasion to be told that Oliver Marlow was your late uncle and that you inherited Rushmere over the head of his well-to-do widow, with whom you live."

She bit deep into her lower lip. "You may find this hard to believe, but never once have I denied that Oliver Marlow was my father or said that Amelia is my aunt. The tale was—spread. For reasons I don't feel able to disclose, one of them being my father's last request of me through this will, I haven't contradicted the story, because it would only reveal private matters that are best kept from the ears of outsiders."

"Such as Amelia having been your father's mistress?"

She went pale. "Has that become common knowledge too?"

"No, it hasn't. I simply drew my own conclusions after hearing that Oliver Marlow had lived for short periods of each year at Rushmere, more often absent than at home, and that his wife must have been lonely many a time there in the house without him."

"You've discovered the truth of it," she admitted regretfully. Then she hesitated, but felt compelled to ask him the question uppermost in her mind for Nina's sake. "Have you spoken of what you know to anyone?"

"No, I haven't. I've kept my mouth shut. Is the secret shared with any person other than myself outside the family circle?"

"Only one man who knows how to hold his tongue. Otherwise nobody else is aware of the true circumstances."

The corners of his well-cut mouth tucked inward as though he smiled to himself with a certain malevolent satisfaction. "As I thought, a well-kept secret indeed! If the merest hint of the old scandal, linked with the new one of you and your sisters appearing to condone the whole unsavory affair, had leaked out, then I wouldn't mind wagering my last penny that not one of you girls would be at the ball this evening."

She gave an unhappy nod. "I know that well enough. I cannot thank you enough for having kept silent. It isn't often in life one discovers how staunch a friend can be."

He got up from his chair and stood in front of her, taking her chin into his hand and tilting her face upward to meet his downward gaze. "If you did but know it, you shame me with your compassion and your loyalty," he said soberly. "You are the pick of the bunch. It will be a fortunate man who gets you for his own one day."

Such final, final words! She was not the first woman to hear them spoken by a man loved in vain, nor would she be the last. But let him not know, let him not suspect at this late hour the true nature of her feelings for him!

"The present dance is ending," she said, rising to her feet, "and my poor partner will be looking for me everywhere. Come with me to the supper room and I'll explain to him we became lost in talk of old times. Judith will want to chat with you, I know." She scanned his face considerately. "How do you feel about meeting Nina again?"

"I'm looking forward to it," he said on a note that was dangerously soft, although she did not realize it, "but whether she'll be pleased to see me is another matter. At least she cannot order me out. She's not lady of the Manor yet by any manner of means! Taylor himself promised to present me, not realizing I was already acquainted with her. It's probably best if we keep it that way. It will save a deal of awkward questions better not asked, don't you agree?"

"I suppose you're right," she said on a sigh. "I hate all this subterfuge, but at the present time I can see no way out of it."

"Family love and filial loyalty have made you a conspirator against your will. Maybe some good will come of it in the end, you never know." He turned sideways to her, offering his arm. "Come. I'll take you in to supper. You had better warn Judith not to exclaim in astonishment at the sight of me. That would ruin everything."

She rested her fingers in the crook of his arm. "What about Nina?"

"Don't worry about Nina. She has her wits about her. You'll see, she won't know why her future husband is introducing me as a stranger, but she will be thankful for it and play out her part to the letter."

They emerged from the anteroom to join the throng of people drifting in the direction of the supper room. Spotting Judith close at hand, Tansy seized the opportunity to breathe a few words of explanation. Judith, who was on the arm of the young man who had first asked for her dance programme after Dominic, shot an amazed look over her shoulder in Adam's direction and flashed him one of her sweet smiles.

In the supper room, the occasion being in Edward's eyes one of great importance in the long history of Cudlingham Manor, the candelabra on the buffet table were of gold instead of the silver ones normally used, and the porcelain plates and dishes were thickly bordered in gold leaf. Edward, who was an excellent host, was making sure that all his guests were being comfortably seated and attended to. When he saw Adam and Tansy approaching he smiled broadly and singled them out.

"You've made each other's acquaintance already, I see. That

saves one introduction anyway. Now, Webster, you must meet Miss Marlow's sister."

He guided them to where Nina, not yet seated, stood talking to some people. When Edward spoke her name she turned with a graceful swirl of her apple-green skirt, its flounces fluttering, and she was excited and happy, looking more beautiful than Tansy had ever seen her look before.

"Yes, Edward dear—?"

It was as if her vocal cords had snapped in her throat, so abruptly did she cut off her words. Tansy saw her pupils dilate as she stared at Adam standing there, and she went white about her delicate nostrils and around the mouth, yet her smile, although it appeared to have become transfixed, did not falter after an initial quiver.

Edward, blissfully unaware, performed the introductions, to which Nina replied with a certain stiffness. "Mr. Webster knows my cousins, Bertram and George Haversham," he explained to her. "He's the good fellow who's going to rebuild the stables for me. He'll tell you all about it."

She looked startled and held out a hand in appeal to Edward, who was already turning away. "You're not leaving me again, are you?"

"I must make sure that everyone is being looked after. I'll be back in a few minutes." He was gone. At this point Tansy's supper partner, locating her at last, came to sweep her away. Nina and Adam were left to themselves in the midst of the busy, crowded room.

"Where can we talk?" he demanded tersely, his voice lowered against being overheard.

"I have nothing to say to you," she retorted coldly. "It was all said on the evening that you struck me."

"But I have much to say—not necessarily to you if you should refuse to be alone with me for a short time, but to the rest of the gathering."

"What do you mean?" She was still not seriously alarmed. It had been a shock seeing him, but obviously Tansy had had the good sense to warn him against revealing anything about their past village life that could put a dangerous light on their present situation.

"I have only to circulate in this room for five minutes for everybody to pass on to each other the fact that you are not the late Oliver Marlow's niece, but his daughter, and that the woman you profess to be your aunt was his mistress, a former actress from a sleazy traveling company—or perhaps you didn't know about her background? A chance word in a certain quarter gave me the opportunity to find out—I won't bore you with the details. Those whom I entertain with this bawdy tale won't be bored, I do assure you."

She had put a shaking hand to her throat. "You wouldn't! Oh, you couldn't!"

His inexorable expression did not change. "You underestimate me. Now where can we talk?"

Trying to keep from appearing frightened she glanced to the right and to the left to make sure they were not being listened to by straining ears or carefully observed, but amid the settling down to eat and drink no one was throwing more than a casual glance in their direction. "I cannot leave the supper room now," she stammered. "Edward will be back at any moment—"

"Then we had better depart before he comes. I'm not playing games. I mean what I say."

She saw that he did. There was something desperate, almost fanatical about his determination to talk privately with her. As if he had some matter of great urgency to relate that could not wait under any circumstances. She decided she must humor him.

"Let Tansy come with us," she implored. "It will look better if I leave the supper room with her."

"Alone, I said! I'll have no company."

She saw Edward coming back in their direction, although he was stopping here and there to bend over a seated guest or signal to a footman to pour champagne into a half-emptied glass. Time was running out.

"Very well," she capitulated quickly. "There are anterooms off the ballroom—"

"Not secluded enough. Anyone could interrupt us there."

There was only one other place she could think of that was within easy reach of the supper room and from which she could return as quickly as she went. "Do you know where the conservatory is?" He gave a nod. "Then go by way of the ballroom and the drawing room beyond. I'll take another way there and meet you in a minute's time."

He nodded again and went back in the direction of the ballroom, threading his way through the groups of seated and standing guests. She, after one swift glance to make sure Edward was still a safe distance away, hurried toward a door barely discernible in the paneling and slipped through, noticed only by one or two people sitting nearby.

She almost sobbed as she ran along the corridor that backed the anterooms on one side and the full length of the library on the other. Along this carpeted route she had expected to go joyfully hand in hand with Edward, but instead she had to traverse it first for a hateful, clandestine meeting with a man she had thought never to see again.

The only illumination in the conservatory came from the moonlight and a single rose-shaded lamp which had been placed by a white, intricately patterned wrought-iron seat that stood amid the green potted plants and tall palms and feathery ferns. It wrenched her heart to look at it, knowing it was there that Edward would propose. Adam swaggered forward from the shadows.

"Well?" she said impatiently, stimulated by anger now that the danger she had faced in the supper room was removed. "What was it you wished to say to me?"

"You're not to accept Edward's proposal of marriage this evening."

She gaped at him, her mouth falling open. And then she laughed, bravely but not far from hysteria. "You're mad! In less than half an hour he'll propose to me and I shall accept him. Right here in this conservatory. I'm going to be his wife and there's nothing you can do to stop me."

"You misunderstand me. I don't intend to stop you becoming his wife, but it is not to be yet. I want to pick up our relationship where it left off. That's why you're not to say yes to him this evening."

She became calmer, suddenly certain of power herself through this somewhat untimely revelation of the fact that he was still in love with her, and she was more than a little flattered that he should have acted so decisively in a last-minute attempt to gain a reprieve in which to continue to court her. His pretense that he would not eventually bar her from marrying Edward was pathetically transparent.

"I was attracted to you," she confessed frankly, "and had I expected nothing more from life than that which you were able to offer me I might have allowed myself to fall in love with you. But I've always known I wanted more than that. Edward can give me everything I've ever dreamed of. We shall travel abroad, lead a splendid social life, and go to London for all the great events of the season." She clasped her hands together in her ecstasy at the thought of it all, her good humor returned, quite amused that he should have laid his heart at her feet as a final tribute to her single status before she promised herself to another. She decided to be gracious and magnanimous. "You must forget me. I forgive you for your behavior toward me on the night we parted and for all that has taken place now. Being in love can make a person act illogically and without reason."

He gave a derisive snort. "In love? Who's talking about being in love? Not I! And you have yet to learn the meaning of the word. I mean to teach you one aspect of it." Deliberately and insolently he cupped a palm against her breast and squeezed it.

She struck his hand away, all calmness gone from her, suddenly consumed by fear. "This nonsense that you're talking has gone far enough," she stammered. "And your insults, too. I cannot and will not reconsider my decision to marry Edward. Now I must return to the supper room or else everyone will be wondering where I am."

She turned to go back the way she had come, resisting the impulse to bolt like a panic-stricken fawn, but his next words, dry and taunting, halted her. "Suppose Edward reconsiders his decision to ask you."

She stayed motionless, her back toward him. "Why should he do that?"

"Haven't you learned yet that a man like Edward would never think the world well lost for love? Let him catch one whiff of the scandal that trails after your skirts and the doors of Cudlingham Manor will be slammed in your face. By living under the same roof as your father's whore you will have appeared to condone the association, which puts you on the same level socially—the dregs! Mistresses, courtesans, streetwalkers are all ladies of ill-repute and are bracketed together in the eyes of society. Genteel poverty is one thing, but associating companionably with a low woman like Amelia Marlow is another. Not for Edward the ostracism he would have to suffer on your behalf, not for him the turned backs in his club, the dwindling of invitations, the whispered request that he should leave the Royal enclosure at Ascot. A hard truth for you to accept, but Edward will not take a bride from the gutter."

It was as if she had become immobilized in stone, a glowing-haired statue under an arch of foliage, her gown in the diffused light almost as pale as the scoop of her bare shoulders revealed by the low back of her gown, her skin holding the sheen of creamy marble. "This is blackmail," she hissed accusingly.

"Call it what you will."

Still she did not move, but the beautiful curve of her shoulders bowed as though under an invisible weight that she could scarcely bear. "Tell me what you want me to do," she moaned brokenly.

"I thought you understood." Leisurely he strolled across and sat down on the wrought-iron seat, resting one arm along the back of it. "I'm not a spoil-sport. I'll not deny you the pleasure of being proposed to, but you'll just have to avoid giving him a direct acceptance. Tell him you must have more time to reach a decision. Let's say"—he pushed his lips together and tilted his head reflectively as if he had previously given the matter no thought, an action that she was aware of although she did not see it—"six months."

"No!" She came alive in her wretchedness, snatching hold of

her skirts and rushing across to throw herself to her knees on the tiled floor beside him. She clutched at the white-cuffed wrist of the hand that rested on his crossed knee. "We'll starve in that time! I'll have no new dresses to wear to anything and the soles of my only best shoes will be worn through. We're penniless. The gowns Tansy and Judith and I are wearing this evening are made out of Papa's last gifts to us. Amelia has nothing either. She was as improvident as Papa, who left debts behind him that have to be paid. Tansy held back with turning Rushmere into a lodginghouse to make money in order to let me establish myself socially, and how can I ask her to wait another half year? At least when I'm betrothed to Edward I can receive gifts from him of gowns and other garments, for he knows that we're impoverished, and then I'll see that the others are clothed and fed too, but he cannot do that until I've promised to be his wife. Oh, relent, Adam! I'll do anything—anything—if you'll only let me accept the ring he wishes to put on my finger."

He sucked in his cheeks sardonically, viewing her distraught face with a bright and mocking eye. "You are selfish to the core, Nina, and naïvely you still seek to bargain with me. You have nothing to offer that isn't virtually already mine. If you were Tansy you would tell Edward the truth and if he didn't love you enough to go ahead and marry you with feelings unchanged you would think yourself well rid of him no matter what heartache it caused you. But you are not Tansy, and in any case she would never have embarked on such a course as you have taken in the first place."

"Stop talking about Tansy!" She hammered both her fists on his fingers spread out on his knee, and swiftly he moved to capture her wrists in the grip of his other hand, bringing his face close to hers.

"You can thank your lucky stars I am talking about her. I'll not see her suffer privation through any action of mine or yours. I came too near to loving her myself once, and even though it is all over and done with I'll not land her with additional misfortunes. You may accept Edward's rings tonight, but you'll not marry for a year."

"A year!" she cried on a sob of protest. "You said six months before!"

"If you will recall, I said that there was to be that particular length of time before you would give Edward an affirmative answer, but there would have been an additional six months betrothment after that. A year in all. I haven't broken away from my original plan for you, only changed the conditions slightly out of consideration for your sister."

"Am I entitled to no consideration?" she wailed piteously.

He helped her to her feet and held her, she being too crushed in spirit to struggle free, her head hanging. "I've granted you one concession. Be thankful for that. Now do you know the lane—well, it's little more than a track—that the race horses follow every morning through Ashby Woods to the gallops beyond?" When she gave him a weary nod he continued: "I've bought the old house that stands on its own there. It has large outbuildings and a disused brickyard with a pond and a great kiln, which I intend to put into full working order again. Come to the house tomorrow evening at eight o'clock."

"And if I don't come?" she asked, lifting her face with a last flash of defiance.

He shrugged nonchalantly. "In that case, with an evening lying spare on my hands, I shall come back to the Manor to thank Edward for this pleasant ball and regale him with tales of the residents of Rushmere."

She stood dumb in her defeat. He took her face between his hands and kissed her limp, unresponsive lips. Then without another word he left her. She heard his footsteps cross the tiles of the conservatory, clack twice across polished wood, and become lost on carpeting as he made his way back to the supper room. She knew she should return herself, but the thought of facing all those people, many of whom would turn inquisitive glances in her direction in puzzlement at her prolonged absence, was more than she felt able to endure.

With a groan she sank down on the seat that Adam had so recently vacated and put both hands together on the back of it, her head bent to bring her forehead to rest on them. She was stunned that such a catastrophe should have happened to her. It was like some dreadful nightmare out of which she must wake in a few minutes and find that everything was as it had been before. But it wasn't a nightmare. It was reality.

When she heard a door open she sat up with a start of alarm, thinking that Adam had returned to heap some further humiliation on her head, but it was Edward who had come by the same corridor that she had taken to reach the conservatory. When he saw her sitting there on the seat, apparently waiting for him, he stopped by the palm under which she had stood so shortly before, smiling in his delight at discovering her.

"You're here, Nina! I missed you from the supper room and couldn't think where you might be with everyone asking for you." He came and sat beside her, taking up one of her hands to put, palm uppermost, to his lips. "You're trembling!" He sounded doubly pleased, not realizing that her state of strained nerves had been induced by another's presence and for an entirely different reason that the one he had assumed. "How dear of you to slip away to meet me at our rendezvous." He kissed her hand again. "For weeks I've been deciding what to say to you at this moment, and now I'm dashed if all of it hasn't flown out of my head."

She sat with her throat arched, her chin high, and her little smile felt stiff and painful. "How much do you love me?"

"With all my heart!"

"Would you love me if all turned against me and the finger of scandal was pointed in my direction?"

"But it wouldn't be."

"Yet if it *was*, Edward! If none would receive me and I couldn't be presented to the Queen and together we were snubbed on all sides, would you still love me?"

He gave an uncomfortable shrug, displeased with her odd attitude which was unsuitable to the romantic occasion. "Why on earth should a sweet girl like you imagine such impossibilities. You could never become such a person and I would stay a bachelor all my life first, so the situation could never under any circumstances arise."

She gave a deep sigh that sounded curiously resigned to his ears, making him give her a baffled look. "You are right. It couldn't, of course." Tilting her head she turned waiting eyes on him. To herself it was as though she viewed him through the bars of a cage to which he had just thrown away the only key.

Still holding her hand he got up from the seat again to go down on one knee to her, naturally and without embarrassment. "Dearest Nina, I love you. You are everything I ever wanted in a partner to share my life, and during the months we've known each other I have come to hope that you love me in return enough to feel the same. I'm asking you to marry me."

She gazed him. Everything was hers. This man. This great house and all the wealth and social splendor that went with it. And this magnificent ring of diamonds and emeralds that he was taking from his waistcoat pocket. Her moment of triumph was sour. The price she had to pay for it all through no fault of her own was too terrible to contemplate.

"Yes, Edward dear. I will marry you."

"My love!"

The ring slid on her finger. He took his seat again and clasped her to him, his kiss passionate and triumphant. When he let her get her breath she put a hand against his shining shirt front to keep him at a distance, wanting to speak before he could carry out his obvious intention to kiss her again. One last chance had unexpectedly presented itself to her.

"I have the most wonderful idea! Let's elope!" she implored eagerly. "Now! This minute!"

He was enchanted by her notion but did not take it seriously. "We would certainly have a flock of company to see us off."

"No! No! I'll get my cloak and we'll go secretly. Like lovers in a fairy tale."

He laughed lovingly. "To Gretna Green, I suppose."

"Yes, oh, yes! At once!" She was already on her feet.

He frowned incredulously, seeing that she meant it, and he reached out to draw her firmly down to his side again. "Dearest! Nobody could be more eager to wed than I, but there is no question of an elopement. I'm my own master with none to question any decision I make and you have Tansy's blessing on our union. No couple could be more free to wed than we. There's no need for any hole-and-corner marriage for us, and I thank God for it. Elopements always bear the taint of scandal."

"Then marry me tomorrow in the village church," she begged.

He gathered her to him, no longer quite so happy about her eagerness, which was flattering but unseemly. "What you ask is impossible. There are banns to be read and all the rest of it. There's also—er"—he gave a little cough—"well, people sometimes jump to wrong conclusions when a couple marry with unnecessary haste."

Her face became raddled with despair. "If you will not do as I ask it must be a year before I become your bride."

He smiled, patting her hand, overwhelmed that she should love him so much. "A year isn't long officially for a betrothment and I hadn't expected it to be less. Naturally every day will be like a year to me, but you will find that you'll need the time for everything that has to be done. I thought you might like me to take you to Paris to have your wedding gown made—with Sarah as chaperone, of course."

She burst into tears. She, who never cried, who had remained dry-eyed at both parents' funerals, and who always bottled up her emotions, wept brokenheartedly for herself and for the blighted fulfillment of her lovely plans, which would have been perfect beyond her wildest dreams had not Adam chosen to savage them with his vindictive lust. Edward thought he understood. She was overwrought due to the excitement and emotion of exchanging vows. Without doubt she was a passionate creature, something he had long been aware of, in spite of her outward primness, for he fancied that he was experienced and knowledgeable about women. Nina had excited his interest from their first meeting at Ainderly Hall with her shell of coolness, her air of being unawakened to her own sensuality, the hint of blazing fire beneath the ice. It was to be expected that not recognizing her own physical longings she should find expression for them in present tears. But what tears! They were pouring from her eyes in a flood.

"Nina! My love! Hush, hush!"

She did not pull away from him when he took her into his arms, but looped her own about his neck, pressing her tear-wet cheek to his. With a supreme effort she used the minutes of his attempt at amorous comfort, her mind racing, to take a grip on herself. All was not lost. She would be away from Cudlingham—and Adam!—for much of the betrothment year with all the visits far afield that Edward had planned for them to take as well as the trip to Paris. At least she had his ring on her finger and in twelve months' time she would be his wife, no matter what happened in between. For the time being she would not think about the price she had to pay. This was the most important evening of her life so far and she would concentrate only on that.

In the ballroom the second Polonaise was ending when Nina and Edward reappeared and the announcement of their betrothal was made. Tansy and Dominic were among the first to offer good wishes and congratulations. Adam had left long since. Everybody stood back to clear a circular space on the floor for the host and his bride-to-be to dance together in a waltz, ripples of applause following them round and round, and Nina's face as she looked into Edward's eyes was a studied portrait of hope and happiness. Only Judith spotted that she had been crying.

Dominic turned to Tansy. "Shall we?" Other couples were joining in the waltz, and he took her fingers into his and his arm encircled her slender waist, drawing her hard in to him as they spun into the dancing.

"You're holding me too close," she said with an upward glance under her lashes.

He looked down into her face, his eyes dark and glowing and eloquent. "Not close enough. Oh, no, my dear Tansy, not nearly close enough!"

She caught her breath, her pulse racing, and with that extraordinary empathy that seemed at times to enable him to read her thoughts he danced her off the ballroom floor and into one of the anterooms where closed curtains of crimson velvet covered the windows. She made no protest and he spoke no word. As in the anteroom where she had talked with Adam the lighting was soft, a single rose-glass lamp turned low, the pattern thrown out by it lost on the deep-red walls. In the darkest shadows he crushed her to him and buried her mouth in his, obliterating all else for her. No single languishing thought for Adam, no last thread of wistful longing, could withstand the onslaught of his ardent passion, and it was almost as if he knew what he was about.

Some minutes later he asked her a question, still holding her, she quiet and still and warm within his arms, her head against his shoulder. "Have we sealed a truce?"

Her voice was breathy and almost inaudible as she answered him, but he caught the faint undertone of regret. "No, kisses settle nothing. There are still barriers between us."

When the ball was over she traveled home with Judith and Amelia as they had come, in one of the Manor carriages, Nina following with Edward in another equipage. Sitting silently in the corner, barely listening to the others' chatter, Tansy felt the ball had marked the end of an era, Nina having gained her goal, leaving her free to go ahead with her plans for Rushmere. But what of her relationship with Dominic? Was it about to move forward into a more turbulent phase?

Nina was late up next morning. She came into the kitchen with her hand to her head, declaring she had scarcely closed her eyes. "No, it wasn't due to excitement," she argued crossly, by no means the radiant newly betrothed as she had appeared the night before. "It's sharing a bed with Judith. She was continually getting up and walking about again."

"It's true," Judith admitted, looking up from kneading bread dough. "After all that dancing I couldn't sleep for the pain in my limbs. I tried to be quiet, but sometimes a moan escaped me, and all the floorboards do creak."

"I feel that now I'm betrothed I should have a room to myself," Nina stated importantly. "After all, I shall be attending all sorts of functions that will keep me out to all hours and then I'll be disturbing Judith in my turn."

"Well, you cannot have my room," Tansy replied, "because I'm giving that up to get it ready for guests, but you can have the box room I intended to take for myself, if you like, and I'll move in with Judith."

"The box room by the rear staircase that comes down to the scullery behind the kitchen near the back door?" Nina's eyes were alert. She was also remembering that outside the window was the flat roof over two small rooms off the kitchen, which originally must have been housekeeper's apartments. It would be easy enough to gain a footing on the stonework outside and regain entrance to the house by way of the window should the need ever arise.

"I know it has barely room for a bed and a chest of drawers—"

"I'll take it! I don't mind it being small as long as I can be on my own."

Tansy, who had expected a fuss, looked at her in surprise. "That's settled then."

Nina crossed to the coffee pot keeping hot on the range and poured herself a cup from it. "There's another thing. I've told Edward that out of the kindness of your heart you are putting up the racing friends and acquaintances of Dominic and the late Oliver Marlow, who are unable to find accommodation elsewhere for the race week."

Judith managed a half-jocular tone. "I'm sure neither Tansy nor I will let the vulgar word 'lodginghouse' pass our lips."

Nina glowered at her but seemed to decide against any answering retort. She sipped the coffee. "I have something else to tell you. Edward is giving a grand house party the weekend after next to gather together all his cousins and aunts and uncles and any other member of his family who lives far afield and whom I've yet to meet. You are both to be invited, and Roger too. Amelia was included as a matter of course, and for mercy's sake see that she doesn't overdress! Did you see how many rings and necklaces and brooches she was wearing last night? She really is the coarsest creature!"

"Shh!" Judith said reprovingly. "It would upset her if she should hear you."

Nina rounded on her with unnecessary fury. "I don't care if she does! It's all her hateful fault that we were landed in this awful predicament of having to live with her in the first place. Have you forgotten that she was Papa's whore? Or that Rushmere was his own private bordello?"

The ugly, heart-torn, miserable words seemed to hang in the air of the quiet kitchen as she put shaking fingertips over her mouth, her eyes closing tight in an agony of her own suffering. Judith dropped back onto the table the loaf she had begun to shape.

"What's the matter, Nina? There's something new troubling you, isn't there?"

"No, of course not!" Nina snatched up the cup she had poured and took a deep drink, adopting a defiant, blustering attitude. "It's the strain of these past weeks telling on me. Thank heaven, I'll have to spend less time in this house from now on!"

"Edward's house party sounds inviting," Tansy said, deciding it was best to move Nina on to more pleasant paths of thought, "but I doubt that Roger will be able to have time off to go there —or that he would want to, for that matter. If he doesn't call in soon today I'll walk along to Ainderly Hall sometime and see him about it."

Later in the day Nina removed her belongings into the box room. She also tested the stair to make sure she knew which ones creaked and which did not. When it came near the time of her assignation with Adam she made the excuse that she was going for a walk and went up to the closet in the room that was now Judith's and Tansy's where she had left her outdoor garments and some of the dresses that she had no room for in her new quarters. She went to take down one cloak, but then her hand hovered and with a quick decision she took another and swept it around her shoulders as she went from the room, down the stairs, and out of the house.

She had decided it was safer and there was less chance of her being observed if she took one of the paths through the woods instead of going by way of the lane. She knew the house, which had stood empty since before she and the others had come to Cudlingham, having seen it often on walks. It was known locally as the Brick Kiln House, and in spite of its drab name it was a large stone house of pleasing proportions, ivy thick upon its walls, and a big, iron-hinged door. When she approached it from the cover of the woods she saw that the protecting boards had been removed from the windows, but no light shone through any of the curtains.

At the gate she halted, summoning up her courage, wanting desperately to turn and run, but she dared not. The flagged path was newly weeded and there were signs that a start had been made to get the garden into order. She reached for the knocker, but the door opened and Adam, lamp in hand, stood back to let her enter, the glow making bright planes and dark hollows of his face. He was in waistcoat and shirt sleeves.

"You're on time," he said approvingly as if he had not expected her to be punctual. "This way. Follow me."

He led her without preamble up the stairs and across the landing into a large bedroom where a log fire leaped in the wide grate, its dancing glow reflected on the tall mahogany head of the broad bed with its turned-down white linen. He set the lamp on a bow-fronted chest of drawers and closed the door that she had left open behind her. Her hood half-covered her face and he drew it back so that it fell from her head, her hair becoming a blaze of rich color in the firelight. He caught his breath audibly and touched a curling strand of it.

"Did you meet anyone on the way?" he asked thickly.

She shook her head. "I came by a path through the woods that Judith and I discovered one day. It's very overgrown. I don't believe anybody else ever uses it."

"Good." He unfastened her cloak and took it from her to cast over the arm of a chair.

When he turned her about to unhook the back of her gown she crossed her hands instinctively across her breasts for the moment when the bodice would fall from her shoulders, and she was thankful that her face was hidden from him.

"Suppose I—" Her lower lip was quivering violently and she seemed to have no control over it for speech. She made another attempt to voice the awful possibility uppermost in her mind.

"Suppose I find—find myself in the"—she forced out the dreadful words—"the family way!"

He had undone the last hook and he bent his head and kissed the nape of her neck. "You won't. Not unless you ever wish it."

When all her clothes were lying across the chair and every pin taken from her hair he picked her up in his arms and carried her across to the bed.

9.

With Judith beside her on the wagonette seat Tansy drove through the white gates that led direct to the Ainderly Hall stables, the driveway hidden by a high, ancient wall and thick trees from the house and its own grand entrance. It was a fine morning and she would have walked through the village from Rushmere if she had been on her own, but Judith had asked to accompany her and that necessitated the use of the vehicle.

As they drew up in the stableyard they saw several lads going busily about their work, but there was no sign of Roger. Tansy alighted, and a rugged-faced man in a riding coat and leather gaiters came out from an office adjoining the saddle room. He was in his fifties, straight-shouldered, with a full, neatly trimmed sandy moustache, his hair well brushed and brindled with gray. There was a look not unlike that of a well-groomed horse about him.

"Good morning, ladies. May I be of any assistance?" Being bareheaded he had no hat to doff but inclined his head in a slight bow.

"I'm Miss Marlow," Tansy answered, "and this is Miss Collins. I wonder if we might have a word with Roger."

"That can be arranged. I'm Will Kirby, the trainer here." He spoke directly to Tansy. "In your service too, ma'am, since you are part owner with Mr. Reade of Young Oberon. Doubtless you have heard of me."

"I have indeed. I should like to take this opportunity to ask you about Roger's progress."

He looked a little awkward about giving his opinion and ran a hand over his thick hair, but he answered her with a frankness that rang true.

"He's shaping up. In fact, I'll say that he's shaping up very well indeed. The lad works hard, never shirks a duty, and I'm more than satisfied with the manner in which he handles Young Oberon, who has a strong will and can be exceedingly difficult at times. I may well let your brother try out a runner in one of the minor races before long."

"Does he ride that well already?"

"Good jockeys—like Derby winners—are not just made, Miss Marlow. They have inherent in them that special streak that lifts them out of the ordinary class in the first place. Without that streak the best training in the world won't make a champion and, taking it the other way, with lack of good training that streak might never come to light and the Turf would be the poorer for it. Your brother may—I'm not saying he has, mind you, and I ask you to keep what I say to yourselves—but he may have something of that special quality in him. It's early days yet, but rest assured I'm keeping my eye on him."

"That's splendid news. What of Young Oberon? Is he—?"

Will Kirby interrupted her, laying a warning finger against his nose. "Let's say I'm keeping an eye on him too. I'll give you a full report in confidence with Mr. Reade at your convenience any day. I always watch what I say when there could be spying eyes and ears about. Only this morning I set some lads to chase off a tout caught watching some trials at the gallops. Now," he said briskly, changing the direction of the conversation, "shall I send your brother to you or would you like to see him at work?"

"At work, if we may."

Will Kirby took a large gold pocket watch out of his waistcoat pocket and glanced at it. "He'll still be grooming Young Oberon after the day's training at the gallops. I'll take you over to the loose box, but you can't go in, I'm afraid. He's high-spirited and doesn't take kindly to strangers—or even any of the stable lads for that matter—invading his domain." He saw that Judith was about to get down from the wagonette and he hastened round the back of the vehicle to give his hand and assist.

"Is he a dangerous horse, Mr. Kirby?" she asked him, grateful for his aid.

"No, but he's a stallion and proud of himself, liking to assert his presence as though he knew himself to be a winner already. With your brother he's as sweet and docile as he could be, but woe betide anyone else who might handle him a trifle roughly."

"Would he resent a strange rider on his back?"

"No, he's learned to run and to be ridden, and it will be up to any professional jockey to get the best out of him when the time comes. Mr. Reade has two of the best jockeys in the country to bring the winners in for him—that's Nat Gobowen and Arthur Nisbet, and whether young Marlow will match them one day, or even surpass them, remains to be seen."

While talking he had been strolling at their side to lead them across to the loose box at the end of one of the stable buildings from which Tansy had seen the colt led out on her previous visit. They heard Roger whistling before they reached it. The top half of the door was open and Will Kirby rested an arm on the lower half. The warm aroma of horse and oats and clean straw wafted out to them.

"Two ladies to see you, Marlow. Normally I wouldn't allow visitors in working hours, but as your sister happens to be part owner of the colt in your charge I'll allow you five minutes off and you may parade him around the yard for Miss Marlow's inspection if she so wishes it." He turned to the girls once more. "Good day, ladies. Don't forget, Miss Marlow, that I'll be pleased to present that report to you at any time, and if you should wish to join Mr. Reade one morning when we're stretching the colt on the gallops to see what he's made of you'll be more than welcome."

He departed. Roger, eyebrows raised in surprise at the sight of the two girls looking over the half door at him, came toward them with the brush in his hand, with which he had been polishing his charge.

"Tansy! Judith! What brings you here? Not to tell me about Nina's betrothal, I hope. I heard about that soon enough. It put me in a bad light with the other lads, having connections with that lot at the Manor. Their colt, Wild Wind, is going to run against our filly, Merry Day, in the Derby and the St. Leger."

Tansy might have been amused by Roger being unable to discuss anything without linking it to horses and racing if anxiety over his tremendous loyalty to the Ainderly Hall stables did not cause her some worry. Would he deliberately blind himself to any trickery he saw going on there? Or was he so enraptured with his new life that he would see no villainy even if it were flaunted before him? It would be as well, perhaps, if she herself made a point of coming more often to the stables, which should be a little easier for her to do after she had seen Dominic later that same morning.

"It's not to inform you of Nina's betrothment that we came," she said, "because we knew you would have heard of it; the whole village and the district is agog with the news. We're here to let you know you have been included in an invitation we have received to a house party at the Manor—"

She had no chance to tell him more, for already he had started to shake his head firmly, aversion to the idea of being involved in such a social gathering showing on his face. "No, thanks! Phew! What an ordeal! I couldn't go anyway. I should never get time off for half a day, and I thank heaven for it! Young Oberon is going to run next week for the first time. He'll be among the runners in the Hothampton Maiden Stakes, which is a race for colts and geldings that have never won, and I'm going to be with him right up to the starter's flag, and when he gallops home as winner I'll be there at the paddock entrance to lead him in and unsaddle him and tell him how well he has done all the time I'm sponging him down and scraping him dry. Go to a house party! Not me! Not in a thousand years!"

Tansy and Judith both laughed together at his vehemence. "No need to go on so much about it at such length," Tansy declared. "I didn't think for one moment that you would be able to come or would want to, but I had to find out before I wrote our acceptance." She looked beyond him at Young Oberon, who stood as though bored, resting a hind leg, watching them with his dark, melting eyes. "I should like to see Young Oberon in the yard."

"No need to ask me twice!" Roger exclaimed eagerly.

Tansy helped Judith to draw away from the door, which he opened wide and hooked back against the outside wall. Then, taking the colt by the headstall, he led him out into the sunshine as proudly as if the beautiful animal had already won for himself every racing laurel.

Tansy was lost in admiration. Young Oberon had grown and developed since she had last seen him, his coat having a sheen like satin, and he walked as though on eggshells, every inch of him built for speed.

"Is he really going to win his first race?" she asked, thinking of the banknotes she had in her purse as a first payment to Dominic. They were few enough, her savings from her winter money-making efforts, but if she placed that small amount on the race she stood to win a larger sum, which would take her much further along the road to repayment.

"Of course he is!"

"Would it be safe to—to place a bet on him?"

"You couldn't lose!" Roger's eyebrows had shot up. "But a bet. In *money*." He burst out lauging. "Not exactly the action of a lady!"

Tansy laughed with him, clapping a hand over her mouth at the audacity of what she contemplated. Judith frowned in concern, not amused, knowing the double purpose of Tansy's visit to Ainderly Hall that day, and caught her warningly by the arm. "Don't take the risk! It would be dreadful if you lost. You would be back where you started with not one penny to show as a mark of good faith to Dominic. You don't want him to think your promises were worthless, do you? Go to him today with what you have in your purse as planned!"

Tansy's face became resolved and she put temptation from her. "You're right, Judith. If the colt wins, then my half share of the prize money will go toward his keep and training, no matter that Dominic wanted no part of those expenses from me. I'll be thankful for that." She took a few steps forward to meet Roger and Young Oberon as they completed the circuit of the yard. With both hands she patted the sides of the colt's handsome neck, and he blew through his nostrils, which quivered and flared out like rose-tinted shells. "Good luck, my beauty. Maybe one day you will recoup my fortune for me, who knows?"

She stood watching Roger lead him back into the loose box, Then with a final wave to their brother she and Judith returned to the wagonette. A few minutes later Tansy had driven through the grounds to the front of Ainderly Hall. Leaving Judith by her own choice on the wagonette seat in the sun, she was admitted into the house and was shown at once into the study where Dominic sat writing at a desk strewn with racing sheet calendars, race cards, clipped newspaper cuttings, and opened letters. Behind him were bookshelves filled with sporting works, and parallel to them a rack gleaming with double- and single-barreled guns. The paintings on the walls were all of race horses from his own stables. Before he was out of his chair at her entrance he had crossed swiftly to the desk between them and emptied the contents of her purse onto it. The banknotes floated and spread out.

"My first payment," she said, not without pride. "I'll oblige you for a receipt."

He sat slowly down in his chair again, motioning her to take a seat, which she did, and he picked up one of the banknotes and held it by opposite corners, his elbows propped on the desk.

"I know what this money represents," he said, frowning at it. "Early morning and late evening drives in the worst of the winter weather, hours of housework and scratching with a quill pen, and then those sessions selling at a stall in a marketplace, which nearly brought you to your deathbed."

"I could have caught that chill anywhere," she answered. "I would have returned to the stall again when I recovered if there had been anything to sell, but Amelia will not be persuaded to make more of her cosmetic creams and refuses to divulge the ingredients, or else I would have set about making them myself."

"I'm thankful to hear it. You must take care of your health. Judith told me that the doctor warned you to take no risks for some time to come." He picked up his pen again and dipped it in the inkpot pulling a sheet of paper toward him. "You shall have your receipt."

The nib scratched in the silent room. She looked about her, taking in more detail than before. The bay window opened to a lawn where a few tame pheasants pecked, the sun touching their feathers with orange and green and gold. His collection of sporting books appeared to rival her father's, although they were not devoted exclusively to horses and horse racing as those at Rushmere were. Angling, shooting, beagling, hare-coursing, and hunting all took their place among the range of subjects. She glanced at the race-horse paintings in turn, each a winner, the name, race, and date on small silver plates attached to each. So! His stables could boast the Goodwood Gold Cup, the St. Leger, and the Oaks! No mean achievement indeed. It was small wonder that he longed to win the greatest of all races, named after the twelfth Earl of Derby, who founded the race for three-year-old colts and fillies with his friend Sir Charles Bunbury, during a riotous house party at his nearby mansion, the Oaks, which had already given its name to the first running of the famous race for fillies only. The two friends had tossed a coin to decide the name of the new race, and when the first Derby was run the following year in 1780 fate dealt out the honors evenly by letting Bunbury's colt win it. Tansy had heard her father tell the well-known tale many times, and it occurred to her that she had grown up as much steeped in racing lore as Dominic must have been.

The receipt rustled as he handed it across the desk to her and she thanked him, folding it and putting it away in her purse. "You told me once that you had known my father for five years," she said, "but he had owned Rushmere for much longer than that. How was it that you didn't meet before?"

"I must have practically rubbed shoulders with him many a time at race meetings, but to my knowledge we never spoke until I purchased Ainderly Hall and its almost empty stables from a mutual racing acquaintance, an unfortunate fellow on the brink of bankruptcy. Heavy losses and mismanagement had run him into the ground. I've built the stables' reputation up again."

"Some would say it was a tremendous risk for you, a very young man, to take."

"I was twenty-four. I already had race horses of my own, and I had been looking out for a place to buy."

"You must have been most confident of success," she challenged, her sympathies all with the former owner, who could have been the victim of the same racing knavery that had been used by Dominic to propel him to the top.

He leaned back in his chair, tilting it with one foot, an arm slung over the back of it, and answered casually, his lips parting in a smile. "I'm a gambler. But I like to think Lady Luck smiles on me when she knows there's something I really want."

"Perhaps she will tire one day of being coerced," she retorted shortly.

"Coerced?" he repeated with raised eyebrows. "That's a strange choice of word. I should prefer to say that I always wooed her well with a good race horse, a new pack of cards, or a compliment to a pretty woman."

She could see the turn that the conversation was taking and decided to make her departure. "You shouldn't have to wait so long for the next payment," she said. "I'm opening up Rushmere for the Epsom meeting next month."

He walked with her to the door. "How many guests will you be able to accommodate?"

"At least twelve in comfort, and there are six rooms on the upper floor under the eaves, which were servants' quarters, but I'm painting them up and making them more than habitable with extra furniture from other parts of the house. That should mean eighteen guests in all."

"Have you advertised yet?"

"No, but I intend to."

"Don't bother with it," he advised. "There's no need. I have many racing acquaintances who will be more than glad to learn from me of such excellent accommodation within easy reach of Epsom. An advertisement will result in all sorts of unsavory riffraff beating a path to your door. Every kind of thief, pickpocket, and scallawag follows a race meeting, you know."

"I hadn't thought of that," she said in dismay.

"Instead, those whom I know will be glad to pay treble anything you may charge to save the battling and bribing that they normally have to endure to get a roof over their heads in race weeks. It was thought that the extension of the railway line would ease matters, but last year hundreds of people were turned away from the booking offices in London, and the trains that did set off were so crammed with passengers that the locomotives couldn't make it up the gradients and people were left stranded."

"I've heard the roads to Epsom are so crowded as to be impassable at times," she said, "but that people should be left high and dry by the trains too is surely the last straw."

They had come out into the sunshine and she saw that Judith, looking pink-cheeked and pretty, was engaged in conversation with a tallish young man, about her own age, who stood lounging against the wagonette, arms folded, looking up at her.

"I see Judith has met Matthew Kirby, my trainer's son," Dominic remarked.

Tansy felt a pang of misgiving. On no account did she want Judith extending any social connections toward Ainderly Hall. It was bad enough that she herself was involved with it and Roger had been ensnared, but she hoped that Judith would not become embroiled in its meshes in any way. When Matthew turned at the sound of their approach Tansy was forced to admit to herself that he was a personable young man with long, narrow eyes and somewhat pugnacious good looks under a heavy thatch of brownish hair.

"Morning, sir. Morning, Miss Marlow. Miss Collins and I have been passing the time of day. Er—well, I'd better be getting along."

He threw Judith a backward glance over his shoulder and it seemed to Tansy that Judith's eyes followed him as though reluctant to see him go. Taking the reins into her hands when good-byes had been exchanged with Dominic, Tansy glanced sideways at her as they set off down the drive, and she was touched by the unguarded glow in the girl's face.

"Wasn't he nice?" Judith said shyly as the wagonette bowled out of the Hall's huge gates, there being no doubt whom she meant. "He asked me if I would go with him to a magic lantern show in Ewell a week Saturday."

"That's the weekend of the house party at the Manor," Tansy pointed out gently.

"I know," Judith answered on a faint note of regret that suggested she might envy Roger's freedom to turn down Edward's invitation. Tansy refrained from any comment, but was full of sympathy for her disappointment.

During the days that followed Tansy was too busy to think about the approaching house party, leaving the pressing of her gowns and the packing of the clothes she would need to a willing and helpful Judith. She would have preferred not to stay at the Manor and merely attend from home the festivities planned, but Nina was insistent.

Tansy, standing on a pair of steps and hanging curtains at one of the attic windows, frowned slightly at the thought of her beautiful sister, who had always been such a contained, self-sufficient person, not given to outbursts of temperament, and yet ever since the night of her betrothal she was continually giving way to displays of wrath, impatience, and self-pity, even shedding tears at the slightest provocation—or seemingly with no provocation at all.

But there was so much she could not understand about Nina these days: her evening walks for a start. Most evenings she was at the Manor or otherwise socially engaged with Edward, but when she was not thus committed she would go out, sometimes announcing her intention, sometimes not, and always refusing offers of company. What time she returned was anybody's guess, and Tansy could only hope that it remained in the region of eleven o'clock, the hour when she had first called her to task over it.

"Where on earth have you been, Nina?" she had demanded, standing in her nightgown at the head of the rear stairs, having heard the back door close. The candle she held gave a fitful light and Nina's face was only a pale blur at the bottom of the flight. "It's raining and blowing and I've been worried sick about you!"

Nina's voice had answered sullenly: "I have to get some liberty from this house every day or I should go mad."

"That's a ridiculous answer. You took morning chocolate at the Rectory and lunched with Sarah and went driving with Edward into Epsom this afternoon. We have hardly seen you."

She had retaliated like a wild cat. "You mean I'm not doing my fair share of turning Rushmere into a horrible lodginghouse? Is that it? Well, I'm helping in another way. I'm not a burden on you anymore. I'm rarely home to eat, am I? Edward is footing the bill for anything I want in the way of clothes. You should be thankful. Thankful for my contribution toward the well-being of this family. You don't know how much you owe me."

Tansy had hurried down the stairs to her, but Nina had turned her face away from the candlelight, her hair, wind-blown and untidy, looking as if it had fallen loose and been carelessly pinned up again.

"Nina, I'm not annoyed that you're out during the day. I'm glad that you're having the social round you've always wanted. There's nothing in the house that Judith and I can't manage between us, and although Amelia rarely does anything anymore except pass an hour or two in the flower garden, that doesn't matter. I just want to know why you have to go wandering about in the dark until such a late hour. It's worrying."

"This is a peaceful village. Nothing could happen to me."

"I know that too. But where do you go?"

Nina's voice had been muffled. "It's a sheltered place. A secret place, I suppppose it could be called. I don't want to talk about it."

Tansy knew what it meant to be able to retreat at times into one's own solitude, and she had been sympathetic. "I understand. Often I like to be alone. It gives one time to gather one's thoughts when the world seems too busy a place and—in my case —there're all sorts of problems to think over and decisions to be made. I won't ask any more questions. I don't want to pry. But, please, do try not to forget the passing of time when you're out. Try to get home earlier and never, never later than tonight."

"I'll remember." Nina had darted past her and up the stairs into the darkness of the landing, her cloak bundled over her arm. It had not been a very satisfying interview, but fortunately Edward was gradually taking up more and more of Nina's time and the evening walks were becoming less frequent, although no less late.

A step into the attic room behind her made Tansy turn to see who had joined her, although she continued to slide the curtain rings along the rod. It was Amelia. She sank down on the edge of the bed, which Roger had moved up there on his last visit to the house with some assistance from Tansy. She had a wispy lace handkerchief in her hands, which she twisted about her fingers.

"I don't think I'll go to the Manor house party after all," she said petulantly.

"Why, Amelia?"

"Nina doesn't want me there."

It was impossible to deny the truth of that remark. Friction between Amelia and Nina had become almost intolerable, due as much to the acceleration of the older woman's uppishness as to Nina's increasing vindictiveness toward her, which now frequently resulted in shouted words between them, quarrels which ended with Nina flying up to her room and Amelia bursting into tears of rage and stamping her little feet like a spoiled child. Tansy often thought how pleasant it would be to have a quiet sanctuary such as Nina had found in which she could be away from the house's turmoil, secluded from questions and demands, to be released for a while from acting as a buffer between hostile parties. She could not deny Nina's need to be alone when she herself felt the same longing for times of peace and solitude.

"Have you sent your apologies?" Tansy inquired, taking a neutral line, the curtain rings continuing to clink under her fingers. Amelia's hard-done-by air was all too familiar, an immature demand for attention and consolation. Not for the first time Tansy wondered if this weakness in Amelia's character, her constant need of cajoling and reassurance combined with her play of helpless feminity, had not held Oliver Marlow to her as much as her physical attributes. It was possible that his wife's capable independence, her ability to manage perfectly well in his absences, had in some ways emasculated and damaged the protective, loving man that her father had been at heart.

"No, but a note should go this very day." Amelia shrugged irritably, annoyed that no persuasive words for her to consider her decision carefully had come from the girl on the steps. "I suppose I'll have to deliver it myself. It's insufferable that we do not even have a scullery maid to carry out errands. I almost die—truly, I almost die of shame!—when other ladies are talking over their servant problem and I have nothing to contribute."

"You know we have no money to spare for help in the house."

Amelia snorted and went grumbling on, pettishly listing all the comforts she had been accustomed to and now had to do without. Tansy thought that in truth Amelia had little to complain about, for she never gave a hand with the less pleasant chores and had not been seen with a duster in hand for weeks, Judith having taken over that extra chore when Amelia complained that it made her shoulders ache. As for money, it seemed that recently Amelia had known no lack of it in her own purse, for she had made several minor shopping sorties into Epsom, and after joining Sarah Taylor on a day's shopping expedition to London she had returned with a new and expensive bonnet, three pairs of new shoes, and she alone knew what new garments in the box that she had taken straight to her room without opening. A conviction as to the source of this new show of affluence had been growing steadily in Tansy's mind.

"Would you hand me the other curtain, please?" she requested.

The woman gave an elaborate sigh as if there were never-ending demands upon her time and efforts at Rushmere, but she got up to take the curtain from where it lay over the back of the chair.

"Here you are," she said holding it up.

Tansy, turning on the steps to take it from her, looked down into her carefully painted face. "Are you blackmailing Dominic, Amelia?" she asked penetratingly.

Amelia's mouth dropped open in complete astonishment, yet at the same time her face dyed a guilty crimson. She blinked, gulped, and blinked again, taking refuge in outrage and anger. "How dare you! What mad accusation is this?"

"I must tell you that the conversation that passed between you and Dominic on the day I was taken ill came back to me. At first I thought you and he were entering into some kind of plot about the house, and although I couldn't see any way in which you might prise the ownership of it from me I thought it best to bide my time. Not being unprepared, I was sure I should be able to pinpoint the danger when it came. But I have decided that you were pressing for payment from Dominic. I think that through my father you discovered something about his racing activities that wouldn't bear being brought to light and you are extracting money from him. Did he not promise to contact his banker without delay when you threatened that you must have his decision then and there?"

Amelia stared at her for a few moments, seeming to be turning over all that Tansy had said, the first violent color in her face receding, leaving it blotchy, but still high. "So you heard and remembered." She spoke slowly, as if playing for time and needing to formulate carefully the full reply that she must give. "With you at market and Nina and Judith gone to the Manor I had thought to see him privately with no chance of being interrupted and not one among you learning of our meeting. I hadn't expected you to make such an early return, but it hastened a settlement of his decision to pay me the sum I wanted from him." She licked her lips nervously. "I'm not admitting anything, you understand. Tell me first what you propose to do if I should concede that you're right in your deductions."

"I'll not accuse you to a magistrate, if that's what you're afraid of. For my father's sake as much as anything else I'll not see you in a prison."

"Do you intend to enter in any discussion about the matter yourself with Dominic?"

"No, I have reasons of my own for that."

Thoughtfully Amelia moved round and tapped the fingers of one hand on the brass rail at the foot of the bedstead. "Oliver did tell me many things about the Ainderly Hall stables. You are right to suspect Mr. Reade. He is an unscrupulous villain. The reason you father wanted to take the colt away from the place was because he feared the animal's future involvement in shady deals that he knew were going on there. I admit I was wrong to use what I knew to get money from Mr. Reade, but I'm not strong like you, Tansy." She turned her round eyes in Tansy's direction. "You would rather starve and go threadbare than turn against your principles. Not many people are like you."

Tansy began automatically to slip the second curtain into place. A wave of unhappiness had swept over her at hearing that even her father had known Dominic was not to be trusted, stamping out the single remaining ember of hope that she knew she had cherished deep within her that she might one day discover herself to be wrong about him.

"How much of that ill-gotten money have you left?" she asked tonelessly.

"None. It is all spent."

"Oh, Amelia!" Tansy let her hands fall to her sides, the curtain trailing to the floor. "How much was it?"

"Only—only a hundred pounds."

"A hundred pounds! Where has it all gone?"

"As well as a few new gowns and bonnets and shoes and such-like, I bought a ring, too. Your father always gave me something pretty to wear when it came to my natal day." She pouted self-pityingly. "You don't know how much I've missed his gifts and many kindnesses."

Tansy thought despairingly that it was like talking to a child. "You must promise me never to extort money from Dominic ever again."

Amelia nodded, and with a tragic air came to stand meekly before Tansy in the attitude of one who, having received correction with contrition, was bravely resolved to make amends. Almost, Tansy thought, as if she had taken on the role of a character caught up in similar circumstances in one of those past plays during which she had trodden the candlelit boards.

"I know I must do as you say," she said stoutly. "I'll let Mr. Reade know that he need never look to be troubled by me again."

"I'm truly thankful to hear you say that," Tansy replied.

"I'll go straight to my bureau now and write a letter to him. I'll also write to Edward Taylor and withdraw from the house party. It will give you time to enjoy yourself and think less harshly of me and my errors, which I do assure you are committed out of folly and not wickedness."

"I happen to believe that. Don't miss going to the Manor on my account. As long as you put matters right, that is all I ask. We'll never refer to it again."

"Nevertheless I think I'll keep to my decision to stay away. At least Nina will enjoy the house party much better if I'm not there." A twinge of regret sounded in her voice as she contemplated the social pleasures she would be missing, but with a lift of her chin and a hand placed lightly across her breasts to emphasize the sacrifice she was making she swept from the room and down the attic stairs.

Tansy thought wryly that it was an exit that would not have gone amiss on any stage. With a sigh she finished hanging the curtains.

Amelia watched from the window when the day of the house party came and the three Marlow girls departed in the carriage that had been sent from the Manor to collect them. She looked wistful, but resigned. She realized she had been foolish to spend without caution the money she had received from Dominic Reade, but she never could resist spending when she had sovereigns dancing in her reticule and frilly, feminine clothes tempting her in a shop window. She should have known that Tansy would start questioning her, but it was too late for regrets now, and she must be thankful that she had inadvertently been shown a way of escape from too close investigation into the transaction that had taken place.

When the equipage had carried the three girls out of Rushmere's gates Amelia stayed at the window for several minutes after it had vanished from sight, letting her gaze drift over the lawns and flowerbeds and back to the gates. How often she had stood at this very window in the past watching and waiting for Oliver Marlow to return to her. Tears filled her eyes, blinding her with a sparkling sea of them. She swung away from the window and hurried upstairs to her bedroom.

10.

The house party lasted five days and was solely for the families of both sides. Edward's relatives outnumbered by at least ten to one the three girls from Rushmere, who found themselves drawn into social activities from morning till night with various clusters of his aunts, cousins, and uncles. There were even his two grandmothers to talk to and play cards with, both of them having traveled long distances with tremendous stamina, and who hated the sight of each other, holding court in opposite ends of the Manor, only meeting when they had to, which was usually at the family banquets each night.

Nina flitted between them all like some cool and lovely butterfly, watched by Edward with a proud and possessive eye. She went riding, walking, played bowls, ninepins, cards, and chess, danced with every one of the male relatives and was altogether a huge success. She did not, however, go anywhere near the stables, the rebuilding of which was now in full swing under Adam's watchful eye, except on Sunday with one of the grandmothers when no work was going on and every shovel, trowel, and hod stood idle.

Tansy did not join any of the small groups of guests who wandered there to see what progress had been made, but went on her own the last morning before breakfast, finding it impossible to lie abed when the sun was shining and the birds singing. She found the stables site a hive of activity, workmen everywhere trundling wheelbarrows, sawing planks, and climbing scaffolding. There was the smell of wet cement and sand and dust and new wood. Adam spotted her and came across.

"Good day to you. You're the earliest visitor we've had so far. How are you enjoying the house party?" He rested his foot on a stack of pipes and leaned his arm across his knee.

"It comes to an end today after breakfast," she said, thinking how good it was to see him. "It's been a little—exhausting."

He laughed. "I can imagine that." His eyes narrowed. "Has Nina made a good impression?"

"Yes, she has. Even the most snobbish of them—and there's quite a sprinkling of minor titles, you know—have not been able to fault her. I should hate her to have to run the gauntlet of those people if they suspected the skeleton we have rattling in our cupboard."

She had said it half-sadly, half-wryly, and he replied with a curious grin. "It's fortunate you have friends who know how to keep their own counsel."

She nodded gratefully, but wondered at the same time why his remark had made her feel uncomfortable. It was as if there had been mockery behind it, but not necessarily directed at her. "Work appears to be going well," she said, glancing toward the building in progress.

He turned to view it with her, running a hand through his hair with satisfaction. "So far we are slightly ahead of schedule. You're looking at the first step up the ladder for me. One day this whole district and the county of Surrey itself will boast splendid buildings erected by Adam Webster, Esquire."

Her eyes smiled at him. "I don't doubt it. I'm not psychic, but it seems to me that you have an aura of success forming about you."

Before he could reply a heavy wagon, loaded with timber, moved into the stableyard, drawn by four enormous shire horses, their brasses tinkling and glinting in the sun. Adam saw he was needed, some confusion occurring with men unloading a hand-cart in its path, and he bade her a hasty goodbye over his shoulder, leaving her at a run.

She wandered slowly back across the lawn, glad that in an hour or two she would be back at Rushmere, for she was impatient to resume work on it. There were still many last-minute things to be done before the now almost imminent Epsom races. She could expect an influx of guests, Dominic having kept his word about recommending Rushmere to his racing acquaintances. Letters booking rooms had flowed in; some she had gathered up with her before leaving for the house party and had answered and sent them to post with one of the Manor servants during the short lulls in the proceedings when she had had a few minutes to herself.

She was surprised when she passed into the Manor to be told that her brother was waiting to see her and had been shown into the Blue Drawing Room. She found him standing with hands in his pockets, gazing glumly out of the window.

"Roger! What brings you here?" she asked anxiously, seeing that something was wrong.

He turned a face haggard with distress and ambled toward her. "Young Oberon didn't win. He came in next to last."

"Oh, I'm so sorry," she said compassionately, "but it was his first race. He's what Papa would have called a baby yet."

"But he could have won!" Roger insisted desperately. "He didn't pay attention. I watched him. He was looking all round right from the start in the saddling enclosure, flicking his ears as if he had never seen a fellow race horse or a jockey before. He even looked back at me when I let go of his bridle at the line-up. Looked *back!* Instead of being wound up ready to leap off at the start when the flag went down he wanted to know where I was going!"

"What did the jockey think of him?"

"He said Young Oberon didn't stretch himself as he does at the gallops when given the touch."

"Perhaps next time—"

"Next time! It should have been *this* time!" Roger lifted his hands and let them flap down to his sides. Then he managed a rueful grin. "Thanks for listening to me. I shouldn't have come charging in here, but I felt I had to talk to you. Seven false starts didn't help Young Oberon either.

"I'm sure it didn't," she said with a sympathetic smile, putting an arm about his shoulders. He was still shorter than she was, but there was a wiry strength about him.

"At the race before Young Oberon's the jockeys didn't know whether the starter had shouted *Go* or not, there being quite a wind blowing, and some started and some didn't. That sort of confusion happens often."

Together they had walked out into the hall and he took his cap from the footman's white-gloved hand. Twirling it, he turned on the threshold.

"Mr. Reade gave permission to come along and see you. He would like to call on you later today."

She experienced the usual ambivalent reaction at the mere mention of his name, the stab of excitement at the very core of her being combined with an intense abhorrence of all he stood for. "Tell him he will be expected," she said.

When she made her way to the breakfast room she knew well enough why she had found the house party long and tedious: she had missed Dominic's presence, missed his eyes waiting for hers at every turn, desire like black fire deep within them.

She and Judith left soon after breakfast, Nina remaining with Edward to see the departure of the last guests, whom they were to accompany to Epsom railway station. At Rushmere, Amelia did not open the door for them and Tansy had to find her key and unlock it for the groom to carry in their boxes ahead of them, she herself drawing back to give Judith some support with her arm.

"Thank you," Tansy said to the groom, who bowed before leaping back up onto the carriage as it began to move. The hall was dark after the sunshine outside and at first she did not notice the change that had taken place in it, being intent on seeing Judith safe on her stick before releasing her. It was Judith who spotted it first.

"Look!" she gasped. "Everything has gone!"

Tansy jerked her head round and stared in disbelief. The once crammed hall was empty and looked twice the size. The enormous clothes stand, the ornate umbrella pot, the side tables, and the Gothic-backed chairs had vanished. Dark oval and square patches on the green papered walls showed where the many small pictures had hung.

She found her voice. "Amelia!" she cried. But even as she ran forward into the first room, flinging the double doors wide, she knew for certain that the woman had departed, taking everything she possessed with her. Yet not quite everything. In the small drawing room were two chairs, which Amelia had always declared uncomfortable, and the looking glass above the fireplace, which was set into the wall as a fixture within its carved frame. It reflected the white flurry of Tansy's petticoats under her bell-shaped skirt as she whirled back out of the room again, bonnet ribbons streaming. While Judith hurried after her as best she could, Tansy made a lightning tour throughout the house, upstairs and down, and finally they met again on the landing at the foot of the attic stairs.

"She's left only those pieces of furniture that she never liked or were here before she came," Tansy gasped. "Even the best kitchen pots are gone." Then she went white to the lips. "Dear God! Papa's books!"

She hurled herself downstairs again and flew into Amelia's long drawing room, giving a sob of relief when she saw the huge bookcase, which must have been her father's own, still in its place, the contents apparently intact. She pressed herself against it in relief, scanning the shelves to make sure, and saw that Amelia had overlooked, either by intent or through forgetfulness, a number of her own red-, green-, and blue-backed novels with which she had filled the gap that had long stayed empty on one of the higher shelves since the night when Tansy, thinking she had been Judith wandering about, had given her such a start.

Opening the glass doors Tansy reached up and took out the novels to put them elsewhere, the languishing heroines and moustachioed villains within the covers slipping about together as she put them in a pile on the floor. They had never been in harmony with the carefully treasured and collected volumes that took up the rest of the long shelves, but while Amelia had been in the house she had never interfered with their being there. Now she was free to do as she wished.

Judith came into the room, her stick tapping on the carpetless floor. She came to a halt, breathless. "There's an envelope propped on the mantel," she pointed out. "Have you seen it?"

"No, I've been too agitated." Tansy crossed to the fireplace and saw that the envelope was addressed to her. She ripped it open.

"*Dear Tansy,*" she read aloud. "*You must not think that anything you said to me during our talk in the attic room was the cause of my departing. It simply accelerated it. I am leaving Cudlingham to go far away to a new place and a new community where I might live again without the danger of any finger of scorn pointing at me. You see, I have long been afraid that once Rushmere became a hostelry I should find myself received less and less and finally dropped altogether by people of quality in the district, a humiliation I did not know how to face. Nina is secure in her betrothment, and you and Judith are able to command social respect as a natural right, but that has never been my good fortune. There was only one way open for me to change things and I took it. For you and your sisters' sakes as well as for my own, for I wish to leave agreeable memories behind me, I have written short notes to local acquaintances with a white lie to explain my unexpected departure—a sick friend who will wish me to make my home with her—and these letters I shall post in London when I change trains. I regret not being able to leave you sufficient furniture for you to receive those noble guests you had intended to accommodate, but I had to take the possessions that mean so much to me and could not tolerate the thought of leaving them behind. I loved your father and I know that what I have done is not what he would have expected of me, but I hope that in Heaven he looks down and forgives me. I ask you to do the same. Amelia Marlow.*" Tansy lowered the letter. "A hundred pounds," she said under her breath. "It must have been much more than a hundred pounds. More like a thousand pounds for her to set herself up in a new home, wherever it may be."

"What are you talking about?" Judith questioned urgently.

Quickly Tansy took her sister's face between her hands. "I

swear you to secrecy! Not even Nina must know, because she might let fall a word to Edward. Amelia was blackmailing Dominic." At long last she told Judith of the secret meeting she had witnessed and all she had overheard, ending with an account of what had passed between herself and the woman they should never see again. "That's why I'm fearful for Roger. That's why I want you to be wary of Matthew Kirby, no matter how pleasant a young man he may be."

A shadow of regret passed across Judith's eyes. "You need have no fear there on my account. My refusal of his invitation was a rebuff to him." She tilted her head on one side. "Why have you taken this personal crusade upon yourself to bring justice to Dominic? Is being his debtor so increasingly unbearable to you? Or is it that you have come to love him and want to make him see the error of his ways?"

"Love him?" Tansy gave an uncertain laugh. "You're being absurd! I find it exhilarating to challenge such a formidable adversary, and I heard so many tales from Papa of the abominable crimes committed against horses and human beings alike when high winnings are at stake that I'll not rest until I've put to rights at least one small corner of the Turf. As Mama was fond of saying, out of the acorn the mighty oak tree grew. But *love* him? I've never heard anything more preposterous. He is a ruthless, domineering man who is actively aroused by my defiance. He was from the very start. Such men do not love or look for love. It is the chase and the conquest that is all-important to them. I tell you he shall not add me to his conquests!" Angrily she pulled the bow of her bonnet strings undone and snatched it from her head. "We're wasting time talking about him when we should be listing all that has been left in the house and see how we might utilize it all. I've booked every room and I'm not going to cancel those bookings. Amelia's departure gives us extra sleeping accommodation and I shall see that it is used." She swept out of the room and Judith followed her.

Later in the kitchen they sat on the bench at the long table, the smaller one having been taken together with the wheelbacked chairs, and went over the list they had made between them. "We must think ourselves fortunate that Amelia left us most of the beds," Tansy said, "which suggests her new home will not be as large as Rushmere by any manner of means. All the best linen and blankets have gone, but there's plenty of mended sheets and we can switch them top to tail so that the patches don't show. Except for the absence of all those curtains, which took me such a time to hang, the rooms under the eaves are virtually untouched, but the rest of the bedrooms are lacking chairs or chests or washstands—and there's nothing at all left in the room that was Amelia's and the one that was mine. What Nina will say when she finds all her garments out of her vanished chest of drawers on the floor as ours are I cannot imagine. The downstairs rooms present a tremendous problem. There is almost nothing left." She tapped her fingers on the table, looking thoughtful. "Amelia said once there was a lot of old and broken stuff that wasn't sold stored in the stable loft. I looked in there on the first or second day after we came to Rushmere, but it was too dark and dusty to make any close inspection and most of it was covered with ancient tarpaulins. We might find some pieces there that would be usable if Roger could repair them for us." She leaped up and clambered over the bench. "I'll go at once to see what there is. The loft steps are rather dangerous for you. I won't be long."

She was gone almost an hour. When she returned she had the look of one who had seen a vision. There were dust streaks on her face and cobwebs clinging to her skirt.

"What do you think!" she exclaimed breathlessly. "The loft is full of the most splendid pieces! I could only find a few things broken. It's my belief that Papa couldn't bring himself to part with all the furniture that belonged to Rushmere's early days when Amelia wanted it replaced, and he sold some and had the rest put in the loft." She pressed her hands together almost in a praying attitude. "I hardly dare say it, Judith, but I believe Rushmere is going to look again much as it did when my ancestors lived here."

They hugged each other in their exuberance, Judith demanding to know more about all that had been unearthed. Then

Tansy went out to make inquiries from the local saddler as to whether his two strong sons would be willing to move some furniture for her. She returned to tell Judith that they would be coming later that same afternoon. At that point Nina returned.

"What on earth has happened?" she screeched, looking about her in the hall and flapping the gloves she had removed.

"'Amelia's gone," Tansy answered. "Practically lock, stock, and barrel, but things aren't as bad as they look."

Judith broke in eagerly. "Papa Oliver kept a lot of the Elizabethan furniture after all—it's in the stable loft. There's even a magnificent four-poster with a carved canopy."

Nina, her eyebrows high in astonishment, drew in her breath and then flung back her head and laughed. She laughed so hard and so long that her sisters started to laugh too, her mirth infectious.

"She's gone!" Nina choked, doubled over and wiping her eyes with her gloves. "That dreadful woman has gone. I'm so glad! Oh, you don't know how glad!" She flung out her arms and twirled like a top in the middle of the hall floor. "Glad! Glad! Glad!"

She no longer had the others laughing with her, there being some gloating element in her merriment that they did not feel at ease with, and when she swept Judith into an embrace, almost knocking her off balance, Tansy spoke with unaccustomed tartness:

"You'll find it less amusing when you see how your possessions have been taken from their places and not all that tidily. Be thankful that there are walk-in closets in all the rooms or else our dresses would have ended up in the same state."

Nina gave a shriek of dismay and went bounding up the stairs. They heard her banging about in her annoyance, but after a few minutes she was singing to herself. Apparently the disarray she found in her room was nothing compared with the relief of having seen the back of Amelia once and for all.

The saddler's sons, one of whom had an eye for Tansy although she was unaware of it, were more than obliging. They not only brought all the furniture down from the loft, but brushed and cleaned the dust from it all out in the small cobbled yard, giving the girls little to do. One of them had nails and hammer in his apron pocket and had brought his bag of carpenter's tools, so that emergency repairs were done on the spot— several hinges on cupboard doors and chest lids being loose or rusted—and the four-poster, which was in pieces, was soon put together in the room that had been Amelia's. Made of superb English oak, the furniture had mellowed with age to a rich, dark color. The chairs with stout arms and high backs and the long table with its huge, bulbous legs must have seen many a banquet in their day. One day couch had been reupholstered at a later period and when placed in the drawing room gave a warming touch of amber velvet to its setting.

"The house looks beautiful," Judith said when the workmen had departed. "I never realized before how it needed simplicity to show its interior to best advantage." She placed a hand against the oak-paneled wall appreciatively. "As you know, I didn't like Rushmere when I first saw it, thinking it looked a frightening and unwelcoming place, but now at last it seems a little more like home to me."

Nina, about to fetch her cloak for an evening walk, looked round the long drawing room approvingly. "Even these wonderful floors never showed up before with Amelia's carpets and rugs all over them. What are you going to do about the bare windows, seeing how she took all the best curtains with their rods and fittings?" she asked.

"We'll leave them as they are for the time being." Tansy said. "The windows are proudly shaped and inset, and there wouldn't have been curtains covering them in the sixteenth century." She raised a finger, listening. "Ah! The doorbell. That will be Dominic."

Nina flew upstairs, saying she did not want to be delayed, Judith tactfully withdrew to the kitchen, not knowing if he would wish to speak to her sister privately, and Tansy herself went to the door and admitted him.

"Good evening," he said, letting her take his tall hat and cane to place them on a rush-seated chair. He showed no surprise at the otherwise barren state of the hall. "Amelia took everything, did she?"

Tansy straightened slowly. "How did you know she had gone?" she asked warily, determined to give nothing away.

"I received a letter from her this morning, posted in London. I understand we shall not be seeing her again. A sick friend needs her company." His face was unreadable to Tansy, his air relaxed and friendly, but she guessed he was well pleased to be rid of a threat to his security, not knowing another remained in the knowledge that she had gained.

"In a way she has done us a good turn by her departure," Tansy said, leading him into the long drawing room where a fire had been lighted in the wide hearth to keep the evening chill at bay. She gestured toward the furniture. "All these Elizabethan pieces came to light in the stable loft." Briefly she gave him an account of the discovery.

He was lost in admiration for all that he saw, declaring the pieces to be remarkably fine examples of sixteenth-century handiwork. He spent such a long time studying the carved hunting scenes on a large oak and ash cupboard that she began to feel awkward that she had no wine to offer him, Amelia having taken every bottle as well as the crystal decanters. Fortunately some glasses remained for the use of the racing guests she expected.

He came away from the cupboard, almost as if the turn of her thoughts had given him a cue, and he took from an inner pocket a letter, which she saw at once was not in Amelia's writing.

"I happened to receive this letter by the same delivery," he said, sitting down comfortably and informally on the edge of the hearth, almost at her feet where she sat in one of the high-backed chairs. "It's from a racing acquaintance whom I particularly wish you to accommodate. His name is Selwyn Hedley, a North countryman, who probably knows as much about race horses as any man alive. Are you able to do this for me?"

"He shall have the four-poster in the room that was Amelia's. Had she not gone I should have had to refuse you. Every room is booked. It seems as if one gentleman promptly told another after receiving your recommendation, because several mentioned in their letters that my name had been passed to them."

"I'm glad to hear it. Naturally not all those will be known to me, but is there any way I may be of assistance to you, seeing that you have obliged me by letting a number of my acquaintances have first chance to come here?"

"I should like some advice on the matter of wine to purchase," she said. "I learned something about wines and spirits from my father during his affluent times, but maybe you could advise me as to what all these gentlemen might prefer."

He was pleased enough to advise her, being something of an expert in the matter of wines, and she fetched writing materials and returned to sit by him in the fire glow, putting down all he said.

Less than a quarter of a mile away, in the glow of another fire, Nina, still in her cloak, stood looking Adam, who had his back to her, hands deep in his jacket pockets, one booted foot resting on the fender as he stared into the leaping flames, listening to all she had to say.

"So you see," she concluded, "with Amelia gone I'm no longer subject to threats. Should you be thinking of going to Edward with your tales at any time I shall forestall you. I intend to confess to him that I lied about my relationship to Oliver Marlow, but it was to save my sisters suffering the social stigma that living under the same roof as Amelia would have brought upon us. With that woman gone and no danger whatever left of a scandal breaking, Edward will look upon matters in a very different light. He will even be distraught at what I must have bravely suffered in silence when her very presence was abhorrent to me."

He went on gazing into the fire. "You're bluffing, Nina."

"What do you mean?" she retorted.

"You wouldn't dare confess to that mealy-minded future husband of yours. It's too great a risk. You cannot be sure that he wouldn't turn against you. A man's pride is an incalculable force, being a powerful, primeval part of him, linked as it is with his very masculinity and his deepest desires. He would hate you for making a fool of him."

"No, he wouldn't! I know he wouldn't!" she protested, but her voice held a quaver of doubt. Then it changed, becoming fierce and taunting, as suddenly the significance of what he had said struck home. "So that's it, is it? I hurt your pride that night I told you I never wanted to see you again. You, the irresistible Adam Webster, the local Don Juan and captor of village girls' hearts, turned down by someone who could no longer stand the sight of him."

He did not turn and answered her without anger. "You'd better go."

She thought she had not heard aright. "What did you say?"

He did turn now and stood with his back to the fire, feet apart, arms folded. "I said get out. Go. Do as you please. You need never come here again."

She put a hand to her throat and she backed uncertainly. "Yes. That's what I've wanted all along—just to hear you say that."

"That's all right then, isn't it? I've said it. There's the door. You know the way out."

"I've risked everything to keep these assignations with you."

"I know that."

"So you accept I wasn't bluffing about telling Edward?"

"Not at all. You were bluffing."

"Then why are you sending me away?"

Something flickered in the depths of his eyes. Triumph? Satisfaction? She could not tell and his reply was enigmatic. "Go home and think about it."

She moved toward the door and stayed with her hand on the latch, retaliating with a white-hot flash of anger. "I'll never think of you again!"

"You won't be able to forget me."

Her mouth trembled. He had taken her virginity from her, taught her body responses that she had never dreamed existed, abused her, used her, and finally taken from her that sweet moment of her own revenge by dismissing her with complete indifference.

"You've cared nothing for me!" she accused self-pityingly.

He shrugged, not answering her. With a stifled sob she jerked open the door and went out on the dark landing, the door slamming shut behind her. He did not come out after her. She took the first few stairs down the flight at a rush, but then she stopped and looked back over her shoulder, closing her eyes tightly as if to shut out the host of other memories that flooded in on her. The tenderness of touch. His mouth that could kiss her in a thousand ways. The silkiness of flesh against flesh. Whispers and soft moaning and loving caresses.

She took another stair and paused again, leaning her weight on the banisters, her head bowed, taking stock of herself and her feelings. She wanted to marry Edward more than ever before, exulting in the life-style that had already begun to encompass her. She wanted everything he represented and all he could give her. She wanted her children to be cocooned in the family cradle in the grand nursery and grow up by the way of the best education that money and social status could obtain for them. Why then did her feet drag? What prevented her at this final hour from running from Adam with all the speed she could muster? She loathed him, didn't she?

She reached the door and pulled it open, going out into the starry night. Normally she took the utmost care not to be seen, for although the lane was little used except by day, she always watched and waited before emerging from the house, but tonight she walked out as though in a trance, releasing the gate without thought to let it slam closed behind her. It was only luck that none saw her before she entered the dark shadows of the wood and came out near her home on the other side.

Tansy, who was showing Dominic the four-poster bed where Selwyn Hedley was to sleep, heard the back door open downstairs and guessed Nina had returned. She half-expected her to come upstairs, which she usually did after her walks, never wanting to speak to anyone and going straight to bed, but when she did not appear Tansy supposed she must have heard the sound of Dominic's voice and decided to stay out of sight.

"The work on this bed was also done by a master craftsman," he said, holding a lamp to the bedhead in order to see better the quaint figures in Elizabethan clothes that danced and skipped amid the intricate carving that covered every inch of the bed from the enormous posts to the canopy, "and these small recesses were for candles." He tapped one with his finger, and then stood back, viewing the bare boards of the bed. "What about a mattress? Have you one to fit a bed as wide as this?"

"It does present a problem, but—"

"A problem no more. I'll tell my housekeeper to have one sent to you from the Hall."

"I couldn't possibly—"

"Nonsense! There's everything in the linen store. If you're short of bedding or anything else Mrs. Burton can supply whatever you need." When she opened her mouth to protest again he forestalled her with a cynical edge to his voice. "The articles would not be gifts, but only on loan. It's in my own interests to assist this venture of yours in any small way I can. After all, it is to result in financial remuneration for me, is it not?"

"It is indeed," she replied edgily. Somehow he had inveigled her into a position where it would appear she was careless of his acquaintances and their comfort if she was churlish enough to refuse his generous offer. Everything that passed between them was like a duel, each trying to score a point off the other. She made a move to return downstairs and he went with her. "I was sorry that Young Oberon did not win his race," she said as they descended the stairs. "I had hoped that whatever prize money he might have won would have gone toward his upkeep."

"Perhaps he'll do better next time. There is another race lined up for him shortly at Doncaster, and he'll run at Goodwood. The subject brings me to the second and most important reason for my calling on you this evening. As you know, I have high hopes for my filly, Merry Day, in the Derby. Will you come with me on the great day and see her run?"

The Derby! For a moment she was sorely tempted, but she had to refuse. It was not out of pique or animosity or a self-righteous desire to disassociate herself from his racing activities, but the knowledge that with a houseful of guests to sit down to breakfast in the morning and their ravenous return to a dinner of several courses in the evening she could not go flitting off to the

Derby, for she would only have Judith to help her and Nina would not be in the house at all, but would be staying at the Manor to star once again at Edward's house party for race week.

"I cannot," she replied. "I'll be kept far too busy here. It's quite impossible." Then on impulse she added: "But somehow or other, should you ask me again next year, I'll find a way to come with you to see Young Oberon try for the Derby stakes."

He gave a regretful shrug. "You soften my disappointment with a promise I only hope is possible to see fulfilled. My trainer was far from pleased with Young Oberon's performance in his first race and talked bluntly of his having to be withdrawn from next year's Derby at one of the remaining forfeit stages if his performance doesn't improve. I happen to share your faith in the colt, but in the end the facts will have to speak for themselves."

"Why not let Roger ride him at Doncaster. You said yourself you had never seen such affinity between a lad and his horse."

He rubbed his chin thoughtfully. "I'll tell you what I'll do. The Doncaster arrangements shall stand, but in the meantime Roger is to be tried out at a number of smaller race meetings, not on Young Oberon, but on other runners that are being put through their paces. He needs experience—there's always a crush for the best places at the line-up, older jockeys will see that he's pressed into the least advantageous place, and then he has to learn to look for a gap in the field and how to get through without other jockeys crowding him, and a hundred other such points. If he's as sharp as I think he is he'll soon be able to stand up for himself and if he makes sufficient progress I'll let him ride Young Oberon at Goodwood—if you'll agree to come with me and see how he gets on."

He had the most extraordinary talent for getting his own way, she thought. "I'll accept your invitation to Goodwood," she said. "I went there once with my father and I've never forgotten the wonderful time we had."

He took up his hat and cane and gave her a slow smile. "I trust you will enjoy everything twice as much with me."

"That remains to be seen," she said cautiously, but she was

more than happy that she had secured for Roger the opportunity for which he had longed.

Dominic laughed, giving her a sidelong glance as he clapped his tall hat on his head and went out of the door. She closed it after him and ran into the kitchen to tell Nina what she had achieved before seeking out Judith, but of her sister there was no sign and the back door was swinging on its hinges.

At that precise moment Nina was running back through the woods to Adam's house. She saw from the light in the window that he was still in the bedroom where she had left him. Through the gate she charged and into the house. Up the stairs she went and threw open the bedroom door, her cloak swinging about her. He lay in the bed, his fingers linked under his head on the pillow, a sheet covering his nakedness. Their eyes held across the room.

"I've been watching the clock," he said without mockery or scorn, his voice low and curiously tender. "You've taken three minutes longer to come back than I anticipated."

With a cry she ran to him and he sat up to catch her as she hurled herself into his arms. "I love you! I love you!" she cried. Then their mouths met in a frantic fury of kissing.

She returned home in the early hours of the morning, Adam going with her for the first time through the woods to see her into the lane near the gates of Rushmere, more than reluctant to let her go. They clung together in yet another parting kiss before she went from him and slipped silently into the sleeping house. When she got into her own narrow bed and had pulled the covers over her shoulders she hugged the pillow to her face with one arm. She loved Adam, but she was still going to marry Edward, who would one day inherit a title of his own and make her Lady of the Manor in every sense of the word. That was her plan and she would not swerve from it. But, oh! could Edward ever love her as she had been loved this night? Thankful that her marriage was still many months distant she drifted into sleep on a cloud of especially erotic memories which had been created in those few past hours.

11.

The day before the Epsom races the traffic began converging on the town, much of it passing through Cudlingham. Gypsy caravans, tent show wagons, horse boxes, coaches, and every kind of vehicle rolled past Rushmere. Tansy, busy with her preparations, scarcely had time to look out of the window, but the butcher boy, delivering the meat, told her the stream of traffic was nothing compared with what it would be like the next day, and he spoke with authority when he stated that on Derby Day itself complete chaos would reign. Nina, who had not lifted a finger to help, departed at noon to stay at the Manor. In the afternoon Judith took to her bed for a much-needed rest and the house stood ready and waiting. Tansy, wearing a freshly laundered striped blue and white cotton dress, was wandering about restlessly when she saw a spanking four-in-hand come bowling up the drive. She flew to receive her first racing guest. Selwyn Hedley had arrived.

"Good day to you, ma'am. Miss Tansy Marlow, I presume? Pretty name, pretty face to go with it. No impertinence intended, I assure you. Delighted to make your acquaintance. Hedley is the name, don't you know. Selwyn Hedley. If you a fancy a flutter on the Derby or any of the other races, just you have a word with me. There ain't a gee-gee running that I don't know its chances." He laid a yellow chamois-gloved finger in a roguish, knowing way against his bulbous red nose.

He was, she thought, the most vulgar-looking man she had ever seen, black-browed, huge-faced, and coarse-featured and heavy-bellied, his hands of a size that a blacksmith might have envied. His voice matched his physique, loud and deep and throaty with rich living. His clothes were of finest cloth and well cut, but the check of his frockcoat rivaled the brilliance of his waistcoat, across which was looped a thick gold watch-chain with a jeweled sovereign case dangling from it. His servant, a wiry, ferret-faced man, as thin and short as his master was large and broad, was unloading a portmanteau and some other baggage. Hedley jerked a thumb in his direction. "My man, Silas. You've a place for him to bed down, I suppose. The stable loft will do. He has his own bedding."

Tansy had known a second of panic, no mention having been made of accommodation for a servant when the booking was made. "The stable loft is new-swept and clean," she said, sending silent thanks toward the saddler's sons who had even carried out that chore for her. "I'll show you to your room."

Hedley trod heavily but agilely, the stairs creaking under his weight, and the floorboards of the wide landing groaned. He looked about his room approvingly. "You have good taste, ma'am. They don't make furniture of quality like these pieces nowadays. Oak, ain't it?" He slapped a great hand round one of the bedposts, giving it an experimental shake. "I declare this great bed could have been designed specially for my bulk. I'll sleep right comfy in it and still have plenty of room to spare for a companion, what say you? Eh? Eh?"

She ignored the leering innuendo with a stony face. "I'm sure you would like some tea. I'll take it into the small drawing room when I hear you come downstairs. Dinner will be at eight o'clock when the other guests will have arrived."

She was fuming as she stamped down the rear staircase into the kitchen to put the kettle on the hob. What a fat, detestable toad! How dare he! And how dare Dominic ask her to take such a man into her house! She wouldn't trust Hedley in any way. He looked thoroughly dishonest, for all his expensive clothing and fine carriage, which Silas had taken under cover, unharnessing the horses. Dishonest? She pressed her fingertips to her cheeks. Could he be one of Dominic's confederates? Dominic had certainly been most anxious that she should take the man in. If

Hedley was one of the racecourse villains, she was glad to have him under her roof, for there was always the chance that she might get a lead into something of importance. She looked over her shoulder and gave a start, seeing Silas standing by her. She had not heard him in his soft-soled boots. He gave a gap-toothed grin.

"Will there be a cuppa goin' fer me? I'm real parched. Like I allus was afore a race. Still get it when there's racin' in the air. Excitement, y'know."

"You may have a cup, of course," she said, taking a kitchen cup down from the cupboard. She had set one of the best left by Amelia on a tray ready for Hedley. "I'm about to toast some muffins as well. Were you a jockey in your day?"

"I was that. Rode in all the Classics and on every racecourse in the land. Mr. Hedley's a big-hearted gent. Took me on as his personal valet, coachman, and bodyguard when I was unjustly accused of a crime what I never committed and banned from ridin' the course for life."

"Whatever crime was that?" she exclaimed.

He showed more gaps in his dirty teeth as his grin broadened. "They said I savagely whipped and spurred a runner to the bone to bring him in a winner. As if I would do a thing like that. Me, what loves horses! I told 'em all the blood was due to the colt gashing himself on the rails, but they didn't believe me." He gave her a nudge with his bony elbow. "Know what I've been called ever since? Bloody Silas. But none can deny I've ridden more winners than most other jockeys alive today. Mr. Hedley is using his influence to get my ban lifted. Talents like mine shouldn't be lost to the Turf."

She felt sick. For a whole week she would have to put up with this evil little man eating in her kitchen. She had yet to discover who was the worst of the two men, the master or the servant, but for the time being Silas was in the lead.

She had just taken the tea and toasted muffins in to Hedley when other guests began to arrive. By dinnertime they had all gathered, being twenty in all, one gentleman having brought his wife without advance notice, but Tansy was able to switch them to a larger room, and five more servants had come to join Silas in being fed in the kitchen and allotted sleeping space in the stable loft. Among the guests who came without a manservant, arriving on a fine chestnut mare, was a lean, elegant man with prematurely white hair, which was singularly attractive with his olive-skinned, youngish face. There was something about him that made Tansy feel she had met or seen him somewhere before, but how or where she could not recall, the certainty bothering her as the tongue worries a broken tooth. Not even his name meant anything to her: Thomas Brett.

Hedley, however, recognized him instantly and greeted him with a geniality that was belied by the steely look behind the jovially crinkled eyes. "Ah, Mr. Brett, I do declare! Ain't seen you in quite a while! I trust you are in good health."

"Excellent, I thank you."

"Good! Capital! Wouldn't like to see you ailing. What would happen to the Turf if you weren't around?" His laughter rumbled deep in his chest and he clapped Brett's shoulder with a familiarity that was obviously resented by the recipient, whose thin, aristocratic mouth tightened considerably.

Tansy, who witnessed the whole incident from where she was waiting by the dining-room door to show her guests through, saw how quickly Brett drew ahead of Hedley and made sure of sitting at the opposite end of the table to him. He exchanged greetings with the other racing gentlemen, all of whom knew him, but Tansy could tell he was one to keep to himself and his conversation was restrained.

She was proud of the menu she had planned and grateful for the advice she had received from Dominic's housekeeper as to the dishes that would be appreciated, as well as to the rates she should charge her guests for their bed and board. Clear Royal soup was to be followed by sole with cream sauce and some of Judith's delicious lobster patties, which had been one of Oliver's favorite delicacies, on the side. Then would come fried sweetbreads, the beefsteak and oyster pie, the saddle of mutton, the roast pork, the veal fillets, the braised venison, and the stuffed woodcock. To round off the meal, after the cherry pie and the wine jellies, there was a dessert course of fruit both fresh and crystallized, as well as bonbons and biscuits. Not nearly as many courses as would be served at Ainderly Hall and the other grand houses around, but a well-planned menu with plenty of everything.

It was when she was serving the beefsteak and oyster pie, which Judith was cutting up into slices for her, that it came to her where she had seen—no, not seen, but heard—Brett before. It was a slight deepening in the timbre of his voice as he addressed another guest across the table which triggered off her memory. The plate she was holding wobbled in her hand and she set it down hastily in front of the person for whom it was intended. Brett had been the unidentified stranger in the carriage when she had overheard Dominic talking to him in the darkness at the roadside. Was it possible that she had two of Dominic's fellow conspirators under her roof? What game were the three of them playing?

The talk around the table was all of racing and the betting ring. She heard that Merry Day was established as the favorite for the Derby, the odds having been shortened against the filly since her success at Newmarket and subsequent wins at other meetings, and the general feeling around the table appeared to be that it would not be for lack of courage or fighting spirit if the stouthearted little Merry Day failed to win the greatest race of them all. When the conversation flowed on naturally to the chances of the other local entry, Wild Wind, several shook their heads and there was little interest. Hedley was not slow in voicing his opinion about everything, although whether what he said reflected his real ideas was another matter, for he was decidedly cagey when certain pertinent questions were put to him, but his voice boomed out continually as he shoveled food into his mouth, his appetite gargantuan and his thirst apparently unquenchable, his wineglass ever in need of replenishing. He moved with some difficulty from his chair when all rose to go into the long drawing room where coffee was to be served. The one lady in the company, who had left the table before the port was brought in for the gentlemen, returned to the dining room where Tansy was clearing glasses from the table.

"Allow me to thank you for a most excellent dinner, Miss Marlow. I cannot remember when I last tasted so delicious a sole in cream sauce or such tender roast mutton."

Tansy thanked her for her praise and the lady, whose name was Mrs. Wyatt, chatted on about recipes, obviously having been bored by the earlier racing talk and thankful to turn to a more feminine topic. Being a sensible person without pretensions she began almost automatically to help Tansy remove the glasses to a trolley, which Roger had made in his spare time to help speed the dishes from the kitchen, but she held back from Hedley's glass grimacing distastefully at the mess of spilt wine and spat-out grape pips and skins left in his place. "That revolting man! I declare my heart quite sank at the sight of him. He is one of the most notorious characters on the Turf today."

Tansy paused in the clearing up. "In what way, Mrs. Wyatt?" she asked with interest. "I never set eyes on him before this afternoon."

Mrs. Wyatt put a finger to her lips, went to the door to look out into the hall, and then closed it before returning to speak in a lowered voice. "One cannot be too careful. That vile servant of his creeps about and listens in for him and spies on other men's horse trials to discover when a possible winner is coming to light. For the sake of politeness and out of courtesy to you Hedley was accepted into the conversation around the table this evening, but my husband for one—and I should say more than half the others—would not normally pass the time of day with him under any circumstances."

"But why?"

"He was mixed up in that dreadful scandal at the Derby four years ago when the horse Running Rein won. It turned out that the horse was a well-developed four-year-old impostor—not the real three-year-old Running Rein at all but another called Maccabacus. Naturally there was a disqualification, but nothing was proved against Hedley, who had stood to win fifty thousand pounds, but his partner, a rogue named Goodman, bore the brunt of the blame and had to flee the country. That's the sort of man Hedley is."

"I read of a similar case of substituting an older horse for a younger one at Newmarket earlier this year. Is it a common trick?"

"It probably takes place more often than anyone realizes. It's a great shame that Hedley and others like him give the Turf a bad name. The Jockey Club, an organization made up of gentlemen of honor, is vigilant in its attempt to banish crooked dealing from the racecourse, but my husband says there will be no improvement until it is given more power and the rings of villainy cracked up once and for all. Mr. Brett is an investigator for the Jockey Club. He's respected, but not much liked, I'm afraid, but there're many who fear his probing."

Tansy stared at her, aghast at what she had heard. Brett was the biggest scoundrel of them all, secretly lining his own pockets while publicly rooting out the knavery of others! Had she not overheard his plotting with Dominic she would never have believed it possible. Then, before she could make any sort of reply, the door opened and Silas put his head into the room. Both she and Mrs. Wyatt started at the intrusion.

"Your doorbell was ringin', Miss Marlow. I took the liberty of answerin' it. Mr. Reade to see Mr. Hedley. They've gone into the small drawing room to talk private. They'd like brandies sent in. Right?"

"Er—yes. Thank you. I'll see to it."

He gave them each a sly look before withdrawing again, almost as if he had guessed what the talk had been or had even overheard part of it. Mrs. Wyatt gave a little snort. "Mr. Reade indeed. A name unknown to me, but another bird of the same feather, I'll be bound!"

As Tansy approached the small drawing room with the two brandies on a tray she passed Brett, who was strolling toward the foot of the stairs, taking his time over lighting a cigar. Silas was also in the hall, leaning his hand on one of the double doors of the room into which she was to go, absently biting his fingernails and spitting out the bits.

"I'm just waitin' to see if Mr. Hedley requires anythin' else," he said blandly. "I like to think of meself as his faithful shadow. You won't never find me far from his side." Then his sandy eyebrows shot up as from within the room there came the sound of Dominic's voice raised in anger.

"No, damn you! No!"

The doors were wrenched open, Silas stepping back quickly, and Dominic came striding out, his face like thunder. He paused briefly when he saw her with the tray.

"I'm sorry. I'll not be staying for the brandy after all."

He half-thrust Silas aside and snatched up his hat from the chair. Although his wrathful gaze swept past Brett, who was sending a cloud of cigar smoke billowing, not a sign of recognition passed between them. He went slamming out of the house.

"Temper, temper," Silas mocked under his breath in a singsong taunt, aping Dominic's departure.

From a chair in the small drawing room Hedley snapped his fingers at Tansy. "Bring me the brandy, my dear. It shall not go to waste, I promise you." He saw his servant hovering and made a gesture of dismissal, which was promptly obeyed. Tansy took the brandy across to him where he sat with his bulging, food-stained waistcoat well exposed, his legs stretched out and crossed at the ankles. He poured one brandy into the other glass, which he then raised to her. "To you, ma'am. A filly to beat 'em all!" She made to move away, her duty done, but his hand shot out and caught her by the wrist. "Don't go," he coaxed with a wet-lipped smile. "For a kiss I'll place a sovereign for you on the Derby winner that'll bring in enough of them to match up with every bright hair on your pretty head!"

She saw that he was drunker than she had realized and quite prepared to take by force what he had asked of her if she did not act with caution. His hand was clamped like an iron shackle on her and it was all she could do not to claw at it in what would be a vain attempt to release herself.

"That's an idle boast," she said mildly, hoping to bring him off guard with a slackening of his hold. "No one knows what the result will be."

"I have the gift of foresight," he said thickly, his gaze running over her. "For more than a kiss I'll guarantee you a fortune of your own—"

He broke off, a step having sounded in the still-open doorway. Brett stood there. "Could you spare me a moment of your time, Miss Marlow?" he inquired in his quiet, cultured tones. "I should like to know how early I might breakfast tomorrow morning."

With a grunt Hedley released his hold on her and gratefully she went with Brett, out into the hall. "As early as you like," she declared. He gave her a quiver of a smile. "Eight o'clock will do me well enough. I just thought to make sure."

As he went strolling off to join the rest of the company in the long drawing room she gave him a thoughtful glance before returning to the kitchen to help Judith with the washing-up, convinced that he had made the interruption deliberately on her behalf. She reflected on Hedley's boast that he knew the winner of the Derby, his tongue loosened by the vast amounts of liquor he had consumed and his own lecherous thoughts. Did it mean that once again the great race was to be tarnished by evil-doing? But it could not be with the substitution of one horse with another this time, for the stewards would be alert to that kind of mischief with the affair of Running Rein being comparatively recent. Some other plan must be in the wind, and it seemed very much as if Dominic and Hedley had quarreled about how it should be carried out. And why had Dominic not acknowledged Brett, who had shown an equal lack of recognition?

Later, going from bedroom to bedroom to turn down the sheets for her guests, she entered Hedley's quarters with some reluctance even though she knew him to be safely installed downstairs. She was unable to put down the lamp she was carrying on the table beside his bed, seeing that its space was taken by a medicine chest of polished mahogany, the type that doctors invariably took with them on their rounds for emergency dispensing. Was Hedley a hypochondriac? From the way he ate and drank, if this evening was anything to go by, it was more than likely that he suffered from digestive upsets. But so large a chest! It must contain any number of flasks and pillboxes, and the padlock on it was small, but appeared to be a secure fastening.

She was to remember that chest whenever she saw him guzzling or imbibing with gusto, but if he suffered from dyspepsia afterward and had to resort to the chest's contents he never showed it and appeared to be continually in the peak of health. But on the whole she was too busy to ponder much on anything except all the work there was to do. The days became a routine of serving large breakfasts, packing picnic baskets, and preparing vast dinners for the evenings when her racegoers returned tired, hungry and thirsty, their mood varying from jubilation to quiet disappointment, sometimes annoyance, and occasionally depression. Hedley alone gave no indication as to how he had fared, his bland smile and jocular attitude being a front behind which the man hid his true self.

When it came to the evening before Derby Day, Tansy, who had registered more of Hedley's moves and actions than she had realized, became almost instinctively alert and acutely observant, knowing that if any racecourse misdeed was to take place it should be within the next few hours of darkness, for little could be done amid crowds of people in the full light of day. She served dinner as usual, and learned that a colt named Surplice had suddenly soared to favorite after being previously condemned by adverse reports, and she recalled Hedley's boast that for the bet of a sovereign he could make a pile of them. Had he placed his money on Surplice when the odds were as long as they had been, the winnings if the colt should come in first would be considerable. But how could he be sure that Surplice and not Merry Day would win? The answer to that was simple: there was dirty work afoot and he was part of it! So she had been right about that from the start. But what it could be and how Dominic was involved she could not begin to fathom. All she did know was that Dominic had been far from pleased with the plan set out for him, for he had not been back to see Hedley since the night he had stormed out of the house. She felt certain that he would have returned, even just on a pretext to see her, if he had made up his quarrel with Hedley during one day or another at the races. Yet all this was supposition and she had no proof of anything.

When Hedley asked her for two bottles of brandy late in the evening after dinner and retired with them to his bedroom she experienced a sensation of relief that his nocturnal activities were to be confined to drinking himself insensible on his own and not to setting out on some nefarious venture that would most surely have been beyond her powers to interfere with or prevent, however good her intentions. With this worry eased from her mind she went contentedly about the last task of the day, which was the final tidying up of the kitchen in readiness for the morning. She believed that Silas, together with the other servants, had retired long since to the stable loft, and it was sheer chance that when coming from the pantry after putting away the remainders of a mutton joint, she caught a glimpse of him going out through the back door into the night. As always he had moved silently, and a second later she would only have known he had passed through the kitchen by the quiet clicking down of the latch. But she had seen the way his coat had flapped against his thin body. He had had a brandy bottle in each of the two side pockets in his coat.

She ripped off her apron and ran for the dark green cloak that she had removed to a peg in a downstairs cupboard since she and Judith had taken up temporary accommodation in the side rooms off the kitchen to set free an extra bedroom for her guests. At that precise moment Judith was collecting coffee cups in the long drawing room, most of the guests having already gone to bed, but there was no time to dash in there and let her sister know she was about to go out after Silas or else she might lose all trace of him.

At first she thought she had already missed him, but her eyes, adjusting quickly to the darkness after the gentle lamplight, soon spotted him, a black, hurrying figure amid blacker shadows of the night, making his way in the direction of the village. He was not walking openly in the lane or on the grass verge, but kept stealthily to the edge of Ashby Woods, making no more sound outside than he did indoors, not as much as a twig snapping underfoot. She began to follow from the opposite side of the lane, keeping about fifty yards behind him, and she kept her cloak drawn closed over her full skirt, for it had a distinctive scarlet lining that could shine and flicker in the gloom. At any other time she would have thought it unusually generous of a master to give his servant two bottles of superior brandy, although accepting the possibility that Hedley had had a lucky day and wanted to be munificent toward his hireling, but this evening it was a different matter altogether, for tomorrow was a day in the year unlike any other day and the giving of the bottles had taken on a sinister significance. After all, why had Hedley taken them up to his room first? He could more easily have handed them over direct to Silas, who had been in the same room when she brought the bottles from the cellar.

Her mind flew to the medicine chest by Hedley's bed. Suppose some drug from it had been substituted for the brandy. What more innocent way to carry about a lethal dosage for a horse than in ordinary-looking brandy bottles? But which horse? Not Wild Wind, for they had passed the gates of Cudlingham Manor, and in any case Edward's colt was said to offer no threat to either Merry Day or Surplice. Then, as she followed Silas on through the village by one of the less frequented routes by the river she realized that he was making for Ainderly Hall. She glanced swiftly over her shoulder, having the uncanny feeling that she was being followed in her turn, but decided that the tautness of her nerves was playing tricks with her imagination.

From the cover of a coppice she watched to see what Silas would do when he reached the main gates, knowing this was the crucial moment when the terrible suspicion gathering in her mind would be either confirmed or denied. It was confirmed, and she hurried on after him.

Had he turned in at the main gates she might yet have wondered if the brandy was being sent as a sly peace-offering before Derby Day from Hedley to Dominic, but instead Silas became even more cautious and difficult to keep in view, giving the tall wrought-iron entrance gates a wide berth and darting past them along by the thick hedge on the opposite side of the lane, almost in the ditch. Then suddenly he was gone from sight as completely as if the night had swallowed him up.

Warily she approached the spot where she had last glimpsed him, afraid he might be lurking there, but the stretch where he had hurried along was deserted. Still taking care herself to keep to the darkest and most sheltered places, she hastened on along the lane until she came to the wide, white-painted, five-barred gate which opened to a separate drive that led to the Ainderly Hall paddocks and the stables, shrouded now in blackness, the trees and bushes creating a tunnel of foliage.

She had no doubt that it was the way that Silas had taken. The business he was about was evil and it had all become crystal clear to her. Hedley was determined that Surplice should win, for without doubt he had laid heavily against the horse when the odds were long, and the only serious threat to Surplice's chances lay with Merry Day. For once Dominic must have drawn the line at interference in a race, seeing that his own filly was involved, and when he had refused to instruct his jockey to "pull" her and hold her back from winning, which would have enabled him to win as hugely as Hedley on the other horse, Hedley had taken matters into his own hands. Silas had been dispatched to inflict some harm on Merry Day that would prevent her from racing on the morrow.

There in the darkness, pushing open the gate, she almost wept in rage against their wickedness and in terror for the safety of the beautiful creature sleeping quietly in her stall while danger crept up silently out of the night. Any nervousness for herself being out alone and unprotected vanished before the thought of the vulnerability of Merry Day, and she half-walked, half-ran on the soft, turfy verge of the long graveled drive in a determined effort to catch sight of Silas again and to be ready to raise the alarm when he reached the stables. Her feet were soundless and there was nothing to hear but the beating of her own heart and the rustle of the branches overhead and on either side.

When the drive curved, following the paddock fence beyond the trees, she glimpsed ahead at the end of the black, leafy tunnel the archway into the stableyard where a few lamps made illuminated patches on the whitewashed walls of the buildings and caused the cobbles to gleam like gray pearls. Then her attackers struck.

With united shouts that resounded like a clap of thunder they sprang out from the blackness, and their fists, aimed wildly, caught her blows across the face, in the stomach, over the breasts, and something hard crashed against her head. With the breath knocked from her she uttered no more than a rasping gasp, blood flooding into her mouth, and she collapsed on the ground, two heavy bodies tumbling on top of her with more pummeling blows. It was then that her third assailant, who was still on his feet, opened the lantern he was carrying and gave a hoarse shout.

"It's my sister! Get off her! Get off her, I say!" He pulled like a madman at the two stable lads, who had stopped raining blows at his shout and drew back amazed to see it was a girl they had attacked. Roger dropped to his knees beside her. "Tansy! Speak to me! We didn't know it was you. We're on guard to see that no intruder gets in to try to nobble Merry Day." He lifted her head helplessly between his two hands, aghast at the terrible pallor of her face and the blood running from her lip. "Say something to me!" He was in tears.

"'I'll get help!" exclaimed one of his companions, leaping up and dashing through the archway, his boots clattering on the cobbles. The other lad picked up the lantern that Roger had thrown down and held it awkwardly, not knowing what to say or do. The gormless lass! he thought between pity and contempt. Fancy creeping about in the darkness near racing stables on the night before Derby Day. She should have known there would be stable personnel on the lookout for intruders, even though Merry Day's own lad was locked into the loose box with her, a cord in his hand ready to sound an alarm bell should anyone start tampering with the lock and trying to get in to them. Mr. Reade had come to check himself that neither Mr. Kirby nor the head stable lad had overlooked anything, a most unusual occurrence, but then it was not every day that Ainderly Hall had a possible Derby winner within its boundary walls.

Tansy had made an effort to sit up and Roger was putting his arms about her to support her against him. She took from him the kerchief he had whipped from about his neck and held it against her lip in an attempt to stem the blood.

"I'm not badly injured," she croaked half-humorously, still dazed, but wanting to reassure her brother, for he looked desperately alarmed and frightened, "only a little knocked about."

Her head was swimming with pain and her body shrieked out where the blows had landed, but she was dismayed when the head stable lad arrived at a run with a stretcher, others with him, and she protested when he insisted that she be lifted onto the stretcher. "No, Mr. Harris. I'm well able to walk."

"We're taking you up to the Hall, ma'am. You may need a doctor and this affair is something Mr. Reade must know about without delay."

A plaid blanket was put over her and she was carried at a swift pace away from the stables and through a side door into the Hall, another lad running on ahead to take word of what had occurred. By the time a couple of yards along a downstairs corridor had been traversed they were met by Dominic in evening clothes, a footman who had conveyed the stable lad's news in his wake.

"Carry her in here," Dominic said, opening a door. "I've already sent for the doctor."

Roger stayed with her, the rest departing, and he and Dominic between them lifted her from the stretcher to the sofa where she lay propped against cushions, her cloak removed. She was shivering with shock and Dominic tucked the blanket, which smelled faintly of bran and horses, closer around her. The realization of why she was there in the first place came swooping back to her.

"I must tell you—" she began, but Dominic interrupted her.

"Don't talk," he said calmly. "Plenty of time for explanations later."

"No, it cannot wait! I believe Merry Day to be in danger. I've no proof, but I'm certain that Hedley's man, Silas, means mischief. I followed him from Rushmere."

Dominic's glance became guarded, but he was undisturbed by what she had told him. "Nobody can get at Merry Day before the race. We've taken the utmost precautions."

"Suppose the filly was left unprotected when all those people came to look after me!" she cried, clutching at his hand. "Please make sure. Please!"

He smiled reassuringly, folding her fingers over his, and sat down on the edge of the sofa, facing her. "Every precaution has been taken. Those keeping watch over Merry Day's loose box have had instructions not to leave their posts under any circumstances, but if it will set your mind at rest Roger shall go back there now and tell Harris I want him to make an extra round to make sure that all is in order."

She relaxed, feeling that everything was in safe hands, and saw Roger depart. He passed in the doorway a middle-aged woman in neat black, whom Tansy recognized as Dominic's housekeeper, Mrs. Burton. She was carrying a tray of tea, and over her arm she had a snowy white blanket to replace the one from the stables.

"I've brought Miss Marlow a hot drink to alleviate the shock," Mrs. Burton said in explanation to Dominic, who withdrew from the sofa and let her take over. Before long the doctor arrived and then he left the room.

"No broken or cracked ribs," Dr. Westlake said with satisfaction while Mrs. Burton hooked up the back of Tansy's dress again. "You've a cut lip that's in no need of a stitch, a black eye that a pugilist wouldn't be ashamed of, a sore spot on your head that's going to be tender for a long time, and more than a fair share of bruises, but that's the sum total of your injuries." He went to the door to admit Dominic back into the room again and repeated what he had said. "So if Miss Marlow can be shown to a room now and rest quietly for a few days—"

"No, I cannot do that!" Tansy exclaimed agitatedly, snatching up her cloak to swing it about her shoulders. "I must go home at once. I have a houseful of guests to look after. My sister cannot manage alone."

They tried to persuade her against leaving, but she was adamant. Finally Dominic turned to Mrs. Burton. "I know you have my houseful of racing guests to take care of, but can two maid-servants be spared to assist Miss Marlow over the next few days?"

"Yes, sir. I'll see that they're at Rushmere by five-thirty tomorrow morning."

Tansy was given no chance to have a say in the matter, Dominic thanking the doctor, who was making his departure, giving her final instructions not to put her foot to the floor for twenty-four hours, and then Roger arrived to report that Mr. Harris said all was well in all quarters.

Dominic took her home and saw her into the house. Judith, who had been at a loss to know where she had gone, cried out at the sight of Tansy's cut and swollen face and had to be quickly reassured. Tansy spoke to Dominic as he was about to leave.

"One moment!"

"Yes?" he turned inquiringly on the doorstep.

"I wish you good luck tomorrow. I hope Merry Day wins."

"Your good wishes mean more to me than you realize." Then he was gone.

The next morning Tansy was stiff and aching in every limb. Thankfully she lay in bed while the two Ainderly Hall maids and Judith managed everything capably between them, explaining her non-appearance to the guests as her involvement in a slight accident. But when it came to late afternoon she decided she had carried out the doctor's instructions long enough for one day, and she dressed, put on the black eye-patch he had given her, tying it with ribbons behind her head, and with a veil over her face she went out to the gates to ask the result of the Derby from the first home-coming racegoer who passed by.

Two men on horseback soon came along, the cut of their flashy clothes telling her they were connected with the racing world, and she darted out into the lane to hail them with a little wave. "Please tell me, who won the Derby?"

One of the two answered her glumly, which left her in no doubt that he had had a thin day. "Surplice, ma'am. He held a good position throughout the whole race. There was a last-minute challenge by Springy Jack, but Surplice won easily."

"It weren't no popular win," his companion joined in, "and there were a right rowdy reception that 'ad Sim Templeman, Surplice's jockey, looking real scared, but it were nothing to do with 'im or the colt, 'cos they both gave their best and it showed. No, it were the fact that all those rumors about Surplice 'aving lost 'is form 'ad obviously been circulated deliberately to give people in the know a chance to rake in tremendous winnings. You should 'ave seen those shaking fists and 'eard the abuse! On second thoughts, maybe it's as well that you didn't, ma'am."

"What of Merry Day?" she demanded impatiently.

"She came in far back." The man looked questioningly at his friend. "Nineteenth, weren't she? Even Wild Wind were ahead of 'er."

"Why?" Tansy cried. "What could have gone wrong?"

"That's easily answered. I 'eard it on all sides. 'Er jockey, Nat Gobowen, 'ad been on the booze all night and were drunk in the saddle. Not that it noticed in the enclosure, 'cos 'e always sits tight and quiet before a race, never opening 'is mouth, but as soon as the race started it were clear that 'e 'ardly knew what 'e were doing."

"Thank you," Tansy said almost inaudibly, drawing back inside the gates. The men nodded amiably to her and rode on. She stayed where she was, eyes shut, leaning back against the closed gates. So Hedley had won after all! Silas had not been bound for the stables, but for the cottages on the Ainderly Hall estate where the jockeys were housed overnight or during times of prerace trials. Merry Day had had no need of all that elaborate protection. It had all been skillfully bypassed and the filly's loss of the race neatly ensured in a way that nobody else had thought of.

It was quite late that evening when Dominic came to see how she was, bringing her a nosegay of flowers set in a lace frill and tied with peach satin ribbons. She received him in the room off the kitchen where she was continuing to keep out of the sight of her guests and their servants.

"I'm sorry about the result of the race," she said when she had thanked him for the flowers and they were both seated opposite each other in cushioned wicker chairs.

"You were right about Silas being up to no good, but not in the direction we had imagined," he said with a heavy sigh. "Nat Gobowen said that Silas called on him with a gift of the brandy and to wish him luck. They had ridden against each other many a time in the past, and although Nat had been on his way to bed he allowed himself to be persuaded to take one drink and saw no harm in it. He remembers almost nothing after that."

"I think the brandy was drugged." She told him of her original suspicions.

"I'm certain you're right. The brandy bottles have been examined, but there's no sediment, nothing except a faint, slightly sickly aroma that soon dispersed. One of two people couldn't even discern that, so we're without any proof. I can tell you now that here in this house Hedley offered me five thousand pounds to withdraw Merry Day from the race at the very last minute. He wanted me to stake my money on Surplice instead as he had done."

"That's why you were so angry," she mused.

"I had good reason to be doubly so," he said enigmatically, more to himself than to her.

She decided it might be the right moment to show her hand. "Why did you pretend not to know Brett on that occasion? He was in the hall, but you passed him as if you had never seen him before in your life."

He was visibly shaken by her disclosure that she knew more than he had realized. "I'll not lie to you. I do know him, but there are the most urgent reasons why you should keep your discovery to yourself. How did you find out?"

"I was sitting on a stone by the river on the night you and Brett met at the bridge. I recognized him from his voice the first evening he arrived at Rushmere."

He shook his head in mingled astonishment and incredulity. "To think we believed that none would see or overhear us. He was passing through the district and I thought that such a place to meet was safe enough, it being important that he should not be seen at my home. To the best of my knowledge my servants are trustworthy, but there can be spies everywhere when high winnings are at stake, and the visit of a Jockey Club investigator would have been reported. It was imperative that Hedley in particular should have no cause to wonder whether Brett had come to seek or receive information." He gave her a long look. "I wasn't happy about letting Hedley book accommodation under your roof, but it was a way to give Brett the unique opportunity of keeping him under close surveillance."

"I suppose that means he went through Hedley's belongings to see what he might find," she exclaimed.

"He opened the medicine chest twice with a key of his own. It contains all the usual drugs to make a horse unfit to run or render a jockey incapable of riding, but that's no proof." He spread his hands wide. "All of those decoctions have domestic uses too. After the Derby, Brett opened the chest a second time and found that there was less opiate in one phial than before, but Hedley could swear that he needed it for toothache or rheumatism or anything else he cared to name."

"Isn't Hedley taking a great risk in using such potions? Suppose he misjudged a dose and brought about some unfortunate jockey's death?"

"He specializes more in bribes to make jockeys *pull* a race, but Nat Gobowen is a jockey of high principles who has never run a dishonest race in his life, and Hedley knew that. So you see why he had to use the method that he did. I had to have an assurance from Brett, whose idea it was that Hedley should stay here, that he would keep a close eye on you all the time the man was in your home, because Hedley is without scruples in all fields." He gave a rueful smile. "Brett was greatly alarmed when you set off to follow Silas just ahead of him. He decided to stay a little distance behind you, and when you turned into the entrance of the stable drive he thought you still had Silas in view and followed after. He was too far to prevent the attack on you when it came, but before he could reach you your brother had shone the lantern and he decided you would be in good hands. He tried to pick up Silas's trail again, but in vain—as I was so soon to discover to my cost."

"Surely Hedley's attempt to bribe you is proof enough for the stewards to see that he was responsible for interfering with the race—or is it that you dare not risk laying the evidence before them?" There was a fierce challenge in her tone, her expression one of despairing anger.

"Dare not?" He gave a nod. "Yes, for the time being I dare not, for there was none to bear witness. I hadn't counted on Silas closing the door and keeping guard over it after I had carefully left it ajar. Hedley is no fool."

"Was Brett to be that witness?"

"Yes. Both he and I had hoped that Hedley might let slip some word to reveal what skullduggery he had in mind for twisting the results of the Derby to suit his own ends, but when I heard Silas close the door I knew the chance had been lost again."

His answers puzzled her, for he had spoken consistently as a man with no guilt of his own to hide. She deliberated briefly. "I think I could help you to get the evidence you missed before."

"Brett and I will support you in every way," he replied with rising interest.

Unhappy impatience got the better of her. "How can you be so false when I heard with my own ears your plotting with Brett to fix the race at Newmarket with an older horse bearing another's name!"

He stared at her with lifted eyebrows and widening eyes. Then he laughed uproariously, tilting back his chair and showing every white tooth in his handsome head. "You thought that of me, did you?" He let the front chair-legs crash back to the floor again and with his heels he brought himself and the chair sliding forward in a single motion, his knees coming hard against her skirts, and he seized the wicker arms on either side of her, making it impossible for her to move back away from him. "No wonder you've been as touchy as a spitting cat more times than I care to remember!" His eyes, half-closed, glittered with merriment. "What Brett will say when he hears what you thought of him I cannot imagine! We were exchanging points on how to thwart *Hedley's* attempt to commit that very crime you thought us guilty of. We realized that if we failed it could jeopardize all chance of pinning him down at a later date, but we considered it worth the risk, having gathered plenty of information about what was afoot. We did manage to get the switch revealed, but he was crafty enough to dispose of the evidence, getting the horse away in the nick of time. It has been imperative all along for me to appear to be linked with the renegades of the racecourse while working in close co-operation with the Jockey Club, whose aim is to clear the Turf of scoundrels like Hedley and his ilk, who will stop at nothing to achieve their nefarious aims."

She was between laughter and tears in her relief at his words, radiant in her happiness.

"I thought my father mistrusted you and that's why he wanted to remove Young Oberon from your stables."

"No, no. It was simply for the reasons I gave you. I'm no saint —far from it, I fear!—but I've never taken part in a crooked deal in my life and your father knew that."

"But Amelia was blackmailing you!"

"What?" He laughed again. "Good God! Whatever gave you that idea?"

"How else did she get the money from you to leave Rushmere and start a new life elsewhere?"

"A simple business transaction. She had three old and precious books that your father had given her several years ago as security against her old age after deciding to leave you the house, and she gave me first chance to buy them from her for my own collection. They had been valued at a considerable figure, but she pressed me for a much higher and quite exorbitant price." He compressed his lips, eyeing her warily. "You won't care to hear it, I suppose, but in truth I considered them cheap at three thousand guineas, because I guessed I was being instrumental in procuring you your freedom from her. It was no surprise to me when her letter came telling me she had left Cudlingham."

She was looking down at her hands folded in her lap, remembering the gap on her father's bookshelves that had been filled with rubbishy editions that she had removed. "Were they books on horses by any chance?" she asked hesitantly.

"Yes. Three superb volumes printed once and once only in the late seventeenth century for a private individual, who had the most exquisite illustrations, some drawn, others watercolors, inserted into them. Scenes of racing on the Epsom Downs in centuries gone by."

"Tell me about some of them," she requested, scarcely able to comprehend Amelia's deceit in stealing and disposing of them.

"Well, there's the racing that took place in Henry II's time, and some splendid views of Nonesuch Palace—gone now, more's the pity!—when Elizabeth stayed there and with her court watched her gallants compete on horseback for the favor of a Royal glove or riband. Farther on there's a picture of James I enjoying the sport. Best of all I like the amusing illustration on that day in 1618 when the country fellow, Henry Whicker, couldn't get his cattle to drink water in an Epsom field—the discovery of the mineral spring that was to bring people from afar to sample its medicinal properties, and eventually to produce by refinement the famous salts. A series of pictures shows the people coming in their coaches and wagons—first to drink the water and then to attend the races, while all the time Epsom village grew on its new prosperity."

"What else is there?" she asked with wistful fascination.

"A double page shows the panorama of Charles I and his cavalry gathering on Epsom Downs to do battle with the Parliamentarians, and there are several delightful contemporary illustrations of Charles II and his ladies, trailing scarves and fans and the Royal spaniels, arriving and staying at the King's Head tavern in Epsom for the races." He frowned in smiling puzzlement. "I can't understand why Amelia did not show the volumes to you. You may look your fill of them now at any time."

Those books had been the jewels of her father's collection and, in that respect, hers too. The words of Amelia's farewell letter came back to her with a new meaning. Almost incredulously Tansy recalled the toil and labor she had gone through, the millstone of debt about her neck that would weigh her down for many years to come, and all the time she had had a fortune at Rushmere, which Amelia had taken from the bookshelves—yes! on the very night of her arrival at Rushmere—and hidden away. Those books, given to Dominic in lieu of payment to settle Oliver's debts, would have set her free. Free even to love this man who was still divided from her by a gulf of those outstanding obligations that had never pressed harder on her than at this moment.

Wrenching her mind away from a vain contemplation of what might have been, the chance of it gone forever, she drew breath and spoke again on the matter of gathering evidence against Hedley.

"When Epsom race week comes to an end," she said, "two gentlemen, as well as Hedley, will be staying on to attend another meeting at the Redstead course, which is only a comparatively short ride away. Let Brett stay on too." Briefly she outlined the plan she had in mind.

Dominic looked doubtful. "I don't know that we should try it. It could place you in grave danger."

"How could it? With you and Brett on hand to protect me nothing can go wrong," she said confidently, with a smile.

His gaze was warm and very tender. Taking both her hands into his he drew her forward, leaning over himself from the waist to place a kiss on the corner of her mouth. She became self-conscious about her appearance, dropping her head to hide the black patch over her eye, knowing her lower lip was still swollen, her cheek darkened by a bruise, but he continued to pull gently on her hands and as though it were the most natural thing for her to do she obeyed his unspoken request and pushed her chair away to slide onto his knees. His arms enfolded her and her head came to rest on his shoulder, her brow against his neck.

It was as if her heart surrendered at last after its long and vigilant battle against him. She knew only joy and contentment and peace in his arms. Though she was temporarily disfigured and unsightly, he still found her beautiful and showed it in his gentleness. With a lover's sensitive fingertips he stroked her hair away from her face.

"I love you, Tansy," he said softly. "I tried to tell you once before when I took your glove from your hand on the stairs at a party, but you gave me no encouragement. I have longed for this moment to come."

Even now she could not tell him that she loved him in return. The bright flicker of her independent spirit made it impossible. She had to be free of him to become his. One day she would be able to tell him. One day. When there were no more barriers between them.

On the wall the ugly kitchen clock, not wanted by Amelia when she departed, ticked languorously, its pendulum swinging to and fro, but neither Tansy nor Dominic noticed how the minutes passed and the hands moved on. Cocooned in love, she did not wish to stir, and he, holding her to him, inhaled the young bouquet of her, the fragrance of skin and hair, and marveled, as though he were a boy again in love for the first time, at the magic wrought upon his heart by her nearness. But perhaps it was the first time. Never, indeed, had he loved as he loved her.

It was Judith who finally disturbed them. Hearing no sound and thinking he must have departed, she opened the door and was in the room before she saw that Tansy was seated on his knees, his arms about her.

"I'm sorry," she stammered, blushing at her own intrusion. "I didn't know—I mean, I thought you had gone, Dominic." Then she saw by the way they smiled at each other, Tansy moving as lazily and luxuriously as a contented cat disturbed in sleep, that something inexplicable and wonderful had happened to make their enmity a thing of the past. The impact of what it meant to her personally made Judith speak out on a gust of relief: "I can tell all is well between you at last. It gladdens me for many reasons, and an ambition close to my heart can now be realized."

Tansy looked at her in mild surprise, her face still blissful. "What is this?"

"Some time ago—at the first musical evening we spent at the Manor—Dominic said he had a mare that would make a very quiet ride for me if I would like to make use of her. When I said I didn't know how to ride, never having been very strong, he said it should prove the best exercise for weak muscles and he would arrange that Mr. Kirby's son, Matthew, should teach me. I refrained from doing anything more about it, knowing how angry you were with Dominic and everything to do with Ainderly Hall at the time, but now!" She was radiant as she spoke. "Now I intend to have my first lesson very soon!"

Tansy swept forward and hugged her. "What a spendid idea." She knew Judith understood that she was giving a blessing on her falling in love with Matthew.

When Dominic left them they stood with arms about each other's slender waists. He kissed them both, Judith on the cheek and Tansy on her loving lips.

12.

Epsom race week came to an end. All the guests, except the four men staying on, Brett having fallen in with Tansy's plan, settled their bills with much voicing of appreciation. Judith dealt with them, as Tansy had kept out of sight of her guests and their servants since the night of the attack on her person, not now because of her unsightly appearance, but because it was decided that an element of surprise should be used in the trap that was to be set for Hedley.

Nina came home the same day. She brought no baggage with her, a bedroom having been set aside for her at the Manor where she kept overnight necessities and some of the new clothes that Edward had paid for. At first she would not leave her plain and serviceable underwear to be laundered there in her absence. But since it now had been replaced with the frilliest of petticoats, the most delicate chemises, and pantalets afoam with lace and ribbons, which she had purchased on shopping trips with Sarah, who was her close friend and constant chaperone, she was able to flit to and fro between Rushmere and the Manor with not so much as a comb to carry in whichever dainty little reticule was swinging from her wrist.

After sympathizing profusely with Tansy's bruises, having received an account of the attack, although the true reason for Tansy's presence in the vicinity of the Ainderly Hall stables had been kept a secret in spite of the incident being common talk in the village, Nina flitted about the room adjoining the kitchen. Tansy sat with a ledger, doing the accounts, while Nina pulled her French kid gloves from her hands by the tip of each finger, recounting the quite marvelous time she had had at the races. Judith paused in her sewing to listen with rapt attention. At first Nina was full of a tale being circulated about Lord George Bentinck, a prominent figure in the racing world, in whose party she had been with Edward and Sarah on Derby Day. All his life Lord George had longed for a Derby winner and he had sold Surplice with his stud only two years before, so his state of mind was one of regret and distress, to say the least.

"When he returned to the Houses of Parliament the next day," Nina continued, "he was sitting in the Library there—very glum, as you can imagine—and Disraeli came to offer his condolences. Lord George gave a long, deep groan, poor man! But here's the interesting part—Disraeli called the Derby the Blue Riband of the Turf. He was comparing it to the Order of the Garter, which has that special riband and is the highest honor in the land, as you know. I tell you, the phrase has quite caught on. Everyone is using it now to describe the Derby stakes."

She also had a fund of other tales to tell, accounts of her meetings with famous people in the political world and other spheres of society, her head quite turned with it all, the compliments paid to her repeated with relish and at great length.

Yet in spite of her turning up her nose at Rushmere, looking about her with a disparaging air as if after being at the Manor any other surroundings were hard to live with, she did not seem sorry to be back. Tansy noticed how often she glanced at the clock as the evening wore on, although no mention was made of a walk and all three girls went to bed at the same time. With Tansy still keeping away from the others in the house, she and Judith retired as usual to their room in the kitchen quarters, but Nina went upstairs to the box room, the guest who had occupied it having departed. Judith fell asleep almost at once. It took Tansy a little longer to drop off, because she thought she heard a faint creak on the rear stairs and then a sound that might have been the click of the kitchen door latch, but she knew herself to be mistaken, having bolted it with her own hands on the inside before retiring.

Every detail of the plan to trap Hedley was worked out among

Dominic, Brett, and Tansy herself. The two men decided that Judith should be told, as she would be in the house at the time, but not Nina, who would again be staying at the Manor for some event, the fewer people who knew of the plan the better. When Judith discovered that Hedley did not intend departing on the same evening as the other two guests, but would be leaving the following morning, Brett and Dominic came to the conclusion that it would be the right night to carry out their plan. Only Silas had to be reckoned with, but he normally retired to the stable loft before his master, who was always late to bed, went upstairs. Judith was given the task to keep watch and make sure he was out of the way.

Tansy woke on the morning of the appointed day with an uncomfortable flutter of nerves in her stomach. She could tell that Judith felt the same, and she was glad that Nina was at the Manor and out of it all. The day seemed incredibly long and she was reminded of Nina again many times in her own constant glancing at the clock as if the passing of time were all too slow an affair.

The two last guests returned from the Redstead races to collect their baggage and depart. Hedley arrived soon afterward and Tansy felt a twinge of misgiving when she saw that he was driving the four-in-hand himself and Silas was not with him. Obviously Hedley did not expect Silas to return to Rushmere within the next hour at least, for he unharnessed the horses himself and fed and watered them. Watching him from behind the kitchen window Tansy thought he appeared to be in a black mood, pulling on his thick lower lip, his huge black brows drawn into a straight line bushy as a hedge. She put a hand across her heart, aware of its nervous beating, when she heard his heavy footsteps go past the baize-lined door as he made for the stairs. When next he went up them she would be at the top of the rear stairs, ready to challenge him as he crossed the landing, coming face to face.

When it came to his dinnertime Judith wheeled the courses in and out of the dining room on a trolley, which enabled her to dispense with her stick, except when setting something down singlehanded on the table. She made conversation, letting him know that he was the last guest in the house, Brett having appeared to leave with the rest, but being in fact already installed in Nina's box room. While setting the fish course under its silver cover on the sideboard Judith inquired as casually as she could when she might expect Silas back for supper.

Hedley, slurping up the last spoonful of soup, a napkin tucked in his cravat, took a piece of roll and stuffed it into his mouth before replying in a spitting shower of crumbs. "I ain't certain." His voice growled with ominous displeasure that boded ill for his servant. "Shove a bowl of leavings on the stable loft steps. That's good enough for him if he should return."

At that point, quite without warning, the dining-room door opened and Silas came sliding into the room, a wide, gap-toothed grin on his ferrety face, his expression one of supreme satisfaction, but the grin vanished and fear became stamped upon his features when Hedley gave a great roar at the sight of him, threw his chair back, and sprang across with an amazing speed for a·man of his bulk. He seized Silas and shook him like a dog with a rat.

"You infernal idiot! You brainless fool! You lost me a pretty pickings and made me pay out half my Derby winnings in the bargain."

"I couldn't help it!" Silas whined on a high, shrill note of terror. "How was I to know they had switched stalls—"

"Shut your gab!" Hedley dealt the wretched man a violent blow across the mouth. "We ain't alone!" With a jerk of his head he indicated Judith, whom Silas had failed to notice. She was standing stunned by the scene. Hedley threw his servant from him contemptuously. "Get out of my sight!"

Silas needed no second bidding. Hedley returned to his chair and fell back in it. He had dropped his napkin in the skirmish and Judith picked it up and handed it to him.

"Thank you, my dear." He managed a kind of sick smile, but his thoughts were faraway. He ate the rest of his meal absently and with none of his usual gluttonous relish.

In the kitchen, with Tansy out of sight in the side room, Judith served Silas his supper. He was even more talkative than usual, telling her that the racecourse he had been to over the past two days could not compare with Epsom. "Not fashionable like Epsom is with the gentry," he said, tucking into his supper, his appetite unimpaired by the treatment he had received. "You wouldn't like it. No fancy bonnets and touch-me-not shawls, but solid racing folk aimin' to make a bit of money and have a bit of good sport like what they do at smaller meetings all over the country."

Judith made Hedley's coffee and took it in to him in the long drawing room. When she came back Silas had his elbows on the table, his food finished, and was picking his teeth with a splinter of wood.

"Mr. Hedley was within his right to lose his temper with me," he continued with such elaborate nonchalance that it was obvious he had suffered some discomfiture. "Gave him the wrong tip. A tout gave me the whisper and I thought I'd put Mr. Hedley on to a good thing. He knows I'm not often wrong about a horse, but I was in this case." He got up from the bench and came across to where she had started to wash up. "Here! I'll give you a hand."

"No, thank you, I would much rather you didn't," Judith insisted, but he seemed eager to be sociable, as if convivial company would be balm to his injured feelings, and he took a drying cloth and set to work. Unhappily she was aware that the cutlery, glass, and crockery used by Brett for his dinner, which had been taken to him secretly earlier, were among the things to be washed up. She did not think Silas would notice or count, nor place any significance to a few extra pieces if he did, but she decided it was best to keep him talking and his attention diverted. Unfortunately she was becoming increasingly nervous and when she dropped a glass she started as if the smash had been as loud as cannon fire.

"My, my! You're jumpy this evening," he said jocularly, getting a dustpan and brush to sweep up the fragments for her. "That's one down and how many to go?" He cast an eye over the rest of the glasses, meaning it as a joke, but Judith, who had never had to deceive before in her life, became even more agitated.

"There's no need to count them. Tansy had a guest for dinner anyway. Oh, I do wish you would leave the drying up to me!"

"That was nice for her," he said, watching Judith as he reached for another glass to wipe. "Havin' a guest, I mean. Company for her. Glad to know she's feelin' better."

A jingling of one of the bells on the wall made her glance with relief in its direction. "Someone at the door. I must go and answer it."

She removed her apron, took her stick, and hurried as fast as she could into the hall. To her astonishment and delight it was Matthew Kirby who stood on the step, dressed most dapperly in a check frockcoat and trousers. He doffed his hat and held it, smiling at her.

"Miss Judith! We meet again. I hope it's not too late to call on you, but Mr. Reade told me you were eager to start your riding lessons and I wondered if you would like your first turn in the saddle tomorrow."

"Oh, I would!" The wild rose tint was high in her cheeks and her eyes sparkled, all else forgotten before this vision of young manhood about whom she had dreamed, sighed, and languished over ever since that brief but momentous meeting in the grounds of Ainderly Hall. "Come in!"

In the small drawing room he sat opposite her, seemingly as much taken with her as she was with him, his wide, friendly mouth curved in a happy smile. She thought again how dear he was, how kind his eyes, and how pleasing his voice, which was mapping out how the lessons would progress.

"So I'll bring the mare along at ten o'clock then," he said, rounding up the arrangements. "With Patient Lady on the leading rein—and never was a mare better named!—you'll gain confidence in no time."

"I'm looking forward to it immensely," she said between shyness and gaiety. "It's most obliging of you to be my teacher."

"It's an honor," he replied eagerly. Then they both fell silent, aware they were on the brink of some experience that would be new to both of them, a fulfillment of the promise that each had felt in the other's presence when she had sat on the wagonette seat in the sun and he had looked up into her face and thought he had never seen a sweeter girl.

"What have you been doing today?" she asked in a rush, afraid he was on the point of leaving and wanting to extend his visit for as long as possible.

"I went with my father to the Redstead races. Oh, yes! Here am I forgetting to tell you. Roger Marlow was riding again. That's the sixth time he's worn the Ainderly Hall colors, and he did better in his race today than he has done any of the times before. There was a real determination in his face when my father gave him last instructions and told him to ride to win."

"Did he win?" she inquired eagerly.

He looked sorry to disappoint her. "I'm afraid not, but he held a good position all the way and came in third. In his other races he's been well back and once he was last, so this was a big stride forward."

"He'll be the greatest jockey England's ever had one day," she said serenely and with perfect confidence.

"I hope you're right. I had dreams like that once, and then suddenly I grew like a weed to my present height, and so now I'm learning to be a trainer instead. Anyway, my father was pleased with Roger's performance, but it was a good day spoiled for everybody by the discovery that one of the runners in the most important race of the meeting had been 'got at.' Bloody Silas, as everyone calls him, was questioned by the stewards for over an hour. He's been staying here with his master, Selwyn Hedley, hasn't he?"

"They're still here. They don't leave until the morning. What happened?"

"Well, this runner—a dappled gray colt—had been nobbled by a most fiendish and cunning method. A silk kerchief had been wrapped about his leg and then that leg beaten until a sinew was sprung. The stewards had a report that Bloody Silas was seen in the vicinity of the stables some time yesterday, but he was able to prove he was elsewhere. The stewards might have been less easily persuaded of his innocence if his master had raked in a big win, but strangely enough Hedley had his money on that very colt and suffered a heavy loss."

Judith's gentle face showed her distress and horror at the dreadful deed. "Such cruelty! How can men be so inhumane! You mentioned a silk kerchief—"

"It was found in some straw mucked out from the stall. The discovery was made after nearly everybody had left, and it must have been dropped accidentally by the wretch who committed that foul act. My father and I were having a drink with one of the stewards in a local pub when the kerchief was brought in for him to see. It was expensive silk—a gentleman's kerchief—but there are hundreds like it."

"Does Silas know of the discovery of this clue?"

"No, he doesn't. But as I said, he has already cleared himself."

"Suppose Tansy or I could identify it as being like one of Hedley's? He has a variety of them that he wears flowing from his tail pocket. He is quite a dandy, but in the worst possible taste."

He looked doubtful. "You would never be able to prove it was Hedley's, although there's no harm in your having a look at it. I'll ask the steward to arrange it. They would be glad of anything they could chalk up against Hedley, but this is one crime that can't be laid at his door."

She was tempted to tell him of that revealing snatch of a sentence spoken by Silas before Hedley silenced him. Silas must have injured the wrong colt because he had mistaken the stall or else the horses had been stabled differently since he had learned of the whereabouts of the one he had been instructed to maim. It was best to save that information for Dominic and Brett and Tansy for the time being. That reminded her that time was ticking by and she should be making sure that Silas was on his way to the stable loft.

"I haven't a proper riding habit," she said, reverting to the original topic of their conversation.

"It's no matter," he said, thinking how she would have outshone the haughty Nina, who rode with Edward Taylor and parties from the Manor, had she the same fine habit to wear. "Just put on a simple dress, a jacket for warmth, because there can be a cool wind blowing sometimes across the slope of the Downs where I'll be taking you, and a band to keep your hair in order."

She did not know how she would be able to wait until morning came, for he had conjured up a picture for her of the two of them alone with the wind and sky and grass and flowers, two quiet horses taking them wherever they wanted to go. "I'll not sleep this night for thinking of the morning," she exclaimed happily.

"Nor I," he answered, pleased to see how the color flowed up into her cheeks again. He could have stayed talking to her until it was the very hour of their appointment, but he knew he must take his leave without further delay.

She went with him to the door. Accidentally their hands touched and it fired their eyes to swift meeting, each seeing the other's own deep pleasure at the contact reflected there.

"Until tomorrow then," he said, dawdling on the step.

"Good night, Mr. Kirby."

"No—Matthew, please!"

"Very well, Matthew."

He turned round a dozen times in the drive, his step buoyant, to wave his hat and make sure she was still there, standing in the lamplight, smiling and waving back to him, watching him out of sight. It was an image of her that he was never to forget, an image that was to stay with him till his long life's end.

Back in the kitchen Judith found that Silas had finished washing up and had put everything away. To her dismay he had settled himself in the rocking chair with his clay pipe and showed no sign of moving off to bed as he usually did.

"I really must ask you to retire," she said firmly. "It's getting late and I want to lock up."

He took several more puffs on his pipe, watching her closely, and just when she was afraid he was going to ignore her request he acquiesced with a nod, stirred himself lazily, and tilted the rocking chair forward as he knocked out his pipe against the cooking range.

"Yes, it's gettin' late." He swung himself leisurely toward the back door. "I bid you good night then. I'll be right sorry to leave this comfortable place tomorrow. The grub has been real tasty."

She shot the bolt home on the door with as much noise as possible to make sure he heard it as he went down the path. Tansy emerged from the rooms off the kitchen at the same time.

"I thought he was never going!" she exclaimed, her face taut with tension. "Hedley hasn't gone upstairs yet, has he?"

"No, he's emptying a bottle of brandy in the long drawing room. But listen to what I learned this evening!" Swiftly she recounted all that Matthew had told her, linking it with what Silas had blurted out in the dining room.

"That's splendid. It will give me extra verbal ammunition to use if I should need it. Is the front door locked?"

"Yes, I fastened that after Matthew left."

"Then go to the long drawing room and make sure that Hedley is still ensconced in his chair. I'll go upstairs to our old room and watch to make certain Silas has settled down in the stable loft and then you come up and take over from me to see he doesn't come sneaking over to the house again."

"What about the back door?"

"I'll unbolt that ready for Dominic afterward. He'll be waiting for the signal of the kitchen lamp going out and then he'll come in."

Tansy took from a cupboard a hidden, emptied brandy bottle, one of two that Dominic had recovered from his jockey after the debauch, and then she sped up the rear stairs. At the top she rapped with her knuckles once on the box-room door. Brett replied with two taps to let her know he was alert and ready to bear witness to anything Hedley might be trapped into revealing. She ran on into the unlit bedroom that gave the best view of the stables. She breathed a sigh of relief. The lamp that Silas used there was alight. There should be nothing more to fear from him.

Shortly afterward Judith arrived, breathless with effort, and she collapsed in the chair pushed up to the window. In the darkness she smiled at her sister, reaching out a hand. "Good luck, Tansy!"

Tansy clasped it and leaned forward, their cheeks coming together in a swift pressure of affection. "I'll do my best!"

Somewhere in the house there came a faint thud. "What was that?" Judith whispered tensely.

Tansy went to the door and listened. "I think it was Hedley moving about downstairs. I must go."

She flew down the rear stairs again, shot back the bolt on the door, doused the lamp, and returned to take up her position at the head of the same flight. A single lamp burned on the landing. She would see Hedley coming up the main staircase before he would see her. How loud her heart was beating!

Downstairs she heard the latch of the door lift and felt the rush of a cool draft. Footsteps entered quietly, but without secrecy, telling her that Dominic had come to install himself beyond the curve of the flight in that well of darkness. The latch fell into place again and all was still. With confidence she squared her shoulders, hearing Hedley's heavy footsteps leaving the long drawing room to take him on his way to bed. There was no need to be afraid.

Outside the back door Nina, who had slipped indoors to replace her light cloak with the dark one on the downstairs peg, adjusted the hood as she set off at a run across the lawn, making for the gates into the lane. When she reached them she paused, seeing that the carriage in which Edward had brought her home from the Manor to these same gates was well and truly out of sight. Then she bolted down the lane in the opposite direction and turned into the path leading through Ashby Woods, which she had made her own. Edward had wanted her to remain at the Manor until the morrow, but she could not stay one night more away from Adam—he would be frantic for her.

In her haste she failed to realize that for once she had been seen and someone was in pursuit of her. Dominic, emerging from the distant cover where he had been waiting, did not connect her with the carriage he had heard pass by some minutes ago but had glimpsed her cloaked figure speeding from the house and thought at once it was Tansy fleeing in terror. Something must have gone desperately wrong with their plans! Had Hedley used violence against her?

"Tansy!" he called urgently. "Wait!"

The running figure did not hear him and when he reached the gates he glimpsed the distant flick of a cloak vanishing from the starlit darkness of the lane into the blackness of the woods. He called her name again, but when he reached the spot where he thought she had disappeared he could find no trace of a path and the thickness of the trees shut off the sound of his voice and made it rebound. Pushing her way at a run through the foliage, which snapped back into place behind her with a wild rustling of leaves and creaking of branches, Nina was deaf already to the outside world, her ears hearing only the whispers of her lover that were to come.

At Rushmere, Hedley had reached the top of the stairs and was pausing to get his breath and his balance, for he was deep in liquor, and he leaned his weight on the huge, powerful hand that rested on the balustrade of the landing. He lifted surprised eyes when Tansy moved from the deepest shadows where she stood, the lamplight falling across her skirt and faintly illumining her face.

"Hey! Who's this then? Miss Marlow, I do declare! Recovered, are you? You'll know better than to go visiting unannounced at Ainderly Hall on the eve of another Derby Day, won't you?"

She moved a step forward, bringing more light onto her face, the patch on its ribbon showing black over her eye. "I wasn't visiting that night. I was following Silas and lost him when he went on to give Nat Gobowen the brandy which had been laced by the drug that you keep in your medicine chest."

Hedley breathed strongly through his wide nostrils. "You're a brave young woman to throw such an accusation at me. Who's putting you up to this?"

"I made up my own mind to tell you what I know." Out of the folds of her skirt she brought the brandy bottle, which she had been hiding behind her. "There is money to be had for such bottles, and I managed to get them returned to me." She embarked on her huge bluff, conscious of no more than a drain of brandy swilling in the bottom of it. "No bottle can ever be completely emptied. What would you say if I told you that the faint aroma of a certain opiate still lingers?"

"I should say you were lying."

"Indeed? Then you have no objection if I take this flask to a knowledgeable person—"

"Take it to whom you please," he scoffed. "That bottle is no different from any other and you know it. I'll also remind you that it's no concern of mine if my servant chooses to get drunk with an old racing comrade."

"Silas wouldn't have touched a drop of the contents of this bottle or the other, even though to Nat Gobowen's eyes he may have appeared to. He knew—as I do—that after you had taken the two bottles into your room first, a certain phial in your medicine chest had less liquid in it than before." She held her breath, waiting on tenterhooks to see how he would react.

A terrible scowl congested his face. "If I thought my medicine chest had been tampered with I'd wring that white neck of yours!"

"It was opened twice—once before and once after Nat Gobowen's night of drunkenness."

"You dare to confess it!" His voice was a bellow and he took a few lumbering, bull-like strides toward her, enormous fists clenched at his sides. "What's your game? Blackmail? You wouldn't try it if you knew what had happened to others who have attempted it in the past!"

"Tell me," she taunted. "I'm not afraid."

He lowered his head, looking under his thick brows. "I don't believe you are," he said slowly, "but then you don't know what it means to have a cracked skull or a lamed leg or a crushed foot."

"Is that what you inflict on jockeys who think to pay you back in your own coin? Some injury to prevent them ever riding again?"

"None tries to trick me and gets away with it! Not jockey or tout or bookmaker—or anyone in debt to me! A slip of a girl like you can be silenced easier than any of 'em."

"Not when I have such evidence as this." She held up the brandy bottle again.

He moved with incredible swiftness, thrusting one hand against her shoulder with the force of his weight behind it, and she went thudding back against the wall between the box-room door and the head of the rear stairs, knocking her head a painful blow, and with the other hand he tore the brandy bottle from her and hurled it from him. It smashed against the opposite wall. "To hell with your paltry evidence!" he thundered.

"I have the other bottle," she gasped defiantly.

He brought his enraged face down on a level with hers, his huge shoulders hunched, holding her pinioned with both hands. "You know as well as I do that it can prove nothing! I ain't been going my own way this long to be caught like that. Now tell me what's behind all this!" He gave her another thud against the wall to emphasize his lack of patience.

"I would have won on Merry Day if it hadn't been for you!"

"So that's it!" He relaxed, giving an evil, mirthless grin. "It's compensation you want. Well, threats ain't the line to use with me. I told you the first night I was here that I could be generous when I had good reason to be. You weren't ready then, but it seems you are now. What did you do? Take a gamble and place all you expected to get when your racing lodgers settled their bills on that unfortunate filly? I'm prepared to give you what you might have won, but at my odds and no lagging to the winning post."

He gave a thrust of his thighs against her, his foul breath in her face, and nausea combined with near panic almost overcame her, so great was her revulsion, and she longed to scream and kick and wrench herself free, but all would be lost if she failed now.

"It's not compensation for my loss on Merry Day that I want," she retaliated, "but for you to receive retribution for fouling the Derby—and not for the first time, according to all I've heard—and also for what you ordered Silas to do to that poor colt at Redstead."

His whole body stiffened, every muscle tensing as if a tornado of rage beyond measure was gathering in him and was about to burst free. "What fresh lie is this?"

She spoke through her teeth at him, her mind full of the picture of that race horse in its agony. "I have it in my power to rid the Turf of you and your crooked dealings once and for all. Silas managed to persuade the stewards that he'd had nothing to do with it, but after he left the racecourse a silk kerchief was found in the straw—one that he dropped by accident after the deed was done. One that I laundered for you during your stay here. One that I shall be able to identify."

His rage vibrated down through his fingertips and his grip almost crushed her shoulders. "A kerchief—like a brandy bottle—can belong to anybody!"

"Not in this case. In order not to muddle the many kerchiefs I took for washing from my guests, together with their shirts, cravats, and underwear, I made my own tiny laundry mark on them. A mark known only to me. A mark used by nobody else."

His rage broke. He clamped one huge hand over her face, pinching her nostrils together with a vise-like hold between thumb and first finger, his vast, clammy palm completely covering her mouth. With brain-splitting terror she realized that he was going to smother her. Why hadn't Brett come out of the box room? Where was Dominic?

She let her knees go deliberately, sagging like a rag doll. It loosened his hold and she gulped in air to emit a scream, but his hand was hard over her mouth and nose again and she was completely overpowered. In vain she fought and struggled, but he thwarted her attempts to kick him in the groin, and she was helpless, knowing as clearly as if he had told her that when life was snuffed out of her he intended to hurl her down the stairs, her silence made absolute, her death seemingly an accident.

"Let her go!" ordered Judith's voice. "Or I'll shoot you!"

In his murderous wrath he had forgotten all about the frail-looking girl whose limping form had never attracted him. He released the pressure on Tansy's nose, but continued to keep his hand over her mouth. Judith faced him with a double-barreled sporting gun used for shooting game, and Tansy recognized it instantly as their father's last gift to Roger, which had been found in his saddlebags together with the dress materials brought for them, but it was not loaded and Judith had placed herself equally at Hedley's mercy if he did but know it.

But Judith had loaded it, having seen her brother and father load such a gun often enough. It abhorred her to handle it and her hands were shaking violently. Her balance was also unsteady, for she had left her stick by the bedroom chair from which she had risen in fear when she had heard the smash of the brandy bottle. She had not been able to hear all that had passed between her sister and Hedley, but when the voices of Dominic and Brett failed to come forth her instinct told her that something had gone seriously wrong with the plan. A glimpse through a crack in the door had shown her that Tansy was being manhandled, and without hesitation she had opened the bedroom cupboard and taken down from an upper shelf Roger's gun and box of ammunition. Thus armed she had moved silently and slowly toward the man, using the wall for support until she came to the balustrade.

"Put that gun down," Hedley snarled, his mind racing as to how he could cope with this new and totally unexpected development.

"Take your hand away from Tansy's mouth and let her go!" She moved along the balustrade, her hip sliding against it, and she reached the round-topped newel post.

Knowing he could do nothing while she pointed the gun at him and ever being in the habit of putting first things first, he lunged out with his free arm to jerk the gun by its barrel from her grasp. Judith's finger, bent about the trigger, hooked as she wheeled backward down the rear stairs, thrust completely off balance, and the gun exploded its shot full in Hedleys' face. The noise of it was the last sound she heard in life, Tansy's scream forming piercing overtones, and then her head struck a stair and the next tumble snapped her slender neck.

Dominic, having relinquished his search for the vanished figure in the woods, heard the shot as he charged across the lawn, bent on discovering the cause of her flight from Rushmere.

Wrenching open the door he rushed in to find Tansy herself leaning over the slumped body of Judith at the curve in the stairs.

"Merciful God! What happened?" he demanded hoarsely.

Tansy raised her stunned face to him as he reached her and dropped to a knee at her side. "She's dead."

He felt for the girl's pulse, although the lolling position of her head told him it was all in vain. Seeing no wound on her he looked toward the head of the flight and saw Hedley lying there.

Swiftly he mounted the stairs and at the sight of the remains of Hedley's face he pulled out his own handkerchief and covered it. Turning to the box room he found the door difficult to open and had to push hard. Brett lay unconscious on a rumpled rug as if it might have been pulled from under him, but it was more likely that a blow at the back of the head had been added by an unseen assailant for good measure. Dominic ran to the window, which was unfastened, and threw it wide. Directly outside was the roof of the rooms adjoining the kitchen below. Anyone could have climbed up there and caught the watching and waiting Brett unawares.

Brett was stirring with a groan. Dominic went quickly to help him up into a sitting position on the bed. "Listen to me, Brett! Hedley is shot and Judith Marlow has a broken neck. I know none of the details, but I have to see that Edward Taylor is fetched right away. He's the local magistrate. For God's sake pull yourself together, man!"

"Ouch, my head!" Brett, still dazed, ran a hand gingerly over it. "I think I slipped on the rug or something. The last I remember is cracking my head against the door soon after Miss Marlow rapped on it." He frowned, trying to concentrate. "Hedley's dead, did you say?"

Dominic had already left him. Tansy, dry-eyed and white-lipped, was still leaning over Judith, holding one limp hand to her cheek. Gently Dominic lifted the dead girl up in his arms and carried her through to the long drawing room where he laid her on the couch.

Again Tansy sank down on her knees on the floor and this time she spread her arms over Judith, resting her head on the girl's breast, shocked to a grief beyond tears.

Out in the hall Dominic unlocked the door and ran down the drive. At the gates he saw to his relief a dogcart approaching, its lamps like pale eyes. When it drew near he rushed to meet it, and the man with the reins was a farmer he knew well. A request to go at once to the Manor to fetch the squire on urgent and tragic business to Rushmere sent the farmer whipping up his horse, with no time lost in useless questioning. Dominic, about to go back into the house, remembered Silas, who was most surely responsible for the attack on Brett, and he went through to the stableyard and up into the loft, expecting to find the man had flown. Instead Silas was in bed, apparently asleep and snoring, and when Dominic hurled the covers from him and yanked him to his feet he professed a bewildered innocence at having been disturbed. Dominic, anxious to return to Tansy, left him there, not bothering with what he was sure were unnecessary explanations, and turned the key on him to make sure he stayed there for questioning by Edward and himself later.

In the long drawing room Tansy was still in the same position as if life had drained from her as well, but when he stooped to put an arm about her shoulder she reached for his hand and held it hard, taking strength from his warm and sustaining grip.

Nina walked swiftly and angrily back along the path through Ashby Woods. Her ecstatic coming together with Adam again had been ruined by the quarrel that had taken place afterward. All because she had told him that at the end of the month she would be going to Paris for the choosing of her wedding gown. When he had heard that she would be absent for six weeks at least, he had said it was far too long and she must find an excuse to cut the time short. Then, when she had refused to consider the suggestion, he had threatened to travel to Paris himself in order that they should have a clandestine meeting somewhere. This risky proposition she had also turned down, and it was then that the squabbling had started, not to be mended on this occasion with renewed love-making, but ending with wounding words, and he had not come back along the path with her to see her into the lane for the first time since she had told him that she loved him.

Nearing Rushmere, she was gripped by alarm. The house was full of lights! She had not been overlong with Adam, no more than a couple of hours at the most, but it was long after midnight and by rights all should be in darkness. There was even a lamp alight in the stable loft and the door stood open. Was someone ill? Entering the grounds by the kitchen garden gate she made for the back door and slid through warily. Voices somewhere in the direction of the small drawing room! Quickly she removed the cloak she had about her shoulders and replaced it on its peg. Then she checked her appearance in a looking glass, redressed some disarranged tresses with a pocket comb, and after composing her face into a mask of innocence went through into the hall.

The double doors of the small drawing room stood open. Within she could see Dr. Westlake writing at a side table, the inkpot drawn up into easy reach of his scratching pen, and nearby Silas stood protesting that if he were guilty he would have done a bunk, wouldn't he? Guilty of what, she wondered. Brett, seated in a chair, a hand to his head as if it ached, was listening to him, and also present was Dominic, whose back was toward her. That there was another man in the room out of her line of vision was revealed by his shadow pacing to and fro across the floor.

Silas launched into a fresh tirade, throwing his arms about. "No, I didn't nip out and light the lamp in the stable loft when Miss Judith had a visitor; I did it when I went to bed after she told me she wanted to lock up. I wasn't lurkin' in the garden or climbin' on the kitchen roof to do harm to Mr. Brett here. I allus kept an eye on my master, I admit, and made sure none meant him any harm, but on this occasion I went straight to sleep in the stable loft. As Heaven is my witness, I swear it!"

He is lying, Nina's mind registered as she entered the room. A whole pack of lies, whatever it may all mean. Then she forgot Silas in her shock and dismay at seeing that the other man in the company was Edward. He swung about and glared at her, fury and relief at her return blended with sharp suspicion.

"Where the devil have you been?"

She did not answer him, her gaze traveling to the other men's faces. Silas, thankful for a diversion, was chewing his lip nervously, and the other three looked terribly grave. Something dreadful must have happened, but what?

"Where is Tansy?" she demanded on a sharply rising note, a sick stab of fear in the pit of her stomach that was more deadly than Edward learning of her nocturnal wanderings, for she had long since concocted a tale for such an emergency. "Where *is* she?"

"She is in bed," Dominic replied. "Dr. Westlake has given her a sleeping draught."

"Why? For what reason? What has been taking place here?"

Edward and Dominic exchanged glances. Then Edward came and took Nina by the hand, putting his other arm about her waist to take her with him out of earshot into the dining room on the other side of the hall. After a few minutes there burst forth the sound of her sobbing, hysterical, grief-stricken, and shot through with remorse. Dominic, taking the two death certificates from the doctor, who had finished writing them out, wondered again what had possessed Nina to go wandering about at night. He had been able to tell by the look on Edward's face that he intended to find out the reason why and would allow no more of it. Dominic groaned inwardly. If only her appearance had not misled him. Who would have thought that it would be she in Tansy's distinctive, dark green cloak?

13.

In the early sunlight of an April morning Tansy sat on a low wall shading her eyes as she watched Young Oberon streak past her along the gallops, Roger in the saddle. How that colt could run! How that brother of hers could ride! Nearly a year had gone by since he had been tried out on other horses and now he shone like a rising star and was to ride Young Oberon in the forthcoming Derby, which was to be run on Wednesday, the twenty-third of May, in five weeks' time.

Her hands lowered to her lap, her eyes becoming shadowy with sorrow as she remembered the tragic event that had followed in the wake of last year's Derby. From the moment of Judith's untimely death she had hated Rushmere, and never once since had she used that ill-fated rear staircase, always going up and down the main flight. Nina, too, avoided those stairs. It always seemed to Tansy that something of Judith's sweet presence still lingered there, and with anguish she recalled how it had been Judith herself who had been struck by fear at the first sight of Rushmere and had said that it looked like a place that might harbor a ghost. But whatever it was of Judith that still touched the heart with a gentle warmth whenever one passed the foot of those stairs, her body lay at rest with her foster parents faraway in a Hampshire churchyard. Dominic had accompanied Tansy on that long, sad journey, Nina being prostrate in her bedroom at the Manor, her tumultuous and genuine grief making it impossible for either Edward or Sarah to leave her to attend the distant funeral, and thus her true relationship with Oliver Marlow remained a secret yet.

There was no denying that Nina had changed considerably since the tragedy, becoming highly nervous and emotional. For a time it had seemed she might suffer a breakdown, unable to bear Tansy out of her sight, needing her constant support and comfort, bowed down by some weight of guilt that was out of all proportion to her having borrowed a dark cloak instead of using her own light one to be less conspicuous on her nocturnal walks. "But you don't understand," she had cried over and over again. "I always borrowed your cloak so that if I was ever seen people would think I was you and no gossip would get back to Edward about my wandering about. I didn't care if you were talked about. Don't you see how wicked I've been? Now I've had my punishment. Oh, oh, oh!" She became lost in wailing again.

It was this obsession that she alone was responsible for Judith's death that made the doctor fear for her sanity and advise both Tansy and Edward that she should be taken far from Rushmere on a long vacation that was a complete rest. When Nina refused to go without Tansy it was natural that Edward should implore Tansy to accompany them, which she did, taking Sarah's place as chaperone, traveling with her white-faced, hollow-eyed sister and her betrothed, a retinue of servants in tow, to the South of France and a luxurious villa. A large sailing craft was hired and there were days spent in picturesque harbors or in idyllic drifting along the water within sight of the lush, bright-foliaged coast. Thus it was that Tansy was not at Goodwood with Dominic to see Roger ride Young Oberon to victory, the whole, vast crowd on its feet uttering thunderous cheers at the speed with which the colt passed the winning post, four lengths ahead of the rest of the field. Other triumphs followed. Tansy missed them all, but Dominic wrote her in great detail, and now and again a letter came from Roger, his writing less descriptive, but full of praise for Young Oberon and closing always with the hope expressed that Nina was feeling better.

When it became apparent that Nina was recovering Edward decided that the time had come to move on to Paris, and there, ensconced in the Hôtel du Louvre, Nina came to life again, the nights a round of champagne, dancing, and every kind of social pleasure combined with ardent kisses from a happier Edward, who had brooded long over the discovery of her late night walks, disturbed that she had found it necessary—according to the little she would say on the matter—to be completely alone with the moon and the stars in order to contemplate how much his love had changed her existence and to ponder whether she had truly set his foot and hers on the right course by agreeing to marry him. That she should have been harboring second thoughts about marrying him had given plausibility to such restless behavior, but as soon as she was fully herself again he seized the first opportunity to question her closely.

"Those midnight walks of yours, my dear," he began, watching her keenly under his lashes. They were having tea and pastries one afternoon after taking a ride in the Bois de Boulogne, Tansy having left them on their own for a little while. "Won't you tell me more about them?"

Nina turned guileless eyes on him, dabbing a tiny flick of sugared cream from her luscious lips with a lace-trimmed afternoon napkin. "Of course, Edward dear. What can I tell you? You must remember that my illness has dulled my memory, and it all seems so long ago."

He was torn with uncertainty, and felt himself a boor to persist. Her whole face was innocent, her attitude frank and trusting. How could he harbor those nagging suspicions instead of putting them from his mind completely?

"I just can't understand why you couldn't have confided in me about your worries, don't you know," he said.

She leaned slightly forward to rest her hand on his across the small circular table, her expression loving. "To you least of all, beloved—you would have swayed me with your tender words and I should have come no nearer to solving my dilemma."

"Then you could have talked to Tansy or—or—" He did not care to mention Judith's name, fearing to reawaken all the old distress, but she completed the sentence for him as if to prove her recovery.

"—Judith?" She shook her head, her smile wan and sweet. "How could either of them have understood the special strength of my love? Had I been selfish I'd have given no thought to whether our marriage should or should not take place, but your happiness was more important to me than my own. I had to be sure, and now I am. You have proved it to me over these past weeks."

"But to wander about in the darkness!" he persisted.

She dropped her lashes, with a little frown, almost as if she was losing patience with him, but when she swept them upward again he saw he must have been mistaken, so dewy was her gaze. "I was born in the country. I'm at home with the trees and the grass and the flowers. The quietness of the night amid woods and meadows was balm to me. Is that so difficult to comprehend?" She gave a tinkling little laugh. "Anyone would think you imagined me to be stealing off to meet a Romeo."

So naturally was it said, so openly and with such innocence that he laughed with her, suddenly reassured. Consumed by a swift rise of desire for her, he raised her hand to his lips and kissed her fingers. She flustered prettily, always shy and quick to restrain him whenever he became demonstrative, and he told himself he could not imagine that she—of all people!—would indulge in an amorous escapade.

"This is Paris, my darling," he said happily, noticing how she glanced about in case they were observed. "The city of lovers."

Lovers. The word hung like a tiny shadow. No, he didn't doubt her purity, but he knew himself condemned ever after to watch her like a hawk. When they were married he'd see that she paid him back for all the unnecessary worry and torment she had caused him, and the coin he'd take from her would be smelted in the passion and ardor that had yet to thaw the ice that enclosed her.

Tansy would have left them in Paris and traveled on home if it had been possible, but Nina could not be left without a chaperone and in any case was as demanding as ever of her company, no longer for constant mothering, but for advice and companionship when ordering and buying the vast amount of clothes, bonnets, and shoes deemed essential to her trousseau. Tansy, filled with a hungry longing to see Dominic, whose company she had missed desperately at the time when she had needed him most, took solitary expeditions whenever the chance was presented, wanting to be on her own, and she enjoyed visits to the Louvre and strolls in the parks and under the autumn-tinted chestnuts by the Seine. Twice she climbed up to Montmartre, buying a picnic luncheon of crusty rolls and cheese on the way; there she sat on the grass amid the turning windmills and gazed at the city spread out below.

They stayed long enough in Paris for Nina's wedding gown to be designed, fitted, and completed, and it was in time for Christmas at the Manor that they returned to Cudlingham and found it covered with a blanket of new-fallen snow. As the carriage passed Rushmere, Tansy looked out at it closed and shuttered in the late afternoon dusk. Selwyn Hedley had gone unmourned by any. Not even Silas had shown the slightest sign of grief, although he had been consumed by bitterness for the personal loss of an influential master, who must have paid him handsomely, if nothing else, but the concern to save his own skin had been uppermost in his mind and his talk had been solely to that end. He managed to get away with it, it being impossible to set up any concrete evidence against him. In spite of everything pointing to Silas having been in the box room until the sound of the gun going off had sent him scrambling back out of the window, Brett could not swear to seeing him or to remembering anything except the rug slipping under his feet. Silas must have overheard all that passed on the landing, but he had known that his innocence at Redstead had already been established even if the silk kerchief was proven to be his master's. Tansy's threat of the laundry mark had been the biggest bluff of all. She had indeed marked each article, but what she had not told Hedley was that she removed each colored cross-stitch mark when she sorted the clean laundry back into individual piles. Often she was haunted by the dark, vicious look Silas had given her when he had learned the truth of it, and she could not shake off the feeling that he would seek to get even with her if ever the chance came his way.

At the Manor she was given a room next to Nina's. She had

dressed for dinner in a Parisian gown of creamy velvet, a gift from her future brother-in-law in appreciation of all she had done for Nina and himself, when a maidservant came to tell her that Dominic had called to see her. She hastened at a run down the long corridors, her wide crinoline caught in both hands to lift the hem free of her winged feet, and she came at last to the head of the grand staircase and saw him waiting in the hall below, his cape over his arm. "Dominic!"

She had only breathed his name, but he turned his head sharply and stared up at her with an exultant look of love and longing. Then he was speeding up the stairs to her, and she was flying down. They met halfway, she throwing herself passionately against him, he receiving her with open arms that crushed her to him, their mouths lost in ardent and unassuageable rediscovery. He was still kissing her when he swept her down with him toward the entrance doors.

"Where are we going?" she asked, laughing and breathless.

"To Ainderly Hall. For once I owe you some money and I intend to settle the matter without delay."

"I don't understand!"

He would give her no explanation, but threw his own cape about her, too impatient to let her fetch her own, and he bore her out to his carriage through the falling snowflakes. Within minutes they were at his home. He took her at once into his study, sat her down at his desk, and brought forward an almost new ledger with a shiny, red leather binding, which he opened and set before her.

"There, look at that! See the first entry? Seventeen pounds. That was your first repayment to me of your father's debt. Now see how I invested it."

Incredulously she studied the entries, seeing how he had gambled with the money, placing bets on one horse and then another. There were some losses, but more wins, an accumulated amount being put on Young Oberon at a time when odds were still long against him, and when he had raced home first past the winning post it brought her small original sum to more than a thousand pounds. Not content with that, Dominic had gone on to bet with those winnings again, and now as she stared at the total figure she could scarcely believe her eyes.

"It more than covers my father's debts and the mortgage on Rushmere," she said in a whisper. Then she pressed her fingertips to her lips, too choked for further speech, seeing he had swept away the last barriers between them.

He twisted her chair round on its swivel and crouched down beside her, taking hold of her wrists as he looked into her face. "You're free of me now, my love. In truth, you've been free of me from the start, but it would have been no good trying to convince you. I tore up those promises of payment from your father the day I heard that he had died and shoved the pieces in a packet in my desk intending to throw them on the fire, but I was interrupted and forgot about them until the day you first came to this house with such animosity toward me in your eyes that I knew if I let you go I should never get near you again. I burned them after you left."

She gave her head a self-admonitory shake. "I was foolish and stubborn. I blamed you for everything. How could I have been so blind?"

"It's all over now." He stood up, drawing her to her feet with him, and put his arms about her. "I loved you from the moment you came bursting into that village tavern with your hair disheveled and your eyes blazing. I knew that you were the woman I had been waiting for all my life and the reason why I had never met anyone else I had wanted to marry. I made up my mind then and there that somehow I would have you for my own. My methods may have been unorthodox, but desperate straits need desperate measures."

A little smile played on her lips and she put up her hands to rest them lightly against his face. "I don't know when I first began to love you. Perhaps it happened then, too. I only know that I was aware of and resented the magnetism that existed between us, but the more I tried to resist it as time went on the more prone to it I became."

"Say you love me now. Say you'll be my wife."

"Oh, yes," she breathed, her lids drooping, her face loving and tender and ecstatic. "I love you now and for always."

That Christmas gave her the greatest happiness she had ever known. On her finger she wore a betrothal ring of a diamond set with pearls. Dominic was included in the Manor party and amid the games and the festivities it was their greatest joy to snatch a few minutes alone together to exchange yet another kiss, to whisper and laugh and kiss again. On the morning of Boxing Day when the hunters were brought out and saddled for the benefit of those among Edward's house guests who wished to ride to hounds, Tansy viewed the new stables, the work of rebuilding having been completed before the Lord of the Manor's return. According to Edward, who was well pleased with all that had been done, Adam was already engaged in building assignments of importance elsewhere.

Nina, stem-waisted in her riding habit, was to ride with Edward, who was a handsome figure in his hunting pink, but Tansy, who had no stomach for the chase, merely went to watch the huntsmen gather for the local Meet on the green in front of The Winner. The morning was cold and frosty, the breath of riders and their mounts alike hanging in the air, and she was glad to share the stirrup cup. Dominic toasted her with a smile and a secret look from the saddle of his black hunter as she sipped the warming punch with its thread of curling steam. It was then that she saw Adam come riding up, soberly dressed in the riding clothes he had worn when riding to hounds while living in Hampshire. Ever afterward the aroma of hot, spiced punch was to remind her of the moment when she saw Nina turn her proud head from chatting to someone and sight him no more than two yards distant from her. Nina's face blanched beneath her veil, her eyes growing enormous with an unguarded look that cried out its passion. Then she had wheeled her horse away and lost herself among others gathered there. Adam's gaze followed her, his face all hard, young bones, his mouth set, and instantly, as if the truth had been shouted at her, Tansy understood what had lain behind those nighttime walks of Nina's and was astonished that she should have been so unsuspecting, so completely and utterly taken in.

Shortly after Christmas, Tansy and Nina moved back to Rushmere, taking with them a respectable spinster to act as their housekeeper and chaperone, together with a couple of maidservants whom they were now able to afford. Dominic wanted to marry Tansy without delay, but she insisted that she must see Nina through to her wedding day, for after what she had observed at the Meet she was desperately concerned, convinced that nothing but trouble lay in wait and that she might be needed by her sister as never before. When he pressed her for a date for their own marriage she declared that she did not want it to be the grand county affair that Nina and Edward's wedding was to be, but begged for a quiet ceremony, to which he readily agreed.

"Let's get married on the morning of Derby Day!" she suggested eagerly. "The quietest wedding of 1849 on the busiest day of the whole year!"

He laughed and embraced her. "Anything you wish, my love."

Nina kept her promise to Edward and there was no more going out at night on those supposed walks. She did not occupy the box room again, but moved into the room next to it, which was larger and more comfortable while sharing the same view of the orchard over the roof of the kitchen rooms below the windows. Tansy gave Nina many opportunities to speak out about her love for Adam, but her sister kept her own counsel and there was nothing that Tansy could do except watch and wait and hope that all would be well.

One week followed another, doing nothing to dispel the old feeling of foreboding, which had returned to plague her once more, and at times her thoughts went to Silas, for she was unable to shake off the conviction that she had not seen the last of him. Spring banished winter, and the flat-racing season started again. In the garden the daffodils that Amelia had planted made golden seas of the flowerbeds at Rushmere. As they faded, so did the days leading up to Nina's wedding to Edward melt away with surprising swiftness, the time taken up with innumerable last-minute tasks and arrangements, the wedding gifts pouring in to create a confusion of tissue paper, boxes, and silken ribbons. It was a need to have a quiet hour in each day that prompted Tansy to get up extra early every morning and walk up to the gallops to watch Roger put Young Oberon through his paces.

As she watched the colt streaking away in the distance she knew she should be returning to Rushmere to waken Nina and launch into the eve-of-wedding excitement, the ceremony being at noon the next day. After her sister and Edward had departed on their honeymoon to Italy she would be without family at Rushmere for the first time, but there would be much to keep her occupied, for the house was to be sold and the furniture that she did not want to keep disposed of. To date, the highest bid for Rushmere had come from a gentleman of the Turf who had stayed in it while Hedley had been there, and she hoped the sale would go through, knowing that her father would have been pleased that a keen racegoer was going to live in it.

How it would have delighted Oliver's heart to see his son and his colt making record time back along the gallops again! Tansy watched them thud past her once more, hooves flashing, and then she slid off the wall and retraced her steps home to Rushmere. Later in the morning when Nina was flying about with frantic haste, being due at the Manor for a variety of appointments, Tansy knew her sister's nerves to be at snapping point, so frantic was she when anything went slightly awry, so desperate her gaiety, so false her merriment. Tansy found herself no longer able to keep silent, many months worrying about Nina reaching bursting point.

"It's not too late to change your mind about marrying Edward," she cried out compassionately. "I know you're unhappy. Let me help you."

Nina's hands, tying her bonnet ribbons before a looking glass, paused briefly before completing the bow firmly. "I'm marrying him," she stated with a stubborn thrust to her chin, her voice toneless as though she were repeating aloud a phrase that she had reiterated times without number to herself. "That's what I want and that's what I'm going to do."

"I beg you to reconsider! I've wanted to reach out to you a thousand times, but always you have silenced me with a fierce look or a sharp word. Now I can keep quiet no longer."

"My attitude hasn't changed." She tugged at the ends of the ribbon bow with a dangerous impatience.

"I know how important security is to you. And to me. Do you think I don't remember those times when Papa had had a bad season and there was little money throughout the winter months for food or fuel to keep us warm?"

"He always had enough in his pockets to wager at cockfights and a bull-baiting." Bitterly. "We were the ones who went without. I have many memories to erase from those days, and Edward will do it for me."

"How can he do anything for your happiness when you love someone else," Tansy implored. "Don't go against your heart, my dear!"

Nina was very still. "I don't know what you mean."

Tansy spoke softly and gently. "I saw how you and Adam looked at each other at the Boxing Day Meet. I know you've been seeing each other again since." There was a poignant pause. "Adam has used the kitchen roof to get into the house as ably as Silas ever did."

The guilty color swamped Nina's cheeks and she spun about, her hand over her heart as if to calm its beating. "How did you find out?"

"Did you think you and I could live together in this house without my guessing sooner or later?"

"Why haven't you said anything before?"

"I wanted to, but it wasn't for me to interfere. I could only wait and hope that you would make your choice freely for the man who must mean so much to you without any coercion on my part." She clasped her hands urgently. "Adam can't offer you the riches that Edward can, but he'll take care of you. He'll always be hard-working and industrious—"

"—and willing to take chances. Willing to stake all on a promising project. Willing to risk bankruptcy for the opportunity to put one brick upon another in some grandiose scheme that could come to nought."

"He loves you—and you love him." To Tansy it was the only valid argument.

One corner of Nina's mouth twisted wryly, and her shoulders seemed to sag resignedly. "That's true enough. I love him, but I'm going to be Edward's wife."

"No, no, you mustn't be so cruel!"

Nina's whole face flashed with a kind of desperate misery. "I was well schooled from earliest childhood. Mama never liked me and Papa never loved me. You and Judith were always close, but I was the outsider to you all, the odd one out. I soon learned that what I wanted from life I should have to grab for myself. Well, I've known love from one man as few could ever know it and I'm gaining security and everything else I've ever wanted from another. The best of both worlds, wouldn't you say?"

"Nina, I implore you! For Adam's sake and for your own—and Edward's, too. Don't go through with this marriage. You'll regret it to the end of your days."

"Not at all!" she cried tormentedly. "Edward is solid and reliable—not like Papa in any way, thank God! And, as I pointed out, that's more than I can say about Adam." She snatched up her gloves. "I'm getting everything I want for once. I'm fulfilling my dearest ambition." She turned on her heel and ran from the house to where a carriage from the Manor awaited her. Tansy rushed to the window and watched her go. Poor foolish, unhappy Nina, who was set on ruining her own life as well as those of the two men who loved her. Tansy dropped her face into her hands and wept in pity for the three of them.

It was shortly before midday when the doorbell rang. Tansy, summoned by the maidservant who had answered it, found Adam on the doorstep in traveling clothes, his hat in his hand.

"I've come to say goodbye," he said stiffly, his face drawn.

"Goodbye? Where are you going? Come in, do," she cried anxiously.

He stepped over the threshold but would not go farther into the house. "I'm sailing from the Port of London at dawn tomorrow morning on the American packet *John Adams* to the New World. I sold my business here in Cudlingham and I'm going to try my luck on the other side of the Atlantic Ocean. They say there are fortunes to be made there and I want to turn my back on this place and go as far from it as possible."

"Nina has told me about you two. Does she know you're leaving?" she asked gravely, filled with sorrow. "Why are you going so suddenly?"

He nodded wearily. "A month ago I gave her an ultimatum. She had to tell Edward Taylor that she wasn't going to marry him. This she hasn't done. I cannot endure to be here—or anywhere else in England, for that matter—when she becomes another man's wife."

"I know it's you whom she loves!" she exclaimed, torn by his plight.

"She doesn't deny it, but will not change her mind."

"I tried to talk to her only this morning. Oh, please stay! I'll try again—"

"It's useless. I love her—God knows why!—but I intend to do my damnedest to forget her. I should never be able to manage that in this country knowing that our paths might cross again at any time." He held out a hand. "Goodbye, Tansy. I wish you every happiness in your marriage to Reade. He's a fortunate man."

She put her hand in his, this man who had been her first love. "God keep you, Adam. I wish you a safe journey and a fine new life in America."

For the first and only time he kissed her, a light kiss on the cheek. Then he turned with a swirl of his coattails and went out of the house and out of her life. She knew she would never see him again.

It was late when Nina came home. She burst into the house wearing one of the evening gowns she kept at the Manor, but without shawl or cape, and with one earring missing. Her eyes were wild and her face ashen. Tansy, waiting up for her, dropped her book and sprang up from her chair in alarm.

"Nina! Whatever's the matter?"

Nina clutched at her with shaking hands. "Adam's gone! A

sudden, terrible sense of desolation came over me in the midst of that hateful eve-of-wedding gathering of Edward's relations, and I felt such a longing for Adam that I nearly died. I left without saying good night to anyone, telling a servant to inform Edward that I had gone home to stop him fussing after me, and I ran all the way to Adam's house. But somebody else had moved in there today. They said he had left Cudlingham—that he was going abroad."

Tansy put compassionate arms about her and hugged her tight. "I know. I know." Her own throat was full.

"You've seen him?" Nina could hardly speak, her teeth beginning to chatter with delayed shock.

"He came this morning to say goodbye. Here—sit down." Tansy drew her sister down onto the couch. "Didn't you think he meant what he said?"

Nina gave a long, despairing moan, rocking in her desperation. "No, I didn't. I even believed he would find it impossible to go far from me, and I thought I should go on seeing him sometimes. It was that which made the thought of marriage to Edward bearable. Where is Adam now? Where is he staying?"

"He's on board ship. He sails for the New World before dawn."

Nina went as still as if life had died within her. Her dilated eyes were all pupils, and she gulped for breath. "What ship? From where?" After being told she gave a deep nod, rising unsteadily to her feet, and thrust Tansy's supporting arms from her. "I'm going to my room."

"I'll bring you a hot drink and sit with you."

Nina did not answer, but went up the stairs with her head high. Tansy rang at once for a pot of tea. When it was ready she took it from the maid and went upstairs with the tray to find Nina's room deserted. The evening gown she had been wearing lay in a heap of shimmering, azure silk on the bed, the closet door stood open with some garments missing, and drawers in the chest had half their contents tumbled on the floor. The window to the kitchen roof was flung wide. Tansy dropped the tray and flew to look out. In the same instant the clatter of hooves resounded over the cobbled yard.

"Nina!" she shrieked. She hurled herself back down the stairs and rushed out of the house. Nina had already vanished through the gates, riding to her lover on the horse that had once brought Oliver Marlow home for the last time.

Tansy did not go back into the house, but broke into a run down the drive and out into the lane. She did not stop running until she reached Ainderly Hall. There, admitted by a servant, she almost fell into Dominic's arms and in the privacy of his study she told him all that had occurred.

The next day dawned gray and overcast. Shortly after nine o'clock Dominic drove his hooded phaeton through the gates of Rushmere, Nina a bowed figure beside him. Tansy, her hours of watching for them over at last, ran out to meet them. Nina's eyes were tragic and sunken, but she straightened her back when she alighted as if defying pity.

She spoke in a harsh whisper. "I was too late. Adam's ship was no more than a sprinkle of lights in the distance when I reached the quayside."

"That's what I feared," Tansy said sadly. "That's why Dominic came after you."

A bitter little smile showed briefly on the colorless mouth. "You also feared I might end my life in those same waters if there was no one there to prevent me. Perhaps it would have been better for me if you hadn't interfered. Now I have to live with my longing for Adam for the rest of my days."

She went on into the house. Dominic, bringing from the phaeton the bundle she had packed with such haste only a few hours before, walked with Tansy indoors after her. "She's going ahead with her marriage to Edward at noon," he said gravely.

"Surely not!"

"You'd better talk to her. I found her adamant."

Nina, already getting out of her travel-dusty clothes in her room, spoke before Tansy had a chance. "Get one of the maids to heat some bath water for me. I have half an hour before the hairdresser comes."

"Don't marry Edward!"

Nina looked over her shoulder at Tansy, her face expressionless. "I no longer have any choice in the matter. I'm going to have Adam's baby."

In the parish church of Cudlingham at noon Nina made a pale and ethereal bride in ivory moiré taffeta with a veil of Brussels lace, delicate as gossamer. Her voice did not falter when she made her responses and under a shower of rice her composed little smile remained neatly in place as she hurried with a laughing, happy Edward down the church path amid crowds of well-wishers to the beribboned waiting landau. Only when she was departing for her honeymoon, arrayed from head to foot in cinnamon velvet, did her composure break down and she clung to Tansy with a desperate, limpet-like embrace as though making a farewell not only to the past, but to all happiness itself.

14.

In a private saloon with almond green walls and white Rococo woodwork in the Grand Stand at Epsom the champagne corks were popping. Tansy and Dominic were receiving congratulations and good wishes on all sides, their marriage having taken place that morning with only Nina, Edward, and Roger present. A buffet luncheon table set with damask and silver and crystal, enhanced by a centerpiece of flowers in Dominic's racing colors of blue, amber, and white, was loaded with Sussex lobsters on beds of lettuce, pyramids of prawns, game pies with glossy crusts, garnished capons, rosy hams, and every kind of delicacy, to which those invited guests in the saloon were doing more than justice. As a background to the laughter and the talk there came the outside roar and bustle of the racing crowd of more than sixty thousand people.

Tansy, too excited and happy to eat, moved with Dominic among their guests, her gown a soft iris-blue, her hat a romantic leghorn, its wide brim edged with scalloped lace, its ribbons loosely tied under her chin. As soon as the opportunity presented itself she drew Dominic with her out through the glass doors onto the balcony that stretched the length of the Grand Stand, which itself rose three floors high above the course, its Doric columns giving it the look of a gigantic wedding cake.

"Our wedding day and my first Derby Day!" she exclaimed joyfully, looking down at the sea of people and the famous course shaped like a horseshoe, the whole throbbing, noisy scene cradled on an unsurpassed stretch of the magnificent Epsom Downs, green as velvet under a sky of clearest English blue with a small fluff of white cloud here and there to emphasize its purity. Bands were playing, tin whistles screeching, fiddles jigging, drums beating outside the drinking booths and sideshows, and the tinkling tambourines of the gypsy dancers flashed like small, twinkling suns as they entertained groups in the crowd. Other temporary and private stands of canvas and wood, vivid with flags and bunting, their benches filled with people, faced the course, and the Judge's chair by the winning post, shortly to be occupied by that distinguished gentleman, Sir Giles LeBoare, was a wooden erection painted red and white. Opposite was the Hill, so spread with people and striped booths and every kind of tent and caravan that it looked like a brilliant Persian carpet with a pattern forever on the move, and on the crest of it were innumerable coaches, which earlier in the day had swept up there into their positions with horns blowing and passengers waving, the strained horses steaming.

Stretching for almost a mile along the rails on either side of the course, except where the lawn in front of the Grand Stand made an exclusive enclosure, were equipages of every kind lying five or six deep, from which the occupants would view the racing. In the elegant open carriages the ladies' parasols made pastel-colored mushroom clusters that bobbed and dipped, the fringes dancing, while liveried servants served picnics of exotic foods and poured champagne and hock and sherry. By the Betting Post there was a frenzy of activity, the bookmakers in waistcoats of garish hues, their belts studded with silver coins, and some with feathers in their hats, all taking wads of notes, piles of sovereigns, and fistfuls of shillings from eager punters as fast as the money could change hands. Young Oberon was joint favorite with The Flying Dutchman, the odds lying 2–1, and some lively competition was expected from a colt called Tadmor. All along the roads and lanes that led to the course people were still coming in a constant stream of carriages, donkey carts, and trade wagons turned to racing use for the day, others on foot and many on horseback, and left behind them all like debris in their wake were countless vehicles that had collided, broken an axle, or ended in a ditch.

Dominic was looking through his field glasses and Tansy touched his arm. "Any sign of Roger yet?"

He lowered them, smiling at her. "It's too soon yet. There's the first race of the afternoon to be run before the Derby. We'll see him after the weighing in when the saddling-up takes place. You can wish him good luck then."

"Take me down into the crowd now," she implored eagerly. "I want to see everything at close hand."

He laughed, tucking her hand into the crook of his arm, and bore her with him back through the saloon, everybody parting with smiles and glasses raised in honor to let them through. She picked up her bridal posy on the way with a shining swirl of its satin ribbons and they went out to the huge staircase that took them down to the front of the Grand Stand.

In the room they had left behind, Edward turned to Nina, putting his arm lightly about her waist. "Would you like to wander down there for a little while?"

She twirled out of his embrace, fanning her face with her hand as if any sort of contact was unbearable in the heat of the afternoon, barely able to suppress her aversion to his touch. "Mercy, no! I can't abide crowds!"

He made no reply, but moodily drained his glass and had it refilled. He had not missed her withdrawal. She withheld herself from him in all ways at the least excuse. Shyness and timidity were one thing, but an excess of modesty to the point of fetishness was another. Had he not been brutal with her he would not yet have seen her naked. Their wedding night had almost unmanned him, so terrible had been her tears, so black the despair in her eyes, so absent the passion he had thought to awaken. And yet—and yet? A certain doubt continued to plague him and he could not dismiss it. His gaze followed her with a chill distrust as she moved out onto the balcony to the spot that her sister had recently vacated, her back to him, her fists clenched side by side on the flat-topped balustrade.

Half-dazzled by the sun Nina stared with unseeing, unfocused eyes toward the distant, wooded slopes. Where was Adam now? That he yearned for her as she did for him she knew well enough. One day he would find he could bear it no longer and return for her. Then she would leave husband, child or children, home, and everything else to follow him anywhere, no matter if he had not a penny to his name. One day. One day. It was a dream that was to sustain her for several years to come until at last she was forced to accept the awful realization that he had gone forever and was never coming back.

By a gypsy caravan Tansy was having her fortune told, her palm extended, and held by gnarled, brown fingers, the nails black-rimmed and broken. "You've known sorrow and heartache and pain," the old crone crackled in a high, toneless chant. "There's a woman, young, related to you, who will always have need of your comfort and strength, and her children will be dear to you and ever in your house where there is the love and laughter that is lacking in their place of abode."

"How many shall I have of my own?" Tansy asked.

"I see you with three daughters and when they are almost grown there'll be a son—a boy born out of your man's love for you that will never wane."

"I couldn't wish to be told better than that on my wedding day," Tansy said softly.

Dominic gave the gypsy woman a sovereign, well pleased that she had added to his bride's happiness, whether there should be any truth in the predictions or not. Together they wandered on, Tansy excited and enthralled with all she saw. He bought her a toffee apple and she stood with feet together and eyes shut as she bit into it, remembering another purchased for her by her father long ago on another race day and in another place. They watched the tumblers and the trapeze artists and the strong man breaking chains, gave coins to some of the ragged, barefoot children who swarmed about, gazed at the woman walking the high wire, her red paper parasol jerking wildly, and went on to observe one of the many illegal games of chance going on, which ended abruptly with a snap of the portable table and a flutter of cards when a policeman suddenly appeared out of the throng. Laughing, they strolled on again. They paused to watch pugilists engaged in combat, passed the cockfights, avoided the booths exhibiting freaks, and stopped to shy for coconuts, Dominic removing his frockcoat to take better aim and giving it to her to hold for him. The sight of a toff in his shirt sleeves, his tall silk hat rammed down in a purposeful, forward angle over his brow, delighted the surrounding crowd, who pushed forward to get a better view. When he won a coconut they cheered, and when he tossed his trophy to a little flower girl they cheered once more. While shrugging on his frockcoat again he successfully thwarted a pickpocket, cutting a blow across the man's wrist with the edge of his hand, and then he pushed aside a rabble of touts and tipsters that had gathered about him and managed to whisk Tansy out of the crush without too much difficulty. In another part of the fair he took her on the swings, her hat ribbons flying as they went up and down, her petticoats a snapping flutter, her eyes closed to a fringe of lashes with laughter. When he helped her out of the swing boat the first race of the afternoon had been run.

They joined other owners with their trainers and jockeys in the paddock where the horses were being saddled up and walked around. Young Oberon was being led by Matthew Kirby, whose father was giving last-minute instructions and advice to Roger, a short, restless figure in Dominic's racing colors, his whip beating a light tattoo against his boot. They turned when Tansy and Dominic approached and there was much talk about the race and the conditions.

"I'm afraid you'll find the going somewhat heavy after all the rain of the last few days," Dominic said to Roger. "The ground hasn't yet dried out."

"I'm prepared for that, sir. I walked every inch of the course at dawn this morning to memorize every rise and fall of it as well as those sharpish left-hand corners and the right-hand curve."

"How do you feel?"

"Nervous, sir. I can't deny it. But I'll be all right once I'm up." With a brave show of confidence he tapped in a masterly manner Young Oberon's saddle, Matthew having brought the colt up to them and busying himself tightening the girths. The colt stood as coolly and patiently as if in his paddock at home, having long since become accustomed to the noise and bustle of a racecourse after his initial curiosity about everything at his debut as a two-year-old, although other horses were already sweating with nervousness and excitement.

A voice boomed across the paddock in stentorian tones. "Jockeys! Get mounted, please!"

Matthew gave Roger a leg up and at once he was more relaxed and at ease, completely at home in the saddle. He checked the stirrups and adjusted them. Then he grinned down at his sister in her blue wedding gown. "You look almost as grand in your finery as I do in your husband's racing colors," he joked with brotherly impudence, aware that he made a dazzling figure in his silk jacket and peaked cap, his kid boots polished to a shine that rivaled the gloss of Young Oberon's perfectly groomed coat.

She laughed, and Dominic spoke to him again, clapping the colt's neck. "Good luck, Roger. Make this a win for my bride."

"Yes, sir!"

Roger saluted them by touching the peak of his cap with his whip and then Matthew took the bridle and led Young Oberon to join the other horses in the traditional parade. Dominic, turning to have further conversation with Mr. Kirby, left Tansy alone and it was then that she became conscious of another jockey's gaze fixed on her. He was in the saddle of a black colt, his racing colors scarlet. It was Silas!

"We meet again," he said with a smirk.

She knew fear. "I thought you had been banned from racing for life."

"My late employer, who was murdered in cold blood by that Judith Collins, no matter what any may say to the contrary, had made application shortly afore his death for my case to be reconsidered and the ban lifted. I'm right pleased to say it went through."

"I didn't see your name on the race card."

"I'm a last-minute replacement. The other jockey had—an accident." He nodded sneeringly toward Dominic, who had not seen him. "I suppose you and Reade think that nag your brother is riding is goin' to win this Derby." His voice took on a vicious note. "Well, for Selwyn Hedley's sake I'll see he don't!"

She caught at the bridle. "You shall repeat that threat you have made to a steward!"

He laughed contemptuously, flicking her hand away with a touch of his whip. "I only meant that the best jockey and the best runner are goin' to win. That's me, ma'am, and the colt I have between my knees." A stable lad came running to lead his horse into the parade and Silas was still laughing as he went.

From the balcony of the Grand Stand, Tansy focused her field glasses on her brother, anxiety high in her, Dominic's assurance that Silas's colt, Tempest, had neither the stamina nor the sprinting ability to win the race having done nothing to quieten her fears. The silks of the jockeys flashed their jewel colors in the sun, and she could pick Roger out easily as the roll call was taken. Twenty-six runners in the peak of condition were drawn up on a moving, uneven line, some prancing, some reversing, and only seconds away from the start of the richest Derby ever to be run, the stakes standing at over six and a half thousand pounds.

She gasped and gasped again when one false start followed upon another, several horses covering a number of furlongs before being pulled up and trotted back to the starting post, riders and mounts thoroughly upset by it, and in the resulting mix-up and jostling Roger had lost his good place near the rails and was caught in the middle of the line. Next to him was Silas on Tempest and on his other side was a gray filly, Bonnie, ridden by a jockey named Toby Jakes. As she watched she saw Roger turn his head sharply toward Silas as if retorting angrily to something the man had said. Then at last the race bell sounded and the starter shouted "Go!" as the flag came down. A tremendous roar went up from thousands of throats.

"They're off!"

Young Oberon flew forward like an arrow released from a bow, Roger needing to get in front at once to avoid being hindered at the right-hand curve, which could cut him off, and he succeeded easily enough, Tempest and Bonnie keeping him company. He could tell that Young Oberon was going to run as he had never run before, and after the first furlong he had to pull hard to stop him taking the lead too soon. It was then he realized that he had been picked out for harassment by Silas and Toby Jakes, neither of whom could hope to win, but who were out to make sure that he didn't. Both were already crowding him and he was sure that rougher tactics lay ahead.

With a thunder of hooves the whole field swept uphill, swung round the right-hand curve and then toward the left as the ground leveled out for a stretch. The milepost flashed by and Roger took up sixth position, kept well away from the rails by Toby's persistent crowding, but he knew Young Oberon had the stamina, and was unconcerned on that point. Afraid of being completely shut in, he attempted to ease Young Oberon to the outside, and although he succeeded to a certain extent, again Silas was there with a deliberate jostle. Roger yelled at him in fury:

"Get out of the way, damn you!"

"Pull him, lad!" Silas taunted back, the wind making his peak bend up from his cap. "As I told you back at the line, you're never goin' to make it!"

The course began to descend steeply and sharply downhill to Tattenham Corner and the pace of every runner quickened. Roger hoped to shake off the other two and watched for a gap, knowing it was only a matter of time before Tempest and Bonnie broke down, for they were already being ridden to the limit of their endurance while Young Oberon was skimming along in perfect balance, his power yet untapped, so full of running that it was like a cry of exultation.

Then the catastrophe happened. Bonnie, like many horses who disliked racing downhill lost her stride and bumped, causing another horse to get his legs crossed, and colliding they fell. With terrified whinnies and frightened shouts there was an immediate pileup of five horses and jockeys, Silas and Tempest among them, which threw those behind into panic and confusion, the rest of the field ahead thudding on to Tattenham Corner. Young Oberon, although not caught in that mass of kicking legs and struggling horseflesh, stumbled and went down on his forelegs, almost tossing Roger from the saddle, but he scrambled up again and with eyes wild, snorting and blowing, he reared away into the center of the course and plunged on again. In that lost time all those entangled in the pileup had gone thundering on, and Roger and Young Oberon were last.

"Come on, boy! Come on!" Roger urged, unaware he had tears on his face. "We can do it yet!"

From the Grand Stand, Tansy and Dominic were among those who watched incredulously as Young Oberon, away from the rest of the field, began the last great sprint of his life. On and on he came, Tattenham Corner left behind as he overtook the stragglers. Still with the full breadth of the course lying between, he drew level with the main body of runners as hooves crashed and flashed up the straight, those four rising furlongs that had lost the race to so many in the past. Roger was the only jockey not using his whip. Young Oberon had become his own great ancestor, Eclipse, all over again, running his heart out to the loudest cheers that had ever resounded across the Epsom Downs.

In his chair the Judge was watching closely the horses in the lead, Young Oberon as yet hidden from his view. The Flying Dutchman, a dark bay colt, was being challenged by Hotspur, an outsider, which was enough to turn any racing crowd into a frenzy, and another horse, Tadmor, was only half a length behind. With trained eyes the Judge concentrated on them, sitting on the edge of his chair. As the Roman nose of the dark bay shot past the winning post, inches ahead of Hotspur, he leaped to his feet and shouted his decision:

"The Flying Dutchman wins!"

Even as the words left him he saw to his astonishment that Young Oberon was also past the winning post on the far side and he heard those around him muttering against his verdict. The Judge was no longer young and could count forty years on the Turf, with fifteen of those as a respected racing judge, this being his final Derby and a fitting climax to his distinguished career. He would not have it ruined by any doubts cast upon the quickness of his eye or let it be said that old age had dulled his wits. He could not—no, he would not!—admit to not having seen Young Oberon pass the post.

"The Flying Dutchman is the winner," he declared to the waiting signalman. "Hotspur was second and Tadmor third."

"What about Young Oberon?" ventured someone.

The Judge's face turned purple and his white eyebrows clamped down into a thick bar across the bridge of his arrogant nose. "Fourth!" he spat. Gathering up his field glasses, race card, and papers he stalked down the steps from the chair. Seconds later the results were made known to the crowd and in a wild flutter of wings released pigeons soared high into the air to carry the news to press offices in London and farther afield.

The owner of The Flying Dutchman, a sportsman and a gentleman, sought Dominic out before going to lead his winner in. "Look here, my dear sir, I feel the Judge's verdict must be challenged—"

Dominic, although deeply disappointed that the glory of the day had been snatched from Young Oberon, shook his head decisively. "To all intents and purposes your colt was the winner. He ran a magnificent race right from the beginning. You and I are working together for the good of the Turf. We want only to see the sport freed from all the villainy we know to be afoot. I think we've made great strides toward that end. To question the Judge and undermine his authority at this particular time could do untold harm. Let the verdict stand, and allow me to be the first to congratulate you."

The two men shook hands firmly. Tansy, knowing that Dominic had behaved most honorably, was extremely proud of him, and others showed it too, in the applause that followed them as they made their way toward the enclosure. The Flying Dutchman was led in to thunderous cheers, but the ovation was nothing compared to the tumultuous reception given to Young Oberon, who had run the race of a lifetime, the like of which had never been seen before and might never happen again. But he was an exhausted horse and once past the winning post he had gone completely lame. Roger had dismounted and led him gently off the course, and Mr. Kirby was running expert hands down his foreleg, the foot of which Young Oberon was reluctant to put on the ground.

"I'm almost certain it's a split pastern," the trainer informed them.

Tansy exclaimed in alarm. "Is that very serious?"

"It can be," Dominic answered, "if it doesn't heal to leave him free of pain. It's an extremely fine fracture of the bone running from fetlock to hoof. It means six months' rest in his loose box and he's out of the St. Leger and any other races he would have run this year."

"It must heal properly! It must!" Tansy cried.

Dominic put his arms about her. "He'll have the best of treatment, I promise you."

"And then?"

"I'll not race him again. He shall be retired to stud and become the sire of many thoroughbred winners like his famous ancestor before him."

At that point Matthew came running up. "I've just heard, sir! Bloody Silas has been arrested! The Jockey Club has laid charges against him for fraud and intimidation quite apart from his interference in the race. The wretch thought he had silenced the jockey whose place he took, having been blackmailing him, but the man decided to speak out to the stewards and has given them enough evidence to round up scores of ring leaders in the crooked practices that the late Selwyn Hedley organized. Bloody Silas will most surely be sent to prison for a long time or sentenced to transportation. He'll never get near a racecourse again."

"That's good news indeed," Dominic said thankfully.

That night over a candlelit supper for two at Ainderly Hall, Tansy lifted her champagne glass. "Let's drink a toast to Young Oberon, who brought us together. May the first foal he sires be the greatest Derby winner ever!"

"I drink to that," Dominic replied, smiling at her as he raised his own glass. "You shall lead in that winner of the Blue Riband."

"We'll lead him in together," she answered contentedly, knowing in her heart that this dream of theirs would come true.

They drank their toast and then he kissed her passionately. With arms entwined they left the supper table and the room, his head bent to hers, his love words whispered against her ear. Again and again their lips met as they ascended the wide staircase.

In the stables amid the scent of warm bran mash and clean, sweet hay, Young Oberon slept.